The Malice

Also by Peter Newman

The Vagrant

PETER NEWMAN

The Malice

HARPER
Voyager

HarperCollins*Publishers*
1 London Bridge Street
London SE1 9GF

www.harpercollins.co.uk

Published by Harper*Voyager* 2016
An imprint of HarperCollins*Publishers*
1

A catalogue record for this book
is available from the British Library

HB ISBN: 9780007593163
TPB ISBN: 9780007593170

This novel is entirely a work of fiction.
The names, characters and incidents portrayed in it are
the work of the author's imagination. Any resemblance to
actual persons, living or dead, events or localities is
entirely coincidental.

Typeset in Sabon LT Std by Palimpsest Book Production Limited,
Falkirk, Stirlingshire

Printed and bound in Great Britain by
Clays Ltd, St Ives plc

MIX
Paper from
responsible sources
FSC
www.fsc.org
FSC™ C007454

FSC™ is a non-profit international organisation established to promote
the responsible management of the world's forests. Products carrying the
FSC label are independently certified to assure consumers that they come
from forests that are managed to meet the social, economic and
ecological needs of present and future generations,
and other controlled sources.

Find out more about HarperCollins and the environment at
www.harpercollins.co.uk/green

For Daniel

CHAPTER ONE

In the south, the Breach stirs.

For over a thousand years it has grown. Slowly at first, a hidden cancer under the skin of the earth, a hairline crack exhaling alien wisps, disturbing yet harmless. But beneath the surface, pressure grows until the crack becomes an opening, and the opening splits wide, a gaping womb, a wound in the world, erupting.

Infernals pour forth, shapeless nightmares that slaughter their way into reality, inhabiting the bodies of the fallen and mutating them, taking the natural order and tainting it, corrupting plants, animals, even the air itself.

As the infernals take on physical form, they find identities and names: greatest of them is the monstrous Usurper, who raises itself to power by force of will, who strikes down Gamma of The Seven and breaks her armies. It is the Usurper who heralds the end of hope and the retreat of humanity's influence.

But Gamma's living sword is not destroyed and its continued

presence nags at the marks left on the Usurper's essence, festering, weakening. The Usurper sends its horde in search of the sword, named Malice by the infernals, but their efforts fail. A man takes the sword from them, and in time its power topples the Usurper and a kind of peace returns. Not true peace, too much is broken for the world to simply recover. This is merely a pause, a holding of breath. It is but a temporary thing. For in the south, the Breach stirs.

*

On the other side of the world a man stands by a window, his amber eyes intent on a small figure outside. Her name is Vesper. She is doing nothing of note and yet the man smiles as he watches her, her very existence comforting, warming like the suns.

For a long time he was alone and lost, a vagrant. Now he has a home, a family and more goats than he knows what to do with. It is a good life.

And yet lately a shadow seems to loom around the corner, a hint of coming disquiet. His home is built outside the Shining City, a step removed from people and politics and the expectations of others. News has to battle to get to his door. This is no accident.

Behind him, the sword begins to tremble, rocking back and forth, folded wings tip-tapping on the wall, but the eye remains closed. For years it has slept, deeply, peacefully, a quiet companion.

He turns to it, a smile sliding from his face. Absently, he scratches at old scars, on his thigh, his face, the side of his head. It has taken years to heal. Years of gentle work to make a new life, a safe space for those he loves.

His attention goes back to Vesper, who chats idly with the goats. Slowly, he returns to work but the tapping of the sword continues, like a thorn in his boot, needling, never quite out of mind. Lips form a line. At his sides, fists clench.

The sword is taken to his room, the door shut.

It is not enough.

He wraps the sword, making a thick bed of fabric for it, muffling the sounds it makes.

It is not enough.

Though it no longer bumps against the wall, the sword's unease comes out in half-made notes, little things that catch on the edges of his soul.

He finds himself standing at the door, staring, one hand starting to open it, to reach out to the sleeping sword. It would be a small matter to lift it, to wake it once more, to . . .

'What are you doing?'

He starts, turns to find Vesper standing there, face bright. With her, every day is a marvel. How tall she has become! How reminiscent of her mother.

Her head tilts to one side, trying to see past him. 'What are you doing?'

He musters a half-smile, shrugs.

'Are you okay?'

He nods.

'What's in there? I thought I heard a noise. Can I have a look? Is it an animal? It sounded unhappy. Can I see?'

He waves the questions away and puts a gentle hand on her shoulder, moving away from the room and taking her with him.

Later, when other distractions have led the girl away, he returns to the room with tougher materials and a box.

But it is not enough.

*

Twenty years have passed since the first wave of infernals came into being but the Breach has not ceased. A steady trickle of twisted creatures has dribbled from it, sometimes alone, sometimes in pairs, occasionally in gluts, but always, always, it grows; by inches, getting a little bigger, convulsing, then stretching again.

For eleven of these years, Samael has watched.

He stands on a rusting hill. Once a snake of mechanised metal, now a monument to things forgotten. Beneath his feet native moss does battle with tainted strains. Spongy carpets, yellow and brown, spreading with intent. Samael does not notice, his attention is on the Breach. He first came here on impulse. Drawn by voices he couldn't quite hear, buried deep within his essence. He likes his impulses, just as he likes his habits. They give him direction.

It is twelve years since his second birth, since he was taken from his life on the sea, and only his hair remains unchanged. Beneath his armour, Samael's skin is bone white, fossilised into a mockery of cracked marble. Unlike the rest of him, his hair is full of life. He wears it tied up, a horses tail that flows from a slit in the top of his helmet. A vanity he knows his creator would disapprove of. The thought brings a shudder and a smile.

Of course, his creator, the commander, was destroyed by the Malice, along with the other Knights of Jade and Ash but that doesn't stop Samael thinking about him. Or seeking approval. He wishes it were different.

The armour he wears is a collection of mismatched plates, dug up from the battlefield and roughly beaten into shape. The result is ugly and ill-fitting. It feels right. A second skin he has made for himself. Wearing it has become habitual. Of this at least, his creator would surely approve. He hopes so but cannot be sure. Since the commander's sudden end, he has been left with freedom and too many questions.

A fresh wave of essence bubbles from the Breach. Once, the chasm could not be seen from this hill and a village stood between his vantage point and the great crack. The village is gone now, swallowed by the earth, sucked down to other unknowable realms, deep, beyond the Breach.

Samael does not know how he knows this, but he does. He remembers buildings, faces, their hope fading as he passes them, leaving them to die. This flash of memory that is both his and not his goes as quickly as it arrives, leaving behind a cauldron of unprocessed feelings.

Grudgingly, his mind returns to present.

This is where the demons find their way in. He cannot change what has been done to him, cannot stop the infernals further north from plaguing the world, but here, he can make a difference. Here, he can at least stem the tide.

Clouds of unborn essence begin to form on the Breach's edge, along with a host of skittering, hungry scabs, the lowest of the infernals. The scabs spread out, hunting for food amidst the dirt. The unborn spirits search for a way into the world, needing host bodies if they are to remain.

Samael smiles, knowing they will fail.

The few remaining corpses he cleared years ago, those not already claimed as hosts, condemning any new infernal to haunt the Breach's boundary, dissipating slowly, horrific concepts never finding expression.

He has watched this sight countless times but it never fails to please.

Something is different this time, however. A second wave of unborn clouds confirms it. His half-breed eyes read the patterns in their essences. They are desperate, yes, this is common, but the flavour of fear in their smoky swirls is new. It is not the hostile world they have arrived in that scares them most. It is something else. Something behind them.

They are running away.

A rumble passes through the earth, radiating outward until it shakes the metal hill. Samael throws his arms out, balancing, riding the shockwave until it has passed. Another rumble comes quickly, and the sound darkens the sky, essence spewing from the Breach, thick and black and purple.

Samael is thrown from the hill, landing heavily in the dirt. The half-breed pulls himself up quickly, untroubled by physical pains. The ground still shakes, constant now, as the Breach heaves, trying to dislodge its burden. Earth trembles, gives, and reality retreats a little further north.

The thing that emerges is too big, stretching through dimensions even Samael cannot see. It is both great and small, contained and limitless. But more than that, it has purpose. Without a host, without a birth, it exists.

The Yearning has come.

Samael does not need a second look, the first has already

found a permanent place in his consciousness. He falls back on another old habit, and runs.

*

Far to the north, across the sea, in lands of waning green, lies the Shining City. An invisible field defines its boundary, tuned to the infernal taint, ready to burn. Within this field windows peek from grassy hillsides, hinting at the tunnels, pods and infrastructure hidden within. Pillars of silver punch towards the sky, landscaped gardens attached to their sides and tops. Within the circles of hills and spires is a grand open space. At its centre stands a set of steps, polished, dazzling. They climb fifty feet straight up, ending in nothing. A further twenty feet above the top step, a giant cube of metal floats, turning slowly, colossal, held by invisible strings.

The cube is packed full of secrets, with its own hierarchies and troubles, both above and beyond the world below.

At its heart is the sanctum of The Seven.

Even here, in this haven, miles from any infernal, they feel the quake. Even here, behind walls of denial and power, platinum and energy, the shift in earth and essence stirs them.

Alpha of The Seven is the first to wake. His eyes open, matchless orbs, sparkling with the wisdom of his maker and a thousand years' experience. They sweep across five other alcoves, each a home, a tomb for the immortal within.

Heads turn slowly, moving to meet his gaze. Stone flakes fall from faces as they emerge once more, tentative.

No words are spoken, no songs are sung, not yet. Their

power is there, waiting to be called but there lacks the will to call it.

Alpha feels the question in the eyes of his brothers and sisters. A new trouble has presented itself. They want to see his response. He flexes fingers, freeing them from their stony prison, and looks towards his sword. It is buried, a barely discernible lump, shrouded in grey rock. His siblings' swords are no better, covered in tears of stone, wept in the years of grief.

It is time to take them up again.

Alpha lifts his hand and the others inhale together. Five hands tense, ready to take action.

An invisible force draws Alpha's eyes to the third alcove, the empty one. Once their sister, Gamma, resided there. Now there is nothing.

She is lost to them.

Lost.

That which they thought immutable was brought low, broken by the Usurper's power. If they go to war, will this new threat claim another? Even the idea is too much to bear.

Alpha stills his hand, lowers his head.

Five other hands relax and six minds retreat, returning to darkness and sweet oblivion.

A few miles away, hidden in darkness, wrapped in cloth, wrapped in wood, wrapped in dust, an eye opens.

*

A bird drifts in the sky, lazy. A worm dangles from its beak, frantic, hopeless. With a flap of wings, it ascends, riding the currents, spiralling around a great pillar. At the top sits a gleaming sky-ship and cradled within its turrets are a number of nests.

The nests should not be there. The workers should have scrubbed them away but there have been no inspections, not this year, nor the four before that. Nobody can see the top of the sky-ship from below, so the workers don't clean them. An indulgence that goes unnoticed. There are others. Tiny flaws in the slowly rotting Empire of the Winged Eye.

Shrill voices penetrate the air, begging for food. The bird ignores them, moving towards its own offspring, letting the worm fall towards a trio of gaping beaks before diving away, carried by currents to new adventures.

Far below and several miles distant, a girl watches the bird through an old, battered scope. Her name is Vesper and her feet itch to travel to the pillar, her hands to climb it. But the pillar, along with everything else around the Shining City, is forbidden. They are but images, only dimly understood, no more real to her than Uncle Harm's stories.

She tucks the scope into a pocket and looks around, seeking inspiration. None comes and her eyes go back to find the bird, staring enviously until the curved line becomes a black dot. Soon even this is gone. Without it, the sky appears blank, uninteresting.

Because she is young, because she is sheltered, because she is different, Vesper plays. She spreads her arms and runs, flapping them like a bird. Enthusiasm cannot defeat physics however and she remains earth bound, an amusement for the goats that crowd the fields.

She arrives at the border of her world, panting. No energy

field prevents further travel, just a simple fence and the endless warnings of her family.

Vesper takes a step towards it. She does not need to fly to cross this obstacle. A glance over her shoulder stops the plan before it can form. Her father stands outside the house, amber eyes searching her out. Feigning innocence, Vesper raises her hand, waves. Her father's hand calls her back towards home.

She loves her father and her Uncle more than words but sometimes she wishes they weren't there. Not forever. Just for an hour, or an afternoon. As she trudges back up the hill, she imagines the glories such an afternoon might bring.

Before she gets back, however, an angry bleating demands her attention.

'Here we go,' mutters Vesper and starts to run.

The male goats follow her a few paces, then stop, knowing their place well.

At the top of the hill, next to her house is another, smaller one. Inside, offerings litter the floor, some barely recognizable remnants, others only half chewed. A mutigel cube has been spread thin across the floor, like a translucent pancake. A blanket partly covers it. The goat stands on top, unsteady, her belly swollen with young. Dark eyes regard Vesper bleakly as she arrives. The goat is old now, too old for such nonsense, yet it keeps happening. The goat is not sure who needs to be punished for the latest in a long line of pregnancies and so tends to bite at anybody stupid enough to get close.

Vesper has learnt this the hard way. She stops at the doorway, absently rubbing the old scar on her hand. 'Don't look at me. It's not my fault.'

The birth is quick and blunt, a few moments of sweat

and struggle. A newborn slides into being, deadly still, wearing its membrane suit like a shroud.

The goat eyes the bundle disapprovingly, and waits. During the early pregnancies, she tended her young but she too has learnt.

'Go on!' Vesper urges.

The goat ignores her.

'Quickly!'

The goat ignores her.

With a curse, Vesper pulls a rag from her pocket and starts to wipe the mucus from the newborn's head. Practiced hands find their way into the kid's mouth and nostrils, unplugging goo. Vesper curses again, borrowing words overheard, exotic, adult. Slowly, the gunk is removed, some of it finding its way to the floor, much of it adhering to Vesper's trousers.

The goat's eyes glint, victorious, and she begins to pick at some stray tufts of grass by the door.

Still, the kid does not move, a damp lump, not quite dead but not fully alive either. Vesper strokes the little animal's side.

'Come on, you can do it. Breathe for me.'

Vesper keeps stroking, keeps talking. She doesn't know if the kid can hear her, or if it helps but she does it anyway.

The goat flicks the stump of her tail in irritation and trots over. She gives her child a quick inspection, flicks her tail again, then kicks out.

The kid judders into life, gulps down air, whimpers a little.

Vesper scowls at the goat. 'Was that really necessary?'

The goat ignores her.

Injury forgotten in sudden hunger, the kid looks between the two figures, mouth open and eager.

'I take it you're not going to feed him?' Vesper rolls up her sleeves. 'Didn't think so.' Alert for retaliation, she snatches up a nearby bucket and starts to milk the goat.

Too tired to fight, the goat decides to be merciful.

When she finishes, Vesper stands up, hefting the bucket. 'I need to get a bottle, don't go anywhere, okay?'

The kid watches the girl leave. He turns to his other mother but she has already gone. Tongue lolling, he swings his head back and forth, unsure. He takes his first steps, stumbling into the goat's domain.

There is a thud and a squeal.

A moment later he scurries out, running for safety. He doesn't dare look back.

Tin bowls sound like anemic bells as they are moved, and a soft voice chatters in the kitchen. Vesper attends to the words and pauses, holding her breath. She does not go through or say hello, preferring to wait. If they do not know she is there, they will be their other selves, the ones that worry more, that hint at secrets.

As usual, her Uncle Harm does the talking while her father potters, bringing order to a space bent on chaos. 'You know, a messenger from the Lenses came again today. They wanted to know if everything was alright here. I told him things were nice and quiet. All the usual questions but something felt different this time. He was agitated, kept scratching at something. I almost asked him in for a drink. Poor man seemed exhausted with stress. I suppose they all are up there. Of course, he wouldn't tell me anything.'

A soft whirring begins. Her father must be Bondcleaning the surfaces.

'I'm sure,' Harm continues, 'if you went and spoke with them yourself, I'm sure we could find out more. They're only here for you, after all.'

The cleaning device is clicked to a higher setting and the whirring gets louder, irritating. Vesper takes another deep breath and edges closer, daring a peek into the kitchen.

Her Uncle Harm sits in the good chair, steam curling from the mug in his lap. He raises his voice, managing to keep the tone gentle. 'I know you've made up your mind about this but it wouldn't hurt to know what's going on. Please, go and talk to them? It would put my mind at rest. And can you come over here? I hate talking to you when you're far away.'

The whirring of the machine slows, becomes irregular, stops. Broad shoulders sag. Vesper retreats a step as her father turns and limps across the kitchen. His hair grows long now. Vesper has spent many evenings watching Uncle Harm brush the long brown-grey strands. Even so, it does not hide the scars running through the hairline. Apparently, these could be fixed, just like the missing teeth and the scarred leg, but her father always refuses any offers of surgery. Harm says he's as stubborn as the goat, which makes her father smile. But he never changes his mind.

Vesper likes the scars. They're proof of a different life. When her father was the heroic knight that her Uncle talks about, not this tired man who frowns too much.

Her father stops by the chair, leans on it, stoops forward. Harm's hands fumble their way upwards, searching for his face.

'There you are.' Fingers brush features: a chin that needs shaving, crow's feet deepening around the eyes. They find

13

lines furrowing the forehead and smooth them away. 'They know you're not going to fight again. Nobody's expecting you to. But I think we should at least know what's going on, just in case.'

Soothing hands are taken in callused ones. The two stand peaceably, enjoying the moment.

As usual, Harm is the first to speak into it. 'I hear things. From the people who bring us offerings. There aren't so many as there used to be but *some* still come. Apparently, Sonorous has declared independence and the First has recognised them. There's been no official response from the Empire yet but either way it won't be good. And have you heard about what's going on in the south? There's a rumour that—'

Hands break apart. Amber eyes fix on the doorway. Vesper is caught in their glare. She smiles quickly, and goes in, clearing her throat. 'What rumour is that, Uncle?'

'Ah, Vesper,' comes the bright-voiced reply, 'it's just gossip, nothing important. How's the goat?'

'She's getting worse. Didn't even bother with this one. It would've died for sure if I hadn't been there.'

'That's the third you've saved now, isn't it?'

'The fifth, actually. But each time, she's doing less.'

'If I was her age, I doubt I'd be much better.'

'How old is she, Uncle?'

Spontaneously, both men smile. 'We've got no idea. But old. If she were human, she would be long past having babies, that's for certain.'

'Well, she's having them but she's not feeding them. I need to get a bottle.'

'Go ahead.'

Hands ruffle her hair as she goes past. She feels her father watching her, and moves quickly. In her haste she fumbles the teat, dropping it. 'Any news from the City?

'Why do you ask?'

She crouches down to collect the teat. 'I . . . thought I saw someone come to the house.'

'It's true, we did have a visitor. And they did come from the City.'

'What did they say?'

'Not much.'

'But they must have said something.'

'You know what it's like, there's always something going on –' Harm hears her excited intake of breath '– but nothing for us to worry about,' he adds quickly.

'Oh.'

Getting nowhere, as always, she collects the teat from the floor and leaves.

Fed and full, the kid goes to sleep in Vesper's arms.

She sits on the front step, enjoying the warm weight of him until her own belly demands attention. The kid grumbles as she puts him down but doesn't wake. Vesper lets out a relieved breath and creeps into the house, her mind already busy conjuring images, succulent and mouth-watering.

Out of habit she listens at the kitchen door, hearing nothing but the sound of soft snoring. A peek reveals Uncle Harm slumped in a chair, enjoying his afternoon nap.

The snores continue, undisturbed by clinking cutlery and enthusiastic consumption.

As she leaves the kitchen, she hears a noise coming from the storeroom and freezes. The door is open a crack but not enough to see what's inside. Curiosity and fear briefly battle within her. She hears another noise, a soft scuffing sound that she cannot identify. Whoever is inside is moving carefully, stealthily.

It must be her father. She wonders what he is up to and reaches out to push at the door, praying that it won't creak. Experience has taught her that if she wants the truth, it is better to look for it herself than to ask questions. The gap widens slowly, half-inch by half-inch.

When she sees inside, her eyes widen considerably faster.

He stands with his back to her, fists trembling at his sides. A low humming sounds near his feet, like a hornet, angry.

Slowly, his head shakes from side to side and the humming gets louder.

She can taste the tension in the air, can see the effect of invisible hands pulling at her father, sees him resisting, leaning back, as if fighting stormy winds.

His head shakes again, faster this time, less confident. His jaw moves but if he says any words, they are too low to make out.

Something seems to break and her father leans down quickly, the movement desperate. There is the sound of a box lid slamming shut.

The humming diminishes but does not vanish.

Her father leans heavily on the box for a moment then stands up.

Vesper pulls back from the door but it is too late, he has seen her. He always sees her.

She adopts what she hopes is a neutral expression. 'Are you alright?'

He marches up to the door and nods curtly. His amber eyes are bloodshot, puffy, and she wonders if he has been crying.

They look at each other for a moment and she feels the need to say something, to reach out to him. She has no idea where to begin and offers him a weak smile instead.

His lips move, threatening a sentence and she dares to hope that, for once, he is going to open up, but he cuts it off in its infancy with another sharp nod.

The door closes between them.

With an angry mutter, Vesper plonks herself down on the hillside. The kid comes and sits next to her.

'It isn't fair!' she exclaims, making the kid look up in alarm. 'He never tells me what's going on. And he never lets me go anywhere or do anything. I am so bored of goats and grass.' To take the sting out of her words she strokes the kid's soft head. 'But you are very cute.'

The afternoon is spent watching the horizon, scope in hand. Scanning the distant edges of the Shining City, hoping for glimpses of a place featured in her Uncle's stories but never visited. Today she is rewarded. A group of young people gather in a circle. She maximises the zoom on the scope to drink in the details. Their clothes are all alike, unadorned, white; there is no fashion for the young in the Shining City, and their hair is of uniform cut. There is something formal about the way they stand and she wonders what it is that they do.

The formation is familiar, sparking the chip in her head to take action. It analyses the group, noting formation and age, and categorises them, popping the noun into Vesper's brain: a choir. In the Shining City all young people are grouped into choirs from an early age. This keeps them from becoming too strongly attached to parents or siblings. Every six months the membership of a particular choir changes to prevent social bonds growing too deep. This way, loyalty to the Empire is assured.

Vesper does not see social engineering or the sparks being slowly stifled. She sees mystery and is hungry for more.

For a time, she watches, noting every movement and gesture. She has no idea what they discuss but is certain every word is fascinating.

She does not notice the man until he is nearly upon her. He appears as a giant in the scope, a portion of pale scalp suddenly filling her vision. With a shriek she falls backwards, sending the kid scurrying back up the hill and out of sight.

Embarrassed, she sits up, looks a second time. Without the scope the man is much less scary. His clothes are black, robust, and a badge of the winged eye stands proud on his collar. His hair is red and wiry and struggles to escape, springing wide on the other side of his hairband. One of the Lenses, like the visitor her uncle spoke of.

'Hello,' she says, giving a hesitant wave.

The man looks up the hill at her. 'Good afternoon, Vesper.'

'You know my name?'

'Yes, we've met. A long time ago. I helped your father once, got him into Six Circles and across the sea. My name is Genner, did he ever mention me?'

'Nope.'

Genner stiffens. 'As I said, it was a long time ago.'

'Are you here to see him?'

'I'm here to help him. At least I would be if he'd let me.'

She nods, knowing exactly what he means. 'You think he needs help, too?'

'I have a feeling he will soon. Do you think you could persuade him to come out and talk?'

'I don't know. He's . . .'

'He's what? It's very important you tell me, Vesper.'

Words come and go, none fit. She shrugs. 'Difficult. Something's going on but he won't tell me what it is.'

He comes and sits beside her and they both look out towards the city as he talks. 'I'm one of the Lenses. We watch for trouble and when it comes we guide the Seraph Knights and the armies of the Winged Eye to where they're needed in order to protect us.'

'You know Seraph Knights?'

'Oh, yes. I even give them orders from time to time.' He takes a moment, enjoying the awe on her face, then sighs. 'Something is very wrong in the south, Vesper. The Seven feel it in their sanctum, and we're sure Gamma's sword feels it too. We need your father to take up the sword again, and when he does, I intend to make sure he isn't alone.'

Vesper is quiet while clouds flit by, fluffy, incongruous. 'Is it dangerous?'

'Yes.'

'What if he doesn't want to do it?'

'It doesn't matter if he wants to or not. There is nobody else.' He takes his gaze from the sky and turns it on her. 'What I really want to do is burst in there and order him to help us. But your father is chosen of The Seven, it puts him beyond my authority. I need him to come of his own free will. I need you to talk to him.'

She gets up. 'My father is a hero. When he realises how bad things are, he'll help, I know he will.'

'So you'll talk to him?'

19

'Yes.'

He waves to her as she runs back up the hill. 'Winged Eye watch over you.'

At dinner, the scrape of knife on plate sounds sharp in the ear, the noises of eating too loud. Harm's banter is subdued and her father's attention fixed on food barely touched. Vesper glances at the two of them, uncertain of her chances. She tries anyway.

'I was thinking, now I'm older, it might be time to see more of the world.'

A frown appears on her father's face.

Harm reaches for her hand, finds it and gives it a squeeze. 'Your father and I were talking just the other day, about how fast you're growing, every time we turn our backs it seems!' Her father's frown deepens. 'But to be safe out there –' he nods towards the Shining City '– we feel there are still things you need to learn. To be safe—'

'What if you came with me? Both of you. We could go to the Shining City. It isn't far. That way I could see things and you'd know I was safe.'

Her father gets up, collecting the used plates, and Harm replies, 'Now isn't a good time.'

Vesper's face darkens. 'It's never a good time.'

'I know it feels that way.'

'I'm not a child any more.' Her father looks round at that, an eyebrow raised. 'I'm not! I know something is going on! And I want to help.'

She feels the weight of their attention, hesitates. 'A man from the Lenses spoke to me today. He said things are getting bad. He said they need you to be a hero again, like you used to be, and this time I want to come with you.' Her father shakes his head and she falters. When she finds her voice again it is small. 'You're going to leave me behind.'

'Don't worry,' Harm soothes. 'We're not leaving you behind. We're not going anywhere. Everything's fine.'

'That's not what the man said.'

Harm nods sadly. 'Things out there are never fine. Even before the Breach there were wars and plagues and floods, and goodness knows what else. We can't look after the world.' He glances at her father. 'We've learnt that the hard way. But we can look after each other.'

'He said father had to do it. He said there isn't anyone else that can bear Gamma's sword.'

'That sword can speak for itself. If it wanted to be used again, we'd know about it by now.'

'But it does!'

'I doubt that.'

'I've heard it and so has he.'

'That's enough,' warns Harm.

She looks at her father for confirmation but sees only his back as he does the dishes. A frown of her own appears, a tiny mirror of her father's. Tears of frustration build, and the discussion ends, abrupt, unsatisfactory, with no mention of Genner or the threat to the Shining City.

The frown stays with her for the rest of the day, a constant companion.

Vesper snaps awake, heart pounding. She sits up, peering into the comfortable dark of her room. She is alone. This surprises her. She was sure of the opposite. Bare feet slip onto cold floor and she pads to the window. Outside, the only lights are distant, unable to penetrate the moat of darkness at the base of the hill.

The house seems quiet. Vesper waits for her pulse to settle and listens. She begins to detect the soft murmur of Uncle Harm's voice and beneath it . . . something else. She frowns, unable to place the sound. It is a kind of humming, more felt than heard. It stirs the blood. She remembers the sound from earlier in the day, and her father's fear.

When it comes to sneaking through the house, Vesper knows all of the tricks. Squeaky boards are avoided, obstacles skillfully stepped around or over. Her door is opened just enough, so slow as to be silent. Soon she creeps past her parents' room.

'Ssh,' says her uncle.

Vesper freezes, panic gripped until she realises that the voice is not directed at her.

'It was just a dream. I'm right here. Vesper's asleep next door. We're all okay . . . Ssh . . . Go back to sleep.'

Against all reason, Vesper risks a glance inside. Uncle Harm lies beside her father, propped up on an elbow, stroking his brow. Her father's eyes are closed and Vesper relaxes a little.

As her father drifts back into sleep, tension falls away, making him appear suddenly younger. Not young, Vesper decides, but not as old as he looks in the day.

She doesn't stop to wonder if her uncle is lying or simply unaware, and moves quickly downstairs, determined to do something to help.

Since her previous visit to the storeroom, boxes have been stacked in front of the door, blocking it. Young arms struggle with the weight and she is forced to place them heavily. She winces as each one clunks against the floor, waiting for the tell-tale sounds of her father or uncle being disturbed.

But upstairs, all is quiet.

Sweating, she removes the last obstacle and goes inside. The room is small, more a glorified cupboard than living space. Junk is stacked messily on top of boxes. Vesper begins to pull things down. She is often distracted. An old rubber lung catches her eye. She squeezes it and it sighs for her. The sound is comforting. She sniffs it, enjoying the faint tang. There are other things, half-finished carvings that her father has abandoned. One is of a smiling knight with bulging muscles. Most are of a woman, vague shapes never fully realised.

When she lifts the first box clear the humming gets fractionally louder.

Excitement and youth make quick work of the pile. Boxes are dumped behind her, scattering across the kitchen floor, haphazard. Without them, the storeroom looks spacious.

Vesper frowns, listens again. She searches the corners, now accessible, finding only dust-heavy webs, long vacated.

Nothing. The storeroom is empty.

As quickly as it came, excitement vanishes. Vesper hangs her head. But humming persists, not imagined, invisible. She feels it through her feet. With a vengeance, excitement returns. Vesper presses her cheek flat on the floor and sees a board not quite aligned with the others. Fingers work the edge, teasing it up until purchase can be found. She lifts the board and sees space underneath. She lifts two more, revealing a shallow hole lined in trembling plastic. She dares to touch it, feels the humming through her fingers.

More carefully now, reverent, she pulls it back to reveal a

long dusty box and a pair of old boots. The boots release a heady musk, mixing damp, old sweat, and other less savoury things. Vesper pulls them on anyway. She tries walking in them, imagining herself as a mysterious traveller. But boots soon fall from little feet, one thump, then another. They remain upright, stiff from experience.

The box is heavy and Vesper struggles to lift it out. Twice it slips out of her fingers, sliding back into the hole at an angle. She does not try a third time, instead leaning into the hole and flipping the catch. The lid creaks as it opens, protesting. A cloud of dust puffs out, demanding its tribute of coughs. Vesper obliges, once, twice, thrice.

An old coat has been used to pack the box. Vesper takes it out. The fabric is worn but tough, reassuring. The coat has been stitched together in places. Lower down, scorch marks and bite marks decorate, left by tainted dogs and unearthly fires. She puts the coat on. It is too big for her, almost a robe. The reality of how she looks in it makes no impact on Vesper's imagination and she keeps it on, grinning.

Only then does she look down.

The humming has quietened, softening into contentment. At the bottom of the box lies a sword. Sheathed. Silvered wings wrapping the hilt unfurl, reach up to her. Open, they reveal an eye set in the crosspiece, staring, waiting.

One Thousand, One Hundred and Thirty-Seven Years Ago

In a storm of purple lighting where clouds look like egg sacs and the sky like a cavernous throat, a baby is born. Only the baby can see the storm, however. To the others the sky appears as it always does, a haze of light pollution and smog.

They wonder why the newborn is showing signs of distress. Experts circle her glassy pod, examining. She seems healthy, a good strong set of lungs, a decent heart. All limbs appear in working order. The experts shake their heads, concluding it is just a temperamental issue, merely emotional. They dose the baby with calming drugs and, as expected, it settles down.

Years pass and the baby is given a name, a gender and a social class. The baby becomes a girl, Massassi, and she is put into the lower middle echelons. Her supervisor is warned of her predisposition to irrational outbursts and authorised to medicate where necessary.

The girl becomes an apprentice mechanic and proves skilful. At the tender age of eight, she is assigned work on the great construction mechs, crawling into nooks and crannies, repairing. It is dangerous work. The mechs are automated and held to rigid schedules. They pause rarely and never for very long. The girl must be quick or dead. She darts between pistons, removing blockages, replacing worn parts, squeezing into spaces too tight for adult bodies. For the first year, she is quick enough.

Perhaps it is a mark of respect that she is trusted with such deadly work, or perhaps it is because she does not get on with her peers or her supervisor, or anyone else. Massassi is a brooding, angry girl. Too clever for her age but not clever enough, not yet.

She enjoys the thrill of her work, finds the thought-invading anger that haunts her nights is sated by daily brushes with death.

There is no time off, no holiday to take, but all workers have enforced downtime, carefully scheduled activity changes to maximise efficiency. More than anything else, she dreads the mandatory social gatherings. One day, after three consecutive events, the anger grows so strong that she starts to break things. Immediately, an alarm sounds on her supervisor's HUD and he whispers an order.

Implanted dispensers in Massassi's spine go to work and anger fades, humbled.

She remembers little of these times but doesn't complain, even prefers it that way. When she requests dangerous levels of overtime, her supervisor doesn't check too closely.

Massassi is ten when she has the accident.

Her thoughts are elsewhere, cloudy with free-floating emotion. She is supposed to be fixing the shoulder motors of Superior Class Harvester 4879-84/14 but all she wants to do is tear them apart. For the first time, she wonders why she is different, and if perhaps everyone else is not at fault after all.

Preoccupation, however slight, is dangerous. Massassi combines hers with fatigue and a self-destructive streak. Too late, she realises the Harvester is reactivating. Massassi tries to throw herself clear but her sleeve catches on a piece of wiring, wiring she would normally have secured.

She cannot free her arm.

Engines roar with power, blades spin, lights flash.

The Harvester moves.

Massassi screams.

Blood smears between metal plates, bones grind to chalky powder.

On her supervisor's HUD, an alarm sounds.

CHAPTER TWO

Thoughts come like the tide from a distant shore. They get closer, louder, more insistent. Gradually, they gain form, lifting through the fog, breaking the spell.

As awareness returns, Vesper finds herself leaning into the hole, hands hovering inches from a feathered hilt, perfectly aligned with the upturned wings, like partners before a dance.

The girl blinks, the sword does not.

It glares at her for a few moments, judgemental, then the eye closes with sudden disinterest. Apparently, she is not the one it wants.

She thinks of her father, standing in the same spot earlier that day, and she begins to understand why he was afraid.

It is tempting to repack the room and turn her back on it but she knows that won't work. The sword will keep calling and wearing her father down. He is already tired, it will only be matter of time before he succumbs.

Something must be done.

She swallows, realising that she has come to a decision.

The sword has to go. She resolves to take it to Genner and let him deal with it. There are many knights after all. They will find one and give the sword to them. Afterwards she will come home and it will be safe again. Her father will be free.

She removes the sword from the storeroom to the kitchen and returns its box to the hole, covering it with floorboards. Then she replaces all of the boxes, trying her best to match their original positions. Finished, she shuts the door and blocks it as her father had earlier.

With luck, she thinks, he'll never know what's happened.

Only after she's finished does she realise she's still wearing the old coat. She gives a shrug, happy, deciding to keep it.

Vesper creeps back to her room and dresses in silence, quickly. She collects the sword last, wrapping it in an old plastic sheet. Scared it might wake again, she tries to make as little contact with it as possible, being especially careful to avoid the hilt and the eye twitching within.

When she opens the door a cold breeze touches her cheeks. She shivers and sets off, not noticing the small body curled by the front door. At the sound of her passing, the kid blinks awake, springing up. He looks round, sleep forgotten at the sight of his good mother, and follows.

Both forms are quickly swallowed by the night.

The sword is lighter than it looks, but still heavy for a young girl to carry. In the dark, familiar ground becomes strange, and Vesper stumbles down the hill, jolting her legs, the bundle bouncing in her arms. Despite plastic wrapping, its edge digs into forearms, painful.

She pauses halfway down, looks at the sword again, sure

29

that under the four layers of plastic, it is looking back. She swallows, sniffs. Dust tickles nostrils and she wipes her nose on her sleeve, only to discover her new coat is filthy. Sneezes come.

Paranoia makes her look back towards the house. But instead of her father, watching from a window, she finds the kid at her heels.

Shifting the weight of the sword onto one arm, she points back up the hill with the other. 'Go, off you go. You can't come with me. Go home.'

A warm head butts against her hand.

'No. You need to go back. You need to . . .' Vesper trails off, finds herself stroking the kid. 'I suppose we won't be gone long, are you sure you want to come?'

The kid looks at her, eyes full of love, mouth full of hunger.

She sighs, returning to the house to grab a bottle of milk from the kitchen before hurrying back. 'Come on then.'

Together, they continue, picking their way across uneven ground. More than once, she trips in the dark. 'Stupid! Should've packed a torch.'

The kid bleats, hoping for food.

'Don't worry, I'm sure we'll find our way.'

As if in answer a light winks into existence at the bottom of the hill, illuminating a man in dark uniform, the only decoration a badge of the winged eye at the collar. As girl and goat approach, the figure resolves into a familiar shape: Genner. He shines his light on them. 'Vesper? What . . .? His light travels to the sword and back up to Vesper's face. 'What are you doing with a relic of The Seven?'

'I'm sorry!' she blurts. 'I had to, I—'

Genner's frown smoothes suddenly. 'It chose you!' he exclaims.

'We expected it to call your father . . . but it's you! You . . . you are the new bearer.'

Caught between trouble and truth, she nods, her eyes darting back towards the house with the lie.

He goes down on one knee, lowering his head. Ginger hair refuses to be sombre, springing from its tie like an angry bush. Words are intoned, soft, musical, their meaning lost on Vesper. Genner looks up. 'Thank The Seven. Bearer, we must—'

'Me?' She stifles a laugh. 'I'm not . . . I just thought, well, if my father doesn't want to use the sword, I should take it to someone who did.'

'Vesper, you don't understand. The sword lets you carry it. It has chosen you.'

She remembers the way it looked at her and doesn't believe him. 'I suppose so.' Vesper looks warily over her shoulder.

Behind Genner, the air shimmers as if struck by the summer suns. A beat later, the space is filled by a sky-ship. Vesper's eyes widen, taking in the stars reflected in its surface, and the tapering wings where twin engines spin, murmuring.

Genner smirks. 'That's exactly what I said when I first saw one.'

The kid is less impressed, diving for cover behind Vesper's legs.

'Are you ready, bearer?'

On the side of the sky-ship a door opens, swinging upward on a hinge. 'This way,' Genner says, gesturing to the door. 'We've been waiting for you.'

Vesper allows herself to be led aboard, hesitating briefly as thoughts of her parents flare, worried faces, words of disappointment, and that frown.

The kid panics. Before he can make a decision, the girl and the man have climbed inside. With a cry, the kid dashes after them.

The door shuts before he gets there.

The kid cries out again.

The engines spin faster, light building, taking the weight of the sky-ship, preparing to leap towards heaven.

The door opens again and Vesper's head appears. 'Come on then!'

This time the kid doesn't hesitate.

As soon as he has leapt inside, the door closes again. Light pulses, pushing down, and grass sprays outward. The frame of the vehicle trembles, the air around it becoming opaque.

A moment later, the sky-ship is gone.

The first of the suns begins to rise, charging the air gold. Its light picks up a house on top of a hill. The house is quiet, full of tension. The door opens and a man steps out. He limps quickly across to the smaller house and looks inside.

Dark eyes glare at him.

He ignores them and goes back into the other house. Minutes pass and he appears again, this time with a hand-carved staff. The wood is worn with use, much like the man that carries it. He sets out quickly, wincing as he goes, amber eyes hunting the grasses.

Harm steps out soon after, moving slowly. He also carries a stick but, rather than leaning on it, he lets it brush the earth by his feet, bouncing lightly, testing for bumps.

'Any sign of her?'

Vesper's father doesn't answer, continuing his study of the ground.

Irregular footprints are easily found in the dirt. Nodding grimly, he follows.

The red glow of the second sun tints the clouds as he reaches the bottom of the hill.

He stops, frowning at the carnage inflicted on the ground. Powerful forces have churned earth here, eating the trail. His frown deepens. No tracks appear on the other side.

He looks up, shielding his eyes from the light.

Nothing.

Eventually, Harm's hand finds his shoulder. He allows himself to be turned round, takes a breath to speak but, instead of words, tears fall.

For a long time they stand, two men joined in sadness, their shadows circling, the suns slow-dancing across the sky.

*

Away from the hustle and bustle of the imperial port, three figures haggle. Waves lap the rocks. Gossip and insults fly back and forth, changing hands faster than goods. Underneath gruff exteriors a strange affection lies. Each has survived long enough to weather the distaste of the other. Each has a secret.

One is a woman who fled from the south years ago. As her companions fell around her, she found the strength to move forward, fuelled by their failure. Sometimes she dreams of those days, waking with the taste of raw meat on her lips.

One is a man who steals goods from others, passing them off as his own.

One is neither woman nor man. Appearing to mortal eyes

they appear as a woman of middling years. Perhaps her hair is a little lank, her skin a little pale, but this is hardly uncommon for those forced to live beyond the Shining City's border.

The three hide their true natures, keeping well clear of the Winged Eye's agents, skulking in the fringes.

As they continue their haggling and grumblings, a sky-ship passes overhead, quick, invisible.

Two of the figures do not notice. The third looks up sharply, as if a wasp has stung her on the crown.

'You alright there, Nell?'

She pauses. The others cannot see the essence flow around her. Normally, the First keeps each of its fragments buried deep within mortal shells, to protect them from the rage of the world. However, a link between them remains, faint, a spiderweb drawn in watercolour, more memory than substance, an echo. And while each is distinct, evolved slightly away from the original, they can, for a moment, become one again.

The First takes the moment. Experiences jar together, jumbling, confusing, multiple timelines jostling, arranging themselves, finding order. Briefly, the First breathes easily, unconstrained.

Then the burning starts and it is over.

Lines of essence fade and consciousness divides, shrinking down.

In total, the pause is little more than the heartbeat of a hummingbird, but that is all it takes for the information to pass unseen across the ocean.

Such exertions cause the First terrible pain but impulses are easily controlled. In a dozen different places, faces twitch, stammer and reset to normal.

'Can't complain, Jacky,' replies Nell. 'Reckon we might be havin' a storm soon though.'

'You reckon?'

Nell looks up at the apparently empty sky and scratches at her belly, making the action appear spontaneous. 'Feel it in my bones so I do. It's a storm alright. A big one.'

CHAPTER THREE

Samael walks the last mile to the Fallen Palace. He does not need to slow down. Muscles can be forced beyond human limits and fatigue is a stranger to him, a person passed by in another life, no longer relevant. He walks to appear more powerful. He walks because, despite the growing threat behind him, it feels like the right thing to do.

Mud clings to his boots, to his shins, reaching up to his knees like a desperate lover. Flies buzz in close orbit, circling, never landing, both drawn to and repelled by his rotting body.

Ahead of him the Fallen Palace rises from the swamp. Once it flew, an airborne fortress for Gamma of The Seven. Infernal forces brought it low, smashed it, climbed inside. A haven of demons ruled by the strongest. For a long time the Usurper held that title, now it is in dispute. Infernals turn on one another. The strong fight the weak, crushing them, making followers or bloody examples. Factions form, face off, break apart. Despite several attempts to take it, the Usurper's throne remains empty.

The residents of the Fallen Palace are ever watchful. Any could rise to the top and all are fair game.

This is why Samael walks.

Over the years, the Fallen Palace has begun to sink, like a boat going down in slow motion. In tiny incremental shifts one half plunges lower, exaggerating the tilt of the floor, raising the other half upwards. The increased strain shakes foundations. From time to time, towers break, sometimes caught between their fellows, sometimes sliding into the swamp, piling onto one another, forming new habitations.

Samael works his way up, pulling himself onto a turret that has toppled over and become a path. The slippery curved sides have been battered into rough flatness by many feet. Boots ring out on metal, clanking dully, off key.

Beneath them, things stir. Red and green eyes appear at glassless windows, peering upwards, angry. Samael ignores them, continues at a steady pace. An infernal hauls itself out of a hole, blocking the way. A beast with two backs, joined at the hip, at the chest, at the chin. Like a person pressing themselves against a mirror, it stands on four legs, toes touching their opposites, fused together. With effort, it twists its heads towards him, skin pulling tight where they join.

Samael is forced to look up to meet its gaze, higher ground emphasising their greater size.

In each hand, the creature holds a weapon. A rock, the claw of a victim, a rotting branch and a Dogspawn dangling from a chain. Of the four weapons, only the half-bred hound remains animate, broken legs kicking feebly, mouth still strong, savage.

The sword that Samael carries is a simple piece of metal, sharp but voiceless. He draws it and prepares to fight.

Immediately, the creature swings for him, misjudging the distance, and Samael rushes forward, sword high. The infernal stumbles back, bonded legs unable to accommodate the demands of combat. At the last second it raises all four arms, making an ugly barrier.

Samael continues forward, turning so that shoulder, not blade, makes contact. Not a cut but a push.

There is a slam, then a squeal. The infernal pitches backwards. Soles of feet are briefly visible, then it is gone, Dogspawn and all, swallowed into the swamp.

Samael sheathes his sword and walks on.

His progress is steady. Soon he reaches the point where tower meets floor and steps onto sloping stones. He passes another half-breed, hauling a sack of ill-gotten gains. Her body is naked to the air, the skin healthier, greener. She is one of the younger ones, born tainted. Though both have a mix of mortal and infernal essence, the two could not be more different.

Studiously, they ignore one another.

Many watch Samael as he climbs higher, intent on the Palace's heart, but none dare attack. This last tower remains whole, both broader and taller than its fellows. A place of power, fit for a king. The gleaming metal walls are covered in green veins, thick and lumpy.

Samael finds he does not like this, feels an impulse to scrape them off. It is everything he can do to resist, to not kneel down and tear away the offending growths.

At the base of the tower is an archway, leading to a spiral staircase. He climbs inside and begins to ascend. Because of the way the tower leans, he alternates between using steps and wall to tread. Up he goes, cutting through webs as thick as ropes. The silk patterns are irregular, lopsided, spun by spiders drunk on tainted essence. He feels a surge of pleasure to be destroying them.

He came here once with his creator. The tower did not lean so badly then. He recalls how vacant his thoughts were at that time, when he was merely a follower, a tool. In many ways his own life was facilitated by his creator's death.

Retracing his steps, he muses, half present, half in the past. He walks through corridors, winding, and ducks through angled doorways, pulling himself up the floor until, at last, he comes to it: the tomb.

Fly eggs gather in piles by the door, like swollen grains of rice. Samael has another urge, to crush them under his boot. This he resists.

The door opens before he can knock, revealing the figure he has come to see. Samael pauses, not sure which words to apply to the Man-shape. Friend? Ally? Co-conspirator?

Though the essence that flows within the Man-shape's shell is completely alien, outwardly it appears the more human of the two. Its skin has barely changed since the initial possession and muscles have remained in correct proportion. Unlike most of its kind, the Man-shape wears clothes, choosing them with care. How they remain clean is a mystery.

Its immaculate presentation makes Samael feel like the monster. Reluctantly, he removes his helm.

The Man-shape moves forward, until noses touch.

Samael opens his mouth and the Man-shape does the same, revealing a dark where tongue and vocal cords should be, cavernous.

Two mouths nearly meet, forming a tunnel of sorts. Inside, essences rise, tentative.

Usually, such a sharing would be hazardous between pure infernal and half-breed, but both are careful and the Man-shape excels at treading lightly.

With utmost care, essences brush together, two bubbles threatening to become one.

'You have been away too long. You are needed here, you know that . . . you . . . you are troubled.'

'There is trouble at the Breach. A new threat.'

'There are always threats at the Breach but they cannot reach us at the Palace. You should concern yourself more with what is happening here. We have new challengers for the Usurper's throne: Hangnail, the Backwards Child, Lord Felrunner, Gutterface. You could fight them.'

'You deal with their kind all the time. You fight them. Why bother me?'

'They have been patient, built their strength. I am a king-maker not a king.'

'I am not a king either.'

'What are you then?'

'I . . .'

'I see a man riding land that flows, is this what you are?'

'I . . .'

'I see a man dressing up, playing as something he is not. Is that what you are?'

'No. I . . . I don't know.'

'Exactly. You do not know. But I know. We are what we are made to be. In you the essence of your creator lives on, and the essence of the Usurper was in your creator.'

'Stop distracting me. My place is at the Breach. There is a new threat. It is bigger than anything I've seen before.'

'As big as our master?'

'The Usurper was not my master.'

'As big as my master was?'

'I don't know, I never saw your master, not until its end.'

'I could show you.'

'No. Let me show you.'

'Yes.'

Samael thinks, remembers the Yearning, its strength. Memories rise up like ghosts on glass.

The Man-shape never physically smiles in public, though it practises often in private. Nevertheless, Samael feels the intent to smile. A brief flush of smugness washes over him, not his own.

'What is it?'

'Perhaps I was too hasty before. Yes, I see it now.'

'See what?'

A second wave of smugness comes, more emphatic. 'The answer to all our problems.'

*

Inside the sky-ship, there is little sense of movement. Gyroscopes and energy fields work hard to maintain peace, buffering, adjusting. Padded straps hold Vesper close; she in turn holds the kid and a bottle of milk. Greedy sucking sounds loud above the hushed song of the sky-ship's light drives.

Above and around her, others sit, the lines of seats describing a dome. Men and women, squires mainly, their armour highly polished, their weapons ready, all trying not to stare.

Genner sits opposite, holding himself in a position of authority.

Vesper glances round at the serene faces, then frowns.

She takes a breath to speak, glances again and lets it out, noisily.

'What is it?' asks Genner.

'Are we actually flying?'

'Yes.'

'Where are we going?'

'That depends on you. This –' he spreads his hands outward '– is all to protect you. Tell us what you need and we'll provide it. Tell us where you need to go and we'll take you.'

Vesper scratches the kid behind its ear, contemplating. 'Well, do you think I could have a torch?'

'We are all your torches.'

'Oh. Does that mean I can't have my own?'

Genner's expression flickers between amusement and irritation. 'No – I mean, yes, you can have one but that's not the point.'

Nuances bounce off the girl's smile. 'Then I'd like a torch please. And some more milk for my goat.'

'We'll see you get them. Now tell us, what are Gamma's orders?'

Her smile falters. 'What do you mean?'

'Ever since your father returned Gamma's sword to us, we have been watching, waiting for it to act. Our sole purpose here is to facilitate your mission. So tell me, what are Gamma's orders?'

'I don't know about any orders.'

'Yes, you do. Something made you take up the sword. That was Gamma.'

She shakes her head. 'I just wanted to bring the sword to one of the knights. Then you could use it against the demons and my father's life would go back to normal.'

'But the sword didn't call to me or a knight, it called to you. And if you let it, the sword will communicate its wishes to you. All you have to do is listen.'

Vesper's smile falls away completely as she thinks. The sword is quiet. No sound comes form it, no edicts spring into her thoughts. After a pause, she says, 'You said the problems were in the south?'

'Yes.'

'Then we need to go there.'

'Where in the south? Does Gamma mean to return to the Breach?'

Vesper looks down at the sword for a moment before mumbling something ambiguous.

'I knew it! And she intends to destroy the infernals there?'

A blush creeps across Vesper's cheeks, and she nods.

'And the Breach itself, she's going to seal it, isn't she?'

Vesper's nod, tiny, timid, is more than enough for Genner.

'This is incredible!' he exclaims, and takes a deep breath, freckles fading on reddening skin. 'Forgive me. We have waited a long time for this. You should ask your questions now. There may not be much time to talk when we land.'

'Why is it so important to seal the Breach?'

He looks at her for a moment, calculating, making her worry. 'Outside of the Shining City, the world is very different. It's going to be a shock for you, Vesper, but I'll do my best to prepare you for it. There is a thing called the Taint. Sometimes it can be seen as a kind of smoke but mostly it's invisible to the unaugmented eye. It changes everything it touches – plants, animals, people – mutates them. It's like a poison being pumped into our atmosphere and it all comes

43

from the Breach. And then there are the infernals. The smaller ones will hurt you if you're lucky, eat you if you're not. The larger ones possess people, make them their slaves. An infernal is stronger and faster than we are. They don't get tired and they can twist and break you from the inside. I don't mean to scare you . . .'

Vesper pulls a face at the suggestion. 'You aren't scaring me. My uncle told me about the infernals, but he said they weren't all bad.'

'Yes, well. They've taken control of the south, more or less, and their reach is getting longer. There are thousands and thousands of them and every single one has come from the Breach. The only way for the Empire and humanity to survive is if we close it. And only one of The Seven –' his eyes go to the sword '– has the power to do that. Gamma was chosen for the task and you have been chosen to bear the sword that holds Her remains, to bear Her.'

Vesper opens her mouth to protest but Genner continues regardless. 'But remember, you're not alone. Each person on board is within the top one per cent of the Empire's finest and all of us are ready to fight, and die if need be.'

'Are there knights here?'

'Twenty-five are with us, all veterans hand-picked by the Knight Commander himself. Each has three squires. In addition, we have a small infantry unit packed into the base of the ship.'

Vesper begins looking around again, then points excitedly at the people either side of her. 'Are they knights? Are you knights?'

One stares straight ahead, contemplating infinity. The other looks back at the girl, catches herself and looks away.

'This,' says Genner, gesturing to the two women, 'is Duet. She's a Harmonised, which is incredibly rare—'

'Is that a special kind of knight?'

'Well, no, not exactly. The Harmonised are a subset of the Order. They're guardians, specially trained to protect against infernal influence.'

Vesper nods, disappointment peeking through the gesture. 'That sounds good.'

Despite the girl's lack of enthusiasm, Duet remains stoic beneath her visors.

Genner's reply is earnest: 'It is. Where we're going it won't just be your body at risk but your mind and spirit. Any contact, even just being close to an infernal, is dangerous and there are a lot of infernals between us and our destination. That's why we're travelling fast and light. We should be able to sail straight over the enemy's forces. If the Winged Eye wills it, we'll be able to set you down right next to the Breach.'

Minutes tick by and Genner settles back like the others, meditative. Vesper bites her lip and strokes the kid, who has fallen asleep in her lap. 'How long till we get there?'

'Four hours.'

She tries not to be sick. A lip receives further mauling. Toes wriggle, heels tap repeatedly against the wall. Everyone else remains still.

Nerves overwhelm her. She contemplates confessing but dares not, nearly asks Genner to turn the sky-ship around, but between mind and mouth, the question wilts into something mundane. Anything to fill the silence.

'So we're actually flying?'

Genner opens his eyes. 'Yes. We're actually flying.'

'I wish we could see outside.'

'Only the pilot needs to see.'

'Where's the pilot?'

'In the iris pod.'

Feet pause their tapping. Vesper's brow creases in thought. She begins to open her mouth, pauses.

'What is it?'

'Please, would it be possible for me to sit in the iris pod?'

'That's not standard procedure.'

'Oh. I understand.'

Genner makes a speech, about safety, about protocol, trying to explain, to restore the happy face of moments ago. 'I'm sorry, that's just how it is.' Before he can say more, a square lights up at his throat, then another within his ear.

The communication makes the young man sit up, straps cutting into his shoulders. He speaks rapidly. 'How many? How do they even know we're here? Is the stealth active? Yes. Yes. I'll await your report.'

As lights fade from skin, Genner meets Vesper's eye.

A quaver disturbs the girl's voice. 'What was that?'

'Rogue sky-ships, three of them. They're on an intercept course.'

'What does that mean?'

'It means no more talking. Brace for impact!'

Figures tense, gripping the arms of seats about and above her. No words are said but many mouths move, intoning the litany: *Winged Eye save us, protect us, deliver us.*

Three sky-ships move in formation. Once, they wore their allegiance to the Winged Eye proudly. Now, those signs have been defaced, with blood or with knives, symbolic. They swoop down together, ready to attack. Their target is invisible, hidden from mortal sight. This does not stop them, for the First guides their hand, finding the needle in the sky and plucking it.

Missiles fire, and the three ships peel away, keen to avoid retaliation.

The target makes an optimistic attempt to evade the attack. It spins, dives, spits balls of light in its wake, distractions that sparkle, tempting.

But the pilot's manoeuvres are as out of date as the countermeasures. Superior missiles find their mark, shattering shields, tearing engines.

In a gasp of fire, the Light-drives fail.

As the sky-ship begins to fall, a cloud of pods explodes from it in every direction, like a sneeze. Each pod is just bigger than the adult it carries. Orders mobilize them and they streak towards the nearest landmass; a formation of white-tailed comets heading to a half-made island, home of the Harmonium Forge and the airy prison: Sonorous.

Part prison colony, part port, Sonorous looms up from the water, buildings bolted onto a vast semicircle of rock. Within the sheltered waters, ships rest. Lifts sway gently as they move between the different sectors, from the dock level at the bottom to the watchtower three miles above. The prison is built on the outer curve, cells dangling from chains over the open ocean.

Tiny roads spiderweb between crammed buildings on the lower levels. By contrast, Sonorous' main road, the Tradeway, sprawls out like a fat tongue, running from the port to the mountain's edge. From here it angles mildly up, a leisurely spiral snaking towards the mid-level, where it meets the machine factories.

Only the Tradeway is large enough to support the four crawlertanks as they groan from their hangars. Mechanised legs bear heavy oval bodies, packed with troops. They travel the length of the Tradeway at speed, warming cannons as they go, for the island kingdom has only recently declared independence and when its rulers see the flurry of pods streaking overhead they assume the worst.

Fearing that the Empire of the Winged Eye has come to reclaim its wayward colony, they summon their soldiers, send a message to the First for aid, and hide in custom-made bunkers, prepared for just such an occasion.

Above, the pods decelerate and spend the last of their reserves in fields of energy, dazzling, sparking as they take the impact of landing.

They come down, some in the streets, some punching through walls. Metal rain that destroys noisily.

People run. Unable to tell which way is safest, they go in random directions. Dust plumes around them, lending a gritty mystery to the scene. Gradually, noise settles. Air clears.

A pod sits in a trench of its own making. A rectangle of white fades up along one of its sides. Soon after, there is a popping sound, soft, anticlimactic, and a segment of metal falls away, allowing a man to stumble out. He brings a hand to his forehead. His fingers come away moist, a much darker red than his hair. He wipes them quickly, then pulls a gun free from its holster.

He scans the streets, counting pods, watching them disgorge

their contents onto the floor. Aside from his own people, the streets are empty.

They will not stay that way for long.

The man intones his name, not Genner, his real one. In answer, knights clank to attention, drawing swords, saluting. Squires rush to their sides and soldiers come limping, come running, moving as best they can into formation.

Duet does not join them, choosing instead to watch through a hole in a cracked wall. She stands either side of a pale-faced Vesper, fencing her between steel and stone.

The girl straightens, trying to peer through the hole. 'What's—'

Duet's hands find her shoulders, silencing, pushing her back down.

Before the wall cuts the scene from her eyes, shots ring out. A squire catches a bullet with his hip, spinning twice before falling. The bullet continues on its merry way, barely slowed, bouncing off walls, looking for more targets. Knights and soldiers disperse, returning fire.

Behind the wall, Vesper struggles to make sense of the chaos outside. She hears more orders being given. They are under attack. More shots, shouts, the sudden belching of fire and screaming, like pigs being savaged by wolves. Pushing aside Duet, she manages to catch a glimpse of the action. Bodies twisting and tearing, people running, some of them on fire. She does not know who is dying and suddenly it does not matter. Nobody should suffer this way.

Vesper ducks down, unwilling to see further.

But the sounds continue, forcing past hands pressed over ears. Fire rumbles, steady, underscoring the highs and lows of battle, constant against the chatter of guns and screams of the injured. Time stretches, each moment heaping age on Vesper's shoulders. She weeps, but war cares little for tears or the children that shed them.

Then, twenty-five voices rise together, thrumming along sacred blades, irresistible. And even though their judgement is not directed at her, even though the girl knows that this is the sound of the Seraph Knights joining the fight, she shivers.

In her arms, the sword is heavy and cold.

Hands release their pressure from Vesper's shoulders but they do not leave. Duet nods, two heads moving as one. 'It is safe –'

'– For now.'

Her voices are complementary, not identical but seamless in the way they join their sentences.

Vesper looks from one to the other, quickly wipes her eyes. 'I don't understand . . . they weren't infernal, they were just people. Like us. All the blood!' Her mouth twists with horror. 'I'm sorry. I can't . . .'

Duet looks down at her and her sentence dies, unfinished.

'They are –'

'– Calling us.'

'We must –'

'– Go now.'

Duet guides her around piles of rubble. On the far side of the street, Vesper can make out something charred, smoking. Fascination and horror come hand in hand. For a while she cannot tell which side the body belonged to. No, she thinks, it is not one of theirs. Flecks of magenta in the uniform identify the unfortunate as Sonorous independent military. The realisation brings little relief.

A palm presses in the small of her back, moving her on. There is so much wreckage for such a small skirmish, she cannot take it all in, nor can she stop looking. Limbs, bits of clothing, unrecognisable hunks of meat, still sizzling on the stone. Smells invade nostrils, snake up into the brain to make memories, lasting.

On broken chunks of brick, she sees blood glistening. The sight makes her stop. There are no corpses here, just bricks flecked crimson and a dark puddle spreading between them. The strangeness of it holds her, troubling a traumatised mind.

'What happened here?'

'It doesn't –'

'– Matter.'

'But how did the blood get here? Who did it belong to? This doesn't make any sense.'

'This is war –'

'People die. That's –'

'– All.'

'But there has to be more to it than that!'

Duet exchanges an exasperated look with herselves. 'They are traitors –'

'– Who side with demons.'

'It's them –'

'– Or us.'

Vesper's eyes are too wide, staring but not seeing.

'We have –'

'– To go.'

She doesn't hear Duet, doesn't catch the urgency in the Harmonised's tone. 'But who were they?'

'We have –'

'– To go.'

'This was a person once.'

One of Duet tuts, the other sighs heavily, and both take one of Vesper's arms, dragging her the rest of the way.

As they get closer to the main group, Vesper sees that Sonorous has lost many troops this day. Their own forces have fared better. Only one knight has fallen. Squires attend their dead master, reclaiming armour and sword. Such items are priceless, made by the creator when the Empire of the Winged Eye was born. Stripped of office and dignity, the corpse is placed with the others. There is no time for ceremony, so the soldiers move quickly, levelling their lances, incinerating remains. A knight's death is regrettable, an untainted corpse left behind for the infernals, unforgivable.

Genner strides over to meet them. 'You're unharmed?'

Duet answers for the young girl. 'The bearer –'

'– Is unharmed.'

'Then all is not lost. Help is coming but it will take time to reach us. We're going to take the forge and hold out for rescue.'

'This is wrong!' Vesper exclaims, clutching the fabric of Genner's uniform in her fists. 'These people have died because of me! I'm not the bearer. I'm just a stupid girl. You take the sword. Here.'

He leans closer to her ear, lowering his voice. 'It's too late for that. You are the bearer, you have to believe that and they –' he gestures to the troops and squires, patching wounds and forming up behind him '– have to believe it too.'

Tears stream down cheeks, mixing with snot on her top lip.

Genner turns to the Harmonised. 'She's in shock. Get her some stims and keep her under cover until we're ready to move.'

There is a pause that threatens to become a protest but Genner kills it in its infancy. 'Step to it!'

Duet salutes and escorts Vesper back towards the wall. One of her hands is firmer on the girl's shoulder. Vesper grits her teeth, stifling complaint.

They climb through a dusty hole into a washroom. Vacuum pipes coil untouched in transparent cases. A crashed pod covers most of the space, spearing the cleaning booth, like a dart in a board. Duet releases Vesper in a corner, then turns, wrenching the door from the booth and placing it across the hole.

Vesper's thoughts are a jumble, she doesn't know what to do or say or think. To her surprise, she sneezes.

She blinks. A moment later, she sneezes again.

Dust is tickling her nose. She looks up, sees a trickle coming from a crack in the ceiling in bursts, uneven.

In seconds, Duet is by her side.

Through the silence, footsteps can be heard, multiple and fast, each one sending a fresh spray of dust as it passes overhead.

From outside, a new noise invades: a rumbling, heavy and distant, heralding the coming of metal beasts.

Duet moves either side of the door and raises her swords, ready.

'What should I do?' asks Vesper.

'Hide –'

'– In there,' replies Duet, pointing to the booth.

Before she can go further, invisible forces hammer the door, wrenching it half from housings to swing drunkenly open. Vesper's mouth mirrors the spirit of the movement.

A metal ball the size of a baby's fist rolls into the room. It stops, clicks.

Instinctively, Vesper leans back.

And Duet is moving, breaking harmony. One throws herself at the girl, trying to push her clear, trying to put herself in harm's way. The other's sword sweeps down, flicking the ball back the way it came. The move is quick, sure, too late.

Halfway out of the room the ball explodes, filling the air with corkscrew slivers, burning hot. They carve through Duet's chestplate, biting a hundred times into flesh beneath.

She takes two paces back, then two more, sword slipping from her fingers. She sways like a reed in the breeze before following her blade, a graceful slide onto her knees. While one woman goes down, the other leaps up, eyes intent on the doorway.

Bullets come first, fired wild to clear the way. Figures follow, vaulting into the space at angles, making room for more behind. Even hurrying, they are stealthy, magenta battle suits muted to shadow grey. They see the injured woman and the young figure curled in the corner. They see the other woman flying at them, sword glinting as it falls.

They do not see the gun in the injured woman's hand.

Lights and sharpened steel flash, strobing the room.

Vesper watches the silhouettes on the ceiling, making their jerky way towards death.

When it is over, a dozen bodies lie contorted in a thin puddle of blood.

Duet reunites. Worried hands rest on shoulders, move to take off a battered helmet.

They are pushed away. The gesture is not hard but it sends one half reeling, uncertain.

Alone, the injured woman opens a panel on her bracer. From it she pulls a tiny needle and injects it under the strap of her helm. Alone, she stands.

The noise outside is louder, closer.

Genner's face appears at the broken wall; it does not flicker at the sight of the bodies. 'Report.'

'The sword –'

'– And the bearer –'

'– Are intact.'

Genner nods. 'And you?'

'We are –' There is a beat, barely noticeable as one glances towards her battered counterpart.

'– We are fine.'

Whatever else Genner might say is superseded by the floor starting to shake. 'Move!' he shouts, pointing towards the door opposite. 'Move now!'

CHAPTER FOUR

Vesper and her escort run, weaving through houses, forcing doors with boots and cannon, trampling on privacy, bursting onto streets again. Soldiers move in packs around her, protective. Light bombs and smoke canisters are deployed often, signalling location but obscuring individuals.

The roar of the enemy is close now. But the Crawler Tanks cannot reach them easily. Each time the group change direction they gain a little time while tanks force their bulk through too-small gaps. Great cannons fire on them anyway, trying their luck. Shells arc over rooftops, decimating homes, obliterating a pair of unlucky squires. New holes appear in the roads, some so deep that water breaks through in hissing streams.

Tanks stop and men and women, armed for war, spring from their metal bellies. On fresh legs they give chase, magenta shapes cutting stark through swirling grey.

Vesper runs in the eye of the storm, surrounded by guardians arrayed in concentric circles. Soldiers form the outermost, followed by squires, then knights and, finally, Duet, who orbits her like a pair of angry bees. Her wide eyes cannot see far and her brain doesn't bother trying to process the madness. Thoughts recede, tucked away under a blanket of adrenaline.

Sometimes Duet is close, pulling her unpredictably, sometimes the Harmonised abandons her for a few frightening seconds, swords dancing over and around one another, spearing smoke, snipping the legs from would-be assailants. They pause by a cluster of bins, crouching, then running, turning, turning again. Perspective and direction are lost, abandoned with the bodies of the fallen.

Up ahead, the enemy cobbles together a barricade. Portable generators power panels of solid light, springing up across the street. But such relics grow rare and there are not enough to seal the way on. More low-tech means are used to make up the shortfall, chairs and cabinets thrown on their faces and piled into the gaps.

Genner raises his hand and, immediately, his forces pause. Sub-vocalised orders come through to every ear. 'They're trying to funnel us towards the Tradeway and those Crawlers. Attack! Punch through the barrier.'

Soldiers comply without question, surging forward into open ground.

The enemy have inferior weapons and nobody with knightly training, but there are more of them and they are not in a rush.

Using the last of their grenades, Genner's forces rush across the space. For such a short distance the tax is high, paid in bravery and blood.

Bullets spray, continuous. In the open, skill and experience mean little, knights and squires falling alike.

Vesper sees the people thinning around her, sheared away one by one. She has time to think that she may die, to marvel that she lives, to be certain the next step is her last.

And then they reach the barricade.

Swords sing, metal sparking on barriers, song penetrating. Generators overload and a panel of light vanishes. With it goes the courage of the defenders. Most run, making targets of their backs. A few, more foolish, surrender. While the knights decimate what's left, opportunistic squires swipe portable defences. Two minutes later, the group moves again.

Behind, tanks continue to threaten and foot-soldiers harry, but ahead, the way is clear. High rocks loom ever higher until, at last, they reach the natural border of the island. Huge power generators nestle into the rock, taking energy from the sea and passing it to the Harmonium Forge, housed in a great block of silver. Genner leads his people to the wall it makes, taking cover between the humming metal pillars.

'Set up a barrier,' he orders. 'Let's hope their power supply is more important to them than killing us.'

Squires comply, using the stolen Light Shields to create a curving fourth wall.

Two hundred metres away, a building falls over and four tanks lumber into view. Squads of soldiers march alongside.

Collectively, Genner's troops hold their breath.

There is a pause, filled by heartbeats, fast, excitable.

The roar of the Crawler's engines becomes a grumble. Cannons power down.

Collectively, the troops exhale.

Genner quickly gives orders. Shifts are divided. Some take watch, some tend to the injured. The lucky ones rest.

Satisfied, he turns his attention to Vesper. She appears somewhere between shock and despair. Duet stands close by, one of her standing next to the girl while the other lies back, allowing a field medic to attend to her injuries. The medic holds a magnet over her chest and Genner watches as metal shards leap up from her wounds, one by one, like tinkling rain.

'Vesper, we're at a crossroads here. It may be that support will arrive in time, it may be that it doesn't. I want to know if Gamma has any commands for us. Has the sword spoken to you?'

Vesper blinks, comes back to the world.

'I said, has the sword spoken to you?'

'Once, I think. Back at home. It called me and it . . . it's hard to put into words.'

'Do you think you could speak to it again, now?'

She looks down at her hands, mesmerised by their trembling. 'No.'

Genner turns his attention to the Harmonised. 'Did you stim her?'

From the ground, Duet speaks: 'We were interrupted.'

Then from Vesper's side she adds, 'And we thought –'

'– Purity would –'

'– Be better –'

'In the presence of –'

'– The Seven.'

Heat rises in Genner's cheeks. 'At this point we don't have anything to lose. Stim her now. I'll make sure you're not disturbed.' He looks pointedly into Vesper's eyes. 'Hurry, we don't have long.' The girl nods, her face white under the dirt. Genner glances back to Duet. 'And just so we're clear: if we survive this, your inability to follow simple orders is going to be a special feature of my report.'

Duet salutes. She waits until his back is turned to glare. Without ceremony, she produces a needle and punches it into Vesper's arm.

'Ow!'

The noise causes several heads to snap round in her direction.

'Sorry.'

Powerful drugs suppress shock, bringing the makeshift camp into sudden focus. Vesper looks at the field medic applying a new layer of Skyn to Duet's injury. She looks at the soldiers lying on the ground and the eyes that flick away when she tries to meet them. 'I . . . I need some privacy.'

'This is –'

'– As good –'

'– As it gets.'

'Okay. Can you at least turn away?'

Duet complies, one of her sighing pointedly.

Vesper nods and unwraps the sword, lays it down carefully and takes a deep breath. 'Winged Eye save us, protect us, deliver us.' The sword is as still as it ever was. Vesper bends over it, until her lips are inches away. Fine hairs stand up on her neck and arms. 'Hello,' she whispers. 'I'm sorry. I'm so sorry. I should never have taken you and I know you didn't ask for any of this, but we really, really need you. Please. I don't want any more people to get hurt. I don't want any more blood.' A memory brings a sudden shudder with it. 'If they attack again, we'll all die and there won't be anybody to . . .' She trails off, unsure. 'To take you to the Breach.'

She waits, intent on the sword, and time seems to stretch. She stares so hard she forgets to blink. Vision blurs, suggesting movement where there is none. But then, finally, there is something. Not the wings, but something beneath them, as if the eye behind were moving beneath the lid, restless.

The girl dares not speak. She sees a second movement: something is disturbing the sword.

Genner's voice, suddenly close, makes Vesper jump. 'How's she doing?'

'Nothing yet –'

'– But she is getting there –'

'– Slowly.'

'Well, she'd better get a move on for all our sakes. We've got incoming sky-ships, known hostiles. The First is on its way.'

*

Three sky-ships spiral into Sonorous. Engines rotate as they glide to a halt in the air, hovering outside the great watchtower.

Worried faces peer out from windows, nobody daring to move until the ships have finished their leisurely descent.

Thirty feet above the Tradeway, a door in the lead sky-ship's side opens and figures tip out. A line of black dominoes, blank, spotless, falling.

Loose fabric ripples in the wind like water, flowing from outstretched arms.

A pause, not quite two seconds, then stones crack under boots, armoured and black. A cloak settles.

The First straightens, steps forward.

A second later, not quite two, another figure, identically dressed, lands behind it. Gestures are copied, they land, straighten, step forward, following their leader as the next one lands.

Fourteen times, the sequence repeats, exact, as if time was stuttering, caught in a loop. With each one, the cracks in the stones expand.

They walk together through empty streets, following the trail of destruction.

The First stops by an ash pile, slowly scattering in the breeze. It shakes its head, the others behind mirroring the gesture, then moves on.

Above them, three sky-ships wait.

None of the figures carry weapons, though all wear protective clothing, covered from head to toe in lightweight armour, featureless. This adds to the illusion that they are identical. However, there are differences in height, weight, gender and age. In other circumstances they would dress differently too, perhaps favouring the clothes and mannerisms of their original selves. But when the First calls them, awakening the sleeping essence in their bodies, their masks of humanity fall away, irrelevant.

Several times they pause on their journey, distracted by the shape of a broken building, or a bed half hanging through a ceiling. Sometimes the First stops by a body to close its eyes, sometimes it stops to open them. For not everyone has died in the combat: a few hover, hearts fluttering on the brink. On these occasions one of the group comes, scooping up wounded soldiers as if they were dolls made of leaves. Prizes in hand, they fall back, returning to the sky-ships.

When the First reaches the Crawler Tanks, only three of the group still follow empty-handed.

The Sonorous military back away long before the First arrives, allowing it to pass by unimpeded. An officer awaits the infernal, trying hard to hide his nerves, unaware that such deception is impossibe. The First reads souls rather than tone of voice or facial expressions. All of the officer's feelings are laid bare before the First's gaze.

'Welcome to Sonorous. I'm Captain Ujim, and, on behalf of the council, I want to thank-you for your quick response. I've been authorised to give you every support. The enemy is well armed and well trained.' He is suddenly aware how small he appears, reflected in the First's faceplate. His throat dries, his voice shrinks. 'They used the terrain against us, so we haven't been able to bring our Tanks to bear. And they have knights, at least fifty of them by our reckoning.

'Still, now that you're here, our combined strength should be more than enough. We're ready to attack on your order.'

The First stares into the captain. Behind it, three heads shake. 'In my dealings with your . . . people over the years, I am always surprised how eager you are to kill each other.'

The First moves past the captain, leaving the protection of the Crawler Tanks behind.

'Wait,' stammers the captain as the identical figures walk by in single file. 'What are you going to do? What are our orders?'

The fourth figure pauses as it passes. 'I am going to do what you should have done from the beginning . . . I am going to make them an offer.'

*   *   *

63

'Someone's coming out, sir. Is that him? Is that the First?'

Genner squints through the spyhole in the makeshift shelter. 'It's not a him, private, it's an infernal. And, yes, it's the First.'

'I've got him, it, in my sights now. Should I take the shot?'

'Not yet. Keep ready but no-one fires until I say so.' Genner turns to his troops. He sees fear in them, mixed with eagerness. Many of the knights have lost sisters and brothers to the First, many of the squires have grown up on bitter stories. 'If we get the chance to rid the world of the First, we'll take it. But remember, our primary mission is to protect the bearer, keep the sword safe, and take it to the Breach. We cannot let it fall into enemy hands. I want options.' He points as he talks. 'You two, see if we can climb the wall behind the cover of these generators. Demolitions, see if there's any way you could punch through to the sea from here and, if you can—'

'Sir, I think it's about to do something.'

Genner spins back to look through the gap. 'Shit!'

The First stops, midway between the tanks and the bunker. It raises its hands, palms open, then removes its helmet. A face is revealed. A young woman, hairless, pock-marks on her cheeks. 'I am the First and I am not here to destroy you. Not unless you . . . invite me.' The First walks closer, face slack as it thinks. 'I do not . . . enjoy the idea of fighting. Something offered is so much more valuable than something taken. This body was given to me. The woman that wore it was sick. Not through contact with my kind. This was an infection native to your world, though no less . . . deadly for it. I am told such a condition used to be treatable but your science is in retreat, your medicine rare and costly. The woman had neither the friends nor the resources to get the treatment she needed. And her . . . community was afraid. Could she be infectious? Would her sickness spread? They did not know. The knowledge was lost to them. And so, she came to me. And though your kind would consider her rotten, to me she was . . . pure.

'A part of her lives on within my essence. Not in any way that you would understand, but be assured that she does. She had no illusions about what she would become. I tell you this because in taking on this form I made an observation that I would like to share with you.' The First pauses, seeming to stare through the wall of light to the many eyes on the other side. 'Humans are desperate to live. Given the choice between an existence of any sort and death, she chose life. Once against the disease, carrying on despite the knowledge that it would kill her, and then once again when she met me.

'Soon you will have to make that same choice. To die here and now or to continue a little longer. In the heat of the moment, it is easy to court death. But we are not yet at that moment. Wait. Think. Listen to what I have to say. I do not speak to your leaders alone, I speak to every one of you. If you wish to live, it is simple. Shatter your swords and swear yourselves to peace, and to me. I cannot allow the knights to leave but I promise that I will treat them fairly. The rest of you may do as you please. Stay, go, or come with me. Above all else, the Malice must be destroyed. Do these things, these . . . simple things and not only will I spare your lives, I will see to it that you can return home, or start anew. Whatever you wish.'

The helmet is raised once more, put into place.

'Consider my words . . . carefully. I will wait for your answer.'

Behind the barrier of light, all eyes go to Genner, then to the girl leaning over the sword, whispering, frantic.

One Thousand, One Hundred and Twenty-Six Years Ago

Thought fragments float across Massassi's consciousness, pieces of mosaic, disconnected. They blend with voices, also floating, near her head. She cannot tell which belong to the past, which to the future as she drifts through them, a happy phantom.

Words become clearer, more pressing. She recognises the speaker, identifies the words but their impact is distant, barely felt.

'. . . And all I'm asking for is a moment of your cooperation. Then everyone can get on with their lives. Surely, you'd agree, that's for the best?'

Massassi goes to speak but a mask stops her. Her eyes flare and she coughs, choking on the tube jamming her mouth, running deep.

'Ah, I think she's waking up.'

A second voice joins in, less familiar. 'Let's not get hasty. The body is recovering, yes, but cognitive function has to be verified if you want her statement to stand.'

Someone bends over her. She tries to bring the shape into focus. It is a head, blurry but recognizable. It belongs to her supervisor. He looks tired, bags like baby slugs sit heavy under his eyes.

'Doctor, look! That was a smile. She recognised me, I'm sure of it.'

'That's hardly conclusive. It may just be a muscle spasm.'

'Massassi? Massassi, can you hear me?'

She manages a nod.

'Good. That's good. Now pay attention: you were in an accident, a serious accident. We need to talk about what happened. There are arrangements that need . . .'

The words start to fall away, dropping into a chasm that opens up between them, her eyes closing.

'We're losing her. Do something.'

'Her body has been under incredible strain. It's natural that she'll want to rest.'

'But for how long?'

'Difficult to say. It could be days, it could be more.'

'That won't do. We need to close the file and move on. We've spent too much on this already.' The supervisor begins to pace, hands folded behind his back, reminiscent of a woodpecker strutting on a branch. Massassi smiles again. 'I can't go back without an answer. We need to wake her up.'

'I can't force her to wake.'

'Yes, you can. Give her a stimulant.'

'With the levels of pain she's in, coupled with her medical history, I don't advise that course of action. If I wake her suddenly, the shock to her system could be catastrophic. She needs to be stronger before she learns the extent of her injuries.'

'I only need her conscious for a few minutes. Once she gives consent, you can keep her here as long as you like.'

'I want it on record that I don't endorse this action.'

'Your objections have been filed, doctor. Now get on with it.'

The doctor moves out of sight, makes adjustments.

The feed of sedatives slows.

Pain climbs back inside, making muscles strain and knuckles white. With it comes something else. The world resolves itself in sudden focus, lines so sharp they cut into the brain.

'Keep calm, Massassi, and listen. I promise I won't make this last any longer than it has to.'

Her eyes lock to his, drawn to the lights starting to fizz inside the supervisor's sockets. They have always been there, invisible to normal sight; manifestations of the man's essence.

But not to Massassi's unclouded mind. Not any more.

Unaware of how dramatic his face has become in Massassi's eyes, the man continues, giving a speech repeated so often it has become a script: 'You were in an accident. A serious one. As a result, Superior Class Harvester 4879-84/14 was shut down following emergency protocol. Hours of work time were lost, not to mention the cost of recovering your body, covering your shifts and ongoing medical care.'

He pauses to smile, a practiced calming thing. Massassi notes that it does not reach his real eyes, the ones that glow behind his face. She also notes his second mouth, the one etched in light, pale, remains sour. Around the tube, Massassi smiles back. The supervisor does not note its feral edge.

'I want what you want. To get you back on your feet and

working as soon as possible. You're going to need a new arm, and a partial reconstruct of your upper body. The mods you'll need will be expensive. Now, I've looked at your funds and you have a lot saved up. However, with the enquiry costs and the mounting medical bills, I'm afraid there won't be enough left to restore functionality.

'But don't worry, I've got a solution. If you admit full responsibility for the incident then we can turn this into a criminal issue. We'll lower your echelon class and take full ownership of your rights until the debt's worked off. Heavy, I know, but it will make all the problems go away. I've got pre-approval to fund your operation based on your work record. We could have you back on the mechs before year's end. What do you say?'

She tries to speak, begins to cough.

'Can we take the tube out now, doctor?'

'Yes, hold on.'

A command is given and the tube recoils smoothly into the mask, which the doctor removes, equally smooth.

Massassi coughs, then accepts the water offered by the doctor. A genuine frown appears on her face as she looks at the formless sheet covering her body. 'I've still got my arm. I can feel it.'

Supervisor and doctor glance at each other. The doctor clears her throat. 'I'm afraid that's a common misconception. Your brain is so convinced the limb is still there, it fabricates sensation.'

'I can see it.'

'You want to see it? Well, if you're sure.'

The doctor pulls back the sheet.

A plastic cap is fixed to her shoulder, running all the way

to her right hip. Her left wrist is fixed to the bed. There is no tie for her right wrist. There is nothing there to attach it to. Despite this, she smiles. 'There it is . . . what did you do to my arm? It's . . . beautiful.'

Another glance is shared. They both retreat to the other side of the room, whispering.

'Perhaps this was too soon.'

'I did try and warn you.'

'We'll try again the next time she wakes. If her condition persists, it may actually work in our favour. How long before you can certify her?'

'Normally, a month but, given the circumstances, we can come to an arrangement, I'm sure.' The doctor returns to the pod. 'Lie back, you can rest again now. This will get easier, I promise.'

Massassi does not relax. She sees the spark of thought appear in the doctor's essence, the desire to silence her. 'I'm not crazy, my arm is right here. Look!'

'Yes,' her supervisor says, adopting an expression of polite pity. 'That's good, that's very good. You'll be back to work soon, I know it.'

Drugs are authorised, dulling pain, dulling sense.

'No!' she screams, glaring at the space where her arm once was. At first, they do not see the luminescence, thin as bone, following the line of a lost limb. Then it brightens, thickens, light intensifying, hardening, like silvered diamond. Compared to the light she sees in their faces, her arm glows with a star's fury.

Now they see it, falling back in their fear, legs scrabbling like a spiders on the slick floor.

With her shining fingers, she tears through the bonds on

her left wrist and jumps from the bed. Weak muscles cannot manage the sudden demands and she falls.

For a moment the two adults relax, though they continue to back away.

Massassi extends her arm. One tug is all it takes to slide her over to them. She touches the doctor first. Silver fingers press against flesh, passing through to touch the soft light within. She does not mean to kill, but the action is too quick and anger-fuelled. The bubble of the doctor's essence bursts, burns and is gone.

Like a doll, the doctor's body flops over onto the floor.

'I need immediate assistance in here!' shrieks the supervisor. Suddenly, he remembers his authority, realises that a single command will shut her down. Before he can give it, however, Massassi reaches out and touches his ankle, and through it, his soul.

In the supervisor's mind, she finds thoughts, treacherous. She squeezes them between finger and thumb, molds them anew.

Footsteps pound down a corridor. Burly men burst through the door. Inside, they find a dead doctor, a maimed, unconscious girl and a man on his knees, weeping.

'You called us, sir?'

The supervisor gives a broken nod. 'I was responsible for the accident. It was my fault. I thought I could bury it. I didn't know the girl would wake up and tell the doctor the truth. So you see, I had to silence them. I killed the doctor first and I was going to kill the girl but then I wondered, where would it end? I'm sick. Sick in the head! You need to take me away. You need to process me.'

The men are so intent on the supervisor's ravings that they do not see Massassi's smile.

CHAPTER FIVE

Behind its wings, an eye twitches, restless. Vesper watches it, desperate for it to open and give guidance. She feels the group looking at her, expectation pressing down. As tension rises, nerves break out in quiet ways. A foot shuffles. Throats are cleared. Armour creaks.

The pressure to do something, anything, becomes too much.

Vesper stands, the sword cradled in her arms. Heads tilt up, following the motion. All shuffling stops.

The girl walks towards the glowing barrier. As she does so, soldiers and knights and squires kneel. Even the wounded stir themselves, biting back pain to demonstrate proper deference.

She thinks of her father's sure hands. How they have always carried her, kept her safe. She wishes she had inherited their confidence.

The sniper at the barrier moves aside for her and Vesper looks out over shimmering light. She sees the First waiting, and double takes, sure it would be larger. Beyond the infernal she sees soldiers massing around Crawler Tanks, like waves around rocks, and beyond them she sees the First's sky-ships.

There are so many of them she cannot believe they could fight and win. All she can think of is the blood that will be shed, the blood that will be on her hands.

She feels movement in her arms. Metal feathers slide over one another as wings part. An eye opens, flicks up at the girl, then fixes itself on the infernal outside, narrowing.

Vesper turns back. The kneeling figures wait, letting heads hang, weary. Many are injured. Together they number less than a third of the forces outside. She looks at Duet, one half of the Harmonised standing watchful, hopeful, the other less so, the holes in her chestplate like the sky punched clean of stars.

The sword tugs towards the First, towards battle. To Vesper's surprise, the motion drags her with it, till her elbows rest on the barrier. Light fizzes where blade and barrier brush, and the First looks up.

Eyes and eye meet.

The sword begins to hum, soft.

The light barrier quivers and the First tilts as if suddenly struck by a strong wind.

Vesper tries to retreat, feels resistance. Young biceps strain, bobbing under sleeves like a pair of apples, and she steps back.

It seems as if the sword wants to fight and she wonders what that might mean. For a moment eyes squeeze shut. No, she thinks. No more fighting. Unable to bear it, she tests the lie in her mind. It feels wrong but anything is better than more bloodshed. She clears her throat. 'The sword has spoken to me.'

Beside her, Genner lowers his head. 'We are yours to command.'

It is hard to tell if the sword vibrates or the girl's hands shake. 'Gamma . . . Gamma of The Seven . . . does not want you to fight today.'

A few look surprised, most simply accept it.

Slowly, an eye swivels away from the barrier and back to the girl, glaring.

From the back, a voice murmurs. 'And so it was, for Gamma knew when to strike and when to hold back.'

'And so it was,' intone the others.

Vesper nods, finding a little confidence. 'You can't beat them today. Gamma doesn't want any more of you to die. If you surrender, you can live on. And when the time is right, you can fight again.'

'But what about our swords? They cannot be replaced.'

A bead of sweat escapes Vesper's hairline. 'I'm sorry, Gamma didn't say anything about the swords.' A muttering passes between the assembled knights and she quickly adds, 'Maybe they can be remade. With The Seven's grace.'

'With The Seven's grace,' they echo, but another question drowns it out: 'What about the knights? The First won't let them go.'

'They'll be prisoners, yes, but they'll be alive.'

One of the older knights looks up. 'You won't forget us?'

Caught in the veteran's gaze, Vesper finds herself speaking. 'I'll come back for you. I mean, Gamma will, I promise.'

The old knight salutes and others follow. 'So be it. But I beg you, give our sacrifice here meaning.' His eyes hold hers as he speaks. 'Make it count.'

'I will,' she says, meaning it.

Genner stands up. 'Gamma has shown us the way. The bearer will go south to finish the mission. It is our job to make that possible.

'We will stall the First here as long as we can while the bearer escapes. Demolitions, we need an exit and we need it now.'

A hand goes up. 'The moment we start blasting, they'll be on us.'

'No,' the old knight replies. 'They won't hear a thing. The death song of our blades will drown you out.'

Genner nods. 'Good. Go to it then.' While soldiers spring into action and knights prepare their farewells, Genner kneels before Vesper. 'I'm sorry things have turned out this way. We have a contact in Sonorous. Another of the Lenses. She will help you to escape.'

'You're not coming with me?'

'No. I need to report to the Winged Eye and communicate with our allies here. They need to know what you're doing if they're going to help.'

'Can't you do that and come with us?'

'No. When I send the signal, I'll draw too much attention.'

'You won't . . .'

'Die? It doesn't matter about me. The sword is what matters.'

Vesper bites her lip, blinks hard.

Genner's face softens. 'If it makes you feel better, I'm not planning on it. If I can escape, I will. And don't worry, you won't be alone. I'm sending Duet with you.'

'Okay.'

'Yes. Now get yourself ready. You've a long swim ahead of you.' Genner turns to go but is stopped by a lip, trembling.

'Here,' he says, 'we need to fasten the sword to you. May I?'

'Yes,' replies the girl.

'It's too big to sit by your waist, you'll have to strap it to your back. If you wrap it and hold it in place, I'll secure it for you.'

Vesper does as she's told, relieved to cover the sword up again. Genner takes his time, careful not to touch the sword itself. 'There. All done. How does that feel?'

'That's fine.'

'There's one more thing.' He takes his pistol from its holster and presses it into Vesper's hand, singing softly, secretly. Light glows from Genner's palm, flowing around the grip, growing with the note, then fading with it. 'I've keyed the gun to you now. Keep it safe and out of sight.' Vesper nods, slipping it away into the pocket of her coat. 'And do the same yourself, for all our sakes.'

Duet presses the foam into Vesper's ears, covers them with her hands.

One of the knights raises her sword towards Vesper, then the sky. A final salute.

On instinct, Vesper closes her eyes.

The knight brings it down hard but the angle is wrong. Sparks fly and metal screeches. People flinch and grit their teeth.

Her sword doesn't break.

She screams and lifts it once more. This time, her aim is true.

Even through the layers of protection, Vesper feels the sound cutting through her, the sensation sharp enough that she checks herself, half expecting to be injured. She also feels the explosion, more mundane, as demolition charges punch through stone.

Outside, the First sits motionless. Within its shell, essence ripples, pleased.

Inside the shelter, more knights come forward, a queue of mourners, faces stiff with grief. Swords are raised in salute.

Vesper manages a quick bow before Duet steers her to the newly made hole, still smoking. She peers down, hears water sloshing in the darkness.

Duet presses a mask to Vesper's face. Clear plastic that covers her from forehead to chin. The mask adheres instantly, misting over briefly, then correcting, clearing.

Genner smiles at the girl, salutes and jumps down the hole. Red hair waves briefly and is gone.

Vesper mumbles something in return but, through the mask, through the breaking of steel, through the last song of the knight's weapons, her words are lost.

Duet lowers one of herself into the hole. The other helps Vesper, then follows. They slide and climb their way down, the tunnel trembling around them as more swords are shattered above.

Stone is cold but water is colder, smacking legs in the darkness, stealing sensation. Vesper tries to pause, to prepare herself but Duet's boots say otherwise, finding shoulders, urging her on.

Rigid with fear and cold, the girl allows herself to be pushed by Duet, pulled by her, handled through the tunnel and out into wider waters. Away from the rock, light finds its way underwater in fingers of red and gold, like two hands reaching from the heavens. They follow the shafts as if lifted by them, up, up and up, until heads break the surface, bobbing at the cliff's base.

Too heavy to swim easily, Duet drags herself and Vesper along the rocks. It is slow jerky progress, punctuated by bumps, by numb fingers slipping on slick stone, by chattering teeth and unbidden grunts of exertion.

Behind them, perched high on a ledge like a black spider, tiny, Genner begins to signal, shining a light towards the sky that flicks on and off. Code flashes, fast and complex, baffling the uninitiated.

But even the most foolish can understand that a message is being sent and even the most foolish can trace the signal to its source. Before Genner has finished, a sky-ship rises above the rocks. It rotates slowly, opening a side door. A figure climbs out, dressed in black armour and loose black fabric and throws itself into the air without fear. Another fragment of the First.

It plummets, arms spread starfish wide, getting faster and faster until it passes Genner, plucking him from the rock face.

For a long three seconds, they fall. Water splashes, surging up in a circle. Then nothing.

*

In the streets of Sonorous, in a rusting house, a woman watches a window. She reads the distant winking light, stuttering on the underside of the clouds.

When it is finished, the woman stands up, snatches a bag hidden beneath a dusty sheet and goes to the door. She glances out. It is eerily quiet. People hide in their homes, in their workplaces. Too-calm voices speak at intervals, suggesting people stay safe, reassuring that everything is under control.

The woman smirks at that, then moves into the street, closing the door behind her. As she walks towards the docks, a figure peels itself from the shadows and follows.

She hears the footsteps getting closer. She considers running but checks the instinct. Instead preparing the dart hidden beneath the skin of her wrist.

Gradually, the second figure catches up with her, falls into step alongside.

The woman wraps her arms around herself as if cold. Seemingly by coincidence, her wrist now points towards the figure's neck.

The new arrival appears weathered, tough as old meat. 'This may come as a . . . surprise to you but we have something in common. Both of us pretend to be normal residents of this city when in fact our true loyalties lie . . . elsewhere. You are in truth, an agent of the Winged Eye and I am the First.'

The woman cannot help surprise writing itself into the curve of her eyebrows.

'Did you know that there is something that moves faster than light?'

She shakes her head, humouring, thinking, furious.

'There is. I move faster than light. Not this . . . shell, though it is certainly fast by your standards. My true self. And that is why I will always be . . . superior.'

They walk for a few more paces. Despite the cold wind, dark circles grow under the woman's arms.

'I know what you are. I know your plans and they will fail. But all is not lost. I am here to make you an offer. Don't react. Don't fight. Listen. Think. Decide for yourself how much you want this life.'

Abruptly, the woman stops. She flexes a muscle in her wrist and a dart fires.

Not as fast as light, but fast enough, the First moves.

*

Duet does not bother to hide her weapons. There is no-one around, no crowd to blend with. One of her moves ahead, eyes alert for changes. She checks left, checks right, squints at dusty windows, then beckons. The other follows, pulling Vesper with her.

The houses they pass are faceless cubes, temporary structures never replaced. Simple boxes designed for efficient use of space and little else. Aesthetics trampled in the name of speed and cost. In places the cubes are stacked to make flats, or linked up, for more affluent residents. Since independence, the people of Sonorous have begun to decorate, to distinguish. Childlike efforts to create art, without the ease or charm of childhood.

Where the maths goes wrong, or where the space runs out, pathways are squeezed to accommodate extra habitation, resulting in tiny alleys, accessible only to the small and slender.

Duet and Vesper barely pass, sidestepping through, the walls dragging across their chests. They dare not slow, for the sounds of pursuit have already begun. Tanks whirring back to life, soldiers shouting to each other, marching.

Above them, three sky-ships move, searchlights sweeping the streets. Before they arrive and pick them out, Duet shoulders her way into a house.

As the door splits open, a man is revealed. In one hand, he holds an autohammer. Behind him, tucked under furniture, his children squeal.

The tool is already set to maximum strength. He swings it at Duet's head.

One of her ducks while the other steps in, sword held high.

The autohammer swings wide, burying itself in the door-frame again and again.

The man falls backwards, clutching his arm.

Duet steps onto him, boots pressing down on armpits, crushing.

The children squeal again.

'Shut them up –'

'– Or we will.'

For emphasis, Duet charges her pistol.

Vesper reaches for her but the other's hand stops her, firm. She tries to reach the Harmonised with words instead. 'Don't kill them!'

'We won't –'

'– Unless –'

'– We have to.'

The family is bound with wire, hidden behind furniture. It is telling how quickly they capitulate. Vesper turns away, goes to the window. Through the grime, she sees lights pass by. The beams point eagerly, hoping to find a target. Once, twice, thrice, they appear, circling, moving on.

Vesper leans against the sill, resting her head on toughened plasglass. Muscles tremble, allow themselves a brief respite.

Time passes while she stares into space, seeing the outside world but mostly not seeing anything. Then, flitting past her line of sight, a small shape, bleating and frantic. Before she knows it, she too is running.

Duet's voice is a chorus at her back. 'Wait!'

But she doesn't. A sudden burst of energy takes her through the broken door, onto the streets and away. She ignores the sword, heavy on her back, ignores the fatigue.

'Wait,' she calls. 'It's me. It's Vesper.'

At the sound of her voice, the kid stops and looks round.

Vesper slows, crouches, opens her arms.

Little hooves skip across stones. Bleating becomes lighter and the kid throws himself into Vesper's embrace.

'There you are. I'm so sorry, I thought I'd lost you.'

The kid rubs his head against the girl's. Lips clamp gently around an ear.

'Come on, we can't stay here.'

She gets up to find Duet towering over her. Their faces are hidden behind visors but she can guess enough from the two pairs of eyes. She is not afraid though. Compared to her father, their disapproving looks seem amateurish.

'Are we going back to that house?'

'No –'

'– We have to keep ahead –'

'– Of the search parties –'

'– And get to –'

'– The port.'

'Genner said help would come.'

Duet takes her arm, talking as they go. 'Help will –'

'– Find us.'

'Or the First will,' adds the injured one, bitter.

Troops spread through the city, a net of people, threading between buildings. Crawler Tanks speed down the Tradeway, joining others already squatting at the port's entrance. Sky-ships move in random patterns, combing the air.

Harmonised, girl and goat run, hide, run some more.

Slowly, the trap closes around them.

There is no longer time for care and Duet sprints, half dragging, half carrying Vesper between her. The girl tries to keep up, tries to help, but weary legs stumble, unable to find their rhythm again.

Nearby, a door opens and from its shadow, a man gestures, inviting them in.

They take their chances, bundling inside.

Vesper and the kid collapse gratefully into a corner. Duet does not have such luxury. One of her places herself between the stranger and her charge while the second leans against the wall, sword in one hand, the other resting on her injured chest.

The man closes the door quickly, then turns, tanned hands open, empty. 'You'll be safe here for a while. Don't worry, I'm not your enemy.'

'We'll be –'

'– The judge –'

'– Of that.'

'Yes,' the man replies. 'Perhaps this will help.' A bag is placed on a table. Duet investigates, finds supplies. Rations, medicine, money, tools, all marked with the seal of the Winged Eye.

She frowns. 'You are –'

'– Of the Lenses?'

'No. But these things once belonged to one. She would want you to have them.'

Against Vesper's back the sword begins to stir.

'Then who –'

'– Are you?'

'As I said, I am not your enemy. But I am not with the Empire.'

Duet raises her blades.

The sword hums louder.

'Is this your . . . judgement?'

'For infernals –'

'– There is only –'

'– One judgement.'

'Are you certain? You do not . . . appear so. How can you be? The very words you speak are not your own. They are simplistic phrases designed to keep you simple. Only one judgement? If that is so, why are The Seven not here in person? Why do the Empire's people turn away from Their leadership? If there is only one judgement for . . . my kind. Why was I asked to come here by yours?'

Almost imperceptibly, Duet's sword wavers.

'You are called a Harmonised. You are an attempt at a deeper union, a different kind of existence. I understand this . . . need. This desire to be greater than your physical self allows. Through me, you could experience complete fusion. It is not too late. Lower your weapons and I will give you want you truly want.'

The First takes a step towards Vesper. Duet does not move, one of her blocking the way, the other remaining by the wall.

Duet raises a pistol in her spare hand, points it at the First as it advances. 'We will not –'

The sentence hangs, unfinished.

Duet looks to her partner, still by the wall, silent. 'Stay with me!'

The First shakes its head. 'But you are not . . . together on this. You've never truly been together. You are a pretence of oneness. You are a mockery of it.'

The pistol begins to charge. 'Shut up!'

'You would rather fall to violence than admit the truth of your position? How sad.'

She squeezes the trigger. But the First has already stepped aside. Powder explodes from the back wall as she swings the gun round trying to track the infernal.

There is a blur of movement, too fast for the human mind to follow, and a broken gun falls to the floor. Moments later, Duet joins it, groaning in the dust.

The First turns to the other half of the Harmonised. 'And you? What is your . . . judgement?'

She looks at the trembling girl and her dazed counterpart. 'I don't know.'

'But you do. Allow yourself the thought and it will come.'

Her blade lowers. 'She's yours. But I want what you promised.'

Vesper chokes back a sob.

'And you shall have it.' The First crouches by Vesper, leans forward until only inches separate them. 'You are lost. How could you not be? That broken . . . relic cannot help you. It is a reminder of something dead, nothing more. Give it up to me and I will let you go.'

Vesper shakes her head, the movement slight, fearful.

The First reaches out to touch the girl's face. The kid flinches and Vesper tries to retreat. But there is nowhere to go, all she can do is twist away, hiding her face from the inevitable. The First is suddenly presented with Vesper's back and the sword strapped to it.

Humming builds to a sudden roar and metal wings part, flaying the plastic that covers them.

An eye opens.

In the space between the First and the sword, air ignites, burning blue and angry.

The infernal staggers back, stunned, one arm across its face.

Vesper drops the kid and reaches into her pocket. The action swings the sword away, forcing it to glare at an innocent wall.

'So this is the Malice,' says the First, swaying as it speaks. 'I had hoped for more . . . nuance. You are a tool without a user, a shoe without a foot. You are . . . nothing.'

In a shaking hand, Vesper raises the gun. The trigger pulls too easily, activating with little more than a touch. Light pokes a hole through the First's body. Blood spurts and essence hisses.

The First lowers its arm, staring at the new wound. When it speaks, there is no trace of pain in its voice. 'Our . . . agreement . . . stands. Hold her . . . here.' With infinite dignity, the infernal sinks to its knees.

Duet levers herself from the wall, crossing the room with sudden speed. Her sword flicks out, making to disarm.

Too late, Vesper realises the threat. The flat of the Harmonised's blade smacks the gun from her hand. Vesper wants to run but Duet raises the sword again, threatening.

'Don't move. There is—'

The tip of a blade protrudes from her stomach, sudden, cutting her off.

'– Only one judgement.'

Duet looks down to find her counterpart awake, sword

in hand. Last words are gargled through blood, then she falls, beating the First to the floor.

As it sinks down onto its back, body weakening, the First's eyes remain steady, locked on Vesper's. 'I will . . . remember . . . this . . . You . . . cannot—'

Duet's sword comes down, silencing. 'I said: shut up!'

The statement echoes in the bare room, hollow.

She stabs the First again just to be sure but cannot bring herself to look at the other body. Vesper does. She picks up her gun and points, watching intently. Duet's chest is still, like a lake on a calm day. Lifeless. She puts the gun away.

Outside, soldiers move from door to door, knocking, searching, not far now.

Vesper's gaze remains on the two corpses. 'What are we going to do?'

Duet doesn't answer. Her sword droops and blood runs down the blade. Vermilion tears, dripping, heavy.

CHAPTER SIX

Off-colour rain patters on the tilting square. At its edges, things gather. In the centre of the square is a hole, known as the Pit of Whispers, and within the hole lives a lonely creature, all limbs and barely covered bones. The denizens of the Fallen Palace call it Slate. Little sense rattles within its hollow skull but even Slate knows when there is to be a display.

Too stupid to run, Slate presses its face against the dark wall of the pit and, momentarily, the world goes away.

At the top of the pit, the Man-shape waits, Samael by its side, while, in factions, the infernals cross the square to meet them.

First come the Felrunners, carried on an abundance of weeping legs. Their Lord stands foremost among them, proud. Raised to power by the Usurper and gifted with a crown of green muscle, it is as close to popular as any of the contenders.

Next comes Hangnail, alone, head studded with claws, its coat of skins flapping in the wind, ragged.

Then, a small girl riding a large Usurperkin comes: the Backwards Child, stretched neck coiled like a serpent, half-breed followers lumbering behind.

Lastly, comes Gutterface. Sometimes called the Unspeakable, even its peers do not care to look at it for long. Swarms of the lesser infernals infest its many pockets and crevices. An army of dysfunctional young, suckling at a hundred teats.

When all have arrived at the pit's edge, the Man-shape reaches down, finding one of Slate's many appendages and lifting it high. One by one, the others copy the gesture, until Slate is lifted slightly off the ground, murmuring and clicking to itself.

Whenever infernals converse there is danger. Even if both parties are peaceful, essences can mix, desires swapping or implanting themselves. No one challenger dares outright confrontation and yet, to end the stalemate, each needs to display its power to the others. A good enough display could convince the others to submit, giving the winner the infernal throne without conflict.

Slate's essence is weak, allowing other infernals to make contact without risk. They use it as a conduit, a patchy curtain that divides like gauze, keeping them apart but allowing communication.

With careful timing the infernals bring the limb they hold deeper into their shells, until it connects with the essence inside them. Now, when any of them forms a thought, it travels into Slate, into the pit and the others can read the echoes.

Inevitably, there is posturing. Each trying to appear bigger than the other, probing for changes, hoping that time will have made new weaknesses. The Man-shape allows this to happen, keeps itself small, unreadable. It suspects that Lord Felrunner is ready to make its bid for power and that Gutterface has a secret it struggles to contain. The other two give little away.

All share a moment of pleasure that the other challengers have not dared come. Then the Man-shape presses itself onto Slate's essence.

'I was made to serve . . .' the Man-shape begins.

'Lesser.'

'Taste.'

'Evres.'

'Us.' Swirl the responses.

'. . . And for much time, I served the master.' It notes the ripple of unease the reminder of the Usurper still brings. 'Where the Green Sun blazed, there is only void. Which of you will fill it?'

Four answers come, declarations of suitability.

'So you say. But the master did not trifle with words, the master took and others trembled. Now a new master comes, one that will take, and change, and wipe us away.'

Questions come thick and fast and Slate's essence stretches dangerously thin. The Man-shape casts a shadow between them, the image of their new enemy.

'It is called the Yearning and it gathers itself upon the Breach. I pledge myself and the master's throne to whoever can end it.'

There is a pause, quicker than the beat of a hummingbird's wing, an eternity between essences. Then there is noise. Lord Felrunner accepts first, the others immediately after.

Slate is discarded roughly, falling back into the pit while infernals scuttle, stride and shuffle away. Already, plots are forming, plans of attack, dreams of victory and what follows.

On the inside, the Man-shape permits itself a smile and wonders if any will return.

*

Vesper stares at the two bodies, her gun shakily pointing at them. Neither stir. 'What are we going to do?' she asks repeatedly. The question is directed as much to herself as to Duet, who has not spoken for too long.

Eventually, the gun lowers and Vesper's breathing calms. She goes to the bag of supplies, searching for inspiration, nudging the kid's head out of the way as he rummages for food. Most of the objects are identifiable, if not familiar. She touches the block of Skyn, the flexicast and nine different tab containers, presumably medicines of some kind. She finds a mutigel pillow, some water, some powdered food and a set of tools. One reminds her of the Navpack her father used to let her play with. She still remembers his face when she broke it.

She picks up the new Navpack and asks it to activate.

The Navpack does not recognise her voice.

'Activate!' she repeats, desperation making the end of the word rise.

On her back, the sword begins to hum.

Vesper spins round, reaching for her gun, but the First remains where it fell, eyes still staring, glassy.

The sword's hum rises sharply, pointedly, then stops.

With a happy ping, the Navpack activates.

A map shines onto the floor, showing Sonorous from above. The outer wall a thick dark line, curving like an inverted pair of horns, and, within it, a grid of roads, packed either side with little squares, countless. Vesper sees her location represented by a white dot that flashes excitedly. She taps it with a finger and the map zooms in, showing the house they stand in, the neighbouring ones and the criss-cross of alleys nearby.

Beneath them, purple, is another network. Passageways made for secret journeys, known only to the agents of the Winged Eye, entrances scattered about the island.

Vesper's eyebrows shoot up. 'This is it. Duet. Duet! I think I've found a way out.'

'It doesn't . . .' she begins, but there is no-one to finish her sentence. She chokes back a sob.

Using the Navpack as a guide, Vesper moves across the room. The view zooms, scaling itself exactly to the space. A purple square of light overlays an incongruous corner. The girl runs to it, followed by the kid, who shares the excitement if not the understanding.

Fingers search for a gap or a handle, find none. Fumbling becomes frantic, a droplet of sweat falls from her hair, dampening dirt. Then, for no discernible reason, a square of plastic pops up, raising two inches proud of the floor. Vesper grabs it, heaves.

Cheeks turn from red to purple, muscles burn and the panel begins to lift.

With an excited bleat, the kid gets his head into the gap and pushes.

Girl and panel flip over, landing on their backs.

The kid tips forward, hooves scrabbling over empty air. For a moment he wobbles, precarious, then falls into the newly revealed hole.

There is the sound of an abrupt landing and disgruntlement.

Vesper scrambles to her feet. 'Duet, look!'

She does, but nothing changes in her eyes. 'It doesn't . . .' She twitches. '. . . Matter.'

Vesper's hand finds Duet's, squeezes. 'Please come. I need you.'

Duet doesn't squeeze back. Her head gives the smallest of shakes. But Vesper doesn't let go and when Duet feels the pull, gentle, insistent, she is surprised to find herself moving.

Together, they descend.

From scattered places across Sonorous, black-visored figures stop, heads turning sharply. Leaving behind the soldiers at their backs, each one begins to run. Legs blur, making fan shapes beneath them as they race through the streets, faster than should be possible.

Witnesses can only stare and shiver.

Quickly, fourteen identically dressed figures converge on a house.

Inside are two bodies. One is of a man, aged by time outdoors, eyes staring towards infinity. They gather by the body. From two sword cuts and a hole made by angry light, essence escapes in little puffs of smoke.

Working as one, the figures capture the wisps, weaving them together. A coherent ball begins to appear, cupped in protective hands. At the same time, the group begin to excavate the essence in the body, clawing it out from the deep places, adding it to the ball. When they are finished, they close the man's eyes.

Then the ball is taken to the second body, that of a woman, half of an abandoned Harmonised. They press it into the wound in her chest, then bind the cavity shut.

Any last spark of the woman flutters away in the flicker of eyelids.

The First opens its eyes and stands.

Restored, it lowers its head and the others do the same, until fifteen skulls tap together, sharing knowledge, making plans.

Less than a second later they break, ten of them sprint for the door, the other five move to an innocent looking corner of the room, reaching for the hidden doorway, glimpsed through dying eyes. But for the First, the panel refuses to open.

Gauntleted hands clench and the First leans over the rebellious plastic. Fists move like pistons, drumming, hammering, penetrating.

The passageway is narrow, forcing them on hands and knees. The kid bounds ahead, a perfect fit. From Duet's visor a diamond flares into life, pushing back the gloom.

Vesper shoots her an envious look.

'What?'

'Nothing.'

They crawl on. Vesper lets out a sigh, murmurs: 'I wish I had a torch.'

'You've got . . .' She pauses, taps the side of her head irritably. '. . . Two.'

'I do?'

'The Navpack . . . and the . . . gun.'

'They're torches?'

'They're torches.'

Distant drumming reaches them. Then a single crack, a dulled burst of thunder.

Duet accelerates, knocks into Vesper. 'Go faster.'

'What's going on?'

She punches the girl in the back of the thigh. 'Go faster!'

Vesper yelps, complies. Behind them comes a rasping sound, of lightweight plates sliding over stone, rapid and numerous.

In their haste, knees are bashed, knuckles caught on the tunnel's sides, a catalogue of minor traumas to be pored over later. Several times the tunnel divides but Vesper doesn't hesitate, following purple lines held tight in memory.

The sound of the hunters pauses.

Vesper slows, takes a breath to speak but Duet knocks into her, hissing in frustration.

When they come again, the sounds of pursuit are diminished.

'They don't know the tunnels,' Vesper pants. 'We're dividing them.'

'It doesn't . . . matter. Even one . . . of them's . . . enough.'

All at once, light hits the end of the tunnel. A solid wall, decorated by damp, and, in front of it, another hole. Vesper pulls out the Navpack and shines it down. The beam dances on water and bends around the long cylinder of an escape vessel, bobbing leisurely on the surface. Where the light hits the side of the hole, bars glint. Each one is as wide as a giant's hand, inviting them to climb. Vesper does so.

Before she reaches the bottom, the cylinder cracks open, welcoming. Vesper drops from the last bar, her impact absorbed by the cylinder's thick inner lining. Girl and tube wobble in the water but neither tips over.

Vesper rocks the cylinder gently, testing buoyancy. Then she shines the Navpack around the chamber, mapping a shape not much bigger than the boat she sits on. She points the Navpack down, switches it from torch to navigator. Lines of light quickly describe a way out. Vesper frowns. 'The exit is below us, we need to go down.' She pats the side of the cylinder. 'In this. It's safe, I think.'

Above her, in the tunnel, Duet crawls backwards. Slowly trying to rotate in the cramped space. 'No.'

'What?'

'You go.'

'What about you?'

She completes her turn, then tries to work her sword free. 'I'm staying.'

'But why?'

'To protect . . .' Her elbow cracks against the side, painful. '. . . you. Give you time.' Her sword is nearly free but within the confines of the tunnel she cannot fully straighten her arm. The tip remains caught in its scabbard.

'Don't leave me. I need you.'

'It's better . . . this way.'

Vesper lowers her head, hesitates, mouth moving quietly, planning the words before she says them. 'It's not up to you. The sword wants you to come.' Duet edges back, feet dangling over the edge. With effort, she twists her head, craning until she can look down at the girl, suspicious. 'Gamma's sword spoke to me, remember? It needs me to carry it and it needs you to keep me safe.'

Duet just stares, face unreadable behind the visor.

'Don't be stupid! You can't even swing a sword up there. They'll kill you in seconds and you'll have died for nothing. If you want to protect me then you need to come down, now!'

Her voice echoes in the tunnels, repeating and fading, fading and repeating, travelling, retreading their steps. When it has gone, silence follows.

The sounds of pursuit have stopped.

Girl, Harmonised and goat freeze, wondering who else listens in the darkness.

Then, sudden and decisive comes the sound of armoured limbs, battering the tunnel, supernaturally fast, gaining.

With a muttered curse, Duet lets her sword fall back into its sheath and lowers herself into the hole. The descent is controlled and quick, her landing soft. Fractionally, the cylinder dips, high sides untroubled by lapping water.

The kid appears at the top of the ladder, afraid to jump, afraid to stay.

'Come on,' encourages Vesper.

'Leave it.'

'No!' She reaches up, smiles encouragingly. 'Come on, you can do it. Jump. I'll catch you.'

The kid bleats, extends a hoof into space, then retracts it hurriedly.

'Don't be scared.'

Duet speaks quickly, forcing words where she would naturally pause. 'There's no time, we have to go, forget the animal or we'll all die.'

Vesper stands her ground. 'You can do it. Jump.' The sword begins to tremble against her back. 'Come on,' she calls, voice fake and positive. 'Jump!'

The kid closes his eyes and with a final bleat, throws himself into space.

Hooves flail.

Duet swears.

Vesper's smile falls away.

There is a collision. Cries of alarm and pain mingle together. Water sloshes.

Vesper finds the kid in her arms, finds herself pitching backwards. Then Duet's hand finds her collar, pulls her upright.

'Thank you.'

The cylinder is built for comfort, for one. Vesper and Duet wriggle together, making what space they can. Fortunately, one is not full grown and the other's armour is streamlined, built for speed. Even so, the sword is hard on Vesper's back and the bag is crushed between them and contents press outward, sharp edges digging into hips and stomachs.

The kid turns round three times, then sits in the space beneath Vesper's feet.

Without being asked, the cylinder begins to close. Hands and heads are tucked inside, hasty. With a sigh, the split sides of the cylinder meet, sealing instantly.

Tiny holes appear on the outer layer of the metal, greedily sucking in water, taking on weight and, with a sudden lurch, the cylinder drops beneath the surface.

The First reaches the end of the tunnel, stopping by the hole. It peers down, not needing a torch to penetrate the darkness.

There is nothing but water slapping the sides of the chamber below.

Others come from behind, hurrying through the network, their growing proximity comforting.

The First does not wait for them. It plunges into the water, head first, a black shape welcomed into inky depths.

Down it goes, down and down, a silent missile that finds

new tunnels branching away. It reads the eddies and currents, quickly narrowing options until only one remains.

The First does not swim. Instead, feet and hands push against the bottom of its chosen tunnel, propelling it forward in bursts.

Tireless effort is rewarded by the sight of a silvered shape powering away. By the time the First reaches the edge of the tunnel, its quarry is clear of Sonorous, a glinting speck in the open sea.

Extending from the underwater hole like a shadowy tongue, the First shows no signs of frustration. It calculates many things: depth, speed, direction.

The Malice is going south.

The First does not move to follow. Does not need to. It is already where it needs to be, in a hundred fragments, scattered throughout the world. Waiting.

CHAPTER SEVEN

A curved screen on the inside of the cylinder depicts a seascape, clouded and vast, where fishlike creatures swim and coral weeps.

Vesper sees only a slice past Duet's shoulder, tantalised by things half seen.

A catch in the Harmonised's breath draws her attention. Duet's visor is only a thumb's width from her face. So close she can see her eyes are squeezed shut, feel her body shake.

'Duet? Duet? What is it? What's wrong?'

She talks through gritted teeth: 'Pain meds.'

'What pain meds?'

'Mine. Wearing off.'

'Aren't there more in the bag?'

Her eyes pop open. 'Yes.' A gauntleted hand squeezes in the space between them like a spider, fingers vainly reaching for the top of the bag. They strain, stretch, then flop against Vesper's neck. 'No good.'

Vesper takes a turn. Although in a better position, her arm is pinned, stifling circulation, making the girl clumsy.

As the two grunt and struggle, a wet trumpeting sound comes from near Vesper's feet.

Girl and Harmonised's eyes widen together, then they look down.

Neither can see the yellow glob, sliding into being, but in the confined space, the smell provides plenty of information.

The kid makes an unhappy sound.

Vesper turns up the collar of her coat and buries her face.

Duet coughs, the motion creasing her with pain. 'Should have . . . left it.'

'It's not his fault. He's just scared. I need to go soon too.'

'Don't even . . .' A finger presses lightly against her neck. '. . . Think about it.'

Vesper pouts, presses her thighs together, then tries for the bag once more. Slowly, she teases out a tube. 'I've got the dispenser but I can't reach the medgun.'

'Click out . . . some tabs.'

'You're not going to eat them raw are you?'

'I'll manage.'

There is a click and a blue pellet falls past Duet's hand. She grasps for it, misses.

'Sorry. It's really hard to aim all cramped up like this. And my hand's numb.'

'Again.'

A second click and another pellet falls, nimbly avoiding Duet's attempt to catch it. This one rolls down the side of the cylinder into the kid's waiting mouth.

'Again.'

Four more times the rare medicine is squandered. On the

seventh try, she catches it. Perspiration sprinkles the visible space behind the visor now. Unable to get her hand any higher, Duet tips her head forward, bringing armoured forehead hard against Vesper's lip.

Eyes water and a lip trembles but the girl manages not to cry out.

Duet doesn't notice, intent on passing the pellet under her visor.

Vesper watches. 'Wouldn't it be easier to take that off?' She waits for an answer, doesn't get one. 'Is it helping?'

'Not yet.'

Time passes. The ocean stretches out, a blankness, dull and gloomy. Vesper tries to wriggle her arm free. The motion makes Duet inhale, sharp. 'Sorry. Where did you get hit?'

'All over.'

'Oh.'

'Worst is . . . my side.'

Vesper cranes her neck and catches a glimpse of a dent in Duet's chestplate, armour bending in where it should run smooth. Very carefully, she touches it with her other hand. She feels grooves in the metal, four short furrows side by side with deeper grooves at the top. Four exclamation marks left by the single stamp of a fist. Matching dents occur in other places, though none as deep.

She bites her lip.

'Bad . . . isn't it?'

'Yes. Shouldn't we get the chest plate off? I don't like the way it's digging into you.'

'Me neither but . . . it keeps the . . . bone in place.'

She hears the catch in Duet's voice. 'We'll get through this, I promise.'

Pain medication finally kicks in, making eyes droop and words slur, bitter. 'It's a sin . . . to lie in . . . the presence of . . . The Seven.'

'I'm not lying!' she protests. Duet's head lolls forward till it rests on hers. 'I'm not lying,' she repeats. Gradually, Duet's head slips down onto her shoulder, settling there, heavy.

The ocean is not empty. To the uneducated eye it appears dirty and featureless, differentiated only by patches of light and shadow, by degrees of cloudiness. But the clouds themselves are alive. Phytoplankton swarm, innumerable. Once, these creatures were the lowest of the food chain. Years of breeding in tainted waters has changed that. Now they are bigger, tougher than before. Individually, they remain beneath the notice of other creatures. However large a speck becomes it is still a speck, insignificant. But when the specks flock together, drawn by common purpose, they become something else entirely.

A silver submersible streaks through the water on a pre-arranged course. It cuts through the clouds like a knife. But these clouds bleed, smearing themselves in a thin film across its surface. Over time the film becomes thicker, deepening in colour. The mindless organisms excrete a thin paste onto the submersible's sides, trying to digest. Juices do nothing to the armoured hull and the vessel travels on, untroubled.

Yet more clouds are passed through until clumps of green become visible. From the submersible's fins, stringy cords dangle like unruly hair.

Still the vessel soldiers on, getting greener and greener, thicker and thicker until the original shape is distorted, a giant gherkin with a hundred tails, sinking.

Sinking.

Down it goes, into darker waters, where the denizens grow as they please.

And as it falls, other things attach themselves, adding to the weight, feeding. Metal fins struggle to move, locked into place by layers of hungry life and engines automatically shut down to conserve energy.

Then, from the deepest places, there is movement. A rising of the sea bed. Something giant and ridged reaches up. It is hard to say if the vessel meets the land or the land meets the vessel. Either way, contact is made.

For a moment the submersible sits on top, balancing, a decoration on a grotesque tree. Then flesh bends under it, bubble-like, splitting, sliding over, enveloping.

Lights blink rapidly, dazzling. Vesper groans and wakes up. Cramped muscles demand to be moved but scream when she tries. Limbs are contorted, squashed within the confines of the cylinder. Her fingers feel fat and floaty. Despite the alarms, thoughts form slowly.

Duet still sleeps, her head like an iron ball pressing on Vesper's shoulder. Vesper cannot see the kid but snores can be heard and smells, new and pungent, suggest activity.

The screen no longer shows the ocean. Instead, an undulating black fills the display, a living curtain. As she peers closer, she notices little dots, peppered all over. Clumsily, she works the interface, zooming in until each speck grows into a pair of alien lips, spread across the camera's surface, dabbed with white-green glue, stuck fast.

Vesper recoils from the sight.

Darkness shifts within the screen and the cylinder shakes.

She shouts: 'Duet!' But the Harmonised remains deep in drug-induced sleep. By her feet the kid snores on, happily oblivious.

Ignoring the stiffness in her neck, Vesper turns her head, trying to look at the sword. 'Hello? Hello? It's me, Vesper. I really need your help.'

The cylinder shakes again, this time there is a slow grinding-crumpling noise. New lights appear on the overhead display and a section of the cylinder slides back, revealing a transparent face mask.

An automated voice speaks, serene, incongruous: 'Emergency sealant application in seven . . . six . . . five . . .'

Vesper grabs the mask and presses it to her face, misses.

'. . . four . . . three . . . two . . .'

On the second attempt, she manages to align it properly. The mask adheres to her face, pores appearing in the plastic.

'. . . one.'

Nozzles tucked within the cylinder start to spray. They are designed to coat the pilot in a layer of specially altered Skyn, enabling survival in the deep water. It is a good design, efficient, perfect for a single occupant. Faced with three bodies of varying size and species, the design fails. A thin jellylike substance blurts out, covering the kid's belly and Vesper's back, all the way from her head to her heels. Her front remains open to the elements, however. Duet's legs are well coated but her elbow blocks one of the nozzles, her backside another. A thick rim builds around those places, like a doughnut made of transparent paste, setting fast.

For a third time, the outside seems to move and the cylinder is rattled. There is a cracking sound, unmistakable. Vesper watches, eyes wide, as a single drop of water pushes its way into the cylinder. It grows slowly, a miniature world with it's own weather systems swirling inside, black and green and grey. Then it runs down the wall, leaving a trail for others to follow. Drip. Drip. Drip.

'Duet! Duet! Gamma! Anybody!'

The drips come faster now. When the first drop reaches the bottom of the cylinder, it stops, not forming a pool, not rolling onto the floor where the kid sleeps. It waits. Other drips join it, sliding down, merging, giving it a thicker shape. Gradually, a tube of living water forms, not quite tentacle, not quite tongue. Speckled blobs drift inside it, turning to look towards Vesper.

The girl stops shouting, clamps her mouth shut.

With a sucking sound, the limb peels itself from the wall, travelling the tiny space to where the girl quivers. She tries to reach her pocket and the waiting gun but Duet is pinning her arm and she has no time.

The limb touches the gel on the back of her legs, jerks back. Pauses.

Vesper tries again, manages to get her fingers into the pocket.

The limb begins to curl around her, avoiding the manufactured substance, travelling upwards, towards her neck.

She can feel the handle of the gun now, can brush the edges of it.

The limb begins to probe, sliding over the fabric covering her shoulder and up, over the collar to touch the soft flesh under her ear, pure, untainted, perfect.

Vesper screams.

Eager, the limb splits in two, sliding around either side of the girl's throat, tightening. One of these halves brushes the sleeping sword.

Vesper's screams cut off in a gurgle.

Then, abruptly, as if shocked out of a nightmare, an eye opens.

One Thousand, One Hundred and Twenty-Five Years Ago

The prosthetic lies in two halves, its inner mechanisms spread out across the table. In place of motors and sensors, Massassi inserts glass, beautiful, curving.

She has been free of medicine for months now and as her head clears, so too have life's obstacles.

Not long after she left the hospital, they came for her. They wanted her to return to work. They wanted her to pay for treatment. They wanted to make her go away.

They did not say so of course but she knew it. Irrefutable, the truth shone from their faces, the secret ones that only she can see. With her silvered arm, she touched those faces and the men left her in peace.

So they sent new men, with fresh questions and these too she turned away.

The third visitors came with tranquillisers and explosives. They did not bother to question.

Massassi took their weapons, then had them return to their masters to report that she was dead.

A week later, a new citizen is allocated her old living square. His name is Insa. After the initial meeting, Insa does not see Massassi, nor does he question why he lives out of his storage crates and makes meals for two. Advertisers notice the change in his purchasing habits and offer tantalising images of the latest tools and mech designs. Without knowing why, he finds himself buying them.

Insa does not mind. He is happy in his new home, happy to get new things with his meagre savings, even if he does not get to use them.

Equipment litters the space, much of it in pieces, essential parts taken and re-purposed. Massassi sits in the middle of the wreckage, working, always working. As she makes fine adjustments and tweaks to the prosthetic her silvered arm fades slowly, like a happy memory.

Sometimes she stops to glare at it and it burns back into focus, sharp as a laser. But each time, a little more sweat beads on her brow, and each time she returns to her work the arm dims a little faster.

She works through the night, using determination to keep going. She dare not use drugs, no matter how tempting.

When the prosthetic is done she lays her silvered arm carefully along one half. Lenses and mirrors capture the light, focusing and holding. Satisfied, she fixes the other half into place, seals them with liquid fire. This is not a replacement arm, it is a sheath, a second skin. The old one was never truly lost.

Fingers of essence flex and stretch, folding the artificial housing around them. She tests the repaired limb for mobility, rotating the fist, swivelling the shoulder.

At each movement she checks the joins, looking for signs

of escaping essence. She finds none. As fears diminish, the urge to sleep returns, strong and demanding.

Massassi gives in, flopping down in a corner.

She awakes in a good mood. With her arm stabilised, she is free. The world is her plaything and she is eager to start. She waves to Insa and makes for the door.

He neither sees nor returns the gesture.

She pauses at the door, turns and walks over to the blank faced man. Metal tipped fingers rise towards his face and an iris opens in her palm, like an eye. She lets the silver light fall on his face, bringing purpose back to his features.

'Goodbye, Insa,' she says.

'Goodbye,' he replies with a smile, certain he must know her from somewhere.

It has been a long time since she has been outside. As always a smoggy haze clings to the horizon but above it she sees a distortion, a crease in the sky, as if a great weight were pressing down, trying to get in. She sees the angle of it, can guess the rough direction it points in.

A shudder runs through her and, on instinct, she goes the other way.

CHAPTER EIGHT

An eye darts to the left, to the right and narrows, hate filled. Forking either side of it is a limb of living water, filled with taint and hunger. It bends to give the sword as wide a berth as possible, seeking the more appetising girl the sword is fixed to.

Silvered wings stretch up, then cut down, sharp, scattering droplets.

The limb recoils, steam rising, sparks of blue dancing around the severed end, threatening to ignite.

Freed, Vesper swallows air down a bruised throat. She pulls the gun clear of her pocket and sends glances everywhere, alert for new threats.

They are not long in coming. Outside the cylinder, an angry dark squeezes and metal buckles. Each new crack allows more water inside, the liquid quickly taking on more menacing shapes. Even as they finish forming they slide towards the cylinder's occupants, probing for gaps in armour, for places to slide inside.

Vesper fires, concentrating on the cracks in the hull, using the beam to seal the holes. As each is welded shut, the limb of water is snipped free of its maker, splashing to the ground to writhe, semi-coherent.

Outside, the darkness ripples in pain and rage, and the cylinder is shaken so hard that metal tears. Then there is a high squeal, a thunk and the sudden sensation of movement.

Dark is replaced by green dark, and alien waters replaced by ocean, merely tainted. Air leaves the cylinder in huge, gasping bubbles, allowing the ocean to take up residence.

Vesper puts the gun away and reaches down to gather the kid into her arms. Now that the cylinder is partially open, it is easier to move. Unaware of the danger, the kid nestles, snoring, content, the blue of the sleeping tablets smearing lips like gaudy paint.

She spreads the thick paste of the sealant that has collected on the kid's belly over the rest of his body. She pulls it wide around his head, making a crude dome.

With her other hand she grabs Duet's wrist. One more time she implores the Harmonised to wake but her words cannot break through the drug-induced slumber.

Hands full, she uses her feet to push the two halves of the cylinder further apart. It is unclear whether it opens for her by luck or by design. Vesper doesn't care either way. She kicks free, out of the cylinder and into open water. After such tight confinement, the sudden enormity of her surroundings is paralysing.

Vesper's breath mask automatically filters air and Duet's visor seals itself to conserve oxygen. Meanwhile, unaware, the kid sleeps on.

Vesper begins to drift but in the darkness she can only guess the difference between up and down.

Legs kick, frantically trying for the surface. Youthful strength and energy are no match for the combined weight of an armoured Harmonised and a sleeping kid.

They begin to sink. Down. Definitely down.

Vesper continues to kick, stirring bubbles, working hard, harder. Their descent slows, pauses. But she cannot maintain the effort, cannot hope to swim free with her burdens.

Without meaning to, her eyes and thoughts turn to the kid, then to Duet. Surely they would understand? Is it not better that some of them survive?

Suddenly, she remembers her father's hands, always there to pick her up. Never letting go.

She cannot let go. Not now.

Legs already tiring, she continues to kick.

On her back the sword begins to hum. Where its eye looks, tainted clouds of ocean clear, opening a pathway to cleaner waters. Silvered wings beat gently, finding purchase in currents, invisible.

Slowly at first, they ascend, getting faster as wings find their rhythm.

Numb fingers grip poorly, Vesper seeing rather than feeling Duet slip away. She tries to hold on, her hand sliding down Duet's bracer, catching on the heel of the other's hand. Their growing speed makes it harder. It is only a matter of time before she is lost.

Vesper closes her eyes momentarily. She stops kicking, trusting to the sword entirely and wraps her legs under Duet's arms.

Tirelessly, the sword drags them up, until light brushes

red and gold around them and biting cold becomes only cool.

Vesper's head breaks the surface. She looks round and sees grey sand close by.

An eye also sees it. Humming subsides, wings stop their work, folding once more about the sword. An eye closes.

Vesper's head dips below the water.

With frantic kicks, she makes towards the land, not bothering to go up. Shortly, her feet touch rising rock and she manages to stand. With wobbling steps she makes her way towards the island. Rock mixes with sand, dragging at feet but Vesper keeps going.

She lies to herself: 'Just one more step.' Believing just enough to struggle on.

She drags Duet as far as she can before dropping an arm and falling to her knees. It is only when she places the kid upon the sand that she appreciates how still he has become.

Vesper puts her hands flat on the sand, closes her eyes. The sword is heavy on her back. Her arms quiver with fatigue. A tear squeezes out, dropping onto the inside of her mask. She takes a deep breath. Then another.

She shrugs out of her coat and unbuckles the sword, placing the latter on top of the former. She crawls to the kid, breaking the rubbery dome around his head and wipes the last of the blue residue from cold lips.

Shaking hands push on the kid's stomach. Air is blown into the kid's mouth.

He responds quickly.

The first cough is delicate, the second less so. Suddenly the kid is standing upright, belching out coloured water onto the beach. By the time he is finished, Vesper is asleep. The kid bleats at her, then tries nudging her with his head. The girl groans a little but otherwise doesn't move.

The kid looks at her for a while, then at the unfamiliar territory. A conclusion is reached. The kid turns on the spot and settles next to the girl, his chin resting on her stomach. The little head rises and falls like the waves, regular and slow.

*

Samael climbs up the old metal hill. He is careful not to look towards the Breach. An instinct keeps his gaze on the dented, rusty floor. A part of him is afraid to look, knows that he will not be able to unsee whatever waits for him. Somehow, it will be easier to bear when he has resumed his customary watching post.

He plants his feet where he always plants them, enjoying the feeling of belonging. In this place he is rooted. He does not understand why this is, does not care to.

Grounded now, ready, he raises his head.

Four infernal factions race towards the Breach. As expected the Felrunners cannot be matched in pace, their weeping legs flashing underneath them like an army of sticks, a never tangling mess of movement. Hangnail is close behind, running with inhuman speed, casual. Next to the rolling, ugly gait of Gutterface, the others appear almost elegant. The Backwards Child brings up the rear. Unable to run, it is carried on the back of a huge Usurperkin, a twisted pimple on a lumbering mountain.

At last, Samael lifts his gaze further, taking in the horizon and the Breach itself.

Without meaning to, he takes a step backwards.

If anything, the Yearning has grown in his absence. A sizable section of the Breach is blocked by its ephemeral form, a roiling cloud of yellow and green, a slice of otherness, a seed trying to plant itself in hostile soil. Where reality is weak, the Yearning spreads out, expanding into spaces defined by currents of essence, mapping out the lines between this world and the impossible.

Where realities blur, the Yearning pushes, its essence smoking under the glare of the broken suns. Along the border, the Yearning burns, fossilising into crystal, forming trees, strange and starlike. This forest sprouts in the ground and the sky with equal felicity, drawing in the good air and breathing out something else.

The Felrunners are the first to reach the unearthly forest.

Samael watches as their lord plunges between the glassy trunks, leaping and sailing over bubbling earth. By the fourth of these leaps, something begins to change. A distortion of distance. A stretching.

Samael leans forward to better understand. Lord Felrunner's head seems to be streaking ahead of its many legs, body and neck stretching to accommodate.

The other Felrunners hesitate, only to find that it is not just their legs carrying them forward. As they scrabble back, their lord rushes on, like a piece of elastic stretched suddenly over many miles, then gone.

Samael's half-breed eyes just catch the last glimmer of Lord Felrunner's essence, a thin ribbon of ash, falling upward, fading.

Unmade.

Unwilling to follow their lord any longer, unable to stop,

the Felrunners slide towards their end, undignified. The glassy trunks catch their reflections, changing them. Samael cannot make out the images and for that he is glad.

Those that can turn away and make for home, save the Backwards Child. For even in retreat it is ever cursed to be looking where it should not.

Only the Backwards Child and Samael see the Felrunners stretching, essence pushing out through their shells, shredding them. Where the monsters once ran stand a gaggle of new essence trees, thin reedy things like stalks of long grass, fragile straws standing high on an abundance of frozen limbs. From each hangs a bag of flesh, suspended in the air, a flag of defeat.

*

Waves lap at Duet's boots. She remains as she was left, one arm raised by her head, pointing randomly. Above, the suns orbit each other, circling slowly towards the horizon.

Vesper sits nearby, feeding the kid. Next to her, the sword sleeps. When the feeding is done, the kid totters along the beach. He doesn't go far and looks back often, bleating until acknowledgement is given.

Vesper lies down by the sword, her nose in line with the crosspiece. She watches it for a long time. Not quite daring to touch the hilt, she rests a hand on the sheath.

The sword does not react.

She stays like that a while, then mouths a silent thank-you.

A booted foot twitches, splashing weakly. Vesper sits up to see Duet doing the same.

'Where are . . . we?'

Vesper waves to the kid, who begins to race back. 'I don't know.'

'What happened?'

She begins to tell her of horrors half glimpsed under the water and the fight for survival. Before she can finish, the kid stumbles sideways, comic, then falls over. Four legs scurry in the air and the kid makes an unhappy noise. He struggles to his feet, standing at a dangerous angle and barely makes two strides before tottering, falling again.

Duet sounds tired. 'What now?'

Vesper gets up stiffly, like a woman many years her senior and rushes over. 'He ate some of those tabs, I don't know how many. And he swallowed a lot of water.'

'We should have . . . left it behind.'

'Don't say that!'

'I'm just . . .' She pauses, jerking upright, her sentence ending in a strangled gurgle.

The quality of the sound stops Vesper in her tracks. She looks back in time to see Duet pull off her visor and bend forward.

Her mouth turns down as Duet vomits repeatedly onto the beach. Hisses of pain accompany the ejections, and her hand moves to her side, involuntary, drawing attention to impressions left by the First's fist.

Afterwards, she sips a little water while Vesper gathers the kid in her arms.

When she is done, she finds the girl staring. Immediately, her face hardens. 'What is it?'

Vesper blinks. 'Sorry, it's just I've never seen your face before.'

'And?'

She looks again at the Harmonised's features. Only the Knights and the Lenses are permitted to grow their hair, Duet is neither. Stubble dusts her scalp, dark and severe. Something about her nose seems wrong, her ears too, though Vesper cannot see why, the microsurgeries too subtle to leave scarring.

'Well?'

'I didn't think you'd be so young.'

'All Harmonised are. They sync us . . . from birth.'

'What happens when you get old?'

'We die?' She shrugs. 'They never said. I never asked.'

For a while, neither speaks. Vesper draws idly in the sand. 'It's getting dark. We need to find shelter.'

Duet doesn't look at her. 'Do we?'

'Of course we do. We need to rest somewhere safe so we can get going in the morning.'

'Why?'

'For the mission of course.'

'The mission is . . . over. We have no . . . transport. No troops, no . . . support. We're dead.'

She pauses her doodling, leaving a knight half-sketched. 'We still have the sword, and each other.'

'A baby goat! A child! And . . .' Duet searches for the words to describe herself, falls to mutterings. 'We're dead.'

'I'm not much younger than you! Five years at the most.'

'Ten is closer.'

'Ten then. It doesn't matter! You still believe in the sword, don't you?'

'Do you?'

'Yes.'

'Liar! I watched . . . you. In Sonorous.' Vesper looks away. 'The sword didn't . . . speak to you . . . there. It didn't . . . ask for me . . . did it?' Duet nods grimly at Vesper's silence. 'She was right . . . about you.'

Vesper's head remains bowed. 'Who was?'

'Me. Her.'

In silence, Vesper collects her things and walks towards the pockmarked cliffs.

Red light glints on Duet's abandoned visor, then makes way for dazzling gold. One of the suns has already dipped below the horizon, the other not far behind.

Duet sighs, a long and bitter thing and levers herself upright.

Waves creep stealthily up the beach, each time a little higher, harrying the Harmonised as she limps after the girl.

Vesper begins to climb. The rocks are moist, too soft, like clay. Where she scrabbles, long spined things as big as a fingernail flee the disturbance, seeking new holes to inhabit.

The kid bounds ahead, treating sheer walls like gentle pathways.

Vesper, finding a hollow halfway up, climbs in with the kid, huddling together for warmth. When Duet arrives, the front of her armour smeared in mud, Vesper smiles but she doesn't join them, sitting as far apart as space allows, shivering, alone.

Clouds roll across the sky, bullied along by a growing wind. Foam-capped waves strike the cliffs, coating them in crust, glistening.

The kid hops onto the top of the cliff. His dark eyes

expressionless as he takes in the view. Behind him comes Vesper, determined expression glimpsed through mud-streaked hair crusted with salt. Last comes Duet, grunting and cursing with each movement, her usual grace abandoned.

Vesper lets her catch her breath before speaking. 'Have you taken any tabs today?'

'I took two.'

'Two? I thought you were only supposed to take one.'

'I took two.'

'Then this is the best time to have a look at your injury.'

'You're no surgeon.'

'Don't be scared. I just want to look.'

'I am scared. Of infection.'

'The sword will protect us from taint.' She holds up the bag. 'And I've got gel for everything else.'

Begrudgingly, Duet agrees and they find a sheltered spot, a dip in the ground, where two-tone flowers grow and bushes with leaves like antlers.

She takes off the chest-plate. Its original contours have been distorted by many dents. Underneath is a thin layer of padding, smart-adjusting to temperature changes, shock absorbing. Beneath the spot the First hit hardest, blood dries in a ragged oval.

At Vesper's insistence, she peels the padding back too, wincing as fabric tears itself from fresh scabbing. Pale skin makes bruises stark. Together they tell of multiple strikes, fist sized. Vesper smears them with anti-inflammatory gel, getting the easy part out of the way.

'What is it?'

Vesper bites her lip. 'It's so swollen here, I'm not sure if the bone is broken.'

'Do you know . . . what to do?' Duet's voice carries an edge of nerves.

'Not really. I mean, I've set legs before but never ribs.' She doesn't mention if the legs are human or animal.

Duet scowls but doesn't protest when the girl starts work. She plugs the newly torn scabs with fresh Skyn, dabbing the thick paste on with her fingers, like an artist. The Flexicast comes next, which appears like a long, thin sack of liquid until activated. She wraps it around Duet's ribs, adjusting it for size. When it is snug, she lets go and the liquid solidifies, moulding itself to Duet's body, supporting but limiting flexibility.

'How's that?'

'Better.'

Vesper beams at her.

For Duet, indeed for many citizens of the Empire of the Winged Eye, smiles do not come naturally. With pain gone, tension soon departs, making room for fatigue. Before she realises it, the Harmonised has fallen asleep in the soft earth.

While she dreams, Vesper's smile vanishes. 'We have to be strong for Duet,' she says to the kid, scratching behind his ear. 'Even if we don't feel very strong. I wish,' she pauses, sighs. 'I wish I knew what to say to her. And I wish Father was here, or Uncle Harm. They'd know what to do.' She meets the kid's gaze. 'Duet's wound looked bad, didn't it?'

The kid's eyes appear bleak.

Vesper sighs again. It would be easy to give up, to throw herself from the cliff or just curl up in a ball and cry. But she allows herself neither, haunted by the sound of swords shattering and the look in Genner's eyes. He died for her along with countless others. It would be the worst insult to fail them now.

She starts with something small, manageable, and tries to knock out the dents in Duet's chest-plate. She moves a discreet distance away, picks up a rock and begins to hammer. Sometimes she holds it up in front of the kid, encouraging him to kick. Girl and goat play happily. Old dents are popped back, new ones made. Throughout, Duet and the sword sleep.

When Duet wakes, they share some rations and Vesper consults the Navpack. It tells them they are on the mainland. It is wrong, ignorant of the floods or the quakes that have changed the landscape in the years since the Lenses kept accurate records of the south. No sky-ships dare fly this airspace and the eyes that watched the world from above have long been closed, dead spheres circling the heavens, endless, hopeless.

Several settlements are nearby, all marked with unknown or hostile status. This far south, there are no flags of the Empire of the Winged Eye, no safe havens, no friends. 'I'm not sure which way to go.'

'We need supplies.'

Vesper scans settlement names, searching for the familiar. 'What about Wonderland? That doesn't sound too bad. Uncle talked about it . . .'

'You surprise me.'

'What's that supposed to mean?'

'Nothing. What did he say?'

'Um . . . he said it was dangerous. But so were all the places in his stories.'

'Do you remember anything?'

'Anything! That's it. He said that in Wonderland, you could get anything. Anything at all. So I'm sure we'll be able to get supplies there.

'This way!' she says, jumping up with an enthusiasm she doesn't feel. The kid echoes the motion and the two set off. Duet follows with a different demeanour, a balance to their brightness.

They make their way down a gentle slope, the kid naturally finding the safest way. The terrain is soft rock in places, wet dirt in others. Grass grows in patches, irregular, like the scalp of a balding man.

Wind tugs at the girl's coat, ruffles hair. As the view of the south presents itself, Vesper slows. She shines the Navpack on the floor, compares the map it draws with what stands before her. 'Uh oh.'

Where land is expected, there are more waves, and beyond them, distant but visible, a second coastline. She puts the Navpack away, pulls up the old scope and puts it to her eye. In places, the water is shallow and she sees shapes beneath it, shadows of rooftops, tubes trying to float, suspended below the surface by stubborn cables.

She sets off, keen to explore. Duet struggles to match her pace, going just fast enough to keep her in sight but no more.

At land's end, kid and girl skid to a stop. There is no beach here, just rock and grass dipping into water. Vesper extends out a leg, lowers her foot carefully. It goes in up to the ankle, then the knee before finding purchase on a roof. Goosebumps appear all over the girl and she bites a knuckle to stop from squealing. Then she leans forward, testing the roof with more and more of her weight.

It holds.

Vesper wades across, coat turning up, floating around her knees.

The kid bleats, making her turn. 'Come on, it's safe.'

The kid bleats again and backs away from the edge.

'It's cold but you'll be fine. Come on.'

The kid sits down.

Duet works her way down to them. She too stops at the water's edge.

'Come on,' Vesper calls. 'We need to cross while it's still light.'

'There's no other . . . way?'

'I don't know. Nowhere nearby anyway.'

Teeth are gritted, hidden behind the visor and Duet steps onto the submerged platform. Water splashes nearby grass and kid, making both wet and one bleat derisively.

'Can you bring him in?' asks Vesper.

Duet complies, reaching back to grab the kid by the neck. Before the kid can panic, Duet throws him out into the water.

Vesper's eyes follow the flailing arc.

For such a small creature, the splash is impressive.

The kid vanishes beneath the surface. There are bubbles, then a tiny explosion as he reappears, spitting, glaring at the Harmonised.

'I didn't know . . . they could swim.'

'All goats can,' Vesper replies. 'They hate it though.' She retrieves the kid, scooping the sodden creature out of the water, wobbling, then getting her balance.

They press on, moving slowly, wading from roof to roof. Some buildings peek from the water, worn heads sparkling in the afternoon sunslight, others lurk deep, forcing them to half swim, tiptoeing at full stretch to make progress. Vesper chatters breathlessly, alternating between encouraging the others and pointing out interesting shapes in the water. Anything to keep Duet moving, anything rather than think about the burden on her back or the consequences of what she has done. Time passes, deceptive, evening arriving before it's welcome. More than half the crossing remains.

Duet holds up a hand. 'Do you always . . . talk this much?'

Vesper's face creases in thought. 'I always talk when there are animals around, they find it soothing.'

Duet mutters, 'I find it . . . tiring.'

But the girl doesn't hear her. 'My uncle likes to talk. He says talking is a way of getting things out. Like airing a barn. But instead of a barn it's like airing yourself. That wasn't exactly what he said but I think that's what he meant. My uncle's good with words.'

She chatters on, determinedly good natured, as they slow-race the suns to the coastline.

There is no real contest. The suns reach the finish long before the people do, allowing darkness to spread. Stars peek between rushing clouds, offering little illumination.

Vesper has her hands full with the kid, so they rely on the light from Duet's visor to guide them. As night deepens, their world shrinks down, defined by the width of the torch beam and jigsaw memories of what surrounds it.

They move carefully, splashing, mindful of cracks stretching underfoot. Then, fifty metres from the loom of the coast, the buildings stop.

Duet sweeps the beam methodically, searching, finding nothing of substance.

From further off, they hear a cackle, and a voice, rough. 'You won't find nothing down there, nope. Nothing.'

Duet looks up, adjusts her gaze until the light catches a small squatting shape across the water. He covers his face with spindly arms. 'Get your buggerfinding bling out of me eyes, damn you!'

Duet dips her gaze fractionally, keeping the edge of her light by the stranger's feet. 'Better?'

Thin arms cross. 'Better if you'd not come at all.'

Vesper speaks quickly, intercepting Duet's reply. 'Please, we've been travelling all day and we're tired. Is there a way to get across?'

'Might be. Might be I can show it to you. Might be I can help you after an' all.'

'We just need help across, thanks.'

'That all is it? You sound like a stripling. You from the soft north?'

'Yes,' replies Vesper, a moment before Duet's elbow finds her ribs. She looks at the Harmonised, reproachful but Duet's attention is on the stranger.

'Don't say too . . . much. We don't . . . know him.'

The stranger clears his throat. 'How much you want to cross then?'

'We want to cross very much, we need to.'

'What? You been slapped in the head?'

'A little bit.'

Vesper receives another cackle. 'Yes, yes, you gonna be needing me alright. Yes, you is. I'm not giving a dry spit how you is feeling. I wants to know what you giving old Churner to be saving you.'

This time, Duet is the first to speak. 'We don't need . . . saving.'

'Don't you now? Way I sees it, you stuck out there in the darky cold. You tired and empty. You got big bling on your head that will draw all the flies here. And there's lots of 'em prowling tonight.'

Vesper nudges Duet. 'I think we'll have to deal.'

Duet frowns behind her visor. 'He's trouble.'

'Probably, but what choice do we have?'

The frown becomes fiercer. 'We'll regret this.'

Vesper turns back to the man across the water. 'We've got medicine we could trade.'

'What kind?'

'Pain meds, stims, soothers and lots more.'

Churner's toes wriggle with excitement. 'Well, if you got the pills, I got the ills. I wants two handfuls, one for each of you.'

Duet shakes her head, making the beam sweep wide to the left and right. 'You'll get one.'

Churner stands up. 'Two, or old Churner goes across the ways and finds some hungry flies and tells them all abouts you.'

'Two!' Vesper blurts. 'You can have two.'

'Two big handfuls? No tricks?'

'No tricks.'

'Right then, you sees that tall building over there?'

Duet turns her light, following where Churner points. The beam picks out a rusting arm, jutting ten metres into the air like a giant's finger, crooked. 'Yes.'

'You get over there and I'll be waiting. An' I'll be letting you into a little secret.' They turn away, trying to find a route through the dark waters. 'And go quicky smart. Won't be long before the flies get your stink and then they be crawling all over here and all over you.'

CHAPTER NINE

Essence pulses unseen across the world, spiderwebbing light that grows thick over the southern continent, linking a hundred heads. There is a single moment of cohesion, the bittersweet taste of old majesty and then the First becomes fragmented again.

Unprotected essence is burned by the angry suns, diminished by the hate of the world as it retreats back into its many shells.

The First feels a terrible pain, lingering far longer than the instant of bliss that preceded. The First accepts the trade, considers it worthwhile. Gradually, the burning subsides, allowing the First to take action. From its many hiding places, it speaks and rumours spread like a sudden rain: the Malice is returning. The Malice is vulnerable. The one who ends the Malice can name their reward and the First will grant it.

Responses are varied and instant.

The hungry dispossessed at the north end of the landmass lick their lips and sharpen their sticks.

Across the flatlands, Usurperkin tribes compete with Mottled Walkers and Pug Packs, boasting and posturing.

In Verdigris, the news has to compete with the sudden onset of plague, but those in power share knowing looks and guards start double shifts at the gate.

Word even reaches New Horizon. In the high courts of the Demagogue, many sweat, suddenly insecure in their seats of power. Inevitably, news trickles through the rotten city, passed from slaves to spies and gossips, spreading like a virus. Soon, a hopeful takes the news to the Iron Mountain, looking to swap the information for something more tangible. He trades with Doctor Zero, who pays him well. When the man has gone, Doctor Zero adds another scar to the white criss-crosses on his hands and whispers into the blood that beads there.

Flies come, drinking deep of Zero's message before flying further south, where even the First does not care to go; where land blisters and air quakes, where Fallen Palaces lay and beyond that, where madness spits in the eye of sanity, and demons run, fearful.

*

A thin ridge of metal skirts the old tower. Because the structure leans, part of the ridge dips below the water level, part of it rises above, although regular waves cover all when they come.

Vesper and Duet balance on it, clinging to scaffolding that pokes from the structure like rusting bone.

Teeth chatter, as much from exhaustion as cold. 'Do you think he's coming?'

'I doubt it.'

'But why bother to bring us out here at all?'

'It's a better . . . place for an . . . ambush.'

With her ear pressed to the tower's side, Vesper cannot help but hear it creak. The groaning speaks of age, of wear and of imminent collapse.

The wind tugs at them, chilling wet clothes, nipping at skin beneath. Vesper starts to go numb, imagines herself turning blue, save for the oasis of warm where the kid presses on her chest.

After what seems too long, Churner crawls into view.

'Hurry up!' snaps Duet.

'Quiet,' hisses Churner. 'Keep your great gobs shut and lower your bling. I sees the prowlers are out and they is not far.'

Duet turns off the beam. With a satisfied grunt, Churner gets to work. Pulleys squeak and squeal like children, noisy, and the crooked tower tries to straighten. It does not get all the way but enough for slick cables to rise from the depths, making a quivering line from the tower to the coast.

They tie themselves on with halting, trembling fingers, fumbling their way in the dark. Brave feet lift from the tower, trusting to the ancient cable.

It sways but holds.

From the other side, Churner works the engineless winch by hand. As he sweats and strains, Duet is dragged across in uneven bursts, heels skimming the wave tops. Vesper and the kid follow. Their progress is faster, if not smoother.

On the other side, the kid is keen for a reunion with dry land. Vesper drops him and he quickly vanishes into the dark.

'You is getting my pills now.'

Vesper holds out the bag while Churner releases the winch and lowers it back into the water. He turns back to the girl, raising his large hands. 'Kept these beasties to myself till we'd made our deal. Old Churner's no fool, nope, no fool. You is giving me a little bling to pick by. Just in the bag, mind, don't want no prowlers sniffing us.'

Duet complies, the light catching on many different coloured tabs and treatments. Churner's mouth opens with delight, a grim hole with few teeth. Any sense of haste fades away and the man runs his fingers over the contents of the bag, signalling his approval with a series of animal grunts.

When he is done, the bag is notably lighter.

'Goodbye,' says Duet, already walking away. Churner chuckles, making her stop. 'Something funny?'

'You is going the wrong way. Very exposed that way. You be easy pickings going that way. I know another path, a little sneaky twisty thing it is. Much better.'

'How much?' asks Vesper.

'I fancy a munch on that little morsel you has.'

'My what?'

'It's a trottsy one, all juiceful and tender . . .'

Realisation dawns. 'No!'

'Ssh!'

Vesper lowers her voice. 'Sorry. You can't have my goat.'

'I don't needs all of him, just some ribs or a couple of legs.'

'No.'

Churner sniffs. 'What about its tongue? You not wanting the stringy old tongue. You wasting that. Give it to me and I gets you on a safe road.'

Duet nods.

'No. No deal. We'll give you some of our rations.'

The agreement is made in a flurry of quick whispers and the group go on their way. Churner leads them across the coast to a crack in the cliffs, just wide enough for one. They slip through to find it opening up, becoming a rocky path winding inland. A stream draws a line down its centre.

It remains too risky to rest and tired limbs are marshalled for one last march. Through the night they go, until Duet's light brushes over cords, tiny, casting shadows the path's width. 'What's this?'

'Stop!' Churner says, forgetting his earlier caution. 'Oh blood and spit, oh bugger and shitholes!'

'What is it?'

'Tingle traps. Touch one and they'll be all over us.'

Duet's voice is quiet, dangerous. 'Where's that goat?'

Three heads turn as one, finding the kid a little way ahead. He has already crossed the first trapline without incident, standing poised by another. Feeling the sudden attention, he turns back and bleats, innocent.

'Stay there,' says Vesper softly. 'That's it. Stay there.'

The kid bleats again, head drawn to the sound of the girl's voice. He trots a few paces towards them.

'No. Stop!'

The kid pauses, head tilted and quizzical.

Vesper holds her hands out in front of her, fingers spread. Slowly, she moves towards the kid, mindful to step over the cord. 'I'm coming to you. Stay there. Stay there.'

Duet's hand goes to her sword, ready. Churner shuffles from one foot to the other. Vesper reaches the kid, goes to scoop him up but the kid has other ideas, scampering back out of reach.

'Oh, come on!' Vesper mutters, then more sweetly: 'Come on, I've got some milk for you.'

The kid stops, watching keenly as Vesper produces the special bottle. Without another word he scampers over.

Relieved, they start to cross the second trap.

From deeper in the darkness, a single pair of hands applaud, mocking. 'Thanks for saving our supper, girl. But don't sweat too much, we wouldn't want you to get lean.'

Duet draws her sword and lights up the dark. Half a dozen figures lurk on the edge of the beam, eyes narrowed against the glare. They look desperate, dangerous. Their scavenged weapons are crude, scraps of metal or tools, re-purposed; in the right hands, deadly. These hands are stained by a lifetime of murder, animal and otherwise.

From behind them more hunters scrabble down the rock, blocking escape.

The kid sneezes.

Vesper pulls out the gun.

'What's this, Churner?' says their leader. 'You trying to keep the bounty all to yourself?'

The old man throws himself at the leader's feet. 'No, no, Licey. I is bringing them safe and soft this way so I could share them with you. Don't want no others whetting their teeth on our meat, do we?'

The leader steps forward, revealing herself, an angry ripcord swathed in strips of cloth. 'And what else have you brought us?'

'Is this not plentiful?'

'No.' She kicks him and he whimpers, quickly producing a treasure of tablets in cupped hands. 'Very nice, Churner. Very nice.'

While she talks, the other hunters stalk closer, a circle, tightening.

Duet can wait no longer. She spins to the ones nearest her, blade flicking out. Instinctively they lean away, flailing their own weapons in her general direction and only the tip of her sword finds them. It is enough. Throats open, singing red songs and while they gape like pale fish, she kills another.

But the hunters are hard and little surprises them for long. They close in, surrounding her, striking always when her back is turned, opportunistic.

She twirls and strikes, parries and thrusts, moving in a way these people have never seen. Vesper watches, the gun shaking in her hand. She points it towards the melee, not quite firing as the figures pass through her line of fire.

'Stop!' she calls out, raising the gun for emphasis.

She is ignored. Perhaps they don't believe her, perhaps they simply cannot see the weapon in the dark.

The fight begins to turn. The hunters pit numbers and experience against Duet's speed and training. She is too fast for them but they are in no hurry to die, keeping her on the edge of their sticks, taking turns, forcing her always to turn towards the next threat. And sometimes, her training fails her. She fights as if she is not alone, making openings for a ghost that never strikes, realising too late that no partner has her back.

Fatigue and injury play their part, too. A stick stabs into her side, easily turned by her armour, then another, rattling wounds. She gasps in pain, pausing for the briefest time.

Sensing weakness, the hunters attack.

Duet cannot stop them all. She drops her sword, curling

into an armoured ball. Blows rain down, furtive at first, testing, but growing bolder.

Vesper points the gun, squeezing eyes and trigger at the same time.

Angry light lances out, briefly illuminating faces, shocked. Somehow, she misses them all.

They gasp and turn towards the new threat, pausing for the briefest time –

And Duet has a knife in her hand and is spinning again, slashing tendons as she rises, stabbing under ribs to slow-puncture lungs. Several break and run. She stabs them too.

As the last hunters flee, their leader, Licey, leaps towards Vesper, who fires, catching the woman mid-leap, burning a line across the outside of her thigh. Then her hands are on Vesper's wrists, forcing them up, twisting, trying to steal the weapon.

Vesper struggles and the kid runs a few steps away then faints, falling sideway with straight legs.

The woman is not much taller than the girl but she is far stronger. And more brutal. In moments, Vesper lays curled on the floor and Licey has the gun. She turns it toward Duet who is doggedly trying to kill as many as she can before they can escape.

Without warmth, Licey smiles and pulls the trigger.

Nothing happens.

Licey tries again and the gun begins to hum off key. She grunts in surprise and veins pop to attention across her face. The hum continues, sound wavering as the gun quivers in her grip. Muscles in her hand spasm first, then her arm and shoulder. Soon all are straining to breaking point, violent, relentless, shaking her until teeth chip at each other and her heart pops. Fourteen long seconds later, Licey is dead.

Too late, Vesper covers her face. She cannot pluck out what she has seen, cannot wash it away with tears.

As the dust settles, Churner starts to crawl away, keeping low, unobtrusive.

Duet's boots soon fill his vision. She has her sword back now. 'Your turn.'

'Don't be doing in old Churner. I is helping you. I is showing you secret ways and I is giving you a safe path.'

'This wasn't safe.'

'Safer than the way you is trying to go.' He sees her sword start to rise and changes tack. 'Will help you more, show you best ways. And I is stashing many treasures. You would like to be seeing them. You would.'

'We've had enough . . . of your help. We don't need . . . anything from you.'

Vesper chimes in. 'It's not his fault. They were going to kill him too.'

'I doubt it.'

'But they hurt him and stole from him. He wouldn't want that. Please don't do anything to him.'

Duet's sword hovers above Churner's head. 'If we let . . . him go. He'll sell . . . us out.'

'So will the men that ran away. Killing him isn't going to make a difference.'

She sheaths her sword. 'We'll regret this.'

'Oh no, you is wise and generous. I is remembering this. Oh yes. I –' He pauses as Duet scoops the tablets out of his hands. 'What is you doing?'

'We traded for . . . a safe path. You didn't deliver.'

Vesper opens her mouth to speak but Duet silences her with a look and points to the gun in Licey's cold grip. Trying not to sob, she crawls over to the body, breath coming in gasps as she struggles to unpeel fingers, stiff and stubborn.

They leave Churner still kneeling in the dirt, a few pills speckling his palms. Vesper looking back at the last moment to mouth a silent apology.

Alone, Churner starts to mutter. 'I is remembering this. Oh yes. I is remembering this.'

The night passes. One sleeps while the other watches, taking turns, dividing the dark. The kid leaves them to it, soft snores unbroken.

In the morning they continue. The valley ends in a rough set of natural stairs, uneven, tilting things, hewn from the rock by powerful forces. Upon seeing them, the kid begins to bounce.

Duet scowls. 'What's wrong with it?'

Vesper shrugs.

Hooves click on stony ground, drumming, excited, then speeding forward.

The girl and the Harmonised watch bemused as the kid bounds from one step to the next. Each landing brings a new platform into view, even more tempting than the last. Sometimes the kid makes the jump first time, sometimes legs flail in the air before plopping down again. To the kid, it doesn't matter. Progress is erratic but fast. By the time the humans start the climb, the kid is two thirds of the way up, squeaking and joyful.

Exertion soon takes its toll on old wounds. Duet pauses,

leaning heavy on the wall. She raises a hand to her visor, letting her head drift down, taking its weight. Grief grumbles from deep within, threatening to wake. She takes a deep breath, swallows, and looks up.

Vesper is there, one step above her, hand held out as open as her face.

'What?' growls Duet.

'Let me help you.'

'I don't need . . .'

Fractionally, Vesper's hand lowers. 'I, I didn't thank you for saving me, and before that, in Sonorous. There were so many of them and you stood up to them all.' Their eyes meet. 'I owe you everything.'

Duet's frown trembles. Another deep breath, another swallow. She grabs at Vesper's hand, a quick, rough gesture. 'Come on. Let's climb.'

Together, they make their way up. The kid skips down to meet them, bleats, skips up again.

At the top, the ground is mercifully flat and good progress is made. The rocky ground gives way to fields of wild crops. A sudden explosion of life, the giant stalks sprout manically for miles, pale yellow, aspiring to be trees.

They plunge inside, and fall down onto ground a step lower than expected. Soon the world becomes a series of bending bars, fibrous, bowing to make room for more. An unending vista of gold. Often they stop to check their position with the Navpack and breathe deep of the blue square above their heads.

Beneath their feet the soil is thick and dark, rich and squishy. Vesper hears crunching and looks down. Tainted things squirm in the mud, a writhing cluster of cockroach shells. Where the girl's passing has flipped them over, a pink underbelly is revealed, sickeningly soft, featureless.

Ahead, the stalks part to reveal the resting place of an old Auto-farmer. One of the last, for years its bladed arms have hung still while legions of creatures investigate, making homes among its wires, tucked safe behind plates of steel. Earth and machine blend together, one seeming to grow out of the other.

Flowers sprout from its cracked eyes, roots twist about metal toes.

Vesper stares at it for a long time.

Duet notices, stops. 'What is it?'

She smiles. 'It's beautiful, don't you think?'

'No.'

'How do you know? You haven't even bothered to look.'

'Yes I have.'

'No you haven't!'

She grits her teeth. 'This is stupid.'

'Just look. It won't take long.'

'Fine.'

She glances at it and mutters agreement, keen to move them on. In places they push the stalks aside, in others they step around them. The kid stays close, sneezing often.

Vesper nudges Duet. 'What did you think?'

'Of what?'

'You know.'

'Oh, it was . . .'

'What?'

'Different.'

'Different?'

What little patience there is evaporates away. 'What do

you want me to say? What do you want from me? It was a broken machine. So what? It won't help us survive, it doesn't even work.'

Against all sense of self-preservation, the girl smiles.

'Why do you keep staring at me? Oath or no oath, if you don't get that smile off your face, I'll kick it out!'

The smile gets broader still. Vesper holds up her hands as Duet advances towards her. 'I'm sorry. I'm not laughing at you, I'm happy for you.'

'What are you talking about? Make some sense, damn you!'

'Your speech. Since Sonorous, it's been broken but now that you're angry with me you sound natural again.'

Duet stops and slumps against the foliage. Thick stalks sway but don't fall. Hands cover a face covered by a visor. She tries to breathe, tries to swallow it down but this time the grief is too strong. Tears come, thick and fast, misting her visor, misting the world.

One Thousand, One Hundred and Sixteen Years Ago

For years, Massassi roams. She samples food, samples bodies, takes what she wants, breaks what she wants. She is young, angry and, for the first time, free.

Without forcing it, she gets stronger. She sees the light in everyone now, sees their true faces without trying, hears their voices stripped of pretence. People quickly bore her. Each new acquaintance robbed of mystery, just another animal with nothing special to say.

Pleasure is pleasure, however, and she enjoys travelling, exploring the contours of the world. Unrendered food is a particular high.

Mostly, she forgets about the chink in the sky but as time passes she finds it bothering her more and more. Like a stone in her shoe it is trivial yet omnipresent. The feelings recede as she travels north but after a month or two it returns again, and her stomach clenches.

At first, she tells herself that she notices because she has become sensitised. Then she tells herself it is because her new senses are more powerful now. At last, she admits the truth: Whatever is wrong is spreading, getting worse.

Perhaps it is boredom that makes her go south, perhaps it is a late blooming sense of duty or an itch that demands scratching, but south she goes. Jump boots propel her along, their design an affront to all her old safety regulations. Between them and her glider, she makes quick work of the journey.

Massassi arrives at a quarry. A handful of people watch over automated loaders and mining mechs. Scores of tools rise and fall together, regular, tireless, while vehicles rush about clearing the growing piles of rock.

Neither machines nor overseers attend to her arrival. The disinterest is mutual. Massassi focuses on the sky. She sees it, ordinary, cloud painted, part blocked by smog from nearby factories. But she also sees more, the film of blue reality stretched thin like a boil, filling with an alien pus. Directly above the quarry, the sky is folded, as if being pressed towards the ground, a giant inverted pyramid, roots hidden well above the horizon, its apex somewhere within the earth.

She glides closer, careful not to touch it, and spirals slowly down. The tip is not within the quarry itself, not yet, though the diggers aim that way. Massassi lands, boots hissing as they absorb the impact. She detaches her glider, planting the two halves into the ground before the wings have fully retracted and begins to dig.

Before long she finds it: the narrowest point, sharp and focused. But then she finds it is not the end. Beneath her, the sense of wrongness widens again, as if the point she has discovered is not the tip at all, rather the meeting place of two pyramids, one on top of the other, mirrored forces, trying to push into the world. The point she has found is the place of greatest pressure. It is not under the dirt, not literally. Normal geography does not apply. The thing Massassi sees is out of phase. There is no space for it to be here, yet the pressure continues to build.

Sooner or later, something will give.

She reaches out with her metal arm. Silver light spills out as the iris in her palm opens. She hesitates. There is nothing in the world that scares Massassi now but this is something else, something not in or of the world. It is bigger than her.

In spite of this, perhaps because of it, she makes contact.

CHAPTER TEN

A line cuts through fields of crops, three metres wide, stretching from the eastern coast to the western one. In places, it is broken by remains of man-made structures. Once a wall of light stood here, holding back the spread of taint, now it is gone. So have the trains that used to link it to the north, so have the magrails that powered them. Scavenged, buried, stolen or eaten, integrated into a hundred new ecosystems.

Vesper steps into the space, stretches her arms.

On the other side, giant crops continue but are made to compete for dominance. Thick runners drape across the yellow stalks, excreting spore clouds from little holes in their knobbly flesh. Branches like hands sprout from the ground, choking the life from other plants. Among them insects hang heavy in the air, rat-sized, their bellies swollen with blood.

The girl shudders, turning up the collar on her coat, wrapping arms and clothing around herself, tight. Duet hangs back, only exposing enough of her face to peer along the open channel, first left then right. The kid bounces past her, past Vesper, crossing the space with enthusiasm.

Hooves connect with something hidden.

An old cable tightens, snaring legs, bringing the kid to the ground with a thump. A trap set by the First's hunters. Vibrations travel along its length, rapid, determined and half a mile away, a bell sounds, prompting unseen forces into action.

The kid makes his own sound, less subtle. It is clear he finds his predicament unacceptable.

'I told you we should have traded it.'

'Quick,' says Vesper, racing towards the kid.

Duet's reply is whispered from cover. 'Leave it!'

'You can't say that!'

'I can. Whoever set this will be less likely to follow us if they get a meal.' She meets Vesper's eyes as the kid squirms against his bonds, bleating, desperate. After a moment Duet breaks away, abandoning stealth, cutting the kid free.

He springs up and turns a quick circle, happy again.

Duet scowls, remaining uncharmed. 'We'd better get moving.'

They run on, quickly swallowed by the fields.

Vesper is distracted by the abundance of life. Unknown creatures hang like fruit, waiting for night to come. Strange things moan under the earth, sliding worm-like through soil where swollen flowers grow, their stalks so bloated they almost fold in on themselves, their colours too pale, washed out.

Duet grabs Vesper's hand and pulls her along, always forward, cutting a path where necessary.

Often, Vesper glances behind her. She sees movement,

buzzings and crawlings, but no hunters. 'Shouldn't we try and hide our trail?'

'No chance. The ground is too soft here. Our best option is to outrun them.'

'Okay. Do you think we can do that?'

'Not if we keep talking.'

They run on until breath becomes ragged. Eventually, though, they have to stop, weighing wasted time against the need to rest. Sweat glistens on Vesper's head and neck, attracting attention. Some of the insects are too big to fly. Instead they jump from tree to tree, armoured monkeys, gangling, with bladed faces and gemstone eyes.

On the girl's back, the sword hums, restless.

At the sound she looks up to see tainted insects all around her, hanging, four to a stalk.

The kid tucks himself behind Vesper's leg.

Wings thrum all around them.

None move to attack.

Seconds pass, tense, Duet with her sword ready, Vesper with her gun.

The swarm watches them. Within a score of labium, proboscises quiver.

Duet steps forward, sword raised and the swarm fall back, maintaining distance. She steps forward again, testing. Once more, the swarm retreats. With growing confidence, she advances, pulling Vesper with her. Bulbous, faceted eyes fix on the girl and the goat.

She keeps her sword arm extended and herself between predators and food, increasing pace.

The swarm allows her passage, falling back in a rough line.

They walk on, nerves tight. Weapons are lowered but not put away. The action elicits a hum of excitement from the swarm.

Vesper glances about, eyes wide. 'What are they doing?'

'I don't know,' replies the Harmonised, blinking angrily at sweat collecting behind her visor. 'But I wish they'd get on with it.'

One of the swarm swings closer. Duet raises her sword again. It springs back.

Still further they go, stalked by the swarm. Whenever heads droop or steps falter, the swarm inches closer. When Duet or Vesper realises, they snap back to attention and the swarm gives ground, though never quite as much as before.

Back and forth, back and forth, like a sinister dance, playing out to its inevitable conclusion.

When Duet finally speaks, her voice is dulled but firm. 'They won't leave us alone until they've had their fill.'

Pale faced, Vesper nods.

'I'm going to give them your goat.'

'You can't!'

'It's that or I sell myself to them. Unless you have a better idea.'

The girl frowns, thinks. She looks around for inspiration. After a moment, she shakes her head, bitter. 'Okay.'

'Maybe we were right to save it after all.' Duet raises her sword.

The kid looks up at the girl, cute, oblivious.

'Wait! Don't do it yet.'

'Why not?'

'I . . . Just give me some time to think.'

'We have to do this now. Get away while they feed.'

Vesper's eyes flit towards the kid and away, unsure if it is best to watch his end or not. She decides it is nobler to look. Changes her mind. Changes it back. Tears threaten to come. The swarm creeps a little closer. 'Okay. Do it.'

Duet nods, raises her sword swiftly . . .

And all at once, the swarm disperses, buzzing away into the darkness.

Silence pours in after them, shocking and sudden. But not pure. From behind them hushed feet approach. One of them missteps and a shell cracks underfoot, thunderous.

Girl and Harmonised exchange a look, speaking as one. 'Run!'

Fatigue forgotten, they flee. Vesper stumbles, nearly falls but momentum keeps her on her feet. Duet keeps pace, one hand pressed against her side while the kid follows, mouth open, delighted.

Behind them, unknown hunters give chase while all around, the inhabitants of the yellow forest choose whether to run or hide, to watch or pursue.

One Thousand, One Hundred and Sixteen Years Ago

The point where the pyramids touch is small, small enough for Massassi to curl her fingers around it, enclosing the distortion in her fist. From her open metal palm, her essence shifts, exploring, sensing.

The divide between dimensions is thin here, stretched to breaking point. But even the tiniest film remains an infinity, too vast for her to comprehend. There are no cracks or splits, not yet, but what remains is so weak that she is able to feel things on the other side, like touching faces wrapped in plastic.

It is tantalising. There are hints of wonders beyond imagination, of terrors, of oddities that threaten madness, of more.

She strains her senses, tries to understand what is there.

Unformed shapes lurk on the other side, alien things, fluid, vast. She can almost define them now, almost taste them on her tongue. Fear tickles her thoughts, thrills through her body. A part of her wants to stop, does not want to know any more.

Silvered fingers clench and she dares to go deeper.

Her essence finds the weakest place or perhaps it is pulled there. She will never be sure. There is a growing desire to retreat, racing to match the need to go further.

Like a hand on a window, her essence rests against the divide. From somewhere on the other side, things notice. They rise from dark places and storms of swirling madness, forming from unthinkable ideas. Chunks of void break away, becoming hungry holes that swim towards her.

She sees it all then, and understands.

So many of them! Drawn by ethereal currents like scum down a plughole, swirling towards the world, poised to pollute, to change, to destroy. And behind them, gaping open, is an incomprehensible dark, ready to drink the silvered light of her true self whole. For a deadly moment it takes her attention, the other monsters fading from sight.

All becomes empty.

There is nothing.

Nothing.

Noth–

No.

She holds the thought. Forms it a second time.

No.

She has been to this place before. She will not allow it to take her. She will not.

Her hand opens, her palm closes and her arm drops away.

Massassi walks clear, returning to her own solid world. She thinks of all she has seen. Of the multitude that is coming. She has always been alone but for the first time in her life she feels incredibly, painfully lonely.

*

Duet tries to count the hunters as she runs.

Vesper tries not to fall over.

The kid simply runs.

Behind them and the hunters come the swarm, and further back, a host of opportunistic beasts and scavengers.

Vesper sees some higher ground and makes for it. The slope sucks speed from her tired legs but she persists. The hill is covered with stubbly grass. It snaps underfoot, smearing her boots, garish and green.

At the top she sees the crops stretching for miles in every direction. Endless yellow, waving softly in the wind, sickly. Further south however, the stalks are overshadowed by tall buildings and taller spires. Gravity defying roads spiral around and between them.

Wonderland.

It is not as grand as Vesper expected. Her uncle had talked of lights, lights everywhere, with more variety and warmth than the Shining City's cutting brightness. The only lights she sees now are reflected sunsbeams, red and gold, winking suggestively from the highest towers.

Even so, it brings hope.

'This way!' she shouts, running down the other side of the hill, enjoying the sudden burst of speed it gives her.

The kid struggles to keep up.

On and on they run, hunters hot on their heels.

Duet glances back, sees figures flitting between the stalks, details too easy to discern. She sees clothes, old but maintained, and weapons more advanced than sharpened sticks.

Across the narrowing gap between pursuers and prey, darts begin to spit, thin, spiteful things. Several find their mark. They lack the strength to penetrate Duet's armour, lodging themselves into the metal, shallow, to become unwanted accessories.

The Harmonised spreads her arms wide, keeping close behind Vesper.

Only luck and lack of height protect the kid.

One punctures the bag on Duet's back, cracking a small tube within. Soon, tablets weep from the hole, hard and blue.

Vesper keeps the image of Wonderland in her mind. She tells herself it cannot be far and gradually, the world comes to agree with her. Greys and blues become visible between the stalks.

'We're nearly there!' she cries.

She makes it to the first structure before realising that Duet no longer shadows her. Whirling round, she sees the Harmonised doubled over, clutching at her side. Old wounds have rebelled, fed up of being ignored.

As she rushes back to help, the fastest of the hunters arrives. A short man, bulked with muscle. He hurdles a treacherous root, winding his dartgun, firing.

The missile streaks over Duet's bent back and buries itself in the thick fabric of Vesper's coat, half an inch from her neck. The girl raises her own weapon. There is not time for hesitation but no desire to pull the trigger.

She points low, away from the hunter's body, and squeezes.

A searing light stabs out, too fast to avoid. It burns a hole through the hunter's thigh, scorching flesh, then biting into the foliage beyond.

The man screams and goes down.

Duet looks up, intent, forcing Vesper to focus on her. 'Go!'

Instead, she grabs Duet's hand. 'It's not far, come on!'

'No,' replies Duet, shaking her head, giving Vesper's hand a final squeeze. 'I'm done. I . . .'

Before she can finish, the man screams again. This time with words: 'Help me!'

Vesper turns back but the man is not where he fell. The swarm has found the injured hunter, crawling under his legs, hooking into his skin, lifting, dragging him away into depths of the yellow forest. The girl just has time to see the man's face, to register the panic and pleading before he is gone.

Unaware of their colleague's fate, more hunters burst through the undergrowth.

Vesper fires again and figures hurl themselves to the ground, shaking the long grasses with curses. Then she runs, keeping a firm grip on Duet, who adds her own seasoning to the hunter's words but allows herself to be pulled along.

Branches tug, vines threaten to trip. Vesper ducks and jumps where she can, pushes through where she can't. Cuts and stings collect, aching muscles make their presence known but all bow down to the need to live. Adrenaline urges her on and all at once they break clear of the stalks, almost falling into the city.

Suddenly, the ground is hard, shocking legs, and resonating to the pitter patter of hooves.

Duet comes to a stop on her knees. 'I can't . . .'

Vesper points the gun back the way they came. She sees no targets but keeps her guard up and breath held.

Time passes.

Nothing comes out of the forest.

No hunters or wild creatures, not even the hum of a tainted

insect. Were it not for the darts protruding from Duet's shoulder plates and the one still in Vesper's collar, it would be easy to pretend the hunters were never there.

Hastily, Vesper pulls out the scope with her free hand and puts it to her eye. Enhanced sight penetrates the shadows, reveals a group pulled far back, arguing. She cannot read their lips but their expressions are clear enough.

'They're afraid.'

'Of what?'

Vesper shrugs. 'I don't know. Us?'

Duet's laugh is bitter. 'I doubt it.'

'At least they aren't chasing us any more.'

'For now.'

'Good point. Let's go!'

The Harmonised holds up a hand. 'Don't think I can. My busted side can't take any more running.'

Worry lines appear on Vesper, hinting at an older face yet to emerge. 'Okay.' She gathers some debris, a faded piece of panelling and a withered half of a water container. She covers the Harmonised with them, concealing everything save the tip of her helm and the toe of her right boot. 'I'm going to get help. Stay there.'

'Funny.'

'I'll be back soon, I promise.' She looks at Duet, moves closer and reaches around the panelling to take her hand, squeezing the gauntlet tight. 'I promise, okay?'

'You know it's a crime to lie in the presence of The Seven?'

Vesper smiles weakly. 'I know.'

The medical bag is left by her side, along with the last of their rations. 'I don't know how long I'll be but, hopefully, you can last for a few days at least. Not that I'll be gone that long. I should be back in an hour at the most. Maybe two.'

'Enough talking.'

'Right.' She turns to go.

Eyes smile behind the visor, not soft, but softer. 'And the sooner you go, the sooner you'll be back.'

Vesper brightens. 'Right!'

'Right.'

The girl sets off at a run.

From a gap in the side of her cover, a small head appears. Dark eyes regard her a moment more than is comfortable, then the kid bounds away.

Duet mutters to herself, twisting to look through a hole in the panel. The yellow forest remains quiet, mysterious.

Apparently, she is alone.

One hand rests on her side, the other on the hilt of her sword. Both are useless. Another look through the hole reveals an unchanged view. Wincing in pain, Duet takes a blue pill from the bag. It is not enough. She reaches for another, surprised to find the tube broken and empty. Quiet curses fill the air while she investigates the bag more thoroughly. A variety of pills present themselves, several not normally available to citizens of the Winged Eye.

She weighs them in her palm, knowing she should not use them while cheeks flush red, guilty.

*

A fly weaves its way through the Fallen Palace, buzzing past sloping rooftops. The Man-shape waits for it, leaning out of a leaning tower, mouth open. When the fly arrives on tired wings, it does not land as expected, instead zigzagging back and forth over the cavernous split in the infernal's head.

For a moment the Man-shape is confused. Then it remembers, summoning its tongue from deep within and draping it over lower teeth.

Immediately, the fly lands.

The Man-shape's head closes like a steel trap. A droplet of blood spurts, and with it, a whisper of essence.

It digests the message slowly, pondering the contents. Only when the Man-shape steps away from the window does it notice Samael standing in the doorway.

The Man-shape frowns, trying to adopt an expression of displeasure. However it has met very few humans, and those it has have been in states of extreme distress. As a result, all of its attempts tend towards the comic.

A wheeze escapes Samael's lips and his shoulders shake. The half-breed laughs rarely these days, so he makes sure to enjoy the moment.

The Man-shape turns its back on him. Its usual control seems to weaken. Shoulders slump, arms hang slack.

Samael steps closer, curious. He hears the infernal drawing in air, manipulating it.

Within the cave of the Man-shape's stomach, muscles contort and bones shift, a delicate operation. At last, the air is pushed out, undercut by distant buzzing. 'I have been practising my speech again. What do you think?' Samael's shoulders clank as he raises them. 'Is that all you can say? Even the master could not speak. Certainly none of the pretenders can manage it. They say the First speaks as the mortals do. Talk with me. I wish to practise.'

'Why?' Samael hates the sound of his voice. It is too quiet, too full of echoes. Wrong. Since his creator changed him, he has been losing it, a little more every year.

'Because,' the Man-shape replies, 'you are all I have.'

'This place is full of half-breeds.'

'Born here. Their shrieks do not interest me.'

'I am ready to let it go. Take it from me if you want.'

'No. Such cuts always bleed and you must remain intact if you are to save the master's legacy.'

Samael's hair brushes his shoulders as he shakes his head. He is bored of these discussions. His impulse is not to rule but to . . . to what? His steel hill is no longer safe. His desire to watch and defend against the Breach has come to nothing. Next to the Yearning, he is nothing. There is nowhere to go. No purpose to motivate and so he stays. Caught by inertia.

The Man-shape continues: 'Do you ever wonder why we are this way?'

'No.'

'No?'

'Yes.'

'You do. Of course you do. Like you, I do not remember much of my time before the master. Before I came to this place, I had no form, no function. I have always thought that the master gave me these things but lately I have begun to doubt.

'The master's will shaped ours. It created everything. Our hierarchy, the displays, all of it stemmed from the master's wishes. But where did the master draw inspiration?'

'I never knew your master.'

The Man-shape carries on as if Samael had not spoken. 'We are unlike the mortals. Superior, and yet we copy them. I think it began when the master forced itself into the shell of our enemy, taking on her shape and, I think, more than a slice of her thoughts. The master believed her shell fully purged before taking residence but something of the foundation must have remained. And then, during our battles to transform this world, the world transformed us.'

'Where is this going?'

'Yes, where is this going? I wonder that often.'

'The Yearning will take us all soon.'

'Will it? My Zero in New Horizon brings news. The Malice has returned. An old tooth in young hands. It sharpens by the day. That is what will end us all.'

Samael nods, accepting the inevitable, feeling neither joy or sadness.

'Unless,' the Man-shape adds, 'it could be controlled.'

'Impossible.'

'I am going to send word to the others and they will hunt the Malice down and find a way to turn it on the Yearning. It is our only chance.'

'Then do it.'

'I will. But first I wanted to tell you.'

'Why?'

'To give you a head start. Whoever succeeds in this will become our new monarch.'

'I am not interested.'

'Then which of them would you rather serve?'

Samael stops. He wants to say that he does not care

but that would be a lie. Without another word, he makes for the door.

And as his boots ring out on tarnished steps, the Man-shape smiles its inhuman smile.

CHAPTER ELEVEN

Long ago, Wonderland was adorned with necrotic pipes and posts, unliving structures bonded with the steel and plastics of the original city. Only stains of their rot remain now, cleared away by rain and a myriad of creatures, happy to feed on old meat.

Vesper wanders slowly through empty streets, head tilted up to take in the dizzying sights. On the walls of the outermost towers are faded marks: rough warnings repeated on every side. At the base of these towers is a barrier of debris, ten metres high, made from rubbish, mud and yellowing bones. The mud is uniformly grey brown, the bones a maddening variety of animal, human and blends in-between.

She stops in front of it. The kid stops next to her.

'Do you think this is the sort of wall that keeps people out or that keeps people in?'

The kid sniffs at the base of the barrier and quickly steps back.

163

Vesper takes the hint and squeezes her nose before peering more closely.

In places, time has decayed the barrier, sections have partially collapsed, making a climb possible. Rain has begun the excavation of a giant's fleshless forearm. Once the property of a Usurperkin, now a key support in the wall. Vesper marvels at its size for a moment, then eyebrows shoot up, inspired. She extracts an old tube from the wall and pokes it through the gap between radius and ulna. The mottled plastic slides through the mud on the other side, going deeper and deeper until Vesper's arm is passing through the bone and she is leaning against the barrier, drinking in its stench. Loose bits of matter spill down onto her shoulders, clump in her hair. She tries to push away, her hand sinking in a couple of inches before finding purchase. Wet earth fills the space between her splayed fingers and she feels the edge of something else, a horror yet hidden.

The girl jumps back, gagging, pale, and vomit rises in her throat, threatening to appear.

Bemused, the kid watches from a safe distance.

There is coughing, a distinctly wet burp and the danger passes.

'I can't do this,' she says quietly. 'I can't.' But thoughts of Duet haunt her. If the Harmonised dies, it will be her fault and she is already full with guilt. 'I must do this.' She repeats it, a mantra: 'I must do this. I must do this.'

When breathing has returned to normal, Vesper pulls her top up over her mouth and begins scavenging again. Eventually she finds an aerial, bent in the middle to form a circle, approximately neck-sized. She straightens out the metal, then uses it to unblock the tube that she has placed through the muddy wall. Her tools are imperfect and progress is slow.

The kid sits down.

Sometimes the aerial yields before the mud does and Vesper has to straighten it again. She glances around, then whispers a curse, experimental. Cheeks flush with daring and she swears again, suddenly feeling very grown up.

At last, the aerial forces out the last of the blockage and Vesper is able to see through the tube to the other side. The view is limited. A courtyard strewn with debris, some of it human, some of it twitching. Handlings scuttle from one shadow to the next, while bald birds with no feathers and sagging bellies line up on a nearby rooftop.

She looks back to the kid. 'It's horrible over there but I think we'll be okay. Shall we climb over?'

The kid gives her a sour look.

'Okay,' she agrees, glad to move away from the barrier's edge. 'Let's try and find another way in. Come on!'

The kid springs up.

Vesper wanders around the perimeter and finds the barrier continues in a large square, linking the towers and sealing in the gaps.

A noise startles them both, a growl, animalistic. It is not clear what makes it and Vesper has no wish to find out. Legs protest at the idea of further running.

She studies the buildings as the growling draws closer, her eyes alighting on a low window, one of the few to be broken but not boarded. She pulls out the biggest chunks of plasglass from the frame and drapes her coat over the smaller ones.

It is a simple thing to lift the kid over. A rough tongue

laps at her face as she drops the young goat on the other side. Then she pulls herself through.

Dust cakes the room and its contents, muting colours and blending objects. A single chair takes centre stage, cut from a chunk of LiveFoam and still holding the imprint of its last occupant. The chair is tilted at an angle, perfect for reclining or sleep.

Vesper draws the kid close and crouches low under the window. The kid sniffs at her ears and she has the ridiculous urge to giggle. 'Ssh,' she whispers.

The growling creature moves by the wall now. She closes her eyes, unable to stop her imagination creating images, vivid, of the monster outside and how she would look hanging from its jaws.

Outside, the growling stops.

The kid trembles against her as Vesper holds her breath.

The growling sounds again but further away this time. As quickly as the creature arrived, it has gone.

Fear washes away in a tide of relief, followed quickly by a crushing sense of fatigue.

On hands and knees, Vesper crawls across the room and pulls herself onto the chair. The kid follows, settling onto her lap.

'We can't stay here long,' she tells him, stroking the top of his head. 'Duet needs us.'

Vesper lets the chair take the weight from her heels and her head. Her eyes feel heavy but she dares not let them close. As she fights to stay awake a new wonder presents itself. From this angle, Vesper can see sky-ships hanging from the ceiling. A fleet in miniature, suspended in the air, slowly rotating. Every detail is perfectly captured and, unlike everything else, their surfaces are free of dust, glinting, winking as they turn.

She recognises one of the models, matching it to memories of sky-ships soaring about the Shining City. But most of them are unfamiliar, older designs no longer used, or rarer ones, lost in battle or left to rust.

The kid licks the sweat from Vesper's hands before falling asleep. 'You poor thing. You can have a few minutes, just to make sure that creature really has gone but that's all.' She blinks slowly, her eyes reluctant to open again. 'Just a few minutes,' she murmurs.

A moaning wakes her. A distant, hollow noise, evoking a sense of size and misery.

Sitting up, the first thing Vesper notices is the waning light. A brief blink has become a long sleep, her treacherous body stealing back lost slumber. Questions haunt her. How much time has passed? Does Duet still live? How did this happen? Ashamed, she turfs the kid from her lap and climbs out of the chair. It seems reluctant to let her leave. After a short struggle, she hops down and crosses to the door. The sensor above the doorway dimmed years ago and the mechanisms that moved it have stopped forever.

She places her hands against the smooth surface and starts to push it sideways. Both girl and door grunt and groan as it slides slowly into its housing.

On the other side is a much smaller room, covered in empty containers. Vesper crunches over them to get to the window.

Now the moaning is easier to hear. Vesper shudders but goes to look anyway. The kid joins her, stretching up on hind legs, front hooves on the sill.

167

They see the courtyard in all its horrific detail and it becomes apparent why the bodies still twitch. A torso, bereft of legs, head rotting, eyeless, is dragged across the square by two tentacles growing from its back. Bits of string are tangled with its trailing innards and these in turn collect more treasures: a torn bag, a small chain that glints and a branch covered in leaves, green and thick.

Entranced, the kid's eyes follow its slow progress, a long string of saliva dangling from his chin.

But it is not the source of the moaning. Vesper has to look up to see that. A half-alive giant lurks behind a nearby tower. Even a tiny section of its silhouette inspires terror. Hooked legs sprout like horns from its moonlike face, a mane of limbs, shaking, sorrowful.

Vesper ducks out of sight, fighting down the vomit. She sits low, letting the wall press cold into her back and murmurs to herself. 'Can't do it.' She wants to help her friend. She wants to be a hero like her father. 'I can't do it.' Fear crowds out thought and she covers her face.

The kid cannot bear it any longer. He springs up, scattering containers, to wobble on the window's edge.

Vesper looks up to see hooves flying, gone. Her arm stretches for where the kid was, the gesture as wasted as her shout: 'Wait!'

The girl peers out to see the kid scampering across the square. For the moment, the giant has not noticed him.

Hissed pleas to come back are ignored. Getting desperate, she pulls herself half out of the window and raises her voice in a feeble shout: 'Please stop!'

The kid glances back, tongue lolling.

'Yes, that's it. Come back.'

The kid looks again at the torso and its tail of leaves. There is no contest.

Vesper watches, locked with fear as the kid leans down to bite.

Tentacles pull the torso clear of snapping jaws and the kid comes up with nothing. He hops in surprise and goes after the torso again.

The giant's head turns towards him.

Unable to bear it any longer, Vesper jumps down into the square and runs after the kid. She keeps low, back hunched like an old man, head down. She is no less visible for it.

The kid chews happily, branch hanging from his mouth, still tangled with dirty string and stringy flesh. When tentacles pull again, the torso moves and the kid moves with them. Hooves slide on stone, then find purchase. The kid pulls back.

A few hard inches are won before the tentacles continue on their way, mindless, taking torso and treasures and hanger-on with them.

Frowning, the kid pulls back.

Vesper arrives. She grabs the branch and snaps it, leaving one half in the kid's mouth and the other still attached. Then she frowns and looks at the body again. Up close, the horror is less convincing. The eyeless face is more waxlike than lifelike and the tentacles make clicking sounds, regular, their inner working more the turning of wheels than the swirling of essence.

She glances over her shoulder to look at the sword. It still sleeps, unmoved by the theatrics.

While Vesper thinks, the kid chews.

Another moan brings her attention to the giant. It faces

them now, shaking its head in anger. Vesper reaches around to touch the sword at her back. Nothing. Not even a slight quiver. She stands up and pulls out the scope. With magnification, she makes out wires attaching the head to the side of the building.

The moaning gets louder, the head shakes more violent. The mane of legs rattles like a nest of snakes. Then one falls off, landing with a hollow clunk.

Vesper smiles and walks towards it.

Still chewing, the kid trots after her.

The fallen leg is a prosthetic, wrapped in cloth, red dye unnecessarily bright. Vesper nudges it with her foot to be sure.

'Hello?' she calls out. 'Is anyone there?' The giant roars, the kid jumps, fearful. Vesper sighs. 'You can come out. I'm not going to hurt you.'

There is no response from the giant.

She raises the scope to her eye again and traces the wires from the back of giant's head to an opening high in the tower. It is a simple matter to skirt the base of the building until she finds a door. Unlike the one before it opens easily.

A chute runs from the floor up through the ceiling. An oval has been cut from one side, allowing access. Vesper approaches it. Whatever arcane forces that used to propel people up and down have been replaced by a dirty ladder.

'Stay here,' she says to the kid, giving him a last pat on the head before ascending.

Dark eyes track the girl until she is out of sight. Then, the kid sits and gets down to the serious business of eating.

The climb is long enough for worries to surface. Vesper climbs on anyway, not sure what else to do.

Five floors later, and Vesper steps out of the chute into a circular room. In a previous life, it served as a viewing platform, augmented eyes transmitting images via necrotic pipes. The walls that Vesper sees are blank, save for the rows of sockets, dried up, like a score of wizened earholes.

The wires from the giant's head come in through a window, gathering together in a complicated knot at the back of a machine. The front of it is full of levers, and on top, a pair of brassy megaphones sit, one inside the other, humming softly.

By the machine stands a girl, not much off Vesper's height, dressed in baggy clothes with rolled-up sleeves and metal pins in her trousers. Dark hair falls uneven over a purple face.

On Vesper's back, the sword shifts in its sleep. She takes out the gun. 'Don't move.'

The half-breed shrinks back against the wall.

'Now, you'd better tell me . . .' she begins but pauses as she notices the way the other girl's hands shake. '. . . You'd better tell me who . . .' It strikes her how young the girl looks. How scared. She puts the gun back in her pocket. 'It's okay. I'm not going to hurt you.'

The half-breed doesn't meet her eye. 'True like?'

'Yes. I'm Vesper.'

'Runty.'

'What, is that your name?'

The half-breed puffs out her chest. 'Yeah.'

Vesper stifles a laugh. 'Are you alone here?'

'No. There's loads of us. And if you did anything to me, they'd come get you.'

'Okay.'

'And do bad things, lots of times.'

171

'Look, I'm not going to hurt you. I have a friend who is badly injured. Do you know anyone who could help her?'

Runty nods, very serious. 'You need to see Neer. She knows things. She's a fixer.'

'Is she close?'

'She's in the Don't Go, where all the maggots and buzzers are.'

'Will you show me?'

'As long as you swear.'

'Swear what?'

'That you won't make her angry.'

*

Past broken villages and gutted towers, Samael marches. He keeps a steady pace, unfazed by night and day. Legs no longer tire, muscles obey without question. He finds it hard recalling the meaning of rest. With little of the physical to distract him, and only a bleak landscape to entertain, thoughts turn inward, chasing each other, repetitive.

He wonders why he is competing for the Usurper's throne. He cares little for power, cares little for anything. Standing atop his steel hill and watching the Breach gave him a kind of peace. Not happiness but better than anything else. Now, the Yearning has taken that from him, forced him to search for the Malice.

But the Malice scares him. He turns the thought over in his mind. *I am not afraid of death but I am afraid of the sword. Why?*

He cannot fathom the answer, leaving the question to circle, recasting itself with each pass, increasingly irritating.

And if he does fear the Malice, if he does not even want to be part of the Fallen Palace's madness, why do what the Man-shape suggests? The truth is simple: pride. As much as he does not want to rule, the idea of an infernal doing so irks him. They are not worthy. He cannot imagine bending the knee to any of them.

In the dirt ahead, a mangy Dogspawn sniffs for scraps. He ignores it.

It is tempting to stand aside and allow the Yearning to take them all. It would be simpler that way. Let there be an end to it, finally.

And yet . . .

A part of him is not satisfied by that. A part of him imagines the infernals having to bow to him, painting intricate pictures of their rage. How they would hate being subservient to a half-breed. Yes, even more than he would enjoy watching them die, he would enjoy their suffering.

The Dogspawn growls at him as he gets closer, a halfway threat, as if the beast still deliberates whether to attack.

The animal looks thin, desperate but not mad. Somewhere nearby it must have a Handler. He surveys the environment, seeing little. Flatlands stretching to mountains in the east and the horizon in the west. Few hiding places.

He approaches the Dogspawn, noting its mismatched eyes are both unclouded, though the human one droops half closed. A wave of revulsion strikes then and he has the sudden urge to destroy. He raises his sword above his head, moving into range.

Unbidden, a memory rises. So clear it eclipses the present.

He sits on a boat in a tranquil bay. Sunslight dances on the waves, hypnotic. Red and gold and blue and green, a shifting mosaic of beauty. If such things were still possible, he would weep. Around him are other boats, a motley collection of jury-rigged rafts and ships with well-worn repairs. One drifts close, a small sky-ship no longer good for flight, its pilot chatting happily with an alert looking dog on the prow. He remembers how happy the two appeared, how lonely his own boat was in comparison.

When the memory fades, he finds the world terribly grey in its absence.

During the reminiscence, time has passed. Though his sword arm remains up, ready to attack, the Dogspawn has moved off, something small wriggling in its jaws.

On impulse, he diverts to follow it.

They travel surprisingly far. Most Handlers and Dogspawn keep close together, unable to cope if their bond is stretched too thin. Eventually, they come across a set of dips in the ground, giant hoof-prints left long ago. In one of them lies a woman's body, caked in sweat. Shockingly young and painfully thin, with livid red skin covered in irregular grey spots. Her skin is naturally red but the spots are a recent addition, parasites determined to suck her dry.

But she is not dead, not quite. As they get closer the woman contorts, twisting, painful, as if trying to wring her infection out.

The Dogspawn approaches, lowering its head by her side. It opens its mouth and a small beetle drops out, legs waving in the air, broken. Next to it are other insects and scraps of meat, a pile of offerings unnoticed and unappreciated.

Bitemarks decorate the exposed skin on her feet and shoulder. In a few places, the flying leeches still gorge, their veins swelling beneath translucent shells.

The Dogspawn nips at them, tossing them away but it is too late, the Handler is nearly gone, her convulsions easing, her face smoothing out. The Dogspawn sits by her side and whines softly.

Soon, she will die, and soon after the Dogspawn will go wild. A grim future full of madness and death.

The whining continues long after her breathing stops.

Another impulse comes, unexpected, and Samael's hands are reaching down to the woman's still warm corpse. Knowledge guides them, secret arts taken from the Uncivil by his creator and buried deep in his unconscious.

Realising what he is about to do, he hesitates, then takes off a gauntlet and pushes open her eyelids. Her left eye is bloodshot blue and human. Her right a rich brown, canine. He plucks her right with deft fingers, extracting it carefully. His own half-breed eyes see the tether of essence running silver grey from the soft orb to the skull of the Dogspawn.

He pulls off his helmet.

He places the eyeball in the palm of his gauntlet, leaving his other hand free to operate.

There is another hesitation but he finds he wants this enough to continue and reaches up towards his face . . .

It is as if another's will takes him through the procedure. There is pain, brief, and half the world goes dark.

He takes the eyeball sitting in his palm and raises it to the hole.

The physical actions are mere mechanics, the manipulation of essence and inner surgeries immensely complex.

The Dogspawn howls.

Samael remains silent throughout.

When it is done, he replaces his helmet.

New senses flood his own, smells and fears. Hunger has long been irrelevant to him but he finds the return of the sensation refreshing.

'Eat,' he says, pointing to the pile of leavings, and the Dogspawn does.

It is a sad looking creature. Underfed. Reddish fur shaggy and covered in scars from past battles. One ear has been chewed away, the other stands straight and alert.

When it has finished eating it sits and looks at him.

He gropes through the dark sea of his mind, wondering what he should do. The Dogspawn is excited and afraid, he knows this. Haltingly, he touches its head, scratching behind the good ear.

A heavy tail begins to thump on the ground.

And then a sliver of memory comes back and his cracked lips curve into a smile. He kneels down so that he is face to face with the creature. 'I am Samael, your new master. From now on, I will call you Scout.'

CHAPTER TWELVE

The building is small, fin shaped, and barely large enough to house a toilet. Bird shit runs in frozen streaks down its sloping side. A flapping curtain covers the front, struggling against metal clips.

Runty chews at what's left of a thumbnail. 'She's in there.'

'Good. Do we go in?'

'She'll come out.'

Vesper glances up at the fading light. 'We need her to come out soon.'

'Neer comes when she comes.'

'What do you mean?'

'What I said. You got earmould?'

'Do you mean she'll be here in a few minutes, or hours or days?'

'Yeah.'

'That's not good enough. I have to see her now.'

The girl takes a step back. 'Go on then.'

'Aren't you coming with me?'

She shakes her head. 'Me? Go in the Don't Go? Never!'

Vesper takes off one of the clips and lifts the curtain. Behind it is a large circular chute, angling down into the dark. Air wafts up, damp and sweet. 'Is this safe?'

'Yeah, we drop stuff down there all the time.'

'And you think she'll help?'

Runty shrugs. 'Probs. If she wants. Just don't make her angry.'

Vesper climbs into the chute and sits down, patting her thighs. The kid scampers over and joins her. She throws the clip back to Runty. 'How do I get back out again?'

'Climb out. She does.'

She sets the Navpack to torch setting and shines it down the hole. It continues at the same angle as far as the light extends, undamaged. She ties the Navpack to the side of her boot to illuminate the way down, nodding to herself. 'Okay . . .' She presses her hands and feet against the chute's insides, inching forward. Gravity notices and starts to pull, testing young muscles.

Further down they go, slow and careful.

With a sense of casual inevitability, the kid slides off her lap, dropping into the space between her open legs, accelerating.

Vesper reacts quickly, catching the kid with her feet. They hang there for a moment, all of their weight on Vesper's arms. Sweaty palms struggle to grip, squeaking against the smooth sides of the chute.

She has time for three different exclamations before she falls.

The chute is cut from several pieces of metal, fused together. Vesper feels the joins thrumming against her back, like a finger flicking, flicking, flicking.

From side to side they bounce, separating, one rolling, the other spinning. Hooves clatter in the dark, animal noises are made.

Seconds later they spill into a larger chamber.

Vesper checks herself. Old bruises have been remastered, new ones added but nothing worse than that. She sits up, one hand rubbing the back of her head, the other pulling the Navpack off her boot.

The room is moist and smells of death. Bugs carpet the walls, crawling over each other, constant, shifting, giving glimpses of a honeycomb brick underneath. By contrast, the floor is completely clear.

The kid takes one look before burying his face in Vesper's coat.

Vesper looks around for an exit, cannot see one. When she steps forward to study the walls more closely, the sword begins to hum, angry. Insects flee from the sound, flowing away, parting like a black tide. She steps back and the humming softens. Insects pour into the gap, sealing it in moments.

She steps forward a second time, watching as the humming rises and the insects retreat. Stepping back, the actions reverse themselves.

Leaning her shoulder and the sword's hilt towards the wall, she makes a quick circuit of the room. The crawling creatures rush away from her like a wave, revealing a desiccated chalky structure.

And a door.

It opens easily at Vesper's touch and she goes through, dragging the kid after her.

A figure waits on the other side, shrouded in robes and mystery, her voice a hard, dry croak. 'Who are you?'

Vesper's torch beam finds a face within the cowl, a mask of leather stitched to old bone. The Navpack slips from her fingers, landing with a clatter, over-loud, and going out.

A pair of pupils glow green in the darkness. 'Well? Name yourself.'

'Vesper,' she replies, hands fumbling towards her pocket. 'Are you Neer?'

'We're not taking turns, child. You are a trespasser and you will answer my questions first. All of them, if you know what's good for you. And then we'll see what we will see, hmm?'

She nods, then, because it's dark, adds: 'Okay.'

'I should warn you, I'll know if you lie to me.' The figure moves in the dark and bones pop, reconfiguring. The kid makes a soft plopping noise as he faints. 'Where are you from?'

'The Shining City. Well, not the city itself but nearby, on the outskirts. Within the protected boundary but apart from the others. On a farm.'

'What do you farm?'

'Goats mainly.'

'Goats? Untainted goats?'

'Oh yes.'

'Well, well. This is most unexpected. You seem well armed for a farmer.'

Her fingers curl around the gun's handle, finding comfort there. 'Yes, I am. But I'm not here to fight.'

There is a pause. 'I believe you.'

'I'm here to ask for Neer's help.'

'And why would Neer be interested in helping you?'

'Because I can tell her about the north if she's interested, and the Shining City, or I can trade with her.'

'Really?'

'Yes. News, or . . . or supplies. I'll do whatever I can but my friend is hurt and she needs help and she doesn't have much time.'

'What's wrong with her?'

'She got injured in a battle a few days ago. Her ribs are broken. I've done my best but it wasn't good enough and now she's getting worse.'

'Alright my little farmer, I'll see what I can do. No need to cry.'

She sniffs, self-conscious. 'I wasn't!'

'Of course you weren't.'

'Are you Neer?'

'In a manner of speaking. I'll explain on the way.'

Vesper stands at the bottom of the chute looking up. The kid sits in her arms, awake now, but keeping a low profile. Neer stands behind them. 'Are you ready?'

She shivers as Neer's cold arms wrap around her. 'Ready.'

Under Neer's robes are three square spirals of bone, two attached to her hips, one to her spine. As she steps onto the chute, the spirals unfurl, becoming extra legs. Longer than her own, they straighten, lifting all three of them off the ground.

Vesper shivers again. On her back, the sword's wings twitch and an eye cracks open, the thinnest of slits. Trapped in its sheath, it shakes angrily between the girl and the half-alive woman.

Neer chuckles, though her head pulls back from the sword quickly enough.

Without talking, they ascend. Silence punctuated by bones clicking on metal and the sword's rage, muffled.

At the top, she deposits her cargo and Vesper stumbles away several paces. By the time she turns, Neer's extra limbs have lowered her to the ground, retracting beneath the robes again, out of sight.

'What are you?'

'My name is Ferrencia, and I was the Surgeon General to the Uncivil, greatest of her Necroneers.'

Most of the words pass her by, save one. She draws her gun and points it at the half-alive. 'The Uncivil . . . You're an infernal!'

'No, no, no. I'm not the girl I used to be, that's true enough. But an infernal? The very idea!'

The gun continues to point at her. 'You look like an infernal!'

'Seen a lot of them have you? Don't answer that. What you call an infernal is something from another world. And no person, not me and certainly not you can understand what that is. And besides, infernals don't talk. They don't need to.'

'The First does.'

'Clever little farmer, aren't you? Well, yes, the First does, but I think it's the exception, not the rule.'

'So, you're like a Dogspawn?'

Neer folds her arms. 'I'm going to pretend you didn't say that. My essence is human, through and through. It just happens to be attached to a few benign fragments of the Uncivil's essence.'

'But your face . . .'

'Is dead. Most of me is. I was old when the Uncivil recruited me and I'd look a lot worse than this if it wasn't for her intervention.'

182

'If you're not a half-breed, and you're not an infernal, what are you?'

'A human being, like you.' Her hand turns, describing circle after circle. 'Just with a few more years and a some major augmentations. But in here,' she taps her head, 'or, if you're the sentimental type, here,' she taps her heart, 'I'm unchanged.'

Vesper puts the gun away. 'But I thought the infernals take over people's bodies.'

'Some do, like the First. The Usurper and its minions were famous for it but the Uncivil wasn't like them. She believed in independence. She dealt with us one by one, listened to our needs, and if we could help her, she satisfied them.'

'You make her sound like a person.'

Neer's smile is small, her face too set to allow anything more. 'Do I now? She wasn't. I didn't understand her, even after years of working on her. But at least with the Uncivil I knew where I stood and that's a lot more than I can say for most.' Her eyes go pointedly to the sword on Vesper's back, then to Vesper herself. 'Hmm?'

They cross the shadowed courtyard, under a giant head's glassy gaze. Tentacles drag a battered torso across their path. Vesper and the kid don't even flinch.

'Our little show didn't fool you then?'

'It did at first but –' she reaches down to stroke the kid '– when we got close we saw through it.'

'Hmm. Used to be Necrotech powered the whole thing. It was really something then. But each time, a little essence leaked away and even I couldn't find a way to make the seals perfect.'

A ramp waits for them, leaning against the barrier. Neer

strides up and unfolds a rope ladder, dropping it over the other side.

Vesper chews her lip, and scurries down after her.

It is dark now, stars pushing through the fading film of blue, illuminating little. The huge yellow stalks have paled to grey, gatekeepers to a hundred hidden threats.

Vesper listens, wondering if there are hunters nearby, doing the same. Sounds come to her, unfamiliar, nocturnal calls and movements and . . . something else . . . a raised voice, manic.

Neer slows to a stop. 'I take it your friend is that way?'

But Vesper is too busy running to answer.

*

The running figure catches Samael's eye, too fast for an animal, too fluid for a machine. A competitor, one of many known to him: Hangnail. Anger rises and Scout howls in empathy.

His detour has been costly, the head-start given him by the Man-shape spent. There is nothing to do but give chase. He sets off and Scout keeps pace, tail waving like a bloody flag.

He and Scout race Hangnail to the ever open gates of New Horizon.

From a distance the city is characterful. Ruined turrets lean against rusting walls like a crowd of merry drunks. The comings and goings of its denizens appear to obey an algorithm, abstract and colourful. From a distance imagination can paper over the cracks with more palatable illusions.

Sadly, both runners make quick work of the distance.

The Malice

A stab of memory makes Samael stumble. It is quick, barely even an image, gone before he can process it. He stops and stares at the city with renewed contempt, paralysed by the desire to destroy.

Hangnail runs on, extending its lead.

But Samael doesn't notice, held in place by thought shards and feelings, disconnected, disconnecting.

Hangnail runs on, passing through New Horizon's great southern gates and beyond, out of sight.

From further behind Samael comes a broken chorus of shouts and shuffles, burping, popping, boasting and growling. He doesn't notice that either.

Something taps against his armoured thigh. No sensation reaches him but the ringing of claw on metal draws his attention. Scout sits at his feet, one paw raised, uncertain.

He pats its mangy head and it whines, dashing back the way they came to freeze, arrow-straight, head pointing at distant shapes. Samael doesn't need to turn round, using their shared vision to see the new threat.

Gutterface and the Backwards Child travel in full force, close but not together. On one side, a motley crew of muscle-heavy Usurperkin, bearing their diminutive leader above their heads. On the other, a pick-and-mix of the most loathsome infernals, bulging in the skins of rodents and the bodies of chicks burst untimely from dead eggs, all clustered around Gutterface, rubbing against it, affectionate and sickening.

With new incentive, Samael runs and soon the noise of the pursuing infernals is lost to the discordant music of the city.

On New Horizon's streets, people cleave together in packs or move quickly, heads down, avoiding eye contact. Skin is more colourful than clothes here, purples, greens, yellows, oranges and browns stark against pale fabrics. Bruises mark many faces, decorative. And chains, physical or otherwise, link slaves to masters. Samael's eyes cannot help but see them all.

He is an oddity here and they know it. Neither full infernal nor half-breed in any sense they understand. They have heard of Seraph Knights and memories of the Knights of Jade and Ash still have power enough to disturb sleep but Samael falls between the gaps. Neither one or the other, somehow mocking both.

A not quite anything, an ugly mystery.

In New Horizon, the rules are simple. If in doubt: run or hide or die.

And everyone old enough to think for themselves plays by the rules.

For Samael, it is a strange novelty, he is used to being despised rather than feared. The streets clear for him as he walks, the sensible slipping back to their holes of residence, the young watching from alleys or the empty sockets of tortured houses.

A reluctant circle of people breaks at his approach, meat traders and flesh merchants keen to save their own skins. They leave a slave to shiver alone in the road, abandoned. Cables tie him to a metal spike, knots too complex for quick release.

Samael ignores the whimpering as he passes. Scout does not, stopping to sniff. In response, the slave retreats to the other side of the spike and cords dig deep into his neck, holding him in tight orbit.

Saliva collects around sharp teeth, hanging in strands,

thick and stringy. A Dogspawn and its belly growl together. Jaws open, ready to grind against a spindly leg.

Samael turns a corner at the end of the main street.

Tail low, Scout yelps and dashes after his master, slobber swinging back and forth from an open mouth.

The slave experiences a moment of relief, a positive blip in a life filled with despair. It does not last.

Meanwhile, unaware of the many travesties playing out around him, Samael marches on. There is no sign of Hangnail, just street after street of misery. Hunger haunts a hundred faces, sharpening eyes and hardening hearts. Scrawny bodies curl in gutters, too weak to complain. Around them scavengers collect, licking lips, stirring juices.

A round-shouldered woman calls to Samael, asking him to stop.

He ignores her.

She bustles into his path, holding out wide flat hands that sit like lollipops on bony wrists. 'Who are you?'

He steps to the left.

She moves to match him.

Scout arrives. He does not like the way she reaches towards his master.

Samael steps to the right.

Again, she steps in his path. 'In the name of the—'

Her sentence cuts off in a flurry of fur and teeth. As the two struggle on the floor, she manages to get out a word: 'Demagogue.'

'Stop,' orders Samael.

Scout looks up, gore-caked muzzle at odds with his innocent expression, an unidentified chunk badly hidden in his mouth.

'Leave her.'

Scout ducks his head, contrite, sloping off to gnaw on his trophy.

Samael wants to move on, leave this mess of a place far behind but something, an impulse, stops him. He leans down, examining the bite mark.

The woman props herself up to speak through pain-clenched teeth. 'The Demagogue demands your presence.'

'I don't answer to the Demagogue.'

She laughs, despite her discomfort. 'Of course you do. We all do.'

'I'm just passing through.'

'It doesn't matter what you were doing or where you were going. You're off to see the Demagogue.' She offers him her hand. 'Now lift me up will you? If we're late, neither of us will get to see the dawn.'

CHAPTER THIRTEEN

Hunters gather, lean strips of shadow detaching themselves from the greater darkness. One by one they assemble on the edge of the forest of stalks, creeping forward under the stars. Wonderland looms before them. All know the history of the place, the grim and gory stories. Hearts flutter at the thought of them, bowels stir.

'We should go back,' whispers one.

'Ssh!' says another.

'We lost Jacks to the buzzers. We ain't going back to the First empty-handed.' Adds a third.

The others have the good sense to stay quiet.

A hunter crouches down, fingers probing the churned earth. Tracks are found, two pairs of human feet and a set of hoof prints, small. He inches forward, led by the marks until hands reach smooth stone. He sighs. 'They went in. Another feast for the Wonderland.'

'That's it then,' says their leader, 'we're too late.'

Shadows retreat, turning for home.

They are nearly invisible again when a belch rings out, rounded and rich. A stifled giggle follows.

The shadows pause, fanning out, searching. They find a piece of panelling leaning against a wall, and a figure propped up behind it. As they draw closer to the source of the sound they hear a woman's voice, firm.

'I'm dead. I'm dead because of a damned burp.' A laugh bursts from her mouth. Four of the hunters move into position around her. 'It's not funny. It's not!' She giggles again. 'Stop laughing! You're a servant of the Winged Eye on a sacred mission. Act like one!'

The hunters exchange glances. Several shrug. The nearest one pulls away the cover.

Duet sits as she was left, medicine bag in her lap, sword laying parallel to her leg, unsheathed.

Before the hunters can strike, brightness shines from her visor, blinding, cutting a wedge from the nighttime. The closest to her gasp, clutching at faces and raising their arms. Those further back aim dartbows, trying to thread shots between their friends.

Metal spines spit through the air, finding new homes in the wall and Duet's armour. A few catch the flailing limbs of dazzled hunters, burrowing deeper to slip toxins into bloodstreams, paralysing, swift.

'I'm not –' she begins, hacking at the legs of the two nearest '– going to –' In her weakened state, strikes that would dismember, merely cut deep. 'Pitiful!' she shouts, interrupting herself. 'Is that the best you can do? You've always been a disappointment to us.' Duet shakes her head. 'Shut up, traitor. You're not here. I killed you! Shut up!'

Two hunters scream, hobbling out of range, the others

regroup, quickly recovering from their initial shock. Duet rages in the background, monologuing while they confer.

'Let's leave her,' hisses one.

'Yeah,' says the second. 'Wonderland's already taken her mind. It'll be coming back to take her body. That's how it is! That's how it happened to my mother's father's brother! It ain't gonna happen to me.'

The third is unimpressed. 'Crap to your stories and crap on your ancestors. We're bringing home a prize. Look at her, she's lost it. She can't even get up. We can take her if we move together.'

Dartbows are swapped for knives and short sticks. As a pack now, the hunters reengage.

Duet watches them, letting her sword tip rest on the ground. 'I think I can take two with me. Or maybe three. Two? Three? I'm not sure.' A giggle forces its way out and then she half sings, 'Two or three, three or four, I'm altogether not quite sure.' She slaps herself on the side of the head with her free hand. 'Why can't I stop talking? And why don't these sorry fucks get on with it!'

The lead hunter raises his hand. 'On three. One . . . two . . .'

A new arrival gives him pause. Something approaches fast from Wonderland, footsteps sounding like gunshots, and behind them, a tall, robed shape, inhuman eyes flashing from a deep hood.

'. . . shit it!'

Though unorthodox, the order is clear enough. The hunters flee, dispersing quickly into pairs, diving back to the protection of the stalk forest.

Duet rolls her head towards the newcomers. Vesper skids to a stop, blinking down at her. 'Duet, you're alive!'

'I wish I wasn't.'

'Don't say that.'

'I can't help it. It's like my mouth's got a mind of its own.' Confusion appears on Vesper's face. A moment later, the kid catches up. 'It's probably the pills I took while I was waiting. Damn, didn't mean to say that.'

'Pills? How many?'

She laughs again, hysteria catching around the edges. 'I don't know! I was waiting for hours and hours. A lot. More than's safe. Enough that I could die or go a funny colour. Maybe I'll do both. That seems to be the way my life is now. For the love of the Eye, shut me up, I can't bear myself!'

The kid begins to back away.

Maintaining a more dignified pace, Neer finally reaches the group.

Duet adjusts the grip on her sword. 'Vesper, get behind me!'

Neer tuts. 'Really, there's no need for that. I'm here to help you.'

'Damn you and damn your help, monster!'

Vesper tries to think of something to say, fails.

'As I explained to your friend here, my situation is not what you expect. I'm human like you are, just—'

'Shut up! Just shut up!' Duet pulls herself up the wall, grunting as she stands. 'Look at yourself! Born with those eyes, were you?'

The glowing pupils narrow. 'You and I are about to have a misunderstanding.'

Duet's next words are interrupted by a burp. 'Not again!' she wails. 'Not now!' She raises her sword, trying to threaten, then drops it, hands required to tear free her visor. As she doubles over, the face plate sails over her shoulder, bouncing twice before settling.

Vomit splashes hot and wet and acrid. Words and laughter come together, discordant. 'Urgh! Huh, huh, huh! It hurts! Bleaaarch!' There is another round of swearing and laughing, babbling moist words and blowing sicky bubbles and then, sudden, dramatic, she passes out.

Within the secret tunnels beneath Wonderland, deep in the Don't Go, there is a room. The room is full of instruments, proudly displayed on racks, ordered by size and function. A slab of plastic is suspended in the middle of the room, capable of rising or falling, of turning, of tilting.

Duet is strapped to the slab, stripped of armour and consciousness. Neer leans over her, held steady on her tripod of ivory. Initial investigations bring tuts of disapproval.

Vesper sits in a corner, chewing on a nail. The kid sleeps across her feet. 'Do you think you can help her?'

'My dear young girl,' she replies without looking up. 'I have spent a lifetime merging the living with the dead, expanding the very boundaries of life's definitions.'

'But do you think you can help her?'

'Yes, I've just said so, haven't I? I was trusted to carve the paths in the boneways above our heads. I laid the road for the Uncivil's essence to flow. I'm sure I can manage a few cracked and broken ribs.'

The smartcast is removed. New skin has formed over old wounds, stretched tight in places by jagged bones. 'No, no, no. This won't do. This won't do at all.' She picks up a scalpel and readies it, an inch above Duet's body. Eyes close and her left hand moves next to her right, fingers curling into a fist. Over the knuckle of her middle finger, a seam in the old leather opens, unveiling a third eye.

One hand guides the other and she begins to operate.

Blood runs down the face of the slab, funnelled along grooves into holes, stashed away for future projects.

'Living subjects are so much messier than the dead. The Necroneers used to be so artful in preparing the limbs. Stitching and gluing so smart as to become decoration! Ah yes, they were good times. Gone now.'

'Were there lots of you?'

'Oh yes. From the collectors at the bottom, to the cleaners and the pre-ops, to my own order. I'm not sure how many we numbered in total. Always changing, you see. We grew as the Uncivil did, recruiting in a rush to keep pace with her.' Red lines draw four doors on Duet's belly. Neer opens them all, unmoved by new smells rising, clogging the air.

Vesper covers her mouth, presses harder against the wall. 'What happened to them?'

'They died. Terrible waste it was. You see, when the Uncivil was ended there was nobody to replace the essence animating our augmentations. When it faded away, undead limbs became dead and rotten. And nothing spreads so fast as rot it seems.'

'What about amputation?'

'It's not just about removing an arm or a tail. Many of us had been altered at the deepest levels.' Vesper says nothing, a silent confession of bewilderment. 'The bonds weren't neat, they were intertwined with our very essence. You can't draw a line around something like that and cut it. And in any case, by the time we'd stopped grieving, it was too late.

194

Wonderland was dead and the enlightenment gone with it. Within days the economy had collapsed and people fell on each other like hungry dogs.'

'Oh.'

A broken rib is eased back into position. A fragment, half hanging, sharp, is removed. She holds it up, closing her knuckle eye and opening her other two, bone limbs carrying her to a cabinet. On the other side are a collection of skeletons, each one exploded slightly, the gaps filled with careful documentation. Comparisons are made, several times she comes back to a particular match, shaking her head.

'Ah well, it will have to do. Ugly measures for ugly times.'

Long before she is finished, Vesper sleeps. Soon after, the sword stirs, disturbed by something. Wings part and its eye swivels to point south, staring into other places, troubled, before turning its glare upon the sleeping girl.

The work continues. Bone grafts are made and applied, cracks filled with a milky jelly. Swelling is eased, skin folded back into place, tied off neatly with black thread that swirls over pale skin like calligraphy.

Hours pass and Vesper wakes to the smell of soup. She is not in the same place she fell asleep.

The walls are piled high with scribblings, tiny writing crammed onto chunks of slate and recycled lids, on treated skins, even the walls themselves. A stream of consciousness laid bare. Secrets and dreams writ large for any who care to read them.

All Vesper sees is the warm bowl and the kid's tongue, lapping. 'Hey!' she says, sitting up on the thin mattress to push the kid away. To her surprise, the kid pushes back, head firm against her chest, knocking her back down.

The kid sniffs then resumes his feast.

From the doorway, Neer chuckles. 'Not to worry, there's plenty more where that came from.'

'It smells great. What's it called?'

'Compound three.'

'What's in it?'

'Compound three.'

'Oh.'

Neer passes the girl a second bowl of soup. This one is rectangular, cut from the base of a larger container. Vesper takes it and eats, adding her own sounds to the kid's happy grunts.

Neer waits until they are nearly finished. 'We should talk about your friend.'

Vesper looks up, mouth still full. 'Mmm?' She swallows. 'What happened? Did you save her?'

'It was a trivial operation but during it I observed several things of interest. What can you tell me about her?'

'I . . .' She pauses. 'I think you should ask her.'

There is a flash of green, brief, but when Neer speaks again, her voice is level. 'She's been operated on before, extensively. The techniques are strange to me but not so much that I can't guess their intent.' She leans closer and Vesper instinctively does the same. 'She's one of those Harmonised isn't she?'

The hesitation is only slight this time. 'Yes.'

'I knew it! Her essence has been attuned to another's. Her face and body too I'd wager. Where's the other one?'

'Dead.'

'Hmm. I think your friend is going to struggle.'

'Me too.'

'She probably isn't going to be long for this world.'

Vesper looks at her, hopeful. 'Can you help her?'

'I've already done all I can. Assuming you still want to leave, that is. If you and your friend were to stay for the long-term, I might be able to. I'd very much like to try.'

'How long does she have?'

'Try to understand. Half of her is gone. Physically, she is intact but her mind and soul,' Neer spreads her hands, 'are fading. Her essence is trying to find what's been lost. Each time it reaches out, a little more fades away. I'd give her a few months. Perhaps a year.'

'But we can't stay. We have a mission.'

'That's a shame. I'd hate to be the one to watch her degenerate.' She straightens. 'But if you have to go, I suppose the sacrifice has to be made.'

'Wait. I don't know. I'm not sure what to do.'

'It really isn't up to me. What would she want?'

'I think she'd want to go.'

'Are you sure?'

'No.' Vesper frowns, gets up. 'I'm going to talk to her.'

One Thousand, One Hundred and
Fourteen Years Ago

The bird is colourful, golden feathers crown its head and edge its tail. A matching chain hangs around its neck, regal. The man opposite is no less gaudy.

'You see,' he explains to the crowd, 'we talk to each other, she and I. Not with words. A universal language. A language of the soul.'

For two years, Massassi has searched. Going high and low. From the targets of obscure docuvids, to the offices of the best media wizards and thought doctors. Not one of them is like her. The desperate hunt for allies brings her here, to a live show. She does not believe the buzzwords about the performer, does not expect to see any real magic but still, she cannot help but hope.

The man points to a small skateboard mounted on a horizontal ramp. 'Pollyanna, ride the board for us.'

The bird complies, drawing chuckles from the crowd.

Massassi scowls. She is looking for more than mere tricks.

'Beautiful, no? But our bond allows for far more than

play. What you are about to see is a level of power so secret that it has only been achieved by a few masters and only after years of training. I, the Great Suprendus, found these masters and convinced them to share their secrets. Today, I share them with you. For my next demonstration, the bond between Pollyanna and I will be tested to its ultimate limit when I place my life in her hands.'

As if on cue, the crowd gasps.

Massassi sits forward. A grain of truth is woven into his lies. Perhaps this one will be different.

'Behold!' booms the Great Suprendus. 'The wheels of death!' Curtains pull back, revealing a set of twenty-three wheels, clockwork armed for war. A gap, one metre wide and two metres high passes through the middle of them. The wheels leap cross the gap, one after the other, like spinning discus thrown by an unseen juggler.

The Great Suprendus throws a bright blue fruit through the gap. Only pulp comes through the other side.

Obligingly, the crowd gasps again.

'Each of these twenty-three wheels is connected to a switch on this display. Each switch has a code next to it and each wheel, a corresponding code, written across its hub. As I walk between the wheels of death and I see the code, I will transmit it using only the power of my mind and command Pollyanna to press the appropriate switch. Only one wheel can be stopped at a time and so there is no margin for error. Now I will need a moment of silence to prepare my spirit and Pollyanna's. Once we begin, can I ask that you do nothing to break my concentration.'

The man begins to hum softly, closing his eyes.

Massassi studies his true face, is not impressed by what

she sees. The bird is not much better, it looks forward to the food it will be given when the trick is done.

The trick.

Massassi is tired of tricks.

As the Great Suprendus begins to walk towards the wheels, she raises her arm, letting the iris in her palm open enough for a point of light to come through. He does not notice, passing through the first three wheels while Pollyanna dutifully hops from switch to switch. The timing is excellent, a testament to hours of training. Impressive but not magical.

The needle of light tracks over the seats in front of her, over the backs of heads, passing up to the stage itself where it find its target.

Meanwhile, the crowd hold their breaths as Suprendus steps safely past wheels six, seven and eight.

Pollyanna opens her beak wide. 'Stop!' she screeches, then throws back her head and laughs.

The crowd laugh, too, assuming it is part of the show. Suprendus stops, his attention torn between the unexpected development and the blade held inches from his head, spinning, ready. 'Now, Pollyanna, this is not the time for chatter.'

'Shut up, you old fraud,' the bird replies.

A few titters ripple through the audience.

'Fraud? Fraud! I am—'

'There is no bond, no magic. Admit it or I let this switch go.'

A few people glance at their neighbours. Not as many are smiling now.

'Alright, I admit it.'

'Say it,' demands the bird, relentless.

'There is no magic. There is no magic! Now, please, let us finish this.'

'Not yet. Tell me about the masters.'

'Of course, of course. As soon as I am free of the wheels.'

'Now!' Pollyanna screeches. 'Now!'

'I'll tell you everything!'

And he does. The Great Suprendus did hear about a group of masters, he even sought them out but they never taught him. He knows little more but she has a lead. Despite her best efforts, a chink of hope appears in cynical armour.

Massassi leaves the confused crowd behind. They stare at the sobbing man and then at the bird, as it dances on the vital switch, swapping from foot to foot, cackling.

CHAPTER FOURTEEN

Vesper lingers in the doorway. 'Hello?'

Eyes blink open, staring blankly. They blink again, slowly remembering how to focus.

'Hello?'

Duet looks down at herself. 'What is this?' Thick straps hold her in place, tight around bare limbs. The fine hairs on her arms stand up, attentive to the cold. She pulls against her bonds, feels rigid steel beneath soft padding.

'Hold on, I'll get those.' Vesper goes to her side, fiddles with the clasps. As soon as one releases, Duet wrenches a hand free, making Vesper cringe away while she works on the others.

Shaky hands make it difficult. Sweat soon beads at her brow, her face twisted in concentration and discomfort.

'Neer had to reset and regraft your bones. It was . . . How are you feeling?'

'My side aches. Differently.'

'Different how?'

A second wrist is liberated. 'Hard to say.'

'Is it any better than before?'

'It's like the pain is more on the outside now than the inside.'

With both hands free, her ankles are quickly unshackled. Duet looks around. 'Where's my armour? And where are my weapons?' She frowns at Vesper. 'And where's the sword?'

'All our things are next door.'

'Get them, we need them.'

'Okay, I will. But first, I wanted to talk to you about something.'

Duet swings her legs over the side of the slab and puts a hand against Vesper's chest. She looks down at it as the Harmonised propels her back towards the door. 'Sword first. Chat later.'

Vesper stumbles away out of sight, mumbling apologies.

Duet shakes her head, sighs, then takes in the surroundings. Specimens float in all manner of jars, pickling slowly. Her mouth turns down as she struggles to identify the species of donor.

Arms full, Vesper returns to the room. The sword sleeps on her back once more, weighing her down. 'Here we are,' she says, dumping armour and weapons and packs on the floor. 'That should be everything.'

Duet inspects her kit carefully, suspicious. 'It looks in order.' Vesper's lips part, hesitant words not quite ready to emerge. She scares them off with her own. 'Never leave the sword unguarded again.'

'It was only next door.'

'That doesn't matter.'

'There isn't even anyone down here apart from Neer, and she's a friend.'

'Is she? How long have you known her? How well do you know these tunnels? Do you know who comes and goes? Are you sure we're safe? Would you bet our lives on it?' Vesper's head shakes with every question. 'Never again, you understand?'

'I won't. I'm sorry.'

'The Seven don't care about apologies. Nor do the infernals.'

A little colour finds its way to Vesper's cheeks. 'I don't know what you want me to say.'

'I don't want you to say anything!' The outburst leaves her suddenly tired. She rests her head in her hands and time begins to drift.

When she looks up again, the kid is running up and down the outside corridor and Vesper sits in the corner, glum. With one foot she hooks the medical bag and scoops it off the floor. Pills are quickly dispensed into an eager palm and popped.

She wipes her mouth, notices the girl is watching her. 'What?'

'Nothing.'

'Go on. Spit it out.'

'I . . .'

'Go on!'

'Neer thinks you're going to die soon. Because you're a Harmonised and because the other you is gone.' Duet lets the medicine bag slip from her fingers. 'She says you're going to, er, I don't know how to say it.'

Duet's voice is quiet: 'Yes, you do.'

'You're going to get worse, in your head.'

'How long?'

'She doesn't know. A few months, no more than a year.'

Throats become tight, awkward. Skittering hooves slow and the kid peers in at the two silent people. Duet stares at the floor, not seeing. Slowly, her eyes close.

Vesper moves to where she sits, wrapping her in gentle arms. Eyes squeezed ever tighter, she presses her head into Vesper's shoulder.

For a while, they stay that way.

The kid bleats once, pauses, bleats again. When neither respond he runs off.

Duet wipes at her eye and pulls back. 'Thank you.'

'Listen, Neer couldn't promise anything but she thinks she might be able to stop things getting worse.'

'What's the catch?'

'Time. We'd have to stay here.'

There is a pause, then the Harmonised shakes her head. 'No. The sooner we leave here, the better.'

*

The Demagogue's palace has gone through several incarnations. Shortly after the infernal tide first swept through New Horizon, the building collapsed, killing many of the occupants and putting a permanent crick in the Demagogue's neck. Repairs are carried out quickly by a mix of slaves and demons, fear-driven and unskilled. Many die to complete the project, as much through incompetence as the design of the foreman.

At first, the Demagogue is pleased. It has little experience of buildings or aesthetics but is certain that if the Usurper has a palace, it should have one too. A larger one.

Two problems emerge. Both come from Witterspear, New Horizon's half-breed chamberlain. Witterspear talks as most breathe, regular and unconscious. One day in court a stray comment is made, the tail end of a dull conversation.

'Of course, the Fallen Palace is nothing like this one.'

From his high basin, the Demagogue glowers, demanding explanation. It had thought the two were identical.

'I . . . well, for one thing, the Fallen Palace leans at an angle, like this.' The chamberlain demonstrates. 'And for another, it's bigger.' Juices bubble in the folds of the Demagogue's belly and Witterspear tries to backpedal. 'Not much bigger! The difference is marginal, barely noticeable.'

The next day, Witterspear is charged to make the Demagogue's towers taller than the Usurper's, to lean at a more acute angle and to be grander in scale.

More suffer, dragging materials up by hand and claw, pouring sweat into the growing structure. As soon as a new phase of the build eclipses the home of the Green Sun, it starts to collapse. Some say this is due to Witterspear's incompetence. Witterspear says it is because the Usurper is ruler of all and, therefore, no palace can be greater. The Demagogue accepts this until the Usurper is ended.

While some infernals mourn the passing of their monarch the Demagogue orders a new round of building. Shortly after it crumbles, Witterspear's head is added to the scaffolds.

New chamberlains come with designs and plans. Their heads line up together, mute testimony to the Demagogue's displeasure.

Through this legacy, Samael strides. A strange patchwork of history. No one wall matches the other, any sense of the original's cohesion buried in a mess of brick and metal, of glue and gaps. There are many holes in the Demagogue's palace. A mix of struts and supports crowd in the spaces, eclectic, straining to keep the upper floors from gravity's embrace.

Trophies and pictures are thrown up to an alien design, some at angles, some upside down. Several partially obscure each other, creating a collage, accidental. Some of the trophies are still alive; once displayed pride of place in the Demagogue's court, now relegated to hallways or alcoves. They are fed when there is food to spare, and when the staff remember.

His guide leads Samael along passages that wind and coil like ugly knots of string. Windows are everywhere, on inner and outer walls, making little cuts in the floor and great gashes in the ceiling, melted blobs of glass that tint the world in surreal colours. Through these he sees abandoned sections of the palace, unfinished. Stairs that lead nowhere, doorways that open onto nothing.

Scout pads alongside him, communicating unease through linked essence and a heavy tail.

One of the exhibits comes to life as he goes past. A young man, ribs proud and easy to count, eyes and cheeks sunken, hollow. 'Are you?' he says with the greatest of urgency.

His guide waves a hand, dismissive, and keeps going. To her dismay, the exhibit continues to talk.

'Are you?'

Samael stops, annoying the guide who is forced to wait for him. 'Am I what?'

His mouth flaps, fishlike. 'Are you?'

'Come,' says the guide, gesturing him to follow. 'It is not wise to keep the Demagogue waiting.'

He nods, and they continue on their way, leaving the man

on his plinth. Samael is nearly at the passage's end when the man finds the words.

'Are you real?'

This time he does not stop. Of course he is real!

The man sees something recognisable in Samael's armour despite the battered plates and grotesque construction. 'Are you a knight?'

His question hangs in the air, unanswered, ignored.

They pass through a set of doors that are sealed to the walls, forever open. It is unclear whether the gesture is symbolic or just apathetic.

As he walks, Samael wonders. Is he a knight? He is not. But is he? Should he be? The thought troubles him. The idea too resonant to put away.

The last question reaches him though Scout's ears. The Dogspawn hanging back as, in truth, he wishes to himself.

'Are you going to honour your oath?'

He has never taken an oath. His creator did not need oaths to secure his loyalty. He was made to obey. But the question joins the others, swirling in his thoughts, an indigestible chorus.

The Demagogue's court chamber is made entirely of glass. A vast quantity of it, stolen over many years and fused together into a huge sphere of irregularity, thick in places, thin in others. The chamber makes nightmares of anything viewed through or reflected in it. It sits dangerously on top of the palace, an ugly bauble, clashing magnificently with its messy surroundings.

Within the court are half-breed servants and demi-lords, keeping to the edges. A huddle of lesser infernals occupy a closer orbit, a colourful collection of shells, mostly animal.

The Demagogue has forced them into regular essence contact over the years, asserting its dominance. The result is a gradual eroding of boundaries, of identities. Homogenising possible rivals into a simplistic mob.

Towering over them all is the Demagogue itself, a giant mound of blubber bobbing in its basin. Its arms are long wizened sticks capped with spindly twig fingers and its legs atrophied stumps. The shell's original head flops to one side, purple, like a wonky pimple.

Three humans sit on a bench before it, facing towards the entrance, still as statues. They are the voices of the Demagogue, living mouthpieces for New Horizon's infernal ruler. The first man is thick-limbed, well fed and full of beard, the second, young and supple, hairless. The third a tiny girl, wrapped in black.

Samael is brought before them.

Having carried out her duty, his guide makes a quick retreat.

The Demagogue reaches out with a stretched finger to stab the head of the tiny girl. Essence jolts into her, animating, and eyes glare with inhuman intensity.

'What, what, what? What is it? Is it from the Palace of the Fallen? Another one?'

The girl's chin juts towards another part of the room and he realises he is not the first to be invited. Hangnail stands painfully apart from the others, its body still, its essence radiating displeasure. The battered shell of a pink-skinned cat stalks around its legs, trying for Hangnail's attention, tugging at the infernal's ragged coat.

'But wait!' says the girl, looking at Samael once more. 'It was not there when we spilt into the world. It is not a challenger. It is not even of the Jade and Ash. An ashling at best. Which of us do you serve, ashling?'

His response is automatic. 'I do not serve.'

'It does not serve? It will learn. It will see.'

'Enough of this. I must go.'

'Must it? Must it go? Where does it go? Why does it go? It will speak or it will be made to speak.'

The court tenses, prepared to do the Demagogue's bidding. Hangnail's coat of skins twitches, ready to open, though on who it is hard to say.

It is almost impossible to lie to an infernal, Samael knows this. He chooses a truth, hopes it will satisfy. 'I go to find the sea.'

'Later, it goes. First, it waits. Waits on my pleasure.'

'Why?'

Everything goes still, even the infernal cat, wary of what will come.

'Why, it says? Why? Because I wish it. You are the second to come here, not the last. A gathering we will have. Until then, the ashling will wait.'

He has no choice, there are too many for him to take alone.

If Hangnail and he were to fight together, they may have a chance. But he does not trust Hangnail to support him. Does not wish to throw his existence away, at least, not cheaply. So he waits, wondering, questions loud in his mind.

What am I?

Ashling? Knight? King?

Scout begins to growl, turning back to stare at the doorway. He senses it too. The coming of new infernals, familiar. A taste, powerful, utterly repellent and lots of similar, lesser ones.

He waits for them while thoughts swirl, storm-like, and his hand moves to the hilt of his sword.

*

In her dreams, Vesper falls. Ever faster, tumbling into the void. Sometimes she rushes towards it, sometimes it towards her, hungry. There are other details, trivial, changing from one night to the next, that Vesper forgets. Only the falling is constant, and the inevitability of impact.

She wakes in surprise, in a sweat. Across from the bed, leaning in a corner, is the sword, its eye fixed on her.

It does not look happy.

Vesper rubs at her face. For a moment the room seems too solid, too . . . substantial? In her heart, she is surprised to find it still here.

Slowly, an eye closes, glaring while wings curl, returning to their normal position.

She sits up, stretches. The room is just a room again, the sword, a sullen sleeping thing.

Vesper turns her blanket back into a coat, pulling it on. Then she picks up the sword by its scabbard, mindful not to make contact with the sword itself. She is not sure what will happen if she touches the hilt but expects it would be bad. She remembers her father's fear of it, remembers that, unlike her, he was chosen by The Seven. For the first time, the reality of her situation strikes. Someday soon, she will have to use the sword and it may very well be her end.

The kid follows her through passages, dusty and dark, to where Duet rests.

'I think it's time to go,' she says.

'Finally.'

It has been two weeks since Duet's operation. The time is filled with waiting and arguments about her health and the need to leave.

Neer escorts them to Wonderland's edge.

Vesper chats with her, footsteps dragging towards the end. 'Thank you so much for all your help.'

'We could turn back if you wanted. There's no shame in it. You could live with me and I could study your friend.'

'I'd like to stay longer, I really would. But I think the sword wants us to go. And anyway, I have family waiting for me to come home.'

'That must be nice.'

Vesper's eyes brighten. 'You could come with us!' Neer is already shaking her head but she presses on. 'That way you could help Duet and we wouldn't have to part. It's perfect!'

'Perfect? No, no, no. It is a sweet notion but this body is getting too delicate for travel and, besides, what about Runty and the other children? They need me more than you do.'

'You could bring them too.'

'Now you're just being silly.'

'How did you find all those children?'

'Oh, I didn't find them. Others found them, or grew them from cuttings. I just look after them. It's one of the few parts of my job that is still relevant.'

Duet stops, suspicious. 'A Necroneer minding children?'

'What of it?'

'I don't believe it. More likely, you harvest them for parts.'

'Yes. I thought that was obvious. Even the best methods of preservation can't compare to fresh material.'

'It's disgusting.'

Vesper nods, horrified.

Neer tuts at them both. 'Is it? They are given shelter and food and a much better quality of life than they'd have without me. They live for years in relative comfort. For years! Is it any different from keeping animals, my little farmer?' She looks pointedly at the kid.

Vesper frowns.

'Or any worse than grooming soldiers for battle.'

Words struggle out past Duet's rage. 'You can't compare . . . what you do . . . with me!'

'Are you not looked after until such time your purpose is served? Tell me, how does the Shining City treat its veterans?'

'They are honoured.'

'Do you know any?'

'A few.'

'And how many of those are soldier class?' Duet frowns. 'And how many of those are Harmonised?'

'I've had enough . . . of this.'

'Hardly the lively debate one hopes for but I accept your surrender.'

Duet walks away without saying goodbye. Vesper trudges after but cannot help turning one last time. 'But, you don't do that any more, do you? Kill the children I mean.'

'No, no, no. Not any more. The Uncivil is gone, my only source of animating essence with her. What could I possibly gain from further experiments?'

'I don't know.'

She raises a finger skyward. 'Exactly. I'm as fond of the little rascals as you are of your pet. I enjoy the company so I keep them on. It gives me something to do.' She looks past

Vesper's shoulder. 'Now you'd best be moving on. Your friend has already got a head start.'

Vesper nods. 'I'll miss you.'

'If she survives, bring her back with you.'

'I will.'

'And if she doesn't, anything you can retrieve would be invaluable to my research.'

'But if she dies, what would be the point?'

'The future. One must always have an eye on the future.'

*

Through the ever open doors comes the hulking form of Gutterface. Samael watches it shuffle into the room, saggy bulk blocking the exit. Tiny infernals clamber all over it like children, like parasites, sitting in folds of skin and the curls of old wounds, perching on shoulders and hipbones.

Samael notes how comfortable the infernals seem together, essence purring and self-satisfied. He tightens his grip on his sword as other facts come to him, adding up to trouble: Gutterface and its children come without a guide. That means it has been to the Demagogue's court before. He looks between the Gutterface and the Demagogue, positioned either side of him and Hangnail, like the jaws of a trap.

The Demagogue pulls its finger from the girl's head and she goes slack. All eyes follow the too-long digit as it rises, turns and descends upon the bald skull of the young man next to her. He jolts awake, lips pulled back in a smile so wide that skin cracks around his lips.

'Welcome, Gutterface! Welcome!' The lips move, giving voice to the Demagogue's thoughts. 'The gathering gathers

size and is nearly complete. Just one more to come and then
. . .' The man stops talking, his face a smiling mask, frozen.

Samael sees all the little eyes peering at him from the nooks
and crannies of Gutterface's body. He looks at the lesser
creatures of the court and finds hunger in their eyes as well,
identical. At his side, Scout growls.

Hangnail is the first to crack. The lone infernal stretches
out its arms, casts open the coat of skins . . .

Hooks emerge, curling and sharp along its edge. They blur
over the pink-skinned cat sitting by its feet, spearing it. A
single shriek gets out before hooks strip the skin away with
fluid ease, tucking it away to be added later. A skeleton slops
onto the floor, muscle and blood, steaming, red.

The Demagogue's finger comes sharply away from the
young man's head, which flops forward, and finds its way
to the skull of the third figure on the bench. He animates
at the touch, beard bristling, and his mouth foams as he
shouts, storm-like, 'Hang the Hangnail! Tear it! Make me
ribbons!'

As one, the court swarms towards Hangnail.

In answer, the infernal opens its coat wide, like a pair of
ragged wings or the lips of a giant mouth. Hooks glisten
and twitch, ready to strike as the Demagogue's forces attack,
small shapes flying forward, snarling and unfolding, all teeth
and claws and bile.

It is more a scrum than a battle.

Gutterface points its arms towards Hangnail and its children cheer, pouring out of their hiding places to skip towards
the beleaguered infernal.

Samael cannot see Hangnail now for the sheer weight of
enemies between them. Even if they work together they have

no chance of victory. It is time to go. He rushes for the door, sword drawn, Scout keeping pace.

But Gutterface still blocks the door. Samael turns his shoulder, speeds up.

Rotten flesh shudders with the impact but Gutterface doesn't move. Samael swings his sword, trying to cut his way to freedom. The blade slips easily through the meat of the shoulder, cracking bone underneath. He pulls back for another strike but his sword is reluctant to leave, stuck fast in the festering flesh.

Gutterface strikes him in the chest and he sails backwards, limbs trailing after, sword clattering to the floor.

His head slams against the curving wall opposite and lines splinter across the glass, radiating out. His view flickers, like two pictures superimposed, sickening. Through the confusion he senses Scout's rage, and as he focuses on it, he sees Gutterface from the Dogspawn's perspective.

Then it is gone, his mind lurching back and forth, in one place, in another, in both.

He is by the wall, head resting in the new dent he has made.

He is leaping through the air, jaws open and angry.

He is by the wall, trying to stand straight.

He is tearing at Gutterface, watching innards spill like beans from a torn bag.

He is upright, testing his limbs.

There is a crack and a yelp.

He is in pain!

But not true pain. Sanity returns, hard and welcome.

Scout lands nearby, panting heavily. He glances over at the living hill of madness that has buried Hangnail.

Creatures crawl over each other, clawing, biting. Gutterface's offspring on top, stabbing into the mass of wriggling bodies with abandon. If Hangnail still struggles beneath them, he cannot tell. Soon, they will be done and then it will be his turn.

He is without a weapon, hopelessly outnumbered and overpowered.

He charges again.

Gutterface turns toward him, careful to leave no opening. The distance between them shrinks.

Samael's essence is a mix of many powerful things, an exceptional lineage packed with buried secrets but knowledge and history are nothing next to the strength of a pure infernal. Gutterface knows this and is confident.

Samael knows this also.

That is why he diverts at an angle, passing the giant demon, throwing himself at a thinner section of glassy wall.

He hits, a metal plated ram, shattering the wall of the chamber, flying through a second pane and back into the corridor. Glass rains around him, stained and sharp.

A second sense warns him to move and he does so, an ugly sidewards roll. Scout lands in the space. Through their link he senses the Dogspawn's pain and something else. Pride perhaps?

Scout raises his head towards Samael, sword held between his jaws.

Samael nods, impressed, sharing his pride between them, warming. Then he stands up, takes back his blade and starts to run, nuggets of glass crunching underfoot.

All of the Demagogue's forces are occupied behind them, leaving the corridor mercifully clear of infernals, and while

Gutterface is powerful, it is not quick. They are out of sight before the infernal has turned itself round.

Ahead of them, a young man kneels. Samael recognises him as the exhibit who tried to speak to him before. The man's actions are slow and ritualised, tickling memories.

On impulse, Samael slows down.

'My name is Jem. I invoke the rite of mercy. Save me, protect me, deliver me.'

Scout races past him, tongue hanging out to one side, absorbed in the run.

Samael tries to do the same but his feet have stopped. The man's words fill his head, loud as cannon fire, echoing.

Echoing.

A staccato flash of memories, other places, other voices, the same words, charged with purpose.

Back in the present, he sways. The man called Jem is unmoving before him. 'Up,' he says in his dusky voice.

Jem stands up and Samael stares, trying to understand why he feels the need to help this stranger.

Scout bounds back into view, barking at them. He is concerned for his master, keen for him to hurry. He is right to be.

Behind them, there is a great roar, a score of animal throats opening together followed by the sound of tearing flesh.

Hangnail has fallen.

Scout barks again. Jem pulls at Samael's arm. He sees rather than feels the contact. Then, he starts to move. The motion is sluggish at first, as if his body were far away and the dangers even further. He knows their end is coming, is tempted to face it rather than flee, to take some of the filth out of the world before he goes. Instead, Jem and the Dogspawn urging him on, he speeds up.

Together, they run.

Following them down the corridor come the words of the Demagogue, carried by the voice of the big man, booming: 'Bring me the ashling! Bring it! Bring me all of its pieces!'

CHAPTER FIFTEEN

Duet and Vesper stand amid piles of rubble. Size is the only indicator of what made them. The smaller ones, private dwellings or storage pods, the larger ones by-products of communal hives and industrial structures. Each makes a modest hill, piled neatly and surrounded by bushes, green leaves tipped with white fuzz.

Vesper holds out the Navpack, an image projecting by her feet. 'According to this, we're in the right place. It's marked as an active settlement.'

'It's out of date.'

'Yes.'

'Like the others were.'

'Yes. Sorry.'

Duet scowls. 'Stop apologising! This isn't your fault.'

'S—' The girl catches herself and smiles, self-conscious. 'Okay.'

Meanwhile, the kid sniffs at the cottony fuzz on the leaves. Risks are weighed up, options considered. An experimental bite is taken.

Duet sits down on one of the smaller piles and begins rifling through the bag.

The Navpack is powered down, returned to Vesper's pocket. 'What are we going to do now?'

'I'm going to have a pill.'

'Another one?'

'I told you, they help with the pain.'

'But,' she protests, crossing over to the Harmonised. 'Those ones aren't even pain meds!'

'I know. We're out of pain meds.'

'So what are they?'

'Uppers.' She folds her arms but, despite the urge to push Vesper away, finds herself explaining. 'They don't make the pain go away. They just make it not matter so much.'

'You told me the pain was nearly gone.'

'It has. Nearly.' She pops two tablets, one red, one purple. 'Anyway, it's done now.'

'I don't like it.'

'It's done. Leave it.'

Vesper watches the kid stripping the leaves with enthusiasm. 'What we need is food.'

Duet turns her attention to the kid as well. 'Agreed.'

'No, I mean we need to hunt for some.'

'Do you know how to hunt?'

'A little, my father showed me once but he wasn't very good at it. And it was a long time ago. I don't remember much.'

'Not much is more than I've got. What do we need?'

'A place where animals go. A trap and some good bait.'

Duet keeps her eyes on the kid. 'I think I know where we can get the bait.'

221

The girl's stomach growls, scaring off the guilt. 'I suppose, if he wasn't in any real danger, it would be okay.'

Oblivious, the kid keeps chewing.

*

Samael, Scout and Jem huddle in one of the many abandoned sections of the Demagogue's palace. In the darkness, tucked within the ruins of a fallen tower joined by bridge to the main structure, they watch for their pursuers. Each time the wind blows, walls shudder and floors creak, like a man moaning before death.

From their hiding place, they see a gaggle of hunters arrive, small and feral and quick. Without pause the infernal horde leave the relative safety of the Demagogue's palace, spilling out onto the half-finished bridge to the tower.

Samael steps into view, drawing enthusiastic shrieks. Jaws slaver and barbs extend as they rush towards him.

He draws his sword, makes two heavy cuts.

With a ping, the cables holding the bridge fall away, stripping out the structure's spine.

Shrieks turn quickly to wails as the bridge crumples, tin tissue paper folding about them like a heavy shroud.

Samael counts each time they bounce off a wall, marking the crunches and the way the screams change pitch. He finds the sound satisfying.

Infernals at the other end of the bridge struggle to stop. One teeters on the edge, feathered arms making desperate circles in the air.

A small face appears at its shoulder, black eyes glinting malice: one of Gutterface's children. It reaches out slowly, until its small hands touch the infernal's back. It savours the moment, then pushes, siblings leaning forward to watch the infernal tumble, wings flapping, useless.

When the show is over, the eyes all raise to glare at Samael. He glares back.

Then, at some unseen signal, they pull back as one, leaving the corridor suddenly empty.

Jem appears at his side and speaks. Samael cannot recall the last time he has heard a voice so human. His long association with demons giving the man's words a false softness.

'Where will we go?'

'Wherever we go, they will find me. My essence is known to them.'

'Can't we hide?'

Inspiration bubbles from within. Secrets passed from the Uncivil, to his creator and now to him. Sometimes it feels as if his creator still pulls the strings from deep inside, that his own will is but a scab on the wound made by their deaths. 'It will only prolong the agony.'

Jem's hands begin to shake. 'You promised. You promised you would help me.'

'They are not after you. Run now, while you can.'

'And then what? Run where? To who?' Samael stares at him, unmoved. 'You swore an oath!'

Did he? He does not remember and yet he feels it somehow, words that bind as surely as any chains. 'Yes. But first you must do something for me.'

Jem nods, sagging a little, disappointed but not surprised. 'Yes?'

He points down at his feet.

There is a pause and then Jem sinks to his knees in front of the half-breed. 'Yes?'

Samael lifts his right foot, raising it level with the man's chest. 'Help me get my boot off.'

'What?'

'Take off my boot.'

Jem shrugs and sets to work.

While Jem's head is bowed Samael grips at ruined brick-work, steadying himself. Scout begins to whine softly and Samael wonders if the Dogspawn senses his own misgivings at what is to be done. Pushing such thoughts to one side, he raises his sword, bringing it down past Jem's head and into the exposed flesh of his foot.

*

The kid nibbles at a pile of leaves. Around his neck is an old piece of rubber tubing, tethering him to a stake. He does not care about his lack of freedom, fully focused on the task at hand.

Several plastic sheets are staked out around the kid, an uneven square of grey, daubed with glue.

Further out, behind a mound of stones, Duet and Vesper watch.

The Harmonised grits her teeth. 'This isn't going to work.'

'We have to be patient. That's what my Uncle Harm always says. If we're patient, the world will come to us.'

She stands up. 'Your uncle talks a lot of crap.'

Vesper mutters a reply, just loud enough to not be audible as Duet crosses to their trap.

With ease, she hops over the plastic, landing next to the kid. He glances up and she draws her sword.

Vesper gasps.

The kid goes back to chewing.

'Don't!' calls Vesper, half standing in surprise.

Her sword licks the young goat across his flank.

The kid screams, a thin stream of blood running down his side.

Duet hops back and returns to where Vesper gawps.

'What did you do that for?'

'To speed things up.'

They go back to waiting while the kid alternates between screaming, bleeding and shooting dark looks in their direction.

'Sorry,' whispers Vesper, ignoring Duet's exaggerated sigh.

Fresh scents and shouts of distress carry far however and before long, an interested party arrives. Vesper sees it first, pointing with enthusiasm.

A rat the size of a large dog approaches, with horns for eyes and whiskers thick as babies fingers. Its fur is dark, its feet a raw pink with a tail to match.

Despite its appearance, Vesper's mouth begins to water.

It stops just in front of the plastic sheets, sniffing the air, cautious. An unknown smell stands between it and food. Slowly, it walks the perimeter, feet well clear of the treated plastic. The kid tries to get away from it, bleating unhappiness but the tubing holds it close. Two creatures make two circles, one within the other.

The movement squeezes a little fresh blood from the kid's wound and the rat stands on its hind legs, whiskers twitching with excitement.

'Come on,' Duet whispers.

The kid pulls away harder, stretching rubber, legs a flurry, fighting for every inch. While the stake is sturdy, it is not planted deep, the ground too hard and dry for such things.

The rat pauses.

The stake begins to lean.

Vesper can only watch, shaking her head as the kid pulls free, rolling backwards onto the plastic, where he stops, abrupt, stuck fast.

The rat circles round to where the kid lies, stricken.

Duet nudges Vesper. 'Shoot it.'

'What?'

'Shoot it. Right now. Shoot it.'

'Oh!' she replies, fumbling for the pistol in her pocket.

The rat leans out over the plastic, neck stretching, telescoping to add an extra foot to its reach. Long teeth nip at the kid's side.

The kid screams, so does Vesper. The pistol is in her hand now. She points and fires, trying to be conservative, impressively off target.

Unable to see the laser, the rat bites at the kid again, undaunted.

Held on his back, legs stuck in the air, the kid is easy to catch. He cannot run but he can kick. Feet flail and a lucky hoof glances off the rat's skull. The tainted creature startles, one paw landing on the edge of the plastic sheet.

Instantly, the glue hardens, bonding one to the other. The rat lifts its paw and the sheet rises with it. Frustrated, it waves the paw, like a frenzied fan meeting their idol.

Duet breaks cover, starts to run.

Vesper squeezes the trigger again. Nothing happens. She frowns, squeezes harder but the pistol stays stubbornly silent.

She looks back in time to see Duet stab the rat through the neck. 'Finally,' the Harmonised calls back. 'A bit of luck.'

Behind her the kid's eyes narrow to black slits. He kicks out, hooves striking the backs of her knees.

Duet's legs fly outward and her body follows, a half somersault, impromptu.

She lands next to the kid, limbs spread like a star.

For a moment, all three are shocked into silence.

Duet recovers first. 'Right, that's it!'

She returns the kid's murderous look and reaches for her sword. However, the trap has other ideas, holding fast to her head, her back, her hips, her legs and her arms.

Vesper stares at the kid's legs waving crazily, then at Duet writhing and cursing. 'Oh. I'll just . . . huh . . . I'll just . . .' Laughter springs loud and unexpected, a force of nature. She drops the gun, clutching at her side.

'Shut up!' shouts Duet. The kid says something to the same effect.

If anything, Vesper laughs louder, cheeks crimson with mirth, arms pressed to her sides. 'I'm . . . I'm sorry!' she howls, bent double and then she says no more, laughing and laughing, drowning out the threats and the shouts until Duet finds herself joining in.

The kid does not understand. He kicks at Duet but cannot reach her. Dark eyes narrow, plotting revenge.

It is easy to make a space for the fire. Rubble is abundant, the smaller chunks used to outline the fire pit, the larger ones turned into a makeshift shelter to hold back the worst of the winds. Finding fuel for the fire is more difficult. Wood is scarce, forcing Vesper to manage with foraged scraps, abandoned pieces of clothing, of furniture, too damp to burn well.

They make do. Vesper blows gently onto the fire, wincing as the flame flickers away before gasping back to life.

Duet wrestles with the corpse of a giant rat, skinning it with all the skill of a rank amateur. Chunks of flesh are wasted with the skin, piling up at her feet as she hacks, sweating and swearing. By the time she finishes and begins the skewering, Vesper's fire is burning nicely.

Smoke capped flames crackle, chemical tinted.

Together, they lift the rat and suspend it over the fire. A metal bar protrudes from its mouth and rear, each end supported by a pile of rocks. Once in place, the bar begins to bend in the middle, lowering the rat's belly to kiss the fire pit.

The kid puts his back to the spectacle, happy to take the warmth but more interested in stringy weeds sprouting about the rubble.

While Vesper feeds some old netting to the fire, Duet slips a pink tablet into her mouth. The girl shows her palms to the flames. 'That's better.'

Duet grunts agreement.

Vesper looks at the rat's horns curving towards the floor, chews on her lip. 'Are you sure we can eat it?'

'Yes.'

'That's good.' A few seconds pass. 'You're not worried about taint?'

'No. I'm hoping that The Seven will protect us.'

Vesper glances at the sleeping sword. 'Oh.'

'And if they don't, it isn't going to be a problem for long. Not for me anyway.'

'No.'

'And anyway, I didn't go through all of this to not eat.'

Meat slowly reddens. Fat drips down, sizzling. Mouths water.

Turning the rat is stressful. Its weight is uneven, making the bar flex dangerous and hot, scorching fingers despite the rags wrapped protectively around them. When it is done, two smiles shine, fierce in the firelight, each reflecting the other's glory.

They wait again, stomachs growling, impatient.

The kid turns around on the spot once, then twice, then sits. Within minutes, he is asleep.

Vesper chews her lip. 'Can I ask you something?'

'Alright.'

'When did you know you were going to be a Harmonised?'

'Why do you ask?'

'Well, you're not that much older than me—' Duet snorts, loud, but Vesper carries on. 'You're not that much older than me, maybe ten or fifteen years at most, and you have your role in the Winged Eye. I mean, you know what you're supposed to be. There must have been a lot to learn. Did you start when you were my age or earlier?'

Light plays on Duet's face, highlighting its oddities. 'I was young when I knew. There were trials and tests that seemed to take forever. All children in the Shining City take them but I had extra ones for compatibility. The better I did, the more I got pushed.'

'How old were you?'

'They started when I was still in the tube but the first ones I remember happened when I was three. By then I already knew it was a possibility.'

'When I was three I didn't know anything. What did you have to do?'

She frowns. 'What does it matter? You're not going to become a Harmonised.'

'I know that. I'm curious, that's all.'

'It's not natural.'

'You don't have to tell me if you don't want to.'

'It's not that.' She pokes at the fire with a headless spoon. 'I'm not like you. Talking doesn't come easily to me. And for most of my life I haven't needed to talk.'

Vesper takes her time, approaching the conversation as she would a scared animal. 'The other you, what was she like?'

Duet doesn't answer at first and both take a moment to breathe in the smell of cooking meat. 'I don't know. She was me and I was her. So, I'd have to say she was like me.'

'You were exactly the same?'

'No. I used to think we were.' She shakes her head, her tone suddenly bitter. 'I thought our alignment was perfect. In battle, we moved as one, like extensions of each other. I always knew where she was going to be and she knew the same about me. But we weren't exactly the same. She was the Primo and I was the Secondo. Maybe it's the same with all Harmonised but . . .'

Vesper doesn't interrupt, letting the crackling of the flames fill the gaps.

'. . . there were times when it felt like she was keeping something back . . . and sometimes I'd worry it was my fault. What if I wasn't good enough for her to share that last part of herself? What if I was holding us back?'

'I'm sure it wasn't like that.'

'Then why did she drop me for a fucking infernal?' Duet covers her face.

'Maybe she messed up. Maybe you were the stronger one.'

'No. I'm not. You didn't know her. She was . . . perfect.'

'It's true, I didn't know her. But she didn't save me from the First. You did.'

Duet keeps her face hidden. 'I thought about it . . . The First's offer . . . I didn't believe in you . . . I thought we were going to die . . . I was . . . tempted.'

'You didn't sound tempted.'

'Because it was an infernal . . . I thought I was loyal . . . I thought we would never . . .' She tails off, hands pressing roughly against her mouth.

Vesper sighs. 'It's okay. I don't blame you. The truth is, I don't believe in me either. Since I picked up the sword I've been terrified of getting things wrong. My Uncle says that when you don't know what to do, then it helps to pretend that you're someone who does.' A little pride tugs at her lips. 'I pretend to be my father because he was a knight. He always knew what to do. The thing is, I'm not very good at it.'

'I never knew my father, or my mother. They were just codes on my record.'

'Do you know anything about them?'

'No. The Harmonium Forge made me and the Winged Eye raised me.'

Gently, Vesper takes her hands, rests them in her lap. 'For what it's worth, I like you better now the other you isn't here.'

She looks up, disbelieving. 'But I'm horrible to you.'

'Only sometimes.'

She punches Vesper on the arm. 'I think I'm starting to like you, too.'

'I thought so.' Duet punches her again, a little harder this time. 'Ow! What was that for?'

'It's not easy for me, you know. I'm not like you.'

'Okay.'

'. . . Vesper?'

'Yes?'

'I don't want to die.'

She squeezes Duet's hands. 'No.'

Abruptly, the Harmonised stands up. 'I don't want to talk any more. Let's eat.'

One Thousand One Hundred and Thirteen Years Ago

The island is shy, only visible from the shore on a clear day. There has not been a clear day for three centuries now. Mankind makes his own clouds that hang low and heavy, squatting just above the waves, hissing out from rows and rows of metal pipes that sprout like grey grass. Undersea tubes connect the island to the mainland. There are three in total, each divided into two chambers, allowing traffic to flow back and forth. One carries people, another materials. The third is reserved for important items, living or otherwise.

An angry sky flings rain and lightning around the island. Massassi glides through it all, fearless. For her the clouds are easy to read, their bunchings and rollings giving ample warning as to where the next strike will be.

She makes towards the buildings clustered on the island's crown. Six spires carved along the lines of the natural rock finished with iron and gold. They are well-weathered, hard lines smoothed into something more appealing. Between them is a disc, big enough to land a carrier mech. Scorch marks mar its surface, testament to the long relationship between land and storm.

She tips her glider towards it but the winds are strong, shaking the wings on her back. Three times they grab her as she tries to land, spinning her towards the heavens. But she comes back for a fourth time, ready even for a fifth or a fiftieth, and the elements part for her, overcome.

Jump boots absorb the shock of landing, slipping on wet stone. She leans forward, surfing the momentum, tiny waves spraying up either side of her feet.

Opposite, an oval door groans open. In its light, a man stands, one hand raised against the rain. His eyes widen as he sees the apparition emerging from the darkness.

'Ah!' he cries, hopping backwards as she hops inside, wings folding at her back.

They move like dancers, hurried steps matched, legs moving together, until his back meets a wall and Massassi's palms slap against it, framing his terrified face.

'Ah!' he says again.

Her eyes narrow in contempt. 'You are not one of the masters.'

'That's right, I'm not. I just manage the sanitation units. Please don't hurt me!'

'Take me to the masters.'

He complies. She does not even need to compel him. As they weave their way deeper into the complex, her small hopes waver. Perhaps these will be just like the others. Perhaps she is alone in all the world. A freak. A queen amid the worms.

She is led to a laboratory where brains float in tubes, arranged by size and then by normality. Electrical pulses wash over them, regular, matched by soft beeps that issue from a monitor. Light from the screen illuminates a man's face. To Massassi, he looks old and unimpressive.

She pushes her guide out of the way. 'You are a master of thought?'

The man looks up, blinking surprise. 'Hmm? What? Who are you?'

Jump boots activate on minimum power, sailing her across the room. 'You are a master of thought?'

He straightens, chin jutting forward. 'I am a Neuromaster, yes.'

'Show me.'

Wrinkles line up on his brow. 'What?'

'Show me your power.'

'Look, I don't know who you are or how you got in here but it would please me greatly if you used the same means to leave.' His attention returns to the monitor. 'And close the door on your way out.'

Massassi raises her silver arm level with the man's head. White light flashes as the iris in her palm spirals open. 'Show me or I will make you show me.'

He looks up, more irritated than afraid. 'Very well. My primary research is around replacing damaged sections of the brain. Specifically, on the communication between the original and synthetic areas. As with many of my colleagues I have of course had to bend my work towards other, more immediate applications.'

A hatch slides open in a nearby wall and two spheres roll from it. Each is formed of multiple metal bands scored with lines that hint towards hidden compartments. They come to a stop by the man's feet, flanking him. Plates flip down, securing them in place while quivering forks extend from their middle sections, spitting sparks.

'Is this what you had in mind?' the Neuromaster asks. 'I thought as much. You look the type that likes things simple. So let me put it in simple terms. My chip connects me to these drones. With a thought I can manipulate them as easily as I can my own body. If I wish I can turn them on or off, command them to move, or even to kill. So if you know what's good for you, you'll lower your hand and leave me in peace.'

'No.'

Slowly, he shakes his head. 'You are a strange and savage thing. You really wish to die?' The light in her palm begins to brighten. 'So be it.'

The drones tilt, raising their weapons towards Massassi, then past her, turning, pointing them at their master.

Beads of sweat appear on the man's forehead. 'No, aim at her!'

The drones ignore him, weapons humming, full of potential. Slowly, the man raises his arms, crossing them over his chest. He stares at his betraying hands, whimpering as they close around his throat.

'Is this it?' asks Massassi.

The man begins to choke. 'Wait!'

'Why?'

'I'm only . . . one master . . . there are more . . .'

'Better than you?'

'Yes . . . I can . . . show you . . .'

She closes her fist and the man flops forward, head slapping against the monitor, breath rattling in his throat. 'Take me to them, now.'

In minutes she is bursting into another room. This one is small, dark, its walls ridged foam, shaped to give an organic feel. The floor and ceiling are of similar design. In its centre sits a woman, her eyes closed.

'Grand Master Heike,' calls the man over Massassi's shoulder, 'you have a visitor and she was most, ah, insistent. I think she merits our full attention.'

The woman takes a slow breath, lets it out. 'Thank you, Yeorin. You can go now.'

He glances at Massassi, waiting until she waves him away. 'You are the strongest master here?'

Heike smiles to herself. 'That's one way of putting it.'

'Good. Show me your power.'

The woman takes another breath, slow and soft. 'Is that a threat?'

'Yes.'

'What will you do if I refuse?'

'I'll make you show me.'

She makes a noise, something like a chuckle. 'Really? I don't think you will.'

'The other one sneered at me too. He's not sneering any more.'

'Oh I'm not sneering. Do you want to sit down? You must have come a long way. You must be tired.' Massassi nearly growls an insult but the thought interrupts her: what Heike says is true, she has been travelling a long time. And she is tired, right down to the bones. Shrugging, she sits. 'You see,' Heike continues, 'we don't get many visitors out here and those we do get always want something. I'm sure you didn't come all this way just to gather slaves, did you?'

'No.'

'No, you came here because you're looking for answers, for people who can help you.' Massassi straightens. She does want help. 'And I can give you those answers but only on one condition.'

This is more familiar. 'What do you want?'

'If I do all I can to help you and tell you the truth as I see it, you must promise not to punish me for it.'

'I don't understand you.'

'You may not like what I'm going to tell you. Forgive me but you're very young and very strong. I want your word that you'll not attack me and then I'll do all I can for you.' Massassi nods. After all, the request does seem very reasonable. 'Good. It seems we have an accord. You may begin.'

'What?'

'You may begin. Tell me about yourself. Why you have come here. What you want. I can't help you if you don't tell me what you need and why it is so important.'

And so Massassi does. At first, she is self-conscious, halting but soon she is lost in the telling and time passes easily between them. When she finishes, she feels lighter, almost dizzy. 'Well? Can you help me?'

There is a pause.

'I am going to help you, though I suspect you aren't going to like it.'

Massassi frowns. Is this a trick? She looks at Heike's true face but sees neither hope nor deception there.

'I've studied the human mind all of my life. I've benefited from hundreds of years' worth of archives and the company of brilliant colleagues but I have never seen or heard of anyone that can do what you can.

'Massassi, the truth is that you are looking for a master when in fact you should be looking for students. If you want to find others like you, you're going to have to make them yourself.'

CHAPTER SIXTEEN

The tainted creature prowls between rock piles. Like many of the inhabitants it is hard to classify, several generations of crossbreeding, coupled with flowering mutations give it a mythical appearance. Two heads, one beaked, one with a wolfish muzzle, a single feathered wing, as useless as it is colourful and two powerful forelegs that drag its thick, muscled trunk along.

There are many like it, variants scattered further south in the Blasted Lands. Lumped together under the name of Mashups, most barely live long enough to breed. This one is near the end of its cycle and carries a bellyful of growing eggs.

The need to survive, blunt and relentless, drives it on. To feed itself, to feed the eggs, to make them swell with life.

As the suns begin to rise, scales shift hue, taking on the greys and browns of terrain, blending.

It is close now.

Scents sharpen, of food and fire and human prey, the

trail of them carried on the air. Keeping low, the creature accelerates.

Dawn's light washes out the dying fire. Vesper leans over the pit, enjoying the last of its heat. Her stomach grumbles.

Duet's knife is already in her hand. Soon, several strips of meat are cut away and any lingering worries about its safety are banished under a succession of happy groans.

The kid leaves them to it, trotting off to dispense with some morning business.

Duet looks at the remains of the carcass, still mostly intact. Their stomachs, too small from rationed food, have been easily filled. 'That should be good for a couple of days. Then you'll need to get us more.' Vesper nods, warming to the idea of herself as hunter. 'Where are we going next?'

'Good question.' The girl pulls the Navpack out of her pocket and switches it on. Lines of topography sparkle over the dirt, showing settlements and paths of dead rivers and rocky ranges that dissect the land. 'We've still got a long way to go.'

Duet points to the flashing dot in the centre of the image. 'Is that where we are?'

'Yep, that's us.'

'Damn. I thought we'd be further south. What I wouldn't give for a sky-ship.'

'We'll get there eventually.'

'What makes you so sure?'

Vesper shrugs. 'We've got this far. But now we have to get past this mountain range. There's only one road on the Navpack but that takes us through Verdigris.'

'Is that good or bad?'

'Bad.'

'How do you know?'

'My Uncle Harm told me about it.'

'I should have known.'

'He used to live there. He said it was dangerous.'

'Do we have any choice?'

'Well, we might be able to find our own way over the mountains.'

'And risk getting stuck out there? Falling to our deaths or starving? I'd rather face a threat I can fight.'

'Verdigris it is then.' She licks her lips. 'Before we go, I'm going to have some more.'

'Good call.'

While Duet carves, the kid returns, scattering stones as he charges past the fire pit, still accelerating until legs lock, solid, and he topples with comic slowness onto one side.

Duet barks out a laugh. 'That has to be the most useless animal I've ever seen.'

'Something must have scared him. They faint when they're scared.'

'Like I said . . .'

On the ground, by Vesper's feet, the sword begins to hum, interrupting.

Sentence forgotten, Duet readies her knife, turning slowly while Vesper gathers the sword in her arms. Both of them strain for any sign of trouble.

Seconds pass and the landscape appears as lifeless as ever.

Silvered wings flick open, dramatic, and an eye opens. Vesper follows its gaze, seeing an innocent pile of rock. As she stares, teeth appear within stone, stark-white against the grey. And the outline of a body, sliding, coiling, preparing to spring.

'Duet! Look out!'

The Harmonised turns in time to see it fly at her, clocking the many threats: teeth, beak, talons, all coming at once. Her hands come up under one set of jaws, slamming them shut before they can reach her throat. Talons scream down her chest plate, six furrows not quite deep enough to touch skin. The beak punches through much more easily, knocking Duet onto her back.

The creature looms over her, roaring.

Duet's knife is not intimidated, answering with a silent thrust. But thick scales confound the blade, turning it aside with ease. Before beak and jaws can descend again, she throws the knife. It spins towards the canine head which yelps, surprised as the knife bounces off a scaled eyelid.

For a moment the beast is stunned, long enough for the Harmonised to find her feet and draw her sword.

Automatically, Vesper's hand moves towards her pocket. Only when the pistol is in her grasp does she remember the weapon is spent, useless. In her other hand the sheathed sword rattles in fury, tilting towards the tainted creature.

Duet spins away from a snapping beak, striking out on the creature's neck and shoulder. She jumps back from another attack, checks to see if the creature is hurt.

Nothing. No change in the way the head moves, no damage to the neck. The scales are not even scratched.

'Shit.'

There is no time for further strategy. The creature is on her again, harder this time, as if it senses her fading confidence.

She parries and twists, strikes again, trying her luck with its legs. It is like hitting a wall. One of the talons catches her thigh, snagging on her armour, spinning her like an over-enthusiastic dance partner.

Duet falls onto her front.

An eye tears itself from the creature and looks up at the girl.

Vesper meets its gaze, is held by it. The pistol drops unnoticed from her fingers.

The creature's shadows fall over Duet.

Still dazed, she moves blindly, desperately, anything preferable to staying still. The creature snaps at her rolling body, teeth glancing off her armour.

As if in a dream, Vesper's empty hand moves towards the sword's hilt. Wingtips curl, encouraging.

The air becomes tight, holding its breath.

Vesper blinks, looking from her hand to where Duet struggles and back again. Understanding comes, draining the colour from her face. Action is required and the sword is waiting, demanding to be used.

In desperation, Duet scoops up a rock, raising it before her like a shield. The creature snares it in its beak, tossing it over a shoulder.

Unarmed, tired, Duet cries out, a mix of fear and anger.

The creature opens its jaws, opens its beak, rearing back.

A chunk of meat sails past, landing with a wet smack next to the creature's talons.

It pauses, then snaps up the morsel.

Another soon follows, landing next to it.

'Back away,' hisses Vesper. 'Move very slowly.'

Duet edges back on her elbows.

The creature growls at her, baring its teeth.

Duet stops.

Vesper circles into her field of vision, sheathed sword in one hand, a long strip of flesh in the other. 'Here we are. No need to fight. There's plenty to go round.'

The creature watches her warily. It tenses as if to spring but then glances at the sword, pauses.

Vesper lays the meat down. 'Here it is, all for you.'

As soon as she has circled clear, the creature pounces on it, one head eating, the other watching, warning them off.

They pack with forced calm, Vesper sometimes pausing to throw fresh morsels the creature's way.

The kid wakes up. Halfway through a mighty yawn he sees the creature. His eyes bulge, his jaw locks and he flops back where he fell.

Vesper collects him and they retreat, slowly, keeping a measured pace, putting good distance between them and the creature.

Then they run.

Over half the rat and the empty pistol are left behind.

*

Jem runs down a filth-crusted street, clutching something small in his fist. He is not alone. Those with homes go inside, slamming doors shut on reflex. The less fortunate beg for sanctuary. A scant few are shown mercy, the rest do what they always do: they run until they can't run any more, then hide.

Only Jem knows why he is running. The others know that

trouble is coming and that is enough; in New Horizon it is proximity rather than guilt that tends to bring punishment.

Behind them, the Demagogue's forces spread across the tainted city. A mix of infernals and half-breeds, slaves and opportunists, leaking from the palace like a bad smell. Gutterface lumbers out after them, one of the last.

Jem is only a few streets away but already he slows, prolonged malnutrition stamping itself on his health. Thin flanks heave as he bends forward, one hand resting on his knee, the other clenched tight around something small, pressed to his chest.

His heart tremors like a little bird's, fast and fragile. Thudding alongside its delicate beats come the sound of giant footsteps.

He glances over his shoulder in time to see Gutterface arrive at the far end of the street. It surveys the filthy buildings while its children chitter, swarming over its swollen feet, nestling in fatty folds, all impatient for further entertainment.

It has come for him.

A flabby arm is raised, tree-trunk thick, and the impish creatures sing with delight.

He chokes a sob.

It is pointing at him.

Trembling legs carry him around a corner, temporarily away from the infernal's sight. He stumbles on, watching his feet flash in front of him as if they belong to somebody else. The ground is slick with unidentified gunk. He slips and lurches forward, grabbing at random passers-by for support.

His hand snags a sleeve. Worn fabric tears, then holds,

gaining him an angry look and the time to get his footing. All in all, a fair trade.

In other places he would draw attention, a person in his state, hard features locked in fear, in determination, sweat dripping from the ends of his hair, clearly on the run. In New Horizon he fits right in.

Past crusty-faced beggars and long-toothed merchants he goes, never attracting more than a glance. He thinks he is going south but worries he is not. The city has changed during his incarceration, many of the old landmarks have collapsed to be replaced by simpler, meaner structures.

On he goes, slipping into an alley, forcing feet to take yet more steps, till spots dance before eyes and thoughts wander, taking his mind to other times and places, where life was merely grim.

The respite is brief, reality returning with a slap.

Ahead, the alley is blocked.

He stops, staring at the buildings that have folded on top of each other, a scrum of ruined architecture. If he were stronger he might be able to climb it. But he is not and there is no time.

And now he hears them, twisted childish giggles that draw closer with every breath.

He opens his hand, stares at its contents. The sight turns his stomach but there is nothing inside to evacuate.

Swallowing down the bile, he approaches the rubble, full of nooks and cracks, perfect in its own way. Yes, he thinks, it will have to be here.

Gutterface stops suddenly. It knows Samael must be close, can feel the ghost of his essence, faint fingerprints smeared in the air.

And there it is again, the slightest scent of him. It turns and points down a narrow alley and its children screech, delighted.

The alley appears to hold little of interest. One corner contains a woman wrapped in a plastic net, bruises shining through the holes. Another, a man who tries not to look at them. Both exude fear. A few rats abandon their exploration of the woman's leg, scurrying away to their holes.

Gutterface's children rush to take their place, eager to play. One jumps onto the woman's chest, another sinks its teeth into the man's ankle. The woman is too weak to scream, the man is not.

Gutterface points again, over the heads of the beleaguered humans, to the rubble opposite. But its children are too busy having fun, pulling at limbs, prodding, mocking the sounds of people suffering.

Essence flashes with anger and the children freeze. Gutterface picks up one of the nearest and throws it down the alley. The others are quick to follow under their own power.

Soon, the man and the remaining rats are gone, leaving the woman to groan out her last.

As the infernals search, pulling apart the rubble, brick by brick, Gutterface feels Samael is almost close enough to touch, and yet, it had expected a stronger flavour. It had expected more. It had expected Samael to fight, not bury himself in the dirt like this. Perhaps he was injured in their previous confrontation or perhaps the spawn of the Usurper's spawn is weaker than they thought.

Other infernals from the Demagogue's court arrive before Gutterface's children find anything. Some join the search while others flex their claws. There is a chirrup of pleasure and a gaggle of its children scurry back to gather at Gutterface's ankles. A clawed hand tugs at the loose skin of its knee, calling for attention.

Gutterface looks down to see a cluster of faces peering up, hope scrawled on their sharp little features.

They reek of Samael but there is no sign of him. Deep within its shell, Gutterface feels uneasy.

The hand tugs again and it sees they are holding something out, an offering.

A toe, white as marble, capped with half a blackened nail. A hard, dry thing. Within it swirls the merest breath of Samuel's essence. A single thought, repeating itself over and over.

'Here! Here! Here! Here!'

*

Three specks trudge, alone. Around them, the land has flattened out, dull and dusty, stretching off towards the horizon and its distant mountains.

Vesper sighs. Muscles normally content to exist in secret have joined the others, aching, complaining, and within her boots, clusters of blisters grow raw with every step. The sword is ever heavier, rubbing skin red where it brushes against her.

Duet is little better. The split metal of her armour has been bent back into rough shape, jagged edges trimmed away. Sweaty bandages peek through holes.

Even the kid's usual bounciness seems diminished.

A wind blows across them, lacklustre.

Beneath their feet, abandoned goods blend slowly with

the landscape. A clothes rack juts out like the arm of a drowning man. A helmet, half-buried and camouflaged with dust catches Vesper's foot, making her stumble.

The kid snorts but when Vesper looks at him, his attention is elsewhere, his expression innocent.

Vesper opens her mouth to speak but one look at Duet's demeanour changes her mind. Words break down, coalescing into another sigh.

A young man balances on the shoulders of a purple-skinned half-breed, a giant pair of binoculars strapped to his head. They stand atop Verdigris' battlements, alternately scanning the flatlands and looking over their shoulders. They are in a place they should not be. This is nothing new for either of them.

The half-breed wears a resigned expression. 'You have a bony arse.'

The young man chuckles. 'That's because I have a greedy father who keeps all the food and money to himself. But don't worry, Bruise, if we pull this off, my arse will grow so fat, you'll be begging to use it as a pillow.'

'I don't care about your arse. I care about getting paid.'

'The only thing you care about is the smoke.'

'Is it?'

'Well there might be other things . . .' He wiggles his bum against Bruise's shoulders. 'But it's the smoke that gets you out of bed in the morning, or the lack of it.'

'Fuck! Stop that!'

'Why so glum? We're on the road to glory.'

'Doesn't feel glorious to me. If the marshals or your father finds out we're here, we're both in for it.'

'Then stop swearing so loud.'

Bruise pouts, lowers his voice. 'Can you see anything?'

'Patience my friend, patience. Wealth favours the bold but only if they keep their shit together. And sooner or later, the Malice will come.'

'For your sake, I hope it's sooner.'

The young man leans forward. 'Seems like my luck is in then. I see them.'

'You sure?'

'Not many others coming from the north these days. They look . . . they look pretty awful. Perfect!' He slithers off Bruise's shoulders. 'Time to go.'

'What's the hurry? I thought we had to be patient.'

He smacks the half-breed smartly on the backside. 'Fuck patience.'

'Fuck you!'

'Of course,' he replies, grinning. 'But first we get this done.'

CHAPTER SEVENTEEN

The walls of Verdigris are strong, proudly sporting scorch marks from past conflicts; they link the city to the surrounding mountains. Much of the city's past glory has gone but three of the great towers remain, gold tipped and shining in the sunlight.

A flag hangs in the weak breeze. It holds the picture of a woman's arm, bent, bicep firm, fist clenched, unquestionably human.

Vesper smiles. 'That's a good sign.'

Duet sizes up the giant gates. 'Is it?'

'When my Uncle Harm lived here, Verdigris was controlled by the Usurper and the Uncivil. He was part of the rebels that fought against them. They must have won. You see? That flag is their sign.'

'You think they'll open the doors for his niece?'

'Of course! My uncle's really nice. I'll bet he's got lots of friends here.'

Despite fatigue, they find themselves walking faster, thoughts of food and comfortable beds urging them on. Even so, progress is slow, the suns circling past the horizon, taking warmth and colour with them.

By the time they arrive, the gates are a square of black, blotting out the scant stars behind.

'Now what?' asks Duet.

'We could knock.'

'Go ahead.'

'Me?'

'You're the one with the contacts.'

'Okay then . . .' The gates seem much larger close up. Vesper swallows. The kid's head pushes against her dangling palm. 'Okay then.'

Her foot moves forward, hesitant.

An ominous creak comes from the gates and a crack of pale light appears between them.

The silhouette of a man appears in the light, small, almost ridiculous in comparison to the great gates. He scurries forward to meet them.

Vesper raises a hand in greeting. 'Hello.'

Her hand is taken and subjected to a rigorous shaking. 'Hello, my friend, and welcome to Verdigris. There is much to discuss but little time. Is that not always the way?'

'Er . . . who are you?'

'Introductions will come soon, I promise, but now we must go. This way.'

He leads Vesper by the hand, and Duet and the kid follow. They pass through the gates, which clank shut behind them.

A uniformed Usurperkin sweats by a metal wheel, muscles bulging as she turns the old mechanism tight. Her name is

Jo-lee and she is second generation, not as huge as her father but far larger than her untainted grandparents.

The man looks like a child next to her. 'Thank you, dear lady,' he whispers, 'much appreciated.' She nods as he slips something small and flat into her back pocket. 'We were never here.'

He pulls Vesper along, navigating dingy streets with the confidence of a local. 'Not far now.'

Lonely moans sound from time to time. Vesper's instinctive move towards them is checked by the others. 'Nothing you can do for those ones,' whispers the man. 'Best to keep your distance if you don't want to go the same way.'

Vesper frowns but allows herself to be led on.

A door opens in the darkness and the man darts through. Vesper, Duet and the kid follow, the door closing quickly behind them.

They find themselves in a room, small and packed with boxes. The smell of salt and meat issues from nearby. A single lamp sways, its light playing over the room's other occupant, picking out a pair of disinterested eyes and a lean purple chest.

Duet puts her hand to her sword.

Quickly, the smaller man steps between them with raised arms and an easy smile. 'So, here we are. A place to rest your heads. Not exactly home, eh? But, as my father says, the beggar cannot be the chooser.'

Vesper blinks. 'I, ah, thank you?'

'No thanks are necessary. You are a woman in need of a friend, and I am happy to be that friend.'

'Who are you?'

'My name is Ez.'

'We call him Little Ez.' Adds the purple-skinned man.

'Why?'

'Ah, it is not as you'd think. The name is ironic, given to me on account of my huge,' his grin widens, and he waggles his eyebrows, 'blessing.'

Vesper stares.

Little Ez only grins the wider. 'My associate here is called Bruise. No irony there, eh?' He chuckles as the half-breed rolls his eyes. 'I see you have travelled a long way. You are tired, yes? Of course you are. Tired and hungry. Little Ez will bring you food and lay out the finest beds for you.'

'Thank you.'

'It is nothing, the least we can do for such honoured guests.'

Duet takes in the low ceiling, the grubby crates. 'Who are we hiding from?'

'A good question. Clearly there is no pulling the tent over your eyes! Let us be honest with each other. Little Ez sees the sword you carry. Surely such a thing can only have come from the Shining City? They say it is alive. They say it is one of The Seven. Some call it the Malice.'

Duet settles into a ready stance. Only Bruise seems to notice, a muscle twitching in his hand. The kid sneezes.

'Many seek it,' continues Little Ez. 'The First has offered a great reward for any who deliver the Malice to it. And the First is wealthier than what's left of the Empire. So you see, you are hiding from everyone!'

'But,' says Vesper, 'I thought Verdigris was friendly. I thought it stood against infernals.'

'You are a good-hearted girl. I see that. It is beautiful. Like a . . . like a rare flower. Don't you agree, Bruise?' The half-breed shrugs. 'Ignore him, he's a savage with no eye for the sweeter things in life. Where was I? Ah yes, like a flower . . . But my friend, I have to warn you, flowers are delicate things, easily stepped on if you see what I mean. Verdigris will not accept infernal rule but it still needs to survive. We trade with New Horizon in the south and the First's nomads in the north. Not directly, you understand, but we all know where the goods come from. They have Demon fingerprints all over them. A sad fact but there are not many choices, and this city, for all its friendliness, needs to eat.'

'Then why are you helping us?'

'Another good question! And one I am glad you are asking. My associate and I will help you out of loyalty to the mighty Empire of the Winged Eye. We hear the Empire rewards loyalty most generously, true?'

Vesper's agreement is hurried.

'Enough to not regret not going to the First?'

'We don't have much with us,' begins Vesper, wincing as Little Ez's expression sours. 'But we'll see to it that you're richly rewarded.'

'How richly?'

'What about your own island?'

'Ah, a noble offer. But islands are worth nothing unless they are yours to give.'

'Not mine. The Seven's. If you help us,' she licks her lips. 'We'll give you Sonorous.'

Little Ez bows. 'The Seven are indeed generous. We accept their gracious offer. One thing though. How do I know I can trust you?'

Duet's answer is automatic. 'It's a crime to lie in the presence of The Seven.'

They pause, all eyes moving to the sword.

Little Ez smiles weakly. 'Of course, of course. Then it is settled.' He shakes Vesper's hand again. 'I suggest you both rest while you can. We will return with food shortly. Nobody should disturb you here but if they do . . . best to kill first and save the questions for later!'

Under the cover of darkness, a diminutive man and a sour-faced half-breed whisper.

'Interesting conversation, no?'

Bruise rolls his eyes. 'It's just us now, you can talk normal.'

'I thought you liked my sales voice.'

'No, I hate it. You sound like your bloody father. Why do you do it anyway?'

'Lots of reasons. People expect me to sound like him. You know that's not his real voice either?'

'Serious?'

'Yeah. He told me once. Said he made more sales when he used it and he told me that it's easier to lie when you don't use your normal voice. But what do you think?'

'I told you. I hate it.'

'No, you idiot. About our new friends and their very generous offer?'

'I think they're full of shit.'

'You don't think they'll deliver an island to us then?'

'Last I heard, the First helped kick the Empire out of Sonorous.'

Little Ez nods. 'I heard the same. And even if I hadn't, that kid can't lie for shit.'

'Heh. That's true. Nor the woman, thought her eyes were

257

gonna pop out of her head when the girl started lying. You reckon they got anything worth anything under those rags?'

'They look desperate and poor to me. Shame. I was hoping for desperate and rich.'

'I told you didn't I? I said they'd have nothing.'

A finger strokes Bruise's chest, soothing, and the young man gives him a sympathetic look. 'Of course you did. Now you have the joy of being right.'

'Lucky me. I suppose you got a plan though.'

He flashes Bruise a smile. 'Naturally. We go back to plan A: sell them to the First, and fast, before anyone else gets wind they've even arrived. I need to find the money to get a message out of the city. It may take a while.'

'What should I do?'

'Go feed our friends and make sure they don't do anything stupid.'

'You want me to drug them?'

'No. Don't give them any reason to be suspicious. Just be your usual self and don't smile too much.'

'Fuck you.'

Little Ez smiles and pinches the half-breed on the bottom. Bruise's half-closed eyes narrow further. 'Fuck. You.'

'Soon, my lusty friend, soon.'

The wheelbarrow is crudely made but strong. A good fit for the Usurperkin that uses it. His uniform is worn open at the collar, his sleeves rolled back over thick forearms. In each hand he carries a child's body. Even in the dark they are disturbingly still.

First one, then the other is put into the barrow, as gently

as Max can manage. He feels sorry for the parents, old friends of his, and consoles himself that they are not alive to witness the end of their line. He sprays the door to warn off any well-wishers. Another house claimed by the plague. Max sighs, sure that the barrow will be more than full before he's finished for the night.

Footsteps march loudly down the street towards him. They are heavy, purposeful, belonging to his sister, Maxi. He knows from their pace that she is not happy about something. A second set accompany them, stumbling rather than walking, as if being half dragged. He smiles grimly, knowing how it feels to be in their position.

Maxi marches into the light of the barrow's lamp.

Her hair spikes are lightening at the roots, the first signs of getting older. Usurperkin are blessed to grow strong much faster than their human counterparts and cursed to age just as quickly. For now, though, the changes are merely cosmetic.

Self-conscious, Max touches his scalp, aware of the way his body mirrors hers in all things, while his sister hauls her cargo into the light.

'One of yours,' she announces, throwing another Usurperkin down between them.

Young and also uniformed, she looks up at him, pleading.

Max groans. He has many children spread across the city and beyond. Like him they have grown too quickly into adulthood. Like him, they have a tendency to make mistakes. 'What is it this time?'

'This one opened the gates without permission.'

'I dint do nothin'!'

Maxi's hand moves smartly across the back of his daughter's

head. 'She claims she was testing the mechanism, despite the fact the city is under lockdown.'

'Ah, Jo-lee,' he says. 'That was dumb.'

She looks up at him, pleading. 'I dint do nothin'!'

Maxi hits her again. 'You opened the gates. One of mine saw people come in.'

Jo-lee's reply is too slow to be convincing. 'That's spawn shit!'

Max sees Maxi raising her hand and intervenes quickly. 'Hold on! Don't break her.'

'Don't break her? She broke lockdown, took a bribe—'

'I dint!'

'—let suns knows who inside!'

'I dint!'

'And now she's lying to her superiors.'

Max steps between them. His twin takes on the incredulous expression that heralds future violence, while Jo-lee cowers behind him. 'Right. But she's my daughter.' He rubs at the stubble of his chin, slow and thoughtful. 'So I should be the one to beat the truth out of her.'

Maxi folds her arms. 'Alright.'

*

The kid jumps onto one of the crates. He turns slowly on the spot, wobbling a little but keeping balance. Satisfaction is short-lived, however. The rotation has brought another crate into view. A higher crate. It is smaller than the one the kid currently stands on and less secure. But it is higher. The jump required is by no means certain for little legs. The kid chews thoughtfully, weighing the options. He probably shouldn't. He is quite comfortable where he is.

But the other crate is higher.

Vesper sits against a nearby stack, rubbing her empty belly. 'Do you think they'll be long? I'm starving.'

Duet has stood by the door since they left, fingers curled around the hilt of her sword. 'This isn't right.'

'What's wrong?'

'That man. His skin . . .'

'I know. Do you think it hurts?'

She shoots Vesper a quick glare then resumes her vigil at the door. 'Who cares? He's tainted. We can't trust him.'

'The other one seemed friendly.'

'He was oilier than a fish. I say we go now and take our chances.'

'Go where? We have no food. We're exhausted. If what he said was true then we can't just go walking the streets.'

'Maybe he made that up to keep us here.'

Vesper shrugs. 'Maybe.'

Footsteps approach the door, then stop. Vesper instinctively reaches for the pistol that once weighed down her pocket. It is gone, leaving her fingers to make a fist around empty air.

Duet's sword is in her hand, blade held high, ready to strike.

The door opens.

Bruise walks in, hefting a bag. It drops from his fingers when he sees Duet. 'Fuck!' Slowly, he puts up his hands. 'It's only me.'

'I can see that,' she replies, closing the door but keeping her sword up. 'What's in the bag?'

'Food, like we promised.'

'Show us. No fast moves.'

Vesper murmurs an apology as Bruise opens the bag. Inside are a trio of cooked lizards, each the size of a puppy and run through with a stick. They bear expressions of profound surprise.

Duet's sword wavers, her nose wrinkling behind her visor. 'What are they?'

Bruise shrugs. 'Mousespawn or maybe birdspawn. Hard to say.'

For a moment, they all stare at the lizards.

'I think they're birdspawn,' says Vesper, uncertain.

'Really?' replies Bruise.

The girl points. 'I think I can see nubs on the back of the one on the left. Wings could grow from them.'

Duet's sword slides back into its sheath. 'I'm not eating that.'

Bruise takes one of the skewers. 'More for us then.'

They eat in silence, Duet making no effort to disguise her dislike of the situation. Bruise assumes a nonchalant position, careful not to make eye contact.

Silver feathers ripple, restless, as if moved by an unpleasant dream. Vesper watches them, alternately chewing her lip and the unknown meat.

More footsteps approach the door and Bruise is grateful for the distraction. 'At last,' he mutters, getting up. Duet moves to one side of the door, the half-breed goes to the other. No love is exchanged between them.

Bruise's face sours. 'It isn't him,' he hisses. 'Shit, it sounds like more than one of them. Knowing our luck, it's marshals, or worse.'

Vesper hugs her knees. 'What should we do?'

Duet raises her sword but Bruise shakes his head. 'Do nothing. Say nothing. No noise at all. Got it?'

They all wait, bodies rigid, hardly daring to breathe.

The footsteps get closer, louder.

Right past the door they go, maintaining speed, growing quieter as they move on.

Bruise holds his hand up, counselling further silence.

They are so intent on the door that they do not see the kid reach his decision. Do not see him tense his hind legs.

Bruise lowers his hand and Vesper lets out a huge sigh. Even Duet relaxes a little.

The kid jumps.

One Thousand One Hundred and Eleven Years Ago

The quarry has gone, the workers persuaded to go elsewhere. In its place is a large domed building, squatting next to an innocent patch of rock.

People gather outside it, a mix of men and women of varying ages, all hoping to be accepted. They have travelled from the far reaches of the world, from the Dagger States in the west and the Constructed Isles in the east. A few have been sent straight from the growth tubes, three dozen babies frozen inside square cases, presided over by sweating Genetechts.

All seek the master's approval.

The gathering is something of an oddity, forcing an unlikely mix of social groups and designations. Conversation is strained by more than just nerves and all are grateful when the door finally opens.

Collectively, the group shows reverence, through inclinations of the head or body, by raising hands together, palms pressing.

The moment is solemn and dignified. A fitting greeting for their new master.

Massassi sticks her head outside and sweeps them all with a look. A single word is muttered, disparaging, and she withdraws again, closing the door with unnecessary violence.

For a moment the group remain as they are, then nervous looks are exchanged. An older man, uncomfortable in his ceremonial robes, scratches at his head. 'Do you think this is a test?'

Another in the group speaks up, wearing almost identical robes. 'No.' It is the first time members of the Severed Nation have spoken civilly in nearly thirty years but both are too stunned to appreciate it.

'But she said something. I'm sure I saw her lips move.'

The other man sits down on a rock, shaking his head. 'She said: "Crap."'

'Are you sure?'

'I'm sure.'

The first man scratches his head some more. 'But what do you think it means?'

'It means,' replies the second, his voice becoming shrill, 'that we aren't good enough.'

The two men sit together, joined in misery.

A young woman in a blue exo-suit strides past them, servos humming. 'I didn't come all this way to be turned down.' Her boots make deep prints in the ground as she stamps her way towards the building.

Her clenched fist clangs impressively against the door.

There is a pause.

'Open this door!' she shouts, continuing to hammer.

The rest of the group creep back a few paces, underlining the fact that they do not stand together.

With a sudden jerk, the door opens, so fast that the woman cannot stop her hand rushing down towards Massassi's head.

There is a flash of movement and a crunch as the blue fist is caught in a silver palm.

Massassi's and the woman's eyes meet.

The woman swallows in a throat suddenly dry.

'I like you,' says Massassi.

'Th-thank you.'

'Come.'

She leads the woman around the side of the building, still holding her hand, and points towards the empty rocks. 'What do you see?'

'Dust, rocks. A few hills.'

'And?'

'And . . . Is that a yellowback beetle?'

'What else?'

Curved shoulder-plates droop. 'I don't see anything.'

Massassi lets go of her hand. 'Didn't think so.'

'Wait! What do you see?'

Her eyes are drawn to a space several inches above ground level. 'I see a micro-fracture in the skin of our world and the storm that's going to tear it open.' She begins to tilt forward, as if about to fall then checks herself, planting her feet, forcing her eyes down. 'And that's just the beginning.'

'Can you stop it?'

'Not alone.'

'Then –' she tilts her head, trying to catch Massassi's eye '– let me help you.'

'You're not strong enough.'

'Then teach me.'

'Some things can't be taught.'

The woman thinks for a moment. 'They say you can make people do anything you want. Is that true?'

Massassi nods.

'Then make me see as you do.'

Massassi frowns, then smiles. The idea had never occurred to her. 'You're sure?'

'I'm ready,' replies the woman, full of the confidence of youth.

In Massassi's silver palm, an iris opens, bathing them both in brightness. She rests her hand on the woman's chest, extending her energies slowly, memories of burst essence still fresh years later. The woman's essence is stronger than most but even a dazzling firefly can vanish against the radiance of a star.

She wills the woman to be more than she is, charging her spirit, polishing, expanding.

They share a smile, blazing silver, and the light builds between them.

Too late, Massassi hears the screaming. The woman's other face, the true one is growing, stretching like a picture on a balloon, at first merely increasing in size, but then distorting, pulling apart, burning.

An exo-suit clanks to the ground, smoke pouring from its joints.

Massassi staggers back, staring in horror at her hand. When she finally looks up, she sees the rest of the group are watching her.

Old anger quickly returns, hardening her face again. 'Who's next?' she barks.

Nobody answers, except one young man, who retches noisily.

Her mouth curls in disgust and she takes a step forward.

They run without another word. A headdress and a sandal are left behind, along with thirty-six babies, frozen in square crystal.

Lips pressed together to stop them shaking, she picks up the first of the cryo-cases and carries it inside.

CHAPTER EIGHTEEN

Essence lamps lend the room a green tinge and its occupants a sickly pallor. Tough Call, once rebel leader and now Verdigris' chief official, hopes it is only a trick of the light. She has lost too many of her people to illness recently.

One by one, the leaders of Verdigris shuffle into the emergency meeting. Marshals Max and Maxi come first and flank her chair. Neither looks happy and she suspects that the fresh scabs on Max's knuckles are connected. Next comes Ezze, the stripes on his tunic curving around his belly. Cavain joins them soon after, red tattoos looking like bloodstains in the alien light.

Tough Call makes a point of looking around. 'Where are the others? Where's Doctor Grains?'

Ezze pulls at his beard. 'Having more of the fun than we are, yes?'

'Shut up, Ezze.'

'If I may,' begins Cavain, clearing her throat. The woman

irritates Tough Call, always seeming polite but never feeling so. 'Doctor Grains apologises but he cannot attend.'

'Did he say why?'

'I'm afraid it's the plague.'

'Ha!' booms Ezze. 'Even the doctors are sick!'

'Ezze,' snaps Tough Call, 'I refer you to my earlier comment.'

'Many apologies, great leader.'

'What about Snare and Galloway?'

Cavain raises a finger. 'I'm afraid Galloway is sick also. I don't know about Snare.'

'Anyone else?'

Max bends down to her ear, his whispers carrying easily across the small chamber. 'I heard he's on the prowl tonight, boss.'

'He's an architect not a bird of prey. On the prowl for what?'

'Dunno, boss.'

'He's supposed to be here.'

'You want me to go find him?'

Tough Call brings her remaining fist down on the table. 'What I want is for people to do their jobs!' She takes a breath, consciously relaxes her hand. 'No, I'll deal with Snare later. What have you got for me, Cavain? Did Doctor Grains find anything useful about the plague before he fell ill?'

'As you know, our medical supplies are a dwindling resource . . .'

'Just the useful bits, Cavain, I'm well aware of how bad things are.'

'Unfortunately, there has been no definitive progress on how the disease is transmitted and so far, none of the treatments have been effective in slowing or reversing the symptoms. Doctor Grains did note that those with partial tainting survived longer and that there have been no Usurperkin patients so far.'

'Maxi? All of yours still healthy?'

'Yes, boss, we're all good. If it could get us, we'd know by now.'

'Okay, anyone got any good news?'

But Tough Call notices Cavain has a finger raised, her manner imperious, her face a mask of patience. 'Yes, what?'

'Our stockpiles of grain are diminishing . . .'

'The useful bits, Cavain.'

'It happens that the new seeds we brought back from the wallstain are attracting new predators into the city. Some kind of bug. I fear they might have brought this new plague with them.'

'Find out! Drag Doctor Grains off his deathbed, if you have to. This time tomorrow, I want answers. Now, any good news I can tell our people?'

Only Ezze's smile lights the room, too-white teeth shining amid a sea of frowning faces. 'The mother of my children started to cough the other day so perhaps Ezze has hope for new love! No? Too soon?' His smile continues, undaunted. 'Then there is only bad news. Trade is the blood of the city, yes? But you have closed the doors, blocked its flow. The people grow restless. It is not for Ezze that I worry, for Ezze is always prepared. But you must understand, great lady, that many live straight from the hand to the mouth. Trade must go on or they will starve.'

'Get to the point.'

'Tomorrow, the nomads and the caravans come. We must be letting them in.'

'And expose them to the plague too? Out of the question.'

'It is true, some may die. It is a gamble. But Ezze will take bad odds over no odds every time.'

'No. There has to be another way.'

'Ezze could arrange for a . . . ah how to say? A quieter market to be held outside the city. Ezze could buy the goods from our people and trade on their behalf with the others. Then everyone is happy!'

Tough Call has no illusions about Ezze's motivations but her people need to eat. 'Alright, make it happen.'

'Ezze will need the help from those blessed with health and green skin. Perhaps Marshal Max and his many children could help poor Ezze with the lifting and moving?'

'Maxi will go with you.'

'Delightful!' exclaims Ezze, his smile a shade dimmer than before.

'Now get moving, the lot of you.'

They file out much faster than they arrived. Max pauses by the door, glances back. Tough Call watches the sweat weave its way down the creases in his forehead.

'Well?'

'I got some news, boss. Bad news.'

She beckons him closer. 'Then keep your voice down, for suns' sake.'

'Right, boss.' He squats down on his haunches in front of her but she still has to look up to meet his eyes. 'My daughter, Jo-lee, opened the gates.'

'What! When?'

'Uh, just before I came here.'

'I take it they're shut again now.' Max nods. 'But?'

'But she let some people in.'

'Who?'

'She don't know. There were two of them, some kind of soldier and a girl carrying a sword that looked too big for her. Oh and they had a little pet goat with them.'

Tough Call is on her feet. 'Was the soldier in armour?'

'I think so. What's wrong, boss?'

'It's the Malice, you idiot! The Malice is in my city and I bet I'm the last one on the council to know it.'

She makes for the door. 'Meet me downstairs in twenty minutes with everyone you trust.' Pausing, she turns back to the Usurperkin. 'And Max, break out the weapons. The big ones.'

Remarkably, the kid is unharmed. He stands in an oasis of calm surrounded by chaos. Cheap crates have cracked easily, spilling their treasures. Fat beetle corpses glint like gemstones as they emerge into the light, a waterfall of insects, shrieking with voices of broken glass.

Bruise swears several times but the exact nature and colour of the oaths are lost in the cacophony. Vesper and Duet join him anyway.

The noise ends abruptly, leaving echoes to ring in their place, ear filling and awful.

Eventually, they too clear, allowing the sounds of the night back in. Girl, Harmonised and half-breed all strain to listen, hoping that the room has contained the worst of the disturbance.

A brief optimistic quiet is broken by the sound of footsteps returning, more careful this time.

Bruise goes a paler shade of purple.

Duet readies herself by the door.

The kid skips easily up the broken crates until he stands on the highest one, triumphant.

273

Someone knocks from the other side. 'Open up.'

Vesper pushes one of the crates in front of it.

'Open up, I say!'

Vesper grabs another but this one is too heavy for her to move alone. 'Help me,' she hisses at Bruise.

The half-breed's face is a picture of incomprehension. 'What's the point?'

Duet keeps her eyes on the door. 'Don't make me come over there.'

Bruise is no stranger to threats, he assesses this one instantly and sets to work with uncommon vigour.

Knocking turns to pounding and soon the door shakes in its frame. Vesper and Bruise bolster it first with crates, then their own bodies.

The pounding gets stronger, more rhythmic. The strikes of a ram. Each jolt is felt through the door, through the barricade, through their shoulders. And yet, they hold.

The pounding stops. Voices are heard on the other side of the door, the unmistakable sounds of orders being given. A new noise begins, like a helicopter's engine, high pitched and spinning and fast.

Unnoticed by the others, the sword on Vesper's back twitches, an eye opening as if nudged awake.

'Is there another way out?' yells Vesper.

Bruise just looks at the floor.

'Could we try talking to them?' The question elicits a choked noise from the half-breed, part sob, part laugh.

'Then what are we going to do?'

'Save your breath,' replies Duet, 'for the fighting.'

*   *   *

Tough Call hefts the long tube onto her shoulder. Silvered scroll-work runs its length, beautiful symbols unread for more than a millennium. It has been twelve years since she last held it and unlike her, it hasn't aged a day.

A squad of young Usurperkin stand with her, weapons appearing normal in their oversized hands. Several of them are smiling.

Max is still sweating and not from the exercise. 'Bad news, boss.'

'What now?'

'I got the weapons like you said but some of them are missing.'

Her knuckles whiten around the launcher's grip. 'Someone broke in?'

'Dunno boss. Nuthin's broke. But they took some of our big guns.'

Before she has time to retort, they hear the sound of spitting metal, deep and fast.

Tough Call turns towards the sound. 'That came from the north quarter. Go, go, go!'

Humming slugs of metal punch through the door, a swarm of singing death, shredding it and the crates behind. One goes through Bruise's shoulder, another through his leg, tossing him across the room. Vesper barely has time to register the blockade disintegrating in front of her. The sword hums angrily on her back, a counter-note to the singing bullets, urging them away. But the sword is sheathed, its voice muffled. Bullets bend but not completely, stinging an ear, grazing a thigh. Vesper throws herself to the floor, arms and legs spread flat.

A few seconds later, the pain kicks in.

The kid wobbles on his collapsing perch, bleating and jumping clear.

Duet stays by the door, crouched low, waiting. Bullets chip away at the wall, inches from her head. She doesn't move, body clenched in expectation of more injury. This time, she is lucky.

As quickly as it began, the gunfire stops, though the engine continues to whine in the background.

Through the shattered mess of the doorway, people come, hooded and darkly dressed. In their arms they heft guns that are too big for them, long nosed and elegant weapons of another age, meant for better things.

Two clamber over the wreckage, intent on Vesper and the sword at her back. One stays in the doorway, covering them.

Duet kills him first. Her blade flicks out, finding the spot just below his chin. Blood washes over his chest in a sudden gout.

Unaware that their comrade has fallen, the two men close in on the quivering girl. She tries to back away from them but they raise their weapons and she stops, defeated.

From their left comes an angry bleat, followed by the sound of a small head connecting with a knee, the knee buckles with an ugly crack. While one drops, screaming, the other swings round his gun to take revenge on the kid. Instead of a small animal, he is surprised to find Duet there instead, her sword arcing towards his face. Instinct alone saves him as he brings the weapon up.

Sparks fly and her sword lodges deep into the gun, sticking there.

Both try to pull their weapons free. Neither succeed.

The other man on the floor recovers quickly. He realises he has dropped his gun.

Vesper realises this, too.

They both grab for it, both get a hold. Vesper cannot compete with the man's strength but she grips it tenaciously as the man tries to shake her off. Vesper's teeth jangle against each other, her arms jerk angrily in their sockets, but she holds on.

The man changes tactic. He releases one hand and punches Vesper in the face.

The girl screeches, her grip loosens.

The man pulls back again but hears an angry bleat to his left. He turns to find the kid glaring at him, head tilted, rushing forward.

At the same moment, Duet's visor bursts into light, stunning her opponent. He blinks at her, catching brief snapshots of her movements. Her left hand dropping. Blink. Returning, a knife jutting from it. Blink. Stabbing, down, stabbing down. Blink. Mercifully, he feels only the first of the three strikes.

The Harmonised whirls around to find the last man on his back clutching at a broken nose while the kid watches as if daring the man to sit up.

Duet finishes him quickly and returns to the doorway.

Vesper's breath comes too fast and she begins to shake. She looks left, then right, then again, not really seeing. Finally her eyes settle on Bruise's foot, flopping sadly out of some wreckage. The girl closes her eyes. She takes another breath, slower this time. She opens her eyes and stands up. Her legs still tremble but they manage to get her across the room.

Bruise is a crumpled mess. Blood oozes from his wounds

and veins stand proud on his arms and chest, the juices inside them vibrating. His mouth moves but no words come.

'Get down,' shouts Duet. 'We've got more coming.'

Legs suddenly weak, Vesper grabs at the wall for support. 'How many?'

'Too many.'

Max sets Tough Call down on the rooftop. She moves to the opposite edge and raises the long tube until the scope is level with her eyes. Through it she sees a cluster of figures fanning out, stalking towards a warehouse. They are hooded, dressed for stealth, unrecognisable. Their weapons however, are all too familiar.

On the opposite side of the street are three more men and a mounted gun, its barrel spinning with soft song. A relic from another age, a treasure.

Her treasure. Hers and Verdigris', stolen.

'Have your people ready to go on my signal.' She makes a few adjustments to her aim, tracking slightly ahead of the group.

Max nods, signalling his marshals crouched in the alley below.

'We giving them a warning, boss?'

'No Max. They took our weapons and are using them against our city. We're not going to give them a warning, we're going to turn them into one.' The silvery tube is light and she is strong but even so it is hard to aim steady with only one hand. Luckily for Tough Call, her weapon does not require pinpoint accuracy.

The shell fires, seeming to bulge slightly in the air, as if taking a breath.

It lands a little to the right of the group and slightly in front.

Before her eyes shut she catches the frozen moment: hooded figures, tensing, crouching, one trying to dive clear.

The next moment the figures are gone, a portion of the street too, replaced by a red-walled crater. Above, a thousand shreds of fabric float down like blossom, like black snow, mingling with broken glass and dust pluming from cracks in the shattered walls of the nearby warehouse.

Max watches, mesmerised, until she kicks him into action. As he gives the signal to his troops, she notices the blood trickling from his ear holes. Frowning, she lets the weapon slide back over her shoulder to hang from its strap and touches her own ears, relieved that her fingertips remain dry.

She returns her attention to the street. The men around the gun are slowly getting to their feet but by the time they realise the threat the Usurperkin are already on them. Outnumbered and outsized, the battle is short and unfair. Just the way Tough Call likes it.

A thick finger is raised to the sky and Max grunts in approval. 'They managed to catch one alive.'

'I'm impressed.'

The Usurperkin shows her a row of wide, blunt teeth. 'Yeah, they're gettin better.'

She jumps onto Max's back, gripping on to his neck with her arm and his chest with her legs. As soon as she is on, he clambers down the building, hands and feet sure in the dark.

They go first to the recaptured gun, already being dismantled and packed away. Two corpses lay together, the bodies wound riddled, more reminiscent of sacks than men. A young

Usurperkin eyes them suspiciously, almost hopeful they will give him an excuse to fire again.

'Good work, kids,' says Max. 'Let's see the live one.'

A hooded figure is proffered, held in the air like a large doll. One shoulder droops, broken, the other seems only marginally better.

Tough Call slaps Max on the shoulder. 'By the time I get back, I want to know everything they know. Who they work for, how big the operation is, how they got past our security. Everything.'

'Sure, boss. Where you going?'

'To see what all the fuss was about.'

She beckons for two of the uniformed Usurperkin to join her. Max's children move to flank her, taking position as naturally as him and his sister do. Pride swells in his chest as he turns back to the prisoner, flexing his fingers and feeling the knuckles complain. 'Right, let's get this done. If I know the boss, we haven't got long.'

The kid blinks. He is laying on his side. Something bad has happened, a terrible noise, followed by the urge to fall over. Dark eyes dare to open and a small head lifts up, cautious. Everything seems fine now. He stands quickly, blinking against the dust, coughing.

He sees his kind mother slumped in a pile of rubble, clutching at an injured thigh. He sees the one coloured like a giant plum quivering alongside and, by the broken doorway, the other one, part buried. She lies very still, helpless, one arm jutting from the rubble.

The kid trots over to her, watching carefully.

The arm does not move.

The kid turns a hundred and eighty degrees and one leg kicks out, hoof sparking against an armoured shoulder. There is a drowsy groan but nothing more. He kicks it again and the hand reaches for him. Skipping away lightly, he snorts in satisfaction.

Helpless, the hand becomes a fist that shakes at empty air.

From outside a voice calls out:

'My name is Tough Call. I run this city. The people that attacked you are done. What happens next is up to you. If you come out, we can talk. Might even be we can come to an arrangement, save ourselves any more bloodshed. If you stay in there, that'll put me in a difficult spot. It's late, I'm tired and, to be honest, I'd rather lose what's left of the warehouse you're in than any more of my people. So, what's it to be?'

The kid yawns. The woman's voice is far away and doesn't sound angry. Nothing for him to worry about. He sniffs around for some food. His good mother's face is twisted to one side, staring at the big eye in the sword on her shoulder.

Both eye and human seem fixated on each other, allowing the kid to nose in pockets without interruption.

He hears the voice outside talking again but ignores it, having found something that bears further investigation.

'I appreciate you might be wondering if you can trust me. Truth is I can blow you up anytime I want. It's not nice but that's the way it is. So you got nothing to lose in coming out and, for what it's worth, I'd much rather we do things the civilised way.'

The kid is almost there. He worms his snout deeper into the pocket, and nips.

281

Vesper screams, attention suddenly very much in the present. She swats at the kid, who scampers away wearing a hurt expression. The girl is too busy to notice, peering down the front of her trousers with a troubled expression.

At her shoulder, an eye closes.

Vesper breathes a sigh of relief and let's go of her waistband. But relief is short lived. 'Duet?' she asks quietly. 'Duet?'

The Navpack is pulled from her pocket, switched to torch mode. The light swings across the broken room, first illuminating Bruise's prone body, then Duet's buried one. She realises the Harmonised is speaking but the words are too muffled to make out.

From outside, the voice speaks again. 'This is your last chance to do things peacefully. I hope you're going to take it.'

'What?' says Vesper rushing to the side of the doorway. 'Who are you?'

'As I said, my name is Tough Call and I want to talk.'

'Tough Call? The leader of the rebels?'

'That's the one, though I haven't been a rebel for more than a decade now.'

'My uncle told me about you. He was a rebel, too!' The girl steps out into the doorway, immediately picked out by three white lights. She holds up a hand to shield her face, squinting through her fingers. 'My friends are hurt, they need help.'

'Come out and stand aside and keep your hands where we can see them. My marshals will see to your friends.'

Vesper complies, relieved tears pricking in the corners of her eyes. 'Thank you.'

Tough Call walks over, a strange look on her face. 'We'll

do the pleasantries later; right now, I got a question that you better have a good answer to.'

'What's that?'

'Your uncle, you said he was a rebel?'

'That's right. I think he misses you.'

'Huh. You sure that's true? Not many rebels left Verdigris on good terms. You better hope your Uncle was the exception. What was his name?'

'Harm.'

CHAPTER NINETEEN

A shielded essence lamp is the only light in the room. Little Ez holds it up, casting a pale glow across the oversized bed. The covers are expensive, a strange mix of stripes and spots cut from the hide of a creature so bizarre and rare, some consider it a myth.

Little Ez hates the covers. They are a painful reminder of how much money his father is willing to spend on things he loves. Usually, they would swell over a sleeping body. Tonight, they are smooth, flat. The bed is unoccupied, the room also.

He begins to search. The room is packed with furniture and curios, picked for resale value over aesthetics. Together they clash, a painful, mismatched assembly. Little Ez shakes his head and keeps going. Under a statue of a triple-breasted man he finds it: a battered box hidden within the base. The box is guarded with a combination lock, the key to which is a number.

Little Ez tries several. His father's age, both official,

unofficial and in combination, the year of his birth, last year's profit and many more. When he gets the right one he curses himself for a fool. It is the number of lovers his father claims to have.

The box opens on well oiled hinges. Inside is a gemstone the colour of milk, three small brain chips that have been carefully cleaned and a platinum coin that parts the light of the essence lamp with a glow of its own. He hesitates before taking them. He doesn't mean to pause, but before he can continue, a whisper of guilt makes itself known. Little Ez considers closing the box and walking away. Then he considers how much these treasures might be worth and how little of his family's vast wealth ever finds its way into his hands. He considers that it is only a matter of time before he owns these things anyway and so it is not really theft, more premature ownership.

The guilt is swiftly stamped out, the box tucked under his arm.

As he makes his way through the house, he hears the bolts in the front door sliding back, one by one, and voices he knows all too well. With a muffled curse, he closes the shutters on the lamp and dives behind a collection of second hand robes, once worn by the Uncivil's cultists.

'. . . why else would a rat be fleeing? Because Snare is thinking that the city is finished. And Snare is probably not the only one, yes? Tough Call may catch him but she will not catch them all.' Two silhouettes fill the doorway with ease, one impressively wide, the other more generally impressive. Ezze's gaze comes to rest on the disturbed pile of robes. He frowns. 'And here we are. Thank you for the escort, Marshal Maxi, but as you can see, Ezze's home has many locks. He is safe now.'

'I'm not done with you,' the Usurperkin growls. 'We've got things to discuss.'

'The business or the pleasure? There is a twinkle in your eye that is flattering, but even Ezze cannot handle so much woman. It would be his death!'

The door is shut firmly. 'My eyes don't twinkle.'

'Good, that is good. I take it from the look on your biceps that this cannot wait until morning.'

'It can't.'

'The usual, then? Lucky for you, my giant friend, Ezze is well stocked.'

'I think I'll be taking double this time, and make sure it's the good leaf.'

'And why do you think this?'

'Because if you tell me where the Malice is, I won't tell the boss about your little games.'

'Perhaps it is late or perhaps it is the speed at which you speak. Ezze is confused.'

'Jo-lee let the Malice into the city tonight. She was paid to do it by your son.'

'You are sure? There are many handsome young men in the city and Jo-lee is not . . . how to say? The quickest of fish.'

'I'm sure.'

'If it truly is Ezze's son, he will have an explanation.' His eyes settle briefly on the pile of robes badly in need of sorting and narrow. 'Perhaps even a good one.'

'He'd better. 'Cos if I find out you're playing me—'

'Yes, yes. Bones will be crunching, blood will be dancing. Ezze knows. Let us cross that when we are coming to it. For now, we will pay a visit to my boy and be hearing his explanation together. Ezze hides nothing from his friend, Marshal Maxi.'

'Where is he?'

'At this hour, he should be dreaming the dreams of the innocent. Sadly, he is neither dreaming nor innocent.'

'What?'

Ezze sighs, points. 'He's hiding over there.'

'Right.'

Maxi pounds across the room to where Little Ez cowers. Ezze follows, his customary smile slipping away.

*

The bodies have been cleared, Bruise rushed off for emergency treatment and Duet has been dug out. She and the kid exchange black looks behind Vesper's back. In place of the door stands Max, waiting patiently for an opening in the conversation.

Vesper's voice rises and falls, enthusiastic, her arms waving while Tough Call nods, asking questions from time to time.

'And then this monster came, with two heads and huge claws. And Duet was fighting it but her sword couldn't even break its scales and in the end I distracted it with some food and we ran away. And then we walked and walked forever until we got to Verdigris and that's when Little Ez met us at the gates, and he brought us here. I suppose you know the rest.'

Tough Call pinches the bridge of her nose. 'That's quite a story.'

'It is. I probably missed things out.'

'You didn't,' mutters Duet.

287

A tired smirk appears on Tough Call's face. 'I'm glad your Uncle Harm found a way to be happy. And your father, did you know I met him as well?'

'He doesn't like talking about the past.'

'I don't remember him liking to talk much at all.'

Vesper smiles. 'That's true too.'

'Well, he and I didn't meet in the best of circumstances, which is a shame. He seemed like a good man.' She looks at Vesper and pauses until she meets her gaze. 'I'm going to come right out and ask: is that the Malice you're carrying?'

'Yes.'

'Thought so. Is it true what they say about it?'

'What do they say?'

'That the sword is alive. That it's part of The Seven.'

'Well,' says Vesper, screwing up her face in thought. 'I think so. It's definitely alive. It talks to me sometimes, not like we're talking right now. But . . . I don't know how to explain it. Like it's talking into my heart.'

Tough Call gives the sleeping sword a wary glance. 'There was a time when The Seven walked the Empire, long before we were born. Apparently, They used to work miracles. You ever hear about that?' Vesper and Duet nod. 'Good. Because we've both got problems right now and I'm hoping we can help each other out.'

'I'd like that,' replies Vesper. 'What do you need?'

'My people are sick. A plague we haven't seen before. It goes for the untainted first but everyone except the half-breeds are susceptible. I was hoping you might take a look at one of them, and if you could, ask that sword of yours to help him.'

'I can't promise the sword will help but I can try.'

'That's all I can ask, we're in sore need of good news. For my part I'll try and do better by you than I did for you father. Tomorrow, the south gates will be open so that we can trade with outsiders. Be good if we could slip you out then before word gets around of you being here.'

Behind Duet's visor, an eyebrow raises. 'Bit late for that.'

'Like I said, that problem's been taken care of, right Max?'

The Usurperkin's nod is a little late. 'Right, boss.'

'But Snare was just the start. There's a lot of desperate folks out there and the First is offering big for your heads. Up till now we've had no trouble with the nomads but that could change quicker than the wind. And we're in no shape to weather a storm.'

'Can you give us supplies?' asks Vesper.

'Reckon I can stretch to that.' Tough Call offers her hand. 'Have we got a deal?' Vesper takes it eagerly. 'Good. Now, let's see about introducing you to our first patient.'

They march down dim streets, Usurperkin screening off the Harmonised, girl and her goat from onlookers with bulk alone. Ahead of them, Tough Call and Max converse unhappily.

'So, Snare stole the guns, sold us out.'

'Looks that way, boss. You want me to go get him?'

'No, he knows the tunnels even better than we do. It'd be a nightmare trying to sniff him out. Besides, I need you up here. But as soon as he pops his head up again, I want it brought straight to me.'

'Sure, boss.' He sniffs and wipes his nose with the back of his hand.

'You okay?'

'Yeah. I just miss Tina.'

She reaches up for his shoulder and gives a long squeeze. 'Ain't that the truth. Now secure those tears, Max, or you'll set us all off.'

They arrive at a set of three dwellings, piled one on top of the other, a messy sandwich of architecture. The walls of the lower and middle properties bend slightly under the strain of their own weight. Metal struts have been bolted to the outside for support, digging into the rock like the belt of an overweight giant. Original stairs have fallen away long ago, replaced by ladders riveted flush to the walls. Each of the three doors is marked with a circle, with a dot in its centre, the fresh paint glistening in the pale light.

Tough Call stops and points. 'Your patient is in the middle house. His name is Doctor Grains.'

'You're not coming in with us?'

'That house is infected. I'm not going near it! My advice would be to leave your friend here, too.'

Duet shakes her head. 'Not going to happen.'

'But—' begins Vesper, turning to face the Harmonised.

'Not going to happen.'

The ladders creak as they climb. Up close a kind of fungus can be seen winding its way around the rungs, a second skin, spreading slowly. The kid waits at the bottom of the ladder, watching them without expression. As soon as they reach the top, he begins to nibble experimentally at patches on the walls.

Time has warped the door and Duet has to push hard to get it to open. Inside, the air is musty and sweet. Her visor lights up the space. The house has been divided into quarters, each section turned to a different purpose. The one Vesper and Duet stand in is part storage, part kennel. Veins of mould line the walls, their blue vibrant against fading paintwork and a row of battered shoes lined alongside, roguish.

A pack of tame Handlings huddle in one corner, gibbering, rubbing digits together in an approximation of human nerves.

Vesper shivers and moves on quickly, Duet at her back, the Harmonised's sword hanging loosely from one hand.

The next section is full of slides, meticulously labelled and organised, arranged on row after row of tiny shelves.

The third section contains a man wrapped in a sweat drenched sheet. Fever colours his cheeks and a rash twists across his exposed chest, changing shape before their eyes, the patterns never quite recognisable. The man's eyes are closed, most of his eyelashes having already fallen away to land on sticky cheeks. Only his chest moves, jerking up and down, erratic.

Vesper hefts the sword from her shoulder and holds it out over the man, hilt first.

An eye opens, flicking over the man and then straining to turn, silvered wings flapping angrily. Vesper feels the movement, aids it, raising the weapon in her hands until an eye meets hers.

There is a long pause, then Vesper sighs, dropping her gaze.

'What is it?' whispers Duet.

'I think . . . I think the sword wants to be drawn.'

'Then draw it.'

'But I'm scared.'

'So?'

Vesper nods. 'You're right.' She forces herself to look up again, finds an eye looking back. 'Okay,' she murmurs, 'here we go.' She rests the sword on the ground, holding the sheath in one hand, reaching for the hilt with the other.

The sword begins to hum softly, its gaze growing in intensity.

Vesper's fingers pause, trembling. She takes another breath, bites her lip, reaches . . . and changes her mind. Instead of taking the hilt, she rests her right hand under one of the wings, bringing her left up under the other. They curl forward over her fingers, hooking fast.

Vesper lifts and the sheath slides away, the noise of its falling masked by the vibration of triumphant steel.

In the other room, Handlings skitter, their gibbers rising in pitch as they strain against their tethers. Duet glances warily in their direction but stays close to her charge.

Meanwhile, setting the sword's point on the floor and tilting the hilt forward, Vesper is able to bring the man back into its line of sight. Carefully, she sweeps it back and forth.

Between the blade and the man's body, the air sparks blue. Sweat evaporates and the rash turns livid. The man begins to twitch and moan.

Duet sheathes her weapon, stepping quickly around to press down on the man's shoulders.

The rash is smoking now, burning under the sword's terrible scrutiny. Vesper struggles to hold the sword steady, gritting her teeth and willing trembling muscles to stay strong.

Humming builds to a single note, pure and long. It passes through skin and bone, cleansing, changing.

And then it is done.

Duet steps back and all three watch, expectant, daring to hope.

The man's eyes open, tired but focused. 'Hello? What are

you doing in my—' He sits up suddenly. 'Hell and spawn-shit!' Despite his ordeal the man is quick to slide off the bed onto his knees, head bowed. 'By which, I mean, Garth Grains, your servant.'

Vesper embraces the sword, pressing her cheek against the flat of the blade. 'You did it! You cured him! Thank you!'

An eye widens and silvered wings flick straight in surprise, quivering with tension. After a pause, they move to touch her shoulders, resting there.

One Thousand One Hundred and Five Years Ago

Few people come to the old quarry now, and those that do come for the wrong reasons. She warns them to go home but they insist on staying, eager to master the power she possesses. Massassi kills them, one by one. She doesn't mean to. Doesn't even want to. Each time she hopes she will get it right, that her enhancements will be stable. They aren't. Essence disintegrates beneath her silver fingers, leaving empty skin and fresh nightmares.

Meanwhile, the babies grow.

Motherhood does not come naturally to Massassi. She resents their neediness, their noise, their stupidity. It is tempting to alter them, to enforce their obedience, but she worries that such an intervention would weaken their spirits and prevent future growth.

Instead, she resorts to reason and raising her voice, more the latter than the former. Every day, she takes them to the place where the world distorts and tests them for sensitivity. Every day, they fail.

Her own studies verge on the obsessive. When away from the distortion, she worries some critical change will be missed. Checking the anomaly three times a day quickly becomes four, then five, and worrying constantly in the times between. If there is ever an odd noise, an unexpected change in the weather, even a little indigestion, she immediately rushes outside. Soon, the visits become ritualised. They begin with a cursory study, followed by a detailed examination involving careful measurements, painstakingly noted. A third check of both the site and the notes is done to minimise the chance of error, followed by a final check, just to be sure.

If at any point in the process she loses concentration, she forces herself to start the whole thing again.

Over time the anomaly shifts, growing in almost imperceptible increments, shrinking some days, expanding others, an alien tide wearing on her shores, on her mind.

By their tenth year, the children are studious, focused, and very careful not to upset their carer. Despite their best efforts they cannot make Massassi smile, for they are fundamentally disappointing.

Though they try, they cannot understand even half of what she talks about and are of little use to her.

Sleep becomes a stranger to Massassi, brushing past at odd times in the day, leaving before any true rest can be had. She moves a chair outside, spends increasing amounts of her time sitting in it.

Fatigue jumbles memory, sending her back and forth from the anomaly. Often she drifts off partway through a check, restarting and restarting until despairing tears roll down her cheeks.

A hand pulls her from her dreams, gently tugging at her

sleeve. She looks up, recognises one of her charges, Peace-Eleven, looking excited. 'What?'

'I sheen it.'

'Seen what?'

Peace-Eleven can barely contain herself, jumping up and clapping hands against thighs. 'Shmoke.'

Massassi sits up, frowning. 'Where?'

'In the shpecial plache.'

She runs outside to find the other children there, clustered around the worn earth, clustered around the anomaly. Pushing past them she sees it, a thin wisp, pale enough to see through, probing into the world. The light of the sun burns at it, shrinking its potential but still it comes on, fighting to push fully through into the world. Staring at it is uncomfortable, the intruder paradoxical, both alien and familiar, repellent yet mesmerising.

For the first time it becomes aware of the onlookers, stretching towards the nearest, Quiet-Three. The boy gasps as the wisp draws nearer, not realising that opening his mouth, opening anything, is a fatal mistake.

Massassi knows. She can read the wisp as easily as she reads everyone else. Stepping towards it, her fingers spread and the iris in her palm opens.

Quiet-Three giggles as the wisp touches his upper lip. The sensation is hot-cold-sweet-pain and the boy inhales sharply, drawing the wisp inside in one quick gulp.

Essences mix badly within Quiet-Three, the slower moving human essence discolouring and cracking, the wisp of alienness boiling around it, burning itself out.

Massassi clamps her hand over Quiet-Three's mouth, letting her essence reach within. She wraps the writhing energies in bands of glowing silver, one after another, spinning a net around the whole sorry mess. When every inch has been covered, the seal perfect, she squeezes, burning and crushing until nothing is left.

The body of Quiet-Three falls to the floor, reminiscent of so many others.

While the children back away, Massassi turns to what was an anomaly, what is now a breach, a tiny perforation in the fabric of reality. She wraps her hand around it, squeezing it tight, sealing it with fire and will. The Breach pushes against her, fed by forces from another place. It is like a mouth, keen to open, hungry after its first taste of food. Around it, Massassi forms a muzzle, burning it into place.

Sweating, weak, she steps back to survey her work.

The fix is quick and dirty. A temporary solution.

But for the first time in a long time, she feels a kind of peace. The waiting is over and now she sees the problem in a new light. It is time to go back to her roots. She forgets trying to be a master or a mother and focuses on what she knows, becoming an engineer once more.

She turns towards the children, who stare at her with frightened eyes. 'You saw it?'

They don't need to say anything, she sees the answer fear-written in their true faces.

'Good. Then you will be my eyes and you will watch for more while I work.'

Peace-Eleven raises a shaky hand. 'What about him?'

The girl indicates the body of Quiet-Three. Massassi takes a shuddering breath. She had already blanked his death from her memory. The sudden reminder brings back the others, a collage of slack faces superimposed over her vision of the present.

She sways under their weight, then swallows them down with a flash of anger. 'Put him with the rest. Get Quiet-Five to help you.' She looks away, forcing her attention to the present. 'Control-Ten, get my kit and meet me in the workshop. The rest of you stay here. I don't care when you sleep, so long as there are always eyes on the Breach.'

She walks away, designs already forming in her mind. The Breach is re-framed. Not a thing to be feared, not an enemy to be fought.

Just another problem to be solved.

CHAPTER TWENTY

The kid sleeps next to Vesper on the bed. Both flop, completely relaxed, full bellies poking up the sheets. Next to them, the sword rests, equally peaceful.

Although the room is designed for one, its opulence is such that they all fit easily. Duet sits by the door, alternately looking from the small yellow pill in one hand to her visor in the other. Her lips move from time to time, shaping half a conversation. The quiet hours are always the hardest.

She lifts the pill to her mouth, drawing out the moment. Despite rationing, they are running out. The pill's outer shell yields between her teeth and she chews, wishing for the thousandth time that they still had the medgun.

'What?' she says to the visor.

The visor says nothing.

'It's for the pain. I have to stay focused for the mission.'

The visor says nothing.

'I wouldn't need them if you . . . if I was . . .' She stops, tilting her head to listen.

Yes, there is definitely someone outside the door.

Duet puts on her visor and inches her sword free, moving slowly to minimise the sound. Once ready, she raises the weapon and tears the door open.

A man kneels in the doorway, head down exposing a neck covered in curly grey hairs. Behind him are a dozen or so others, also kneeling. Their voices whisper, uncertain, feeling their way around the strange words.

Duet recognises them at once: the litany of the Winged Eye. She halts her blade above the man's neck, twists the edge away and sheaths it. 'Too close,' she mutters.

The man looks up, unaware of how near he has come to death. 'I'm sorry if we disturbed you. I'm Garth Grains, senior doctor of Verdigris, remember?'

'I remember.'

'We were waiting for the bearer to wake up. We wanted to thank her and the Winged Eye. Actually, I was hoping to talk to her.'

'Hasn't she done enough for one night?'

'Oh yes, most certainly she has. We're happy to wait.'

'She's asleep.'

'Yes, I can imagine. As I said, we're happy to wait.'

'Good for you.' She shuts the door and sits back down. Comfort isn't easy to find however, the soft voices on the other side of the door hard to shut out completely.

A long and winding yawn comes from the bed, followed by a voice heavy with sleep. 'What was that?'

'Nothing. Go back to sleep.'

'Were you talking?'

'Yes.'

'Who with?'

'Nobody.'

'You were talking to yourself again?'

Duet scowls. 'What do you mean again?'

'You do that sometimes.'

'No, I don't.'

Vesper props herself up on her elbows. 'Yes you do. You did it at Wonderland and you did it on the way here.'

'You're imagining things.'

'No, I'm not!'

'If you must know I was talking to that doctor you cured.'

'You were?'

'Yes. He wants to see you but I told him you were asleep.'

'Is that him outside?'

She tilts her head again, waits, then nods.

'Okay, we'd better hear him out.'

'But you need your rest.'

'I'm awake now and anyway, I won't be able to sleep because I'm wondering what he's going to say.'

Duet mutters something, then opens the door. 'Just you,' she says to the surprised doctor. 'The rest have to wait outside.'

He comes in quickly, expressing repeated gratitude, and kneels by the bed.

'Hello,' says Vesper.

'Yes,' he replies, head bobbing, unsure whether he should look at Vesper directly. 'What you and the Winged Eye have done for us tonight goes beyond our ability to express. But I wish to try.' He clears his throat. 'On behalf of myself and my fellow victims, we want to offer our gratitude and our loyalty.'

Vesper's smile is natural. 'Thank you.'

'The thing is, well, I don't wish to sound irreverent but there are many others in the city who are sick – the plague seems to spread regardless of our quarantine – but they are just as deserving of care as I was.' He looks at the sword, resting in the corner and swallows. 'Please don't mistake my request for irreverence. I know my place and am entirely at your mercy.'

'How many people are there?'

'In truth, I'm not sure. A few hundred at least. Of course, some of them may be dead by now and there are new cases reported all the time. It's hard to keep track.'

Before Vesper can answer, Duet steps in. 'We're not planning to stay.'

'Of course. I understand.' Doctor Grains allows himself to be escorted out but manages to give one last pleading look over Duet's shoulder before the door shuts him firmly out of sight.

Vesper flops onto her back and Duet flops back into her chair.

The kid snores.

Duet rests her head against the wall. The pill has taken the edge off her cravings, smoothing tension from her shoulders. It also gives her the urge to giggle. Attempts to restrain it result in a noise somewhere between cough and snort. When it has passed, she closes her eyes, inviting sleep to come at last.

The moment is ruined by Vesper's voice. 'I think we should stay another day.' She ignores Duet's groan and continues. 'I can't forget what I've seen. These people, they're dying. We might be their only chance.'

'What about the First? You can't help anyone if you're dead.'

'I know it's a risk but we can't just turn our backs on a whole city.'

'We have a mission, remember. We are here to serve The Seven.'

'But maybe this is the mission!' In her sudden enthusiasm, Vesper is carried onto her feet, disturbing the kid, who kicks out randomly, punishing empty air. 'This is the first time since I picked up the sword that I've felt like I'm doing the right thing.'

'Our mission objective is at the Breach.'

'That's what Genner said but he didn't know, not for sure.'

'Nor do you.'

'No.' Her fists clench at her sides. 'But there are things going on, right here, that we have to do something about. We have to.'

'This place is beyond saving. Look at it! They have mutants as marshals, there are tainted creatures in the gutters. No wonder there's a plague. We should get out of here while we can.'

'I don't like it here either. Those Handlings are horrible and the Usurperkin scare me. But they need me and I can't just abandon them. I can't. Look, if the sword wants us to move on, then we can go. But I have to at least try. Just one more day, I promise.'

'If you do this, Tough Call won't be able to cover it up. Everyone will know you're here.'

'That's why I'll need you to protect me.'

Duet raises her visor to rub at tired eyes. 'This is a mistake.'

Vesper starts pulling on her clothes. 'Thanks Duet. I couldn't do this without you.' She grabs her coat and the sword, lifting it carefully by the strap.

'You're going now?'

'You heard what Doctor Grains said, people are dying. What choice do we have?'

Duet has some ideas but she keeps them to herself, closing her visor and following the young girl out of the room.

The kid watches them go, snorts in irritation and then goes back to sleep.

*

Samael marches across the Blasted Lands, wobbling slightly with every other step. He carries Jem in his arms, a shrunken, shivering thing. He considers him as he travels, leaving Scout to watch the barren landscape for him. Why does the man shiver so? He knows there was a time when his body did such things though the sensations are increasingly hard to remember.

Perhaps Jem is dying. The thought bothers him. It is a vicious cycle. The more he thinks, the more troubled he becomes and the more troubled he becomes, the more he thinks.

Perhaps Jem is cold or hungry. Perhaps he is afraid. Can people be afraid in their sleep? Samael thinks so, sure that he has experienced such things long ago, in his other life.

Whatever the cause, he is sure the man will die if not tended to. He sends Scout off in search of food and sits by a trio of weather-scarred monoliths. Jem has little in the way of clothing or fat to keep him warm and yet heat radiates from a swollen ankle, the veins throbbing around a set of bite marks, black and scabbing over.

Samael touches the injury and Jem jolts, agitated, but does not wake.

Through the contact he is able to learn more. A slight infernal essence spreads slowly through Jem's system, reminiscent of Gutterface. There is no sentience there, just a weak and spiteful poison, corrupting some cells, killing others. He makes a drawing motion with his hand, pulling it free from the skin and catching something ephemeral with his fingertips. Inside Jem's body, the foreign essence becomes sluggish, pauses, then, slowly at first, it begins to be pulled back towards the wound. The tail of it stretches from the man's ankle to spin beneath Samael's palm, faster and faster, reeling itself into a tight black ball of spite.

Samael closes his hand, squeezing until his fist shakes. When he opens his hand again, it is empty.

Not long after, Scout returns, happy jaws holding a fresh kill. Bright blood splashes as the Dogspawn sets down its prize and begins to eat.

With a groan, Jem wakes. Eyelids snap back revealing eyes rolled right up in their sockets. They close and open several times before sense catches up. He takes in the lack of sights and fixates quickly on the fresh meat.

Scout has already torn open the victim's colourful pelt, snout buried in the juicy innards.

Jem approaches carefully on hands and knees, skinny and unsteady, swaying like a newborn calf. As he pulls at a string of meat, Scout growls and he yelps, falling back onto his bottom.

Samael lets his displeasure flow through their link and the growls turn quickly to sorry whimpers. He issues a silent command and Scout's head emerges from the gore, tail dropping. Samael nods and Scout whines one last time, tearing off a chunk and approaching Jem on his belly.

Jem stays very still as Scout leans to drop the meat in his lap. Never taking his eyes off the Dogspawn, he snatches up the offering and begins nibbling at it with small, sharp teeth.

Satisfied, Samael releases Scout to return to his own feast.

When they are done, Scout settles next to Jem and closes his eyes. At first the proximity of the Dogspawn makes him rigid with fear but a combination of exhaustion and warmth lull him swiftly into a deep sleep.

For a time, Samael sits, vicariously enjoying the sensations of a full belly. Periodically, he checks the road behind them, seeing nothing but the native spawns going about their daily business.

He does not understand this new turn of events or where they might lead but for the first time since his creator's death, he is content.

Clouds hang heavy in a breathless sky, creating an illusion of peace as the suns continue their swirling dance overhead.

With surprise, he realises Jem is awake and watching him. It occurs to him that he should probably speak but old resistances die hard. There is nothing he wants to say. Perhaps, he hopes, Jem prefers silence as well.

'Where are we?'

Perhaps not. 'The Blasted Lands.'

Questions come quickly on the heels of his answers. 'Where are you going?'

'North.'

'Why?'

'To find the Malice.'

'What's the Malice? What's going to happen to me?'

'Part of The Seven.'

'And what's going to happen to me?'

'I don't know.'

There is a brief pause in the flurry, then: 'Are there more of you? Are the knights coming to save New Horizon?'

'No. I don't know.'

'How come you have a Dogspawn for a pet? I thought only Handlers could control them.'

'I d—'

'And don't say you don't know!'

'I . . . wanted it.'

Jem looks at Samael, evaluating. 'Are you going to take me north too?'

'Yes . . . Unless you want to go home.'

'I haven't got a home.' His voice becomes flat. 'I haven't got anything.'

'I understand.'

A sudden thought makes him pale. 'Those demons, the Demagogue, are they still coming after us?'

'Yes.'

'And that trick, with your toe. Did it work?'

'Yes.'

'But they're still coming aren't they?'

'Yes.'

'Then, we need to go, right now!' He stands up and immediately regrets it, a wave of nausea returning him to the ground. 'Damn.'

Samael gets up, towering over the man. 'I can carry you.'

'I think you'll have to.'

Jem is light in his arms, barely more than a skeleton. Scout wakes with a yawn and joins them, tail waving from side to side as they set off.

'What happens when we find the Malice?'

'We make it help us.'

'Are all the knights like you?'

'No.'

'I believe you. I think you're one of the good ones.' Samael does not know what to say to that. 'I can see you're different,' Jem continues. 'You may not look exactly like the knights in the stories my mother used to tell but at least you act like one. That's enough for me. Will you tell me your name?'

'Samael.'

He reaches out, grabbing the half-breed by his upper arm.

'Thank you for saving me, Sir Samael.'

*

A new flag flies from one of Vedigris' towers, fresh and colourful against worn stone. The design is simple: a circle with a dot in its centre, with a stylised wing on either side. The Empire's sign has not been seen in the city for many years, abandoned during the time of the Usurper and the Uncivil, and never missed.

Until now.

Alone it flutters, clashing with the more populous symbols of Verdigris' independence.

Max frowns up at it as he escorts Vesper to the outer doors of the council chambers. The girl's shoulders droop with fatigue, their curve a mirror for the smile, still strong, on her face. Duet stays close, a physical barrier between Vesper and the growing troupe of people following them.

Led by Doctor Grains, the group comprises a wide variety

of citizens, united in health and a sudden love of the Empire, their demeanours full of awe and reverence, except when they turn towards Max. When that happens, pupils contract and whispers are exchanged, suspicious and charged with menace.

Usurperkin have always struggled for acceptance here, and every service they have done for the city is weighed against a host of accidents and past mistakes. That Max and his kin are unaffected by the plague is just one more reason to bear a grudge.

Just like its people, the council chambers have survived many masters, a chequered history hinted at by walls re-painted, in colours, in blood, in living tissue, then scraped clean again, stripped back to the original stone. Simple, the way Tough Call likes it.

At Max's nod, the Usurperkin guards open the way. Vesper turns and waves goodbye to the group, delighted at the way their faces brighten, and goes inside, Max, Duet and Doctor Grains following.

It is not long before they arrive at the meeting room. Tough Call and Cavain stand when they enter. 'Welcome back, Doctor Grains.' The Doctor smiles and moves to take his usual seat at the table, while Max moves to flank Tough Call. 'Please,' Tough Call says to Vesper, 'rest your legs. From what I hear, you've earned it.'

Vesper takes off the sword, leans it against the table with the utmost care, as one might a sleeping baby, and flops gratefully into one of the empty chairs. After a moment's thought, Duet sits next to her.

'How are you feeling, Doctor?' asks Tough Call.

'Never better. I've been making time to speak to everyone

who has been blessed by The Seven's grace. The success rate is excellent, with no detrimental side effects for any of the survivors.'

Tough Call's frown is made of many complexities. 'Not everyone survived the process?'

Doctor Grains and Vesper exchange a look and the girl's smile fades noticeably. 'Unfortunately, we couldn't get to everyone in time. And, while victims who are also tainted have a slower progression, they have a harder time being in the presence of The Seven. However, those that survived have been cured of the taint completely.'

'Well,' says Tough Call, 'Verdigris thanks you, Vesper, and you.' She turns to the sword and inclines her head, painfully aware of the way it has started to glare at Max. 'I've prepared all of the things Duet asked for, true to my word. They're good to go as soon as you are.'

Duet stands up. 'Good.'

'Hold on,' says Doctor Grains, also standing. 'You can't possibly leave now!'

'We can,' replies Duet. 'You can watch us, if you like.'

'But we've only helped a tiny fraction of the city. If you go now, the good work will be undone. Don't you see? The plague continues to spread. All of our attempts to contain it have failed and by the time I have isolated its transmission vectors it may well be too late. The Seven's intervention is the only thing that is certain to save us.'

Tough Call waves Grains back to his seat. 'They have their own problems, Doctor, and they've done what they can.' Cavain raises a hand, it is ignored. 'Besides, we had an agreement, and I intend to do right by it.'

Vesper reflects on what she has seen. The tensions in the

city, the grief, the constant eyes on her, hopeful, desperate. 'Well,' she murmurs. 'Maybe we could . . .'

Duet shakes her head.

Cavain clears her throat.

Tough Call sighs. 'What is it?'

'If you recall, I mentioned that we were having bugspawn problems. It's very difficult to persuade my people to go out to protect the crop pods when we're afraid it may be the bugs themselves transmitting the plague. Not to mention that these things are frightfully large up close. I'm sure that if the bearer were to pay a visit, it would scare them off in no time. Even if their leaving were only temporary, it would allow us to set up countermeasures.' She pauses, hand raised to stave off interruptions. 'It is my considered opinion that such action is essential to the long-term survival of the city.'

'I see. But these are our problems and the deal stands.' She looks at Vesper. 'We'd be mighty grateful if you decided to stay but I understand if you have to leave.'

'Well, maybe we could stay a little longer, to help with the crop pods and to contain the plague long enough for you to find a workable cure.'

Duet leans close to her ear. 'What about the mission?'

'Saving people is our mission.'

'I told you—'

'And I told you!' Vesper hisses over her. 'This matters. I have to help.' She thinks of the knights and their broken swords. Of those that died to protect her. She has to make their sacrifice count. Has to do something, anything, to make what she has seen better.

Duet folds her arms. 'What about the First?'

'The First isn't here. This plague is. We have a duty to

311

these people.' She turns away from Duet, looking at the others, lifting her chin. 'We'll stay.'

A faint mantle of gold surrounds the mountains, the red sun already gone. Uniformed Usurperkin work hard outside Verdigris' southern gates, making the most of the day's remains, packing boxes, moving crates, loading carts. In the middle of it all, Ezze stands, conducting with a maestro's skill and a sailor's tongue.

Maxi marches over to him, wiping sweat from her green brow. 'Nearly done. Do you think they'll be happy with what you got?'

'Ha! A good merchant is never happy. But even the bad ones will know Ezze made many good deals today. The caravans left full of Verdigris' finest wares, and we are returning with good money and many things much needed. We are nothing less than heroes, yes?'

'I don't feel like a hero.'

'A good sign. The worse you feel, the more heroic you are being! And that is why Ezze is not making it a habit!' His beard swallows his smile suddenly and he sighs. 'Let us finish here and get back to our beds.'

'Right.' Maxi puts a huge hand on his shoulder and Ezze covers it with his own.

The two part company, Maxi returning to her labouring offspring, Ezze moving away to a single chest set well apart from the others and hidden behind a clump of rocks.

He sighs a second time, and releases the locking mechanism. With a pop, the lid opens, revealing a young man squished tight. A stiff neck twists, and a dirty face squints into the light. 'Father?'

'Regrettably so.'

Little Ez manages to sit up in the chest. 'What's going on?'

'Ah, if only Ezze had smacked you more when you were younger. Then perhaps you would be less stupid.' He prods his son's chest with a merciless finger. 'The only thing going today is you.'

'Going? Going where?'

'Go north, go south, go across the sea, go wherever you wish! But do not go back to Verdigris or Ezze's house. You will never be going there again.'

'So, that's it, you're cutting me loose?'

'So ungrateful! So like your mother, may the suns shine softly on her corpse. You have betrayed your city and a very unforgiving woman with lots of guns. You are lucky to have your head and if you want to keep it you will make hasty with your feet.'

For once, Little Ez has nothing to say, his eyes and face blank, slack with shock.

Ezze pushes a battered box into his son's hands. 'And don't forget this. It is not so full of the treasures now but a man who steals from family must be grateful for what little he is given, yes?'

Ezze climbs onto the lead cart, unusually quiet.

Engines grumble and gears clank, bearing their full load home. Usurperkin grunt as they force the unpowered vehicles to follow.

Maxi runs alongside, waving for attention. Ezze gives it, reluctant. 'Can this not wait?'

She points into the distance. 'Nope.'

Ezze frowns and looks.

313

A lone figure approaches, well wrapped against the winds. They appear unarmed, unburdened.

'What do you think?' asks Maxi.

'Ezze thinks it would be wise to get to the gates before they do.'

'Agreed.'

Verdigris' walls are nearby while the figure comes from far away. Yet each time Ezze looks, they are closer. Horribly, impossibly closer.

Then they are in front, cutting between the caravan and the city, forcing it to halt.

'Hello friend,' calls Ezze, swiftly donning his merchant's smile. 'Are you looking for a bargain? If so you have the most wonderful timing.'

The figure looks at Ezze, looks deep. 'I am looking for something you do not have.'

'A terrible shame. Ah well, good luck in your search. Forgive us but we must be going and goodbyes are always swift in Verdigris.'

'I am the First and I ask for permission to walk among your . . . people.'

'Such things are not possible. The city is closed to outsiders, it is not safe.'

'For your kind. Verdigris' plague cannot touch me.'

'Ah, of course. But no-one of your, ah, inclinations is allowed beyond the gates.'

'I am aware of your city's laws. They were made of history, of conflict with my . . . kin. But the future is as fluid as your nature. Both will bend to my purpose.'

'Ah, friend, your confidence is a thing of beauty.'

'Name your price, man of masks, and I will meet it.' Before

Maxi can move, the First adds, 'And yours, kin of my kin, and those of everyone here.'

The group exchange glances, brows knit in thought. Consciences are wrestled with, thrown to the floor, kicked and beaten. A collective greed settles around them.

For once, Ezze would rather leave well alone but he sees which way the wind is blowing. 'Continue friend,' he says, rubbing his hands together. 'You have our ears.'

CHAPTER TWENTY-ONE

Transparent pods are arranged in grid formation. Each one is ten metres across and four metres wide, joined by a network of tubes to its neighbours. The original design is for a fully automated system but it could not predict the sudden loss of essential parts, or of the specialised tools and skills required to install them. Sweat steps in to fill the gaps. Water is pumped manually through the irrigation systems and harvesting arms are pulled along preset pathways by human hands.

Less than half the pods function adequately and even they do not always provide a full yield.

Environmental controls were among the earliest features to fail, and the pods have been perforated to allow a basic level of airflow. A swarm of insects huddle around these holes, nibbling, burrowing. It is slow going but the swarm work ceaselessly to widen the holes. When one tires, there are two more, ready to take over. It is only a matter of time before the feast will be theirs.

Cavain, Duet and Vesper stand on the edge of the grid, staring cautiously up at the bugs.

On her back, the sword begins to shake and an eye opens, staring the same way. It is devoid of caution.

Cavain pales, making her tattoos appear harsher. 'As you can see, they're here in significant numbers.'

Vesper bites her lip. 'Do they attack people as well as plants?'

'Only if disturbed. If you move close enough they'll make their warning noises. It's an awful sound. Any closer after that and they'll attack. I'm sure you'll understand if I observe your progress from inside.'

'Go ahead.' Cavain gives a slight inclination of her head, grateful, and scurries away. 'You can go too, Duet. If you want.'

'It doesn't matter what I want.' She snaps up a hand, palm out. 'I mean . . . I don't mean it that way . . . I'm going to stay.'

'Good.'

Duet nods, but lips move behind her visor, berating.

Vesper brings the sword in front of her, holding it under the wings. More practised now, she is able to lift and sweep the sword sideways, sliding it clear of its sheath.

Free, the humming of the sword vibrates through Vesper's fingers, travelling outward until it reaches the pods. Those insects nearest to the disturbance stop their attack, rubbing their front legs together, squeaking like a small chorus of violins, badly tuned.

The whole swarm freezes, then turns in eerie unison to face them.

'What do you want me to do?' asks Vesper.

In answer, silvered wings press against her hands, the sword straining to push itself towards them. She holds it as high as she can, and takes a fortifying breath before walking forward.

The pitch of the swarm deepens to a low growl.

Vesper pauses and the wings immediately tighten, squeezing, painful. Fear traps her, telling her to go forward, to run, to go forward, to run.

The greater fear wins, and she takes a step towards the pods.

Before she can take another one, the swarm explodes into action, darkening the sky with black bodies and latticework wings. It swirls around Vesper like a storm, tightening, closing.

Her young arms tremble, with fatigue, with fear and the sword dips. She has a sudden longing to be held by other, stronger hands. Thoughts of home arise, tempting. Her own bed, the company of family and a place where the greatest threat is a disgruntled goat.

She closes her eyes against the tears, forces her arms up again.

The buzzing of the swarm mixes badly with the humming of the sword, both sounds shaking her bones. She feels tiny shapes whipping by her face, scratching at exposed skin.

Then, the humming of the sword rises an octave, cutting over everything else.

Blue light flashes through Vesper's eyelids, like a skyline peppered in tiny white fireworks, detonating rapidly, impossible to count.

The great storming growl disintegrates into a mess of

whines, small and alone. Fire dances across the insects, leaping at random, leaving only husks behind. What is left of the swarm flees in clumps, like rags of paper caught on the breeze.

An eye watches them, not closing until they have disappeared from sight.

Peace descends.

Only then does Vesper dare to look. Relief comes quickly, followed by collapse.

Duet is too slow to catch her. 'Stupid,' she mutters to herself. 'You were always too slow. I would have been there.' She shakes her head. 'But you weren't. You betrayed her. You betrayed us.'

From the floor, Vesper smiles up at her, pretending not to have heard. 'We did it!'

She nods, helping the girl to stand again.

Vesper sheathes the sword once more, thanks it and puts it back over her shoulder. The action overbalances her and she stumbles until Duet puts an arm round her waist.

'You need to rest.'

'I will. And eat, I'm starving! But Duet, we did it. We helped them. Things are finally looking up.'

The nurse frowns down at Bruise's twitching body. 'I'm so glad you're back Doctor Grains. To be honest, I'm out of my depth.'

'What do we know about the patient?'

'Male, half-breed, probably early thirties. Tainting shows primarily in skin discolouration. There's no major muscle augmentation and no additional limbs. My basic exams reveal no evidence of internal reconfiguration but I really couldn't say for sure.'

'He looks familiar, have we seen him before?'

'He works for councilman Ezze.'

'Ah yes. Yes, I remember now. What's his current condition?'

'The bleeding is under control but that's about it. Blood pressure is one seventy over fifty, pulse is one twenty. He has brief moments of consciousness with varying lucidity. He's received multiple gunshot wounds of a kind I've never treated before. The bullets passed straight through him, leaving clean points of entry and exit.'

'But?'

'But he seems to have had an allergic reaction to them. His muscles are locked tight all over, his temperature is currently thirty nine and climbing, and there is severe internal swelling. It's worst at the points of injury but it's spreading. We've managed to preserve an airway, for now but unless we find a workable treatment soon he won't make it.'

'Thank you. You've done excellent work as always. I can take it from here.'

Relieved, the nurse leaves.

Doctor Grains walks around the body, nodding to himself.

A tube extends from Bruise's mouth, running out of sight through a swollen throat. Doctor Grains pinches the end, sealing it.

The sudden absence of air brings desperate consciousness. Bruise tries to move but his muscles won't obey. He looks for help, desperate, making out the doctor through the slits of his puffy eyes. He tries to speak, tries to breathe but nothing gets through the tube.

Doctor Grains leans over him, still nodding. 'May the Winged Eye watch us, measure us, judge us.'

*   *   *

320

Vesper wakes to find a pair of dark eyes watching her, accusing. She sits up and stretches. 'Have you been shut in here all this time?' She wrinkles her nose, catching a hint of something unsavoury. 'Oh, you have.' Vesper looks over to the offending corner and the kid has the good grace to look at the floor. 'I'm sorry. You must be hungry. Let's see about getting you some food.'

Absently, Vesper scratches at her face, only to feel unexpected pain. Surprised, she goes to one of the mirrored walls and examines herself.

Tiny specks of smooth skin pepper one cheek, and her left ear and temple, the remains of insect bites, burned white. Vesper studies them for a while, frowning, tilting her head to display the scars under different lights.

As she does so, Duet opens the door and slips inside. 'What are you doing up?'

'I can't sleep, there's too much to do.'

'You need more rest. It isn't— urgh, what's that smell?'

Vesper looks at the kid.

The kid tries to look innocent.

'I'm okay. I think I'm ready to go back out.'

Duet turns to the kid and shakes her head. 'Well, you can't stay here now. But if you're going to use the sword again, why not use it properly?'

Vesper begins to gather her things. 'You mean like a knight?'

'Yes.'

'I'm not sure, it just doesn't feel right.'

'What are you talking about? What doesn't feel right?'

'It's not the sword. I think the sword wants me to use it, really quite a lot. But . . . something stops me.'

Duet folds her arms, clearly not satisfied. 'Your father did it.'

'I know. Maybe I will too, when I'm ready. Come on,' she adds quickly. 'Let's get going.'

The three go out to enjoy more tolerable air. They pass through a quiet hallway, lit by essence lamps. Each flame dips slightly as they pass, leaning away from the sleeping sword on Vesper's back. Although the main door is open, the way is blocked by the broad back of a Usurperkin, shoulders thick with tension.

They cannot see her face, or the one she argues with, but their voices are clear enough. One of the plague victims has arrived in search of the cure. He is desperate enough to break containment, and unwilling to take no for an answer. When the Usurperkin tries to turn him back, words grow hostile.

A crowd waits nearby, made up of people recently cured who wish to pay respects, and those with loved ones in sore need. By contrast to their sick companion, they present a measured, patient front.

Neither the crowd or the arguing pair hear Vesper's polite hello.

'Get out of my way you big freak!'

'No. Orders say you should be indoors.'

'Screw the orders! Screw you! I'm dying!'

'The bearer's resting. She'll see more of you later.'

'Excuse me,' says Vesper, peering through the space under a large armpit. 'I'm right here.'

The victim sees her and pushes weakly at the wall-like chest. 'Get out of my way, damn you!'

Such efforts are laughable, doomed to failure, and yet, the

gesture and the aggressive feeling behind it stir something in the Usurperkin. Something violent.

'Take your hands off me.'

The request has the opposite effect, and the plague victim pushes all the harder, summoning up last reserves of strength.

'Please stop fighting,' pleads Vesper.

'Move!' shouts the plague victim.

'I warned you!'

With casual strength, the Usurperkin raises a hand, palm out, and shoves the human away. He flies back with surprising speed, feet moving like a crazed dancer trying to keep balance.

Everyone watches, held rapt as the stumble becomes a trip, then a fall, fast and hard. The crack of skull on pavement is crisp, final.

Vesper cries out and tries to push past, wanting to help the fallen, knowing it is probably too late.

The kid retreats into the hallway.

Already close to losing her temper, the Usurperkin is unprepared for new surprises. She feels Vesper pushing her and reacts on instinct, grabbing at the girl and roaring, lifting her one-handed, lips pulled away from massive teeth.

The crowd's shock gives way quickly to outrage, then anger. They have never fully trusted the Marshals or their offspring and now their suspicions, nurtured in the dark, dress up as facts. 'Murderer!' cries one. 'They want to keep us locked up!' shouts another, each one fuelling the fire. And then another: 'She's attacking the bearer!'

Duet's sword is in her hand but Vesper dangles between her and the Usurperkin. She notes the gap beneath Vesper's feet and the possibility of striking the Usurperkin's ankles, and prepares herself.

Vesper tries to speak but cannot get the words past her collar, held tight in green fingers.

At her shoulder, an eye opens, angry.

The effect is immediate. The Usurperkin roars and throws Vesper away from her. The girl sails through the air, back into the corridor, and Duet, who just has time to move her blade clear before becoming a human crash mat. For the Harmonised, it is an unpleasant experience. There is a crunch and a clatter, a grunt, a curse, and a brief glint in the kid's eye.

Too late, recognition dawns on the Usurperkin's face and rage drains away. 'Sorry,' she begins, 'I didn't realise it was you.'

Vesper's reply is only discernible as a wheeze.

And then the crowd grabs at the Usurperkin.

The doorway frames the violence, people jumping at the lone half-breed, kicking, punching, unable to bring her down. From the end of the street, reinforcements come, giant uniformed figures at full sprint. But the crowd continues its attack, and then a knife appears in someone's hand.

Usurperkin blood flows, darker than untainted blood but just as red.

'For the Winged Eye!' shouts a man, holding the knife proudly aloft.

Duet gets to her feet and moves to the door, shutting it and slamming the bolts home. Horrific sights are banished but the noises continue on the other side, relentless.

Finally, Vesper finds her voice: 'No!'

Duet scoops up her sword with one hand and the girl with another. 'Let's find another way out.'

'No,' says Vesper. 'We have to stop them!'

'They're past listening,' she replies, moving deeper into the building. 'Come on.'

But Vesper doesn't follow. With frenzied hands, she unbolts the door and jumps outside.

More people have arrived and even the mighty Usurperkin struggle to contain them.

'Stop!' shouts Vesper. 'In the name of The Seven, stop!'

Most don't hear her over the sounds of melee but a few do, and they add their voices to hers. A ripple of calm spreads out, those on the edges of the crowd kneeling before the watchful eye of the sword. In moments, everyone has stopped, even the Usurperkin, though they do not join the others on the floor.

The air remains tense however, a storm of bloody fists and old hatreds, ready to break.

The moment grows, the pressure with it.

Vesper swallows, licks her dry lips and begins to speak.

A girl's words drift across a crowded street. Bright yet unpolished, the speech is made fresh by its faltering earnestness. 'I don't know you very well. Most of you don't know me either . . . My uncle says it's much easier to hurt people when you don't know them. My name's Vesper by the way. I probably should have started with that.'

Like a gravity well, the gathering draws more and more people to it, over half the listeners are kneeling, and of the rest, most at least appear respectful.

'The sickness in Verdigris is really bad. I mean, of course it is, but what I'm trying to say is that I know that a lot of you are suffering, and I'm doing my best to help. It's just there's so many of you and, well, the sword, it's hard to use. I have to rest sometimes. I get tired.

'I know you're tired too. The Usurperkin are tired as well, I think. They're having to look after the city because they're the only ones the plague can't get. Serra – that's the name of the Usurperkin who was guarding my door – she didn't mean to attack me or that poor man. She was actually trying to help.

'She made a mistake . . . I make mistakes all the time and . . . well, we have to find a way to make the best of this because, if we don't, there'll be more fighting and I won't be able to get to the people that really need us. I won't be able to make them better.

'I know this isn't fair but please, I don't want there to be any more blood. I don't want you to hurt each other any more.'

Heads nod, giving silent assent. The threat of violence remains, however. It hangs in the air, held at bay by the girl and the sword on her back, but not banished, moving through guarded glances and unvoiced thoughts.

Doctor Grains arrives late and is forced to orbit the outer periphery of the crowd. At this distance the girl's words can be heard but not deciphered.

A man peels away from the shadows to stand next to him. Wrapped in well-worn travelling clothes but carrying no weapons, no baggage. Doctor Grains might think this odd were his eyes not fixated on the speaker and his thoughts full of fervour.

326

'That's a good child there,' remarks the man.

Grains pretends not to have heard.

'Makes you wonder why the greenskins attacked her.'

'What did you say?'

'Nasty it was. I saw the whole thing. Innocent man went to the bearer looking for help and the greenskins killed him. When the girl tried to intervene, they went for her as well. Would have had her too, if The Seven hadn't intervened. Bastards, the lot of them, if you ask me.'

'Tough Call will see justice done.'

'Nah, they're as thick as thieves, her and the greenies. She'll cover it up like she always does. I heard she's as tainted as they are.'

Doctor Grains rounds on the man, all too aware that Tough Call stands only a few rows in front of them. 'That's not true. She cut off her own arm rather than live as a half-breed.'

'Yeah, but she kept it didn't she? They say it's still alive.'

'True,' he replies. 'But you don't know her, it isn't your place to judge.'

'That it ain't,' concedes the man, backing away. 'That it ain't.'

Grains turns back, his view blocked by Max and Maxi's hair spikes. He can't help but notice the way an eye glares, baleful, over the girl's shoulder, how one could trace a line exactly from it to the place where Tough Call and her giant lieutenants stand. Many thoughts form, most of them unpleasant. If he were to extend the imaginary line, take it past Tough Call, he would find it piercing the man he'd just talked to. But he doesn't.

The girl's speech comes to an end and the crowd bow their heads, murmuring a prayer to the Winged Eye and The Seven. Though he does not know what was said, Grains eagerly adds his own voice in appreciation.

One Thousand One Hundred and Two Years Ago

Massassi does not know how to close the Breach. But she knows that invaders are coming, in numbers too large for her to take on alone. She had hoped to find others like her, to teach the rest of humanity to see as she does so that they could work together against the threat.

These hopes are gone.

In their place is a cold logic. If she cannot find allies, then she can make an army. Even though they could not hurt it, her charges could see the infernal as it seeped into the world. All she needs do now is give them teeth. Weapons to use against the enemy. But normal weapons will do little to beings of pure essence.

And so she makes swords.

Special blades, infused with her own essence and shaped to cut along reality's lines. Each one is unique, holding a sliver of its creator's intent, refined over time. She designs simple triggers to unleash their power, activated through specific movements combined with song. Even these are too complex for most of her followers and so she designs other, lesser weapons.

Lances of fire, fuelled by echoes of rage, bullets tuned to the sound of fury. Enough to handle the lesser horrors to come, to trouble the greater ones, perhaps.

Soon, she is forced to expand, her warehouses full of her creations, sparkling silver, humming with potential, deadly. There are many more than her two dozen charges can hope to use.

Leaving them to watch the Breach, Massassi travels once more, jump boots launching her skyward, glider holding her there.

She finds the world much changed and yet the same. The mechs are faster, the factories more numerous. Those unfortunate enough to be outdoors stoop low to avoid the heavy smog. She sees their true faces, shining through the filth, full of the same pettiness.

For a while she circles above, wondering why she bothers and what, exactly, is worth saving.

In answer, visions of the Breach swim up from her memory, clenching her stomach, locking her jaw. She descends to ground level, stepping around cleaner-mechs frantic in their futile efforts to control the ever-growing mess of an ever-growing population.

Buildings line up in height order, where tall equals important, and size struggles to compensate for more profound deficiencies. Massassi strides towards the tallest, a soaring tower of gold and glass, its peak lost in the clouds.

Doors open at her approach and, when the receptionist checks a second time, he finds that he does remember her and that she does have an appointment.

She steps into a transit tube and shoots up, passing floor after floor of automated offices, all absorbed in the completion of micro-objectives, fractions of fractions of bigger projects.

The tube deposits her at the top. Thick windows looks out across the cloudscape, making her shudder. For only she can appreciate the distortions in the skyline, deepening with agonising slowness.

She steps into a grand office, enjoying the surprise of everyone around the virtu-table.

'What is the meaning of this?' barks one, imperious.

The journey to this point has given ample time for her to prepare an answer. Half-made speeches come to mind, full of explanations, demonstrations and appeals. Now she is here, she finds she has neither the will nor the patience for any of it.

Of the twelve people attending the meeting, four are physically present. She takes them first, filling their minds with her light, sacrificing some of her new minions' flexibility in exchange for loyalty, complete and unquestioning.

Eight people disconnect from the meeting in horror, blinking out of view. In time, they will return, sending assassins ahead of their armies, mobilising everything they have against the new threat. For now, though, she has secured a victory.

Four heads bow as one and Massassi sits with them, beginning to plan in earnest, sharing ideas that become actions, actions that spread outward, birthing an empire.

CHAPTER TWENTY-TWO

Maxi follows Tough Call to the meeting room. While her leader talks, her mind drifts elsewhere, wrestling with guilt, unfamiliar.

'. . . which is worse. Either way, it's a gamble and I don't like the odds.' Tough Call shakes her head. 'One dead, three others critical. You'd think the plague would be enough for these people.'

They enter the meeting room, both drifting to their habitual places. Maxi feels the urge to run, to fuck, or hit something, anything other than stand in a room doing nothing but feel bad. She begins to twist one of her rings repeatedly.

'Are you alright?'

'Huh?' she looks up, cringing under the scrutiny. 'Don't worry about me, boss. I'm good.'

'Of course you're not.' Tough Call reaches up, puts a hand on her shoulder. 'How's Serra doing?'

Maxi shivers, relieved that her secret is safe, shocked how little her daughter's injury occupies her thoughts. 'They kicked her around a lot. Mostly, little knocks. Grains is with her now. He says he doesn't think anything vital got speared by the knife.' She looks down. 'Lost a lot of blood though.'

'At least she's in good hands. We need her to pull through. Any more deaths and there'll be riots, speeches or no speeches.'

There is a companionable silence, then Maxi adds: 'I don't get it boss, we're on their side. Why can't they see that?'

'Because they're shit scared.' Tough Call takes her hand off Maxi's shoulder to gesticulate. 'You can't see a plague, you can't fight it. It kills folk, no matter if they're good or bad, smart or dumb. It's unfair, plain and simple. People struggle with that. They're scared and angry and looking for answers. They see their own families getting sick and you and yours not even breaking a sweat. That isn't fair either. It's not your fault, it's the plague's. You're just easier to blame is all. Most people see that.'

'You really think so, boss? Feels like most people want us to go down, too.'

'Well, I don't. Verdigris needs you, Maxi. Always has, always will. Having said that, I can spare you for a few hours. Why don't you go see Serra, or just get your head down for a bit. Tomorrow's going to be another long one.' Maxi nods, trying to mask her relief as she rushes towards the door. 'We'll come through this,' Tough Call adds, 'even if we have to knock some heads together.'

Maxi stops suddenly, twisting the ring so hard it rubs some skin off her finger. 'Boss . . . I think . . . I think maybe we've got another problem.'

'What's that?'

She only half turns back, looking at Tough Call from the

corner of her eye. 'Well, I'm not sure. I mean, it might be nothing.'

'When is it ever nothing, eh? Come on, I can take it.'

'I heard that the First might have come over the wall.'

'What? When?'

Maxi takes a step backwards. 'Maybe last night?'

'And you tell me now!' Maxi mumbles an apology but Tough Call is already on her feet. 'I want the council's arses around this table in the next thirty minutes, and bring the bearer too. Drag them here if you have to. No excuses!'

Tough Call looks at the faces around the table, all tired, nerves thin and ready to fray. Ezze is attentive, almost eager. A bad sign. Max appears violent, Maxi distressed, and Doctor Grains keeps staring at her when he thinks she isn't looking. Only Cavain seems pleased, her usually immaculate nails black with fresh soil.

On the other side of the table sits a girl, pale, and her Harmonised shadow. Strangers still, and all the harder to predict because of it.

And these are the people that will fix the city's problems? She suppresses the urge to laugh and gets started.

'So, here it is, suns help us: We got a plague that needs a cure, a people that need calming down, and now the First has infiltrated the city.' She checks in with each of them, making a point of lingering on Maxi a moment longer than the rest. 'Any other problems anyone's heard about?'

The assembled shake their heads.

'Good. Cavain, how are our crop pods?'

'There are, as you are aware, long-term issues with the sustainability of the . . .' She catches the look in Tough Call's eye, trails off. 'That is to say, they are functional again. Bug free, thanks to the bearer.'

'Good. Grains, your only job until I say otherwise is to find a cure. You need anything, people or otherwise, it's yours.'

'But,' says Vesper, rubbing her eyes. 'What about me? I can cure them.'

'I'm sure you could but the First is here, and the longer you stay the worse this is going to get. How soon can you leave?'

Duet looks up. 'As fast as you can open the gates.'

'You need anything for your trip?'

'Already packed.'

'In that case, we'd better open some gates for you.'

A large crowd escorts Vesper to the gates. Some go out of awe, wishing to show respect for The Seven and their servants, most just wish to enjoy the spectacle.

The First follows, blending easily among the bodies. Only the sword, the Malice, seems bothered by the infernal's proximity, tracking it through a narrowed lid, unblinking. The First feels the hate directed against it but, while distracting, the emotion is sheathed, muted, unable to truly harm.

More concerning is the way several of the humans move together, united in their love for the girl, their essences marked with echoes of the Malice's song.

The First resolves to return to the city and stamp out such seeds before they can take root.

At Tough Call's signal, the great southern gates open and the girl stops to wave to the assembled, smiling at them until her companion takes her arm and guides her out.

The First weaves forward, casual, insinuating itself towards the front of the group.

Well-wishers continue to shout until the three travellers are well clear of the city's border.

The First watches the gates begin to close, preparing to move. It judges the distance carefully, so that it will pass through just before they bang together. Even if pursued, it will be able to finish the bearer and her withering protector long before any help could come.

It steps clear of the crowd, moving with inhuman speed, legs suddenly blurring, propelling forward.

With a snap, the First's scarf pulls tight, held horizontal between its neck and Maxi's green fist locked tight around the other end.

Forward motion is arrested, the body moving backwards, the feet forwards.

But the First is not stunned by pain. It stops, heels balancing at an impossible angle, then spins, grabbing the scarf and hauling Maxi towards it.

The Usurperkin is unused to being pulled around, especially by those half her size. Any surprise is quickly supplanted by pain as the First catches her hands, bending back her fingers far further than nature intended.

Free again, the First turns back to the gates, sprinting to make it through what remains of the gap between them.

Too late, it feels the mood around it, sees the weapons appearing in the hands of the crowd. Silvered guns and winged launchers.

Normally it would have detected the trap, reading the mortals as if they were signposts, but the Malice has distracted it.

It tries to call out, to soul-reach across the spaces and warn itself that the Malice is escaping, but bullets sing, stinging its shell and scrambling thought.

Weapons fire, repeatedly, far more than is necessary.

A fragment of the First falls.

And three times the weapons fire again, just to be sure.

Vesper and Duet leave Verdigris and the mountains behind them, packs full to bursting. Before them spread the Blasted Lands, open, barren save for a scattering of hardy shoots, sprouting in tufts from the dry earth. The kid dances between them, teeth whipping down, beheading.

Bright colours contrast with Vesper's faded coat, mementos given in gratitude. Eight bracelets, homespun, line up along her right forearm. New socks cushion her feet. Her hands still tingle from grateful squeezes and her ears ring with kind words.

A wind blows unbroken across the landscape, blocking the view with dusty ribbons. A visor is pulled down, a scarf pulled up. The kid begins to cough. Soon, it passes by. No fresh gusts come, leaving air to settle and feet to fall into the steady rhythm of travel.

'Duet,' says Vesper, breaking the day's silence. 'What do you think about Tough Call?'

'What do you mean?'

'I mean about what she did.'

'She did a lot of things.'

They walk on, except for the kid, who sees a juicy stalk, waving slowly. His head moves in time, mouth watering.

'Well, you know how she got everyone to work together, even though some of them wanted to kill each other?'

'Yes.'

'And how she turned them all on the First?'

'Yes.'

'That.'

Unable to take it any longer, the kid bites at the stalk. Teeth normally suited to the task fail to cut through. The kid pulls but the stalk remains rooted. New tendrils poke out from the cracks, feeling their way. One loops around the kid's ear, another around his front leg.

'I think it was good leadership.'

'But she lied! She said that The Seven wanted humans and half-breeds to work together and that the infernals were the true enemy. But they didn't say that! The sword doesn't like the half-breeds, it grumbles when the Usurperkin get close.'

Duet scowls beneath her visor. 'Why didn't you say something?'

'I thought about it. But it all happened so fast. And to be honest, I was scared of her. But even if I had, nothing good would have come of it.'

'It is a crime to lie in the presence of The Seven.'

'That's what I thought! But what if lying is the only way to make things work, what then?'

'I don't know, I'm only a soldier. But when people disrespect The Seven, they always come to a bad end.'

A strangled bleat distracts them.

The kid struggles heroically, hooves digging new trenches in the ground, muscles straining. The stalk pulls back, trying to squeeze its prey through a crack three sizes too small.

Vesper looks imploringly at Duet.

'Fine!' she mutters, jogging over and cutting the kid loose. Resistance vanishes and the kid tumbles backwards, coming to rest on his back. In his teeth is a chunk of stalk, thick, still alive. It squeaks alarmingly as the kid begins to chew.

Having stopped, they rush down some food of their own.

'I think,' continues Vesper, as if the conversation had never ended. 'That The Seven don't care what we do or say.'

'Careful.'

'If they did, then the sword would have done something when I've told a lie, wouldn't it? And why haven't the other Six come south with us?'

'It's not our place to question.'

'Why haven't they stopped the First already? Why did they let Sonorous fall? Why did they let all those people die?'

Duet puts away her rations and gets up. 'I don't want anything to do with this.'

Vesper shouts after her. 'Why? Nothing is going to happen!'

Backing away to a safe distance, Duet kneels.

The kid edges back also, the chewing temporarily paused.

With horrible certainty, Vesper looks down to the sword resting against her pack.

An eye is open, staring at her. Full of fury, of power, raw and devastating.

Duet drops her head, lips repeating the litany of The Seven.

The kid takes another step back.

Vesper swallows but something in her rises to the challenge. Perhaps courage, perhaps a stubbornness. She meets its gaze, weathers the wave of emotion that suddenly hits her. She sees deep anger within the eye, unquenchable and potent, eclipsing her own emotions, as surely as the suns eclipse a candle. But she sees other things, too, buried deeper.

On impulse, she touches the silvered wings, then takes the

339

tip of one between finger and thumb. Tears come, though she is not sure from where. Being so close to the sword, she feels many things, keen enough to cut, to change, all woven together in a tangled ball.

But she does not feel afraid.

Days of travel blend together. Vesper is unusually quiet and, to her surprise, Duet finds that she misses the sound of background chatter. Anything is preferable to the sound of the kid torturing his tainted plant, rolling it around his mouth as it shrieks. The kid however, enjoys the challenge, wearing his opponent down slowly. A war of attrition with a certain outcome.

Dust and grit blow in bursts, shrouding the travellers, shrinking their world. Little bits of dirt worm their way into everything, in the waistbands of trousers, under nails, behind collars. Wherever they get past protective clothing, skin is rubbed, itched, irritated and even the tiniest grain leaves a lingering taste in the mouth.

As suddenly as they arrive, the dust clouds go, ripped away by the wind like a curtain, revealing the horizon once more.

It is no longer empty.

Sunslight glints off something distant, something moving. Duet wipes her visor clean, double checks. After a few moments she sees it again. 'Give me the scope.'

Vesper complies.

But another wave of dust comes before she can verify whatever it is up ahead.

Frustrated, they travel on.

Like the other dust clouds, this too passes, and Duet is

quick to raise the scope again. 'I see two of them. Both adult. One of them looks armed. The other likely is too. They've got a dog with them.'

'Do you think they've seen us?'

'Hard to say.'

'Can we sneak round them?'

'No, there's nothing to hide behind. We could take a wide berth around them, they might just ignore us.'

'Okay, let's do that.'

They strike out, leaving what passes as a path. Neither of them is surprised when the other group peel off to intercept them.

Duet stops, gesturing for Vesper to do the same. She hands back the scope and takes off her pack, checking the fastenings on her armour, preparing herself. Vesper stares through the scope, squinting against the elements. The more the girl sees, the more confusion takes hold of her face.

The kid waits with them, and chews.

Duet draws her sword.

They all appear wild, each dangerous in their own way. The man is painfully thin, his face haggard with fatigue but Duet notes he keeps one hand low, concealing something. The warrior appears like something out of a nightmare, his armour a patchwork of plate scavenged from dead Seraph Knights and hammered together in awful mockery.

The dog's fur is patchy, its body riddled with old scars, a fighting dog. The mismatched eyes are more disturbing though, one canine, one human, a sure sign of infernal tampering.

Duet remembers her briefings, recognises that this is a Dogspawn, and that means a Handler is close by; perhaps the one in armour, perhaps another, lying low in the dirt.

She looks round but does not keep her eyes off the other warrior for long. His sword is drawn, a simple chunk of pointed metal, dead and without song. She notes he moves with a slight limp, a weakness to be exploited.

The other group stop less than fifteen metres away.

Duet faces off the warrior. Vesper stands opposite the thin man, and the kid tries to avoid the curious stare of the Dogspawn.

Restless but not fully awake, the sword twitches.

Vesper takes a step forward and the Dogspawn growls softly. 'Hello,' she says.

The warrior's voice sounds dry, as if his throat belonged to a much older person. 'You have the Malice?'

'Yes.'

'I . . . need it.'

'You can't have it,' replies Duet.

'Why do you need it?' asks Vesper.

'To stop the Yearning.'

'What's that?'

'I don't know. I have seen many things come from the Breach but this is different. Bigger. I can't fight it. The strongest infernals of the Fallen Palace cannot fight it. I think only the Malice can stand against it. Give it to me.'

Duet assumes a battle stance. 'We'd die before handing anything over to an infernal.'

The man speaks up at that. 'You're wrong. He's a Knight of the Seraph.'

A harsh laugh escapes Duet's lips. 'Save your lies. Knights don't travel with demon dogs. Knights kill them.' She raises her blade. 'And so do I!'

The Malice

With some reluctance, the warrior readies himself, too.

Vesper shakes her head. 'Hold on, you want to take the sword, the Malice, to the Breach, right? We want that, too. There's no need to fight.'

'There isn't?' asks the man.

'There isn't?' mutters Duet.

'No. There isn't. Maybe there's another way.'

There is a long pause. The man looks at his armoured companion, then speaks for him. 'We could help you. And in return, you could help us.'

'We don't need your help,' says Duet. 'And we don't trust you, your demon knight or your pet. You're not fit to travel in the presence of The Seven.'

Vesper glares at her and an eye at her shoulder flashes open. 'That's enough! We're not going to fight each other. We're not, okay?' She takes a breath to calm herself. 'Let's put our weapons away and find a place to rest and eat. We can spare you some of our rations and we can talk. My Uncle says that it's easier to agree on things on a full stomach. What do you say? You look starving.'

'I don't need to eat,' says the warrior.

'Actually,' says Vesper, looking past him to the other man, 'I wasn't talking about you.'

CHAPTER TWENTY-THREE

Jem sits as close to the fire as he can. The hostile woman stays further back, sacrificing warmth for safety, her sword unsheathed over crossed legs. Samael also keeps his distance, uncomfortable in the unexpected social setting.

They shelter in a cave, tucked between some rocks. It looks to have sheltered many travellers over the years, some of whom have left mementos. A few bits of litter, a plastic sleeping mat and doodles, scratched into the stone.

The girl passes around some food, ignoring her companion's expression of disgust. Harder to ignore is the sword, leaning against the natural wall, and the way it glares at Scout when he gets too close.

'My name is Vesper,' says the girl, 'and this is Duet.'

'I'm Jem, and behind me is Sir Samael. The one chasing your goat is called Scout.' They watch the two animals running circuits around the edge of the cave. 'Don't worry,' he adds. 'He's just playing.'

'I didn't know Dogspawn could play.'

'Neither did I.'

Vesper passes a piece of dried fruit to Jem and gasps when he grabs both of her hands. 'You're so warm!' he exclaims, beaming.

'And you're freezing!'

'I know! I've been cold for so long I'd almost forgotten . . .' He trails off, smile fading.

Vesper looks at her hands, still held tight in his. A blush creeps onto her cheeks. 'You can borrow my blanket, if you want.'

Hands part and he nods, eating the fruit slowly, savouring its sweetness. After a while his eyes flicker over the sword before settling on her coat. He begins to frown. 'Where did you say you were from? I feel like I know you from somewhere.'

'I grew up outside the Shining City but I was born in a village south of here. I don't remember it though, I was too young. It got destroyed in the invasion.'

Jem reaches past Vesper to pick another piece of fruit from the open bag. 'Tell me more about the Shining City.'

'There's not much to say,' she shrugs, 'I'm not allowed to go there. What about you?'

'I was born in Horizon, grew up in New Horizon.'

'What's it like?'

'It's bad. The demon in charge is called the Demagogue and it doesn't care much for humans. We're mainly used as entertainment or slaves, or food.'

Vesper shudders. 'That's terrible.'

'That's nothing. If I told you half of what happens in the city you'd die of nightmares. And the worst of it is, nothing's going to change. The Empire of the Winged Eye and its knights, and all of its soldiers abandoned us. Even The Seven. There's no hope anymore. That's why I told Sir Samael we shouldn't go back.'

Duet mutters angrily to herself but the words are easily heard. 'Not a knight. Not fit to speak of The Seven. We shouldn't stand for it.'

Jem's thin frame begins to shake. 'Why? Why am I not fit?'

'Because you're tainted, that's why. I can see it in your teeth.'

His jaw drops in surprise. Shame follows quickly, finding its way onto sunken cheeks. No longer able to meet anyone's gaze he covers his mouth and turns away.

Vesper looks thoughtfully at Jem's back, then to the sword, then at Samael. The kid arrives, diving into her lap and burying his head.

Scout skids to a stop, panting and expectant.

She looks at the muscles playing under the ragged fur. At the mismatched eyes. The human one, blank, the canine one eager, intent on the kid and ready to play.

'And why is he tainted, Duet?'

'What?'

'Why is Jem tainted?'

The Harmonised shrugs. 'Isn't it obvious?'

'Yes. It's really obvious. I can't believe I never realised it till now.' She fixes Duet with a look. 'He's tainted because we failed him. Don't you see? The Empire failed its people. It's failing them every day. We have to change that.'

'What are you saying?'

Vesper pauses, her cheeks flushed. 'I'm not sure yet. But I think, I think things have to change. I think they've already changed and we need to adapt.' She strokes the trembling kid in her lap, aware of Scout's proximity, his head close, his teeth sharp. She reaches out slowly, carefully, giving the Dogspawn time to see what she's doing.

Scout waits, panting softly.

She begins to stroke his head.

Duet looks appalled but says nothing.

Vesper continues to stroke Scout, who settles next to her.

Then, to everyone's surprise, Samael speaks. 'He'd like it if you scratched behind his ear.'

They walk south, towards New Horizon. The soil here has never recovered from the wars or the poisons dropped on it, leaving landscape barren. Chunks of rock are all that break the open bleakness. Though the city is not yet in sight, they all feel it getting closer. Scout bounds along at the head of the group, alert for trouble. The kid joins Duet at the back, preferring each other's company to that of the newcomers.

Jem and Vesper talk often, the conversation easy between them. On her back the sword twitches, alternately watching Samael, Jem and Scout through a narrowed eye.

Then Vesper falls into step alongside Samael. 'Hello.'

Samael looks at the girl, looks away again.

'Jem's been telling me about New Horizon. I understand the Demagogue is in charge and has the support of other demons, but I don't really see where you fit in. Jem doesn't seem to either.'

'The Demagogue ruled New Horizon in the Usurper's name. Now the Usurper is gone, the Demagogue wants to rise to power and rule the infernals in its place. It has allies. Lots of lesser demons. And Gutterface sides with it. There may be others. I haven't paid much attention to the politics.'

'And you're against the Demagogue.'

'Yes.'

'Whose side are you on?'

'I'm not sure. The Man-shape thinks that I should rule.'

'The Man-shape?'

'Another infernal. It served the Usurper. It says that the one who stops the Yearning will have the Usurper's throne.'

Vesper is suddenly aware of the sword humming on her back. 'Wait, are you an infernal?'

'No. Yes. It is complicated. The Usurper made my creator and my creator made me. Before him, I was just a man. Now I am something else. The Man-shape says I am descended from the Usurper, that I was made to succeed it.'

'You don't sound very sure about that.'

'I'm not. I . . . hate them. I can't help myself. When I see an infernal I want to destroy it. But I am one of them, at least, a part of me is. I think it would be better to rule the infernals than be ruled by them.'

'And the Yearning, it that another infernal?'

'Yes. But much bigger than the Demagogue, bigger even than the Usurper was. It doesn't have a shell yet. I doubt there is anything big enough to contain it in this world. It may be it doesn't need one.'

Vesper scratches at an old scab on her temple. 'So let me get this straight. The Demagogue is fighting the Man-shape to take the throne of the infernals and the Yearning is fighting all of you.'

'No. The Man-shape does not fight. It offers the throne

to whoever defeats the Yearning; but if the Demagogue unites enough of the infernals behind it, the Man-shape will have to concede to its power.'

'And you're a threat to the Demagogue?'

'Yes.'

They walk for a while as Vesper thinks, taking it all in. So many ideas, so much to understand.

'Can I ask you something else?'

'Yes.'

'Why did you save Jem?'

'He called to me and . . . and I wanted to help him. I had to.'

'Why?'

'I had to.'

'Do you remember much of your life before?'

'Only little pieces. Some of the pieces don't feel like mine. I have some of my creator's memories inside too and others, absorbed by him and passed on to me.'

'What do you remember? Can you tell me?'

He pauses, a strange expression forming underneath his helmet. 'The smell of the sea. The feel of being in a boat, riding the waves. That I wanted a dog.'

'Do you think this Man-shape would talk with me?'

'Yes.'

'Good. Samael, Jem says you're a knight. Is that true?'

He thinks for a while, then hangs his head. 'No.'

'Would you like to be?'

'Yes.'

'Then help me. Take me to the Man-shape. Protect us. Will you do that?'

'I will.'

349

'Swear it. Swear it to the sword in the name of the Winged Eye.'

He looks at the sword, the sword looks back, a study in hatred. 'But the Malice wants to unmake me.'

'The Malice is angry but not at you. Trust me. Swear it.'

Samael looks at the girl, trying to read her essence past the sword's interference. To his half-breed eyes, she is just a shape, a tiny shadow in the light of a sun. But small as she is, her shape is distinct, enduring. He moves in front of her and kneels. 'Yes,' he says. 'I swear it, in the name of the Winged Eye, I will do as you ask.'

The suns set and stars ease their way into the sky, soft sparkles against darkening blue. None can be seen above New Horizon however. The city is covered in a patchwork of lights, dirty decorations that bleed orange into the air above.

Samael watches the city, Scout sat next to him. The Dogspawn senses the unease, seeks reassurance from its master, transmitting the desire through their essence link.

A moment later, a gauntleted hand pets Scout's head.

Jem joins them. 'Are you sure about this?'

'Yes.'

'I don't want to go back there.'

'No.'

He jerks a thumb over his shoulder. 'They're arguing again. About us.' He glances back at the two figures, makes sure they're not too close. 'That Duet is mental. I don't trust her. And even if we do manage to get past New Horizon, what's going to happen then? How are you going to protect me? I'm not sure you can protect yourself.'

Scout whines softly and Samael turns towards him. 'What did you say?'

'I said, I don't see how you can protect me if we go south.'

'Before that.'

'Before that I said, that they were arguing and that I don't trust Duet not to stick a knife in our backs.'

'You said she was mental. Why?'

'For a start, she hates us. For another thing, she talks to herself. Isn't that enough?'

Samael leaves the conversation, walking back towards the two arguing figures. They stop when he approaches. He is not concerned by the way they look at him. All of his attention goes to Duet, his half-breed eyes tuning into the play of essence around the Harmonised. The proximity of the Malice makes things more difficult, it's bright essence burning, uncomfortable. 'Duet, can I speak to you, alone?'

He does not need to read her essence to recognise the distrust in her eyes. 'I have nothing to say to you.'

'Yes. But can I speak to you?'

'It's feeding time anyway,' says Vesper, backing away.

'Go on then,' snaps the Harmonised. 'Say your piece.'

Away from the Malice's glare, it is easier for Samael to perceive details. Duet's essence ripples in ethereal currents. In places, the original shape has been lost, like a torn flag, edges fraying. Tiny tendrils of it swirl away, leaking. He looks closer, can just make out the faint after image of what was another being, mirroring, joined, now gone. Her essence reaches out to that other self but cannot find it, stretching until its edges thin and fade.

'If you have something to say. Say it!'

'You are dying.'

'We're all dying.'

'Yes. But not like you.'

'How do you know?'

'I can see it.'

Her eyes widen behind her visor, vulnerable. Despite her armour, she is exposed. 'I know what's happening to me.' She looks away. 'And I don't want to talk about it. And even if I did, it wouldn't be with you.'

'I think I can help you.' Her head snaps back up and he continues. 'My creator left understanding in me. Memories. Ideas. I can see your essence bleeding. It needs to be joined to something, completed again or it will collapse. The understanding to do that is in me.'

Horrified, Duet shakes her head. 'Join me? To what? No, I don't want to know. And no, I don't want your help. I'd rather die than become like you.'

She walks away, leaving Samael to think. Is death ever preferable to life? He has often despaired at his own metamorphosis. Struggled to comprehend what he is becoming, wished to be something else. And yet, whenever the chance to stop presents itself, he veers from it. Is this cowardice? Is it courage? He wonders which of these motivates Duet to turn down his offer. He could probably find out, pluck the secret from her essence but an instinct stops him. It feels wrong to find out that way.

Scout howls a warning and Samael allows himself to see through his Dogspawn's eyes.

Infernals spill from New Horizon's ever open gates. Most are aimless, setting off in random directions but one makes towards them directly, getting faster as its confidence in having found its prey grows.

Swift plans are made. 'It is following me,' declares Samael. 'I could lead it away from you.'

'No,' replies Vesper. 'We need you with us.'

'It's only one,' says Duet. 'Let's fight it.'

Jem shakes his head. 'If we fight it, the others will notice. We can't fight them all.'

'Then let's not fight,' says Vesper, picking up the kid. 'Let's run.'

One Thousand and
Ninety-Seven Years Ago

A war rages across the world. On the one side is Massassi and her converts, the growing subjects of a new Empire. On the other, everyone else.

It is hard to know which side will prevail. The numbers are too evenly weighted. While her enemies hole up in their bunkers, secure in rings of steel, she feels precious time ticking away. Because of this, she has made her commanders take risks, pushing forward where caution would be better.

The enemy's news-feeds describe her as mad, a power-crazed dictator with no plan save her own glorification. Her own describe her as a living god.

Massassi sits in a chair suspended high, projected screens forming a globe of lights around it. The globe is divided into sections, each displaying a different stream of data: news both international and local, business reports, updates on production targets, troop distribution, losses and gains, financial and mortal. She lets them wash over her, the globe rotating, twisting to display fresh information as it arrives.

The Malice

Her left hand rests over the arm of the chair, index and middle finger straight out. They point at a screen, fixing it in position despite the globe's movement.

This last screen shows her base in the far south. The place where the Breach lies. Ordinary cameras cannot detect the Breach and so the screen shows only landscape, unremarkable. She watches it anyway, finding the image soothing. Sometimes her charges move into view. Peace-Eleven and Quiet-Five can be seen, chatting idly as they stand watch. Massassi marvels at how tall the children have become. Time moves ever faster, out-pacing her and her plans.

The seat she has taken once belonged to the man that owned her. Or more precisely, the man that owned the parent company of the company that owned the supervisor that owned her. Despite the stresses and troubles she takes a moment to enjoy the reversal of fortunes.

The thought occurs that she could make changes to the current society: lessen restrictions, broaden horizons. Perhaps if her birth and subsequent education had been different, she would have been happier. Perhaps she could change things for the countless souls toiling blind in the factories.

But then she looks at the screen, thinks of the Breach and all other considerations vanish. Let another worry about the shape of the future. Her concern, her only concern is to ensure that humanity has one.

With that in mind she considers her options.

She sees the progress of the war told in a series of numbers. If she could get to their leaders, she could end the fighting in a heartbeat. Unfortunately, the enemy is well aware of the danger she represents even if they do not understand it.

Her face is known to every soldier, plastered across HUD's along with a kill order.

Besides, she is too important to risk. And so she hides like her enemies, sinking to their level, relying on conventional troops and Warmechs to fight her battles.

Some gambles have paid off better than others but overall the numbers are clear that the price is too high to keep paying.

Massassi is not sure how long she has before the Breach erupts, but her estimates suggest anywhere between five and twenty years. Whatever the cost, humanity has to be united before then.

Of course there are always other options, weapons that will be of little use against the coming infernals but devastating to her enemies. Both sides have them but such things are never actually considered, never placed on the menu.

The idea comes and with it the implications, the burdens that will have to be shouldered. Memories of those she has killed surface: her supervisor, her doctor, the ones that came hunting, the supplicants that came to her in good faith, to learn. And then the others, killed on her orders or while following them. Each one burns her a little. She wonders what it will feel like to have whole nations on her conscience.

Massassi clenches her metal fist, calls up the specs of the worst warheads at her disposal. Their designations are surprisingly bland. The RAN Series TK-209. The GANT Series ED-241. Payload, blast radius, fallout range, estimates for soil recovery. Numbers. Just numbers.

When she gives the order, none of her command staff object, none are capable. The missiles are prepped, codes are given by all required and, minutes after the decision is made, confirmation is given of a successful launch.

While she tracks their progress on the screen, the lone figure entering the room goes unnoticed. Under normal circumstances she would sense their intent, read it in the light of their true face. But these are not normal circumstances. She sees neither their face or the gun they carry.

Shocked broadcasts fill the news feeds, all images showing the missiles streaking towards their destinations. The enemy launches countermeasures, and Massassi watches, mesmerised, wondering what the numbers will have to say when it is all over.

The gun is high-powered. A sniper rifle able to punch through tanks from several miles distant. The figure aims it at Massassi. If she were able to see her attacker, she would appreciate how in tune their feelings and actions were, would admire their commitment, would even feel a certain kinship.

The gun fires three times with a pause between each shot for recalibration. Each blast goes through the globe of screens, through the chair, through Massassi's back and out her front, through the other side of the globe and through the outer wall of the room, out of sight.

Massassi bucks in the chair three times, held in place by the straps. Her shocked eyes remain fixed on the one screen not showing the missiles. As before, there is nothing of note. Unaware they are being watched remotely, Peace-Eleven tells Quiet-Three a joke.

Quiet-Three laughs.

The missiles reach their destination.

Massassi's eyes close.

Impact.

CHAPTER TWENTY-FOUR

They take a wide berth around New Horizon, doing their best to stay away from the infernals hunting its perimeter. Vesper often turns her head towards the distant city as they pass by, drawn by the bizarre mix of lights, by the way some flicker and the many shadows they cast.

Jem walks alongside, starved limbs struggling to match her brisk pace. 'Doesn't look too bad, does it?' he says, short of breath. 'Trust me, it gets uglier the closer you get.'

'I wanted to see inside.'

'You don't. You really don't.'

'But I do.'

'Even after everything I told you?'

'No, because of what you told me. I feel like I need to see it for myself.'

'You're weird.'

She looks at him. 'I know.'

Scout races past. Scout races back again, alternating between running circles around Samael at the back of the group and rushing ahead. Jem wishes he had an ounce of the Dogspawn's energy.

It is a small consolation to see that Duet also struggles, though the Harmonised does her best to hide it. Jem takes what small pleasures he can, when he can.

As the last light of the day leaves them, Vesper falls back to walk with Samael, and Jem slows a little too, curious to listen in.

'Are we still being followed?'

'Yes.'

Gutterface follows, not running but keeping faster pace than its human prey. It is content to let the chase run long and mortal muscles grow weak before the fight.

It closes in on them over the night, by inches, drawn out, agonising.

Duet stops and leans forward, hands resting on thighs. 'Enough . . . We stand here.'

'Are we far enough from New Horizon?' asks Vesper.

'Don't care . . . Any further . . . and I'll have nothing left to fight with.'

They prepare themselves as best they can. Duet catches her breath, stretches aching muscles, draws her sword. Jem sits on the floor shivering with fear and cold. Vesper wraps a blanket over razor thin shoulders and helps him to drink. Samael just waits, a metal statue, Scout sat by his feet.

With the need for stealth gone, a diamond of light shines from Duet's visor, allowing the approaching infernal to be seen in all its glory.

It is twelve foot tall, its skin dry and green, curling leather riddled with cracks, held together with dirty staples. Only loosely attached, Gutterface's skin slides over its frame with each step so that when it turns to the left, it briefly appears to be doing the opposite.

Behind it come a small army of infernals. Countless sparks of spite held in the bodies of mutated birds, rodents and children. They scurry wide, hugging shadows, waiting for a chance to cause mischief.

Samael moves to meet the big infernal head-on, Scout flanking on one side, Duet on the other.

Gutterface comes on, unafraid, on a path that will take it directly through Samael's position to where Vesper stands.

Duet prepares herself, waiting for an opening.

Scout tenses, ready to leap.

The infernal's eyes are hidden beneath folds of saggy skin. Its mouth just another of the many creases in what passes for a face. There is no expression there, no acknowledgement of the attackers.

When it steps into range, Samael swings for the head.

Immediately, impossibly fast, arms come up, knocking the blow aside with ease. Gutterface continues to advance, stride unbroken.

A normal man would be unbalanced but Samael is no normal man. His fingers stay firm on the hilt as he steps back, creating room for another attack.

Scout leaps forward this time, jaws closing around an ankle. On the other side, Duet rushes in, swinging for a knee.

Blade and teeth find their mark, slicing through old skin, meeting a wall of thick flesh, sinking in, stopping fast. An abundance of meat clusters around Gutterface's bones, protective.

Again, Samael attacks, is fended off, gives ground.

Gutterface drives on, dragging a Dogspawn behind it.

Duet grabs her sword in both hands and tries to pull it free but her blade barely moves. Heels fail to dig in and she slides along behind the infernal. Next to her, Scout has a similar struggle, four legs faring little better than two.

And then, with a sudden screech, Gutterface's children attack, throwing themselves at Duet and Scout.

The Dogspawn reacts first, releasing Gutterface from his jaws and whirling towards the new threats, snapping at them, trying to hold them at bay. Duet is not so lucky. They grab at her, attaching themselves to legs and arms, screeching and clawing, trying to find a way through her armour. Leaving her blade in Gutterface's flesh, she tries to shrug them off but there are too many. For each one she dislodges, two more jump on and soon the Harmonised is folding under their weight.

As the gap between Gutterface and Vesper closes, Jem tries to stand and falls back with a cry. Fear can only push you so far, and his body is weak, a fever threatening. There is no flight left in him.

The kid more than makes up for his failings, rushing into the night without a backwards glance.

A sick feeling settles in Vesper's stomach as Samael attacks for a third time. Before his blade can connect, Gutterface sweeps him aside with long arms, launching the half-breed into the air for a brief and ugly flight.

Behind Gutterface, she hears Duet cry out she as she is dragged to the ground. There is a chorus of laughter and then jostling as the tiny infernals swarm over her.

It is tempting to run with the kid. There are many reasons

361

why Vesper should not put herself in harm's way. She thinks about them as she steps between Jem and Gutterface.

Vesper looks to her shoulder, eyes locking with the sword's. She sees the usual rage there but something else too, a need. Seemingly of its own accord, her right hand lets go of silver feathers and hovers over the hilt.

It waits for her, glaring, silently imploring to be used. Every instinct warns against making contact. Her father used the sword once and it did something to him. Something terrible. What would it do to her? Her hand begins to shake.

Gutterface looms before her, a silent giant.

She grabs the hilt.

Takes a breath.

And draws the sword.

Free, the sword roars defiance. Vesper tries to sing with it, to give direction but is unprepared for the force of its anger. Her voice is small, untrained, easily drowned out. Sound explodes in all directions, stunning, sparking briefly in the air.

Samael rocks where he lays, as if moved by an invisible hand. Scout cowers away, whining, while the gaggle of lesser infernals cry out, running away as their shells begin to smoke.

For a moment, Gutterface pauses, fundamentally shocked by the waves of rage rippling outward. Instinctively, it retreats deeper into its shell, pulling essence back. But it is only a reflex and one quickly mastered. For alone, the Malice cannot penetrate its defences. Alone its song is not enough to destroy.

Shock marks Vesper's face, her mouth remains open but makes no noise. Her first encounter with the sword leaving eyes glazed, vacant. The sword continues to vibrate, angry, in her hand.

Meanwhile, Gutterface flows back into its extremities, refilling its vast shell. In total it has only been inactive for a few seconds. Long enough for Duet to get up and move round, leaping at Gutterface feet first.

Together, her boots connect with its kneecap, slapping loose skin against wet meat, forcing the hinge of bone too far the wrong way. There is a dulled crack and Gutterface falls sideways.

Samuel and Scout rise together, though the Dogspawn seems shaken, its head lolling, drunk. Both seem braced against an alien wind.

Vesper comes to her senses. She sheathes the sword, ignoring the reprisal in its eye, and helps Jem to stand. 'Come on!' she urges, half lifting, half dragging him away.

Duet pulls her blade free from Gutterface's knee and jumps back as the broken limb stabs at her. 'We should finish it now!'

'No,' replies Samael. 'More are coming.'

'Damn!' She kicks the stunned infernal once anyway, for good measure, and then runs after the others.

For miles around, the Malice is felt. In the gutters of New Horizon, lesser infernals screech in fear, the Demagogue wobbles uncertainly in its bowl and, on the city's outskirts, hunters freeze and turn towards the sound. Most find themselves going in the opposite direction.

Not far away, the mob known as Gutterface's children run until they meet up with reinforcements, doubling numbers. Even so, they continue to wail, intent on fleeing all the way to New Horizon. It is only when the new arrivals direct puzzled looks to the old ones that Gutterface's children realise the

Malice has been silent for some time now. There is an awkward pause, then screams trail off. They exchange looks, guilty, before rushing back to see what has become of their master.

It is already standing when they arrive, though one leg juts out awkwardly, wobbling under the weight.

Before they can shout or climb over Gutterface's craggy body, it raises an arm, pointing after their prey.

If they can remember their recent fear, it does not show, and, with a delighted whoop, they scurry into the night to hunt.

Samael carries Jem in his arms. He does not like the way the man shakes, or the pale tinge his essence has taken. Rest is needed and good food, taken in small quantities. Instead, there is travel and further exposure to the elements.

Exertions take their toll on Duet as well. She lags behind the others, labouring and angry at herself for not being more. Muttered words make a lash to drive her on.

Vesper catches the odd phrase and bites her lip. On her back, the sword's hum is constant. No special sensitivity is needed to know why.

Gutterface is coming. Picking up the chase again. Its children screech and laugh and shout, the sounds sailing easily across open ground. A horde of infernals, too many to fight.

They press on, aware that their pursuers are gaining, the noises behind growing in excitement.

The night presses in around them, playing tricks on human eyes. Rocks ambush toes, tripping, holes in the ground catch unwary feet. Vesper holds Duet's hand, the two wobbling often but staying upright. The kid scampers alongside, mocking them with his grace.

A new smell cuts through the dark, grim, rotten, stirring the stomach.

'What is that?' asks Vesper, one arm across her face.

Samael's voice is quiet, hard to hear against the mob behind them. 'We are on the outskirts of the Fallen Palace.'

Hard earth becomes moist, squelching underfoot. Quickly, each step sinks down, forcing boots to be pulled free from the sucking, lusty swamp.

Scout begins to growl and immediately Samael stops.

Vesper bumps into his armoured back. 'What is it?'

'Put on your light, see for yourself.'

Duet obliges, the beam from her visor illuminating grey mud and finger thick shoots. There are ripples on the surface where shy creatures were but moments ago, and reflected glints, winking where the beam meets a pair of eyes peeking over the surface of the water. As the light travels, it finds more eyes, tucked low within the swamp. Each pair belongs to a half-breed.

As one, the half-breeds rise from their positions, making a fleshy fence that bars the way ahead. The half-breeds are a motley collection, a mix of mutations, of misplaced organs and duplicate limbs. Despite this, three things unite them: none are tall, all have a bright mark on their person, identifying the piece that will be given to their master when they die, and all of them are old by the standards of the Fallen Palace.

By contrast, the single Usurperkin that moves in behind them is huge, a moving tower of rippling muscle. On its shoulders sits the Backwards Child. A girl's body, perfectly preserved save for the neck which twists round too far, always facing the wrong way. A wave of hair cascades down her front, spilling over bent knees to cover the Usurperkin's face.

In truth, the Usurperkin is but an extension of the Backwards Child's shell, the two bodies fused together to make a space big enough to contain the infernal's essence but most forget, treating the child's body as the one in charge.

Vesper looks at the forces arrayed in front of her, doesn't need to look at the forces hot on her heels. She looks at the sword. An eye looks back.

The sword wants to be used. Perhaps together, they would have a chance.

For a moment, she hesitates. What if she tries to use the sword's power and fails to control it. But what cost is there in doing nothing?

She closes her eyes, commits.

Her hand reaches up to her shoulder.

Silvered wings stretch in anticipation.

And Samael's voice cuts in, surprisingly close: 'Hold.'

Vesper blinks, her fingertips tingling less than an inch from the hilt. 'What?'

'I will share myself with the Backwards Child. If it is not part of the Demagogue's alliance, it will wish to know what I know.'

'And if it is one of the Demagogue's creatures?'

Samael offers Jem's body, Vesper and Duet taking him between them. 'Then you should use the Malice.'

The first of Gutterface's children arrive. The small infernals are slowed considerably by the fetid terrain, sinking to their chests, but their enthusiasm powers them on, only flagging when they realise Gutterface is still far behind them.

On impulse, Samael takes out his sword and salutes Vesper.

She forces herself to smile, despite the fear. 'Good luck.'

He nods, moving purposefully towards the Backwards Child and its followers. He sheathes his sword and pulls off his helmet, sliding his long hair carefully through it.

The nearest half-breeds step aside for him and he walks around the Backwards Child until he stands behind it. The girl's body leans back, head bending towards his, eyes intent.

He rests his hands on the Usurperkin's shoulder blades and stands on tiptoes.

One leaning on the other, awkward, their heads come close. The Backwards Child opens the girl's mouth and licks at Samael's eye.

Essences touch and the physical world drops away.

There is always danger when essences meet, the chance that one will overwhelm the other or that ideas will cross over like infections, or worse, that identities will be altered, becoming watered down versions of each other. Samael has touched the Man-shape's essence often but this is different. The Man-shape is the epitome of control, able to hold back its true power, to touch delicately. The Backwards Child is alien, poorly understood even by its fellow infernals. Samael feels the strangeness like a vortex, pulling at his weak sense of self.

He tries to focus.

'I have something to show you—'

He is cut off. The intention to display the events that took place in New Horizon is lost. He intends to show it the alliance between the Demagogue and Gutterface, to show how Hangnail was betrayed, but all of that, all of him, is swept up in other currents.

His essence is like a fragile bubble, held in the Backward Child's grasp. It would be a simple matter to crush it. Instead, the Backwards Child begins to peel.

Samael is made to remember, to walk back through his life.

He stands with the Backwards Child.

He retreats, rejoining Vesper and Duet and taking Jem from them.

Together they chase Gutterface and it's children north but they are not fast enough to catch them.

They encounter a body, on the floor, one leg broken. The shell of an infernal. Duet kicks it and it gets up again, then they chase it towards New Horizon.

From there he goes north, until he parts company with Vesper and Duet and returns to New Horizon, repairing a broken bridge with two swings of his sword and rushing back to install Jem as a piece of living artwork. He leaps into the Demagogue's court in time to see Hangnail throwing off an army of infernals and re-skin a demon cat.

Briefly, a part of him stirs, remembering that this is what he wanted the Backwards Child to see. Before he can form a question, he is moved again, backwards, always backwards.

And on the memories go, passing faster and faster.

Years of watching the Breach.

His creator, rising from the Usurper's deathgrip. Their life together, viewed in reverse, until he experiences his own birth. The moment when his creator's essence mixed with his own, blending.

But the Backwards Child is not done. From the tangled mess of Samael's essence, it finds two threads. One a simple fisherman, mortal, also called Samael. With hopes and dreams, regrets and secrets. The other, his creator, a tangle all its own.

For a moment, he remembers his old life in shocking clarity and then he is moving again, dragged into the infernal part of his heritage, submerged in memories not his own.

The present slips away, ever more distant. He knows that within him lies a fragment of his creator and within that fragment are fragments of other beings, last remnants of the Usurper and the Uncivil. He begins to panic, not wanting to go any further. Marshalling his will, Samael begs for release.

But the Backwards Child is not done.

CHAPTER TWENTY-FIVE

Aged half-breeds face off with Gutterface's children, neither side willing to act until their masters have spoken. Between them, trapped, knee deep in swamp, stand Vesper, Duet and Jem, who wakes up only to wish he hadn't.

They watch the Backwards Child and Samael, leaning together, motionless, and hope for the best. Next to them, Scout throws back his head and howls, making the kid leap straight up into the air and prompting a fresh chorus of laughter from Gutterface's brood.

While Scout continues to howl, the sword continues to hum, setting all of the infernals on edge. The two sides react in different ways. Those that follow the Backwards Child brace themselves, becoming rigid. By contrast, Gutterface's children become agitated. They cannot take their frustrations out on their prey and so they begin jostling each other. Annoyed noises accompany increasingly violent shoves until one unfortunate is thrust towards Duet. A human infant with huge ears and a face full of teeth. It splashes forward, trying to get its balance, coming to a stop only a few feet from the Harmonised.

She looks down.

It looks up.

It smiles, or perhaps it bares its teeth. The expression is hard to judge.

Duet shrugs off Jem, and her sword arcs out as the infernal throws itself backwards, the thick gravy of the swamp hampering its movement.

An ear spins through the air and lands on the surface of the swamp with a wet plop. As one, Gutterface's children watch the ear float for a moment, trembling, before the swamp swallows it. As one, they turn their beady eyes on Duet.

The air thickens and small bodies tense, ready to spring.

Duet starts towards them but Vesper puts a hand on her arm, gentle. 'Hold on.'

She holds, and the infernals do too, drawn by something else. Their collective attention goes over Duet's shoulder, past the waiting half-breeds to the two communing figures. Currents of essence change, barely felt by human or goat and Samael falls away from the Backwards Child like a dead weight.

Scout's howl becomes a whine and he charges over to his fallen master.

The Backwards Child ignores the Dogspawn, moving forward with sudden speed, the little girl bouncing on green shoulders.

Vesper looks at Jem. 'Can you stand?'

'I think so.'

She steps away from him and prepares to draw the sword.

The excitement is too much for Gutterface's children. They attack, arms waving about their heads, shrieking madly.

Duet prepares to meet them, the light from her visor intensifying. Vesper turns to face the Backwards Child. Jem produces a knife and tries to control his shaking body.

The Backwards Child moves around the group of humans and opens her mouths.

Invisible essence flows in the darkness.

And Gutterface's children slow down, their shouts drawing out, deepening, the movement of their arms less violent, more like shrubs swaying in a light breeze.

They come to a complete stop, their cries dying out.

There is a moment of utter stillness.

Then arms begin to wave again, slow, becoming faster. Legs backpedal, carrying bodies away from the fight, gaining speed as they move towards the shallows of the swamp.

It is not long before the night swallows them. Cries of excitement sound in reverse, receding.

The Backwards Child closes its mouths.

Without a word, its half-breed followers create a gap in their ranks, allowing Vesper, Duet and Jem to pass. The kid follows, hopping across slime-coated rocks.

It takes all three of them to get Samael on his feet again.

'Are you . . .? How are you?' asks Vesper.

Samael shakes his head.

Vesper pauses, takes his hand. 'Thank you.' She looks over her shoulder to the Backwards Child. 'And, thank you. I won't forget.'

The Backwards Child says nothing.

Not sure if it can understand her, Vesper bows, aware

of the sword shifting on her back, uncomfortable. She turns and hurries after the others, going deeper into the swamp.

Gutterface reaches the edge of the swamp, limping slowly, doggedly. Shapes appear from the gloom, accelerating towards it, scampering backwards. Its children.

They show no sign of slowing down and Gutterface is forced to scoop up the small infernals as they race by, gathering clumps of them with every sweep of its arms.

Its essence reaches out smartly, slapping them back to their senses.

It tastes the work of the Backwards Child and is displeased.

Shaken by their ordeal, the smaller infernals crawl into familiar nooks and hollows in Gutterface's frame, snuggling close.

Catching them all takes time but the infernal works tirelessly until all of its spawn are united and whole again. Then it interrogates them, drawing essences together within its shell, a cacophony of souls.

'What happened?'

They respond at once, answers jumping over one another. 'We chased the Malice. Yes! We caught it. Caught it, we did. I was the fastest! No, I was! To the hungry grounds, with the sucking sounds, there we found the Malice. Yes, there! I found it there first! And the Backwards Child was there. Waiting. Like it knew we would come. It wants the Malice, too. There was a fight.'

'Who fought?'

'It wasn't our fault! Not my fault! Nor mine. Nor mine. Nor mine. We knew to wait for you, but wanted to taste them so badly. To play. Just a little. Nothing broken not for good. Soften them up for you. Make you happy.'

'Who fought you? The Malice?'

'No fighting. Just a little play, then the Backwards Child spoilt it all. Breathed into our innards, filled them with wrongness. Made us run. Then you found us. You found me first!'

Gutterface withdraws from contact. It can sense the Backwards Child now, a complicating factor, and pauses to consider its options. Perhaps the Backwards Child could be persuaded, perhaps it could be defeated. Either way, the result would be far from certain. Better to withdraw, restore itself and think.

But it must think fast. The Malice is here, the chance for a new dominion with it. Gutterface wants to win, to spread its superior love and bask in its reflected warmth. And if that is not possible then it must at least be on the right side when the fighting is done.

The Fallen Palace looms ahead, a jagged silhouette of slanting structures and teetering towers. Behind it, distant, strange lights flicker on the horizon as if, just out of sight, the world is burning.

This far south, reality begins to bend towards the alien. Air remains air, just less so than it was. Other things are mixed in, unclassified, most too small to detect. Human lungs work a little harder to get what they need, and a primal urge to leave sparks deep in the heart.

An eye at Vesper's shoulder studies its surroundings, seeing hidden depths. Shortly after, the sword hums soft, purifying. Silvered wings stretch and a gentle wind swirls around Vesper, shrouding her in a bubble of normalcy.

'Those lights, are they coming from the Breach?' she asks, pointing past the Fallen Palace.

Samael nods, speaking for the first time since his communion with the Backwards Child. 'You can see them?'

'Yes.'

'How could you miss them?' adds Jem.

'The lights you see are made by the Yearning. It is growing.'

Vesper's eyes widen. 'How big is it?'

'I lack the words. It is like an ocean.'

'I thought it was just a really big demon, not . . . this.'

'It is bigger and it does not seem to need a shell.'

Jem shakes his head. 'You can't fight that.' Nobody argues and he continues. 'We should go north, leave this behind us. Live our lives.'

'Coward!' spits Duet. 'Gamma sent us here to end this demon. It is a sacred duty.'

The young man glances at the sword and lowers his voice. 'Gamma was defeated by the Usurper and that was when she was whole. And from what I heard even the Usurper wasn't as big as an ocean.'

'We must trust in The Seven.'

'Why? Why must we?'

'I wouldn't expect you to understand.'

'Yeah? Well I wouldn't expect you to—'

Vesper holds up a hand. 'Please don't. Don't fight.' She stops walking and the others do the same. 'We can't go back to our lives, not now we've seen this. I'm sorry, Jem. If we don't do something now, then things are going to get even worse. In time, the Yearning would catch us up. And then there'll be nowhere to run.'

'A few years is better than nothing.'

'Is it? How could you live knowing what's coming? I couldn't. The sword can't. It's up to us, we have to find a way. There's nobody else. Everyone's afraid of it, even the other demons. Even The Seven.' She sighs. 'You don't have to come if you don't want. But I think I have to go on.'

Duet nods along as Vesper speaks, the gesture unconscious.

'What do you say, will you come?'

'It's a poor choice, you know? Die here or somewhere else.' He shrugs. 'But I never thought I'd trust anyone again. For the longest time I thought I'd die alone.' He looks at Samael, then at Vesper. 'That thought, the thought of having nobody, still scares me even more than all of this.' He shrugs again. 'I'll come.'

Vesper's smile is both tired and bright. 'Good.'

They help each other out of the swamp and onto the angled floor of the Fallen Palace. There is no sign of anyone, the usual denizens of the Palace scared away by the presence of the Malice and so the group pauses. Food is eaten, weary bones rested. The kid hops with excitement, eager to climb. He bleats at the group, urging them to continue but having sat down, Jem is unable to get up again. He tries several times before giving up. In the end Samael carries him and the young man quickly falls asleep.

Part walking, part climbing, the group make their way towards the Man-shape's tower in eerie silence, uncontested. Even the clouds of flies keep a respectful distance.

Fungus grows over gleaming walls, covering old battle scars and past glories alike. The kid pauses to tear off a spongy strip then trots onward on happy hooves. Eventually, they reach a tower where the walls turn bronze in places, green in others.

'This is it,' says Samael, his voice echoing along abandoned streets.

Vesper cranes her neck trying to see its tip. 'It looks a long way up. Duet, you should wait here with Jem.'

'Is that supposed to be a joke?'

'No. You need to rest and we can't leave Jem here alone.'

'You think I'm going to let you go up there alone?'

'I won't be alone.'

Duet leans closer. 'I still don't trust Samael.'

'I wasn't talking about Samael.'

An eye watches Duet through a half-closed lid. She swallows, kneels. 'I'll be here when you need me.'

'Thanks.' Vesper puts her hand on Duet's shoulder. 'I am going to need you.'

Leaving Jem, Duet and Scout behind, they climb into the base of the tower, ducking under the diagonal doorframe, propping themselves between wall and floor. As they work their way up the spiral staircase, surfaces swap roles, walls sometimes walked on, sometimes leaned on. The kid races ahead, immune to the unbalancing aesthetics. More than once, Vesper slips. Elbows and knees knock on hard surfaces, echoing, adding new bruises to an already impressive collection.

The Man-shape waits for them at the top, standing by an empty window.

While Vesper pauses to catch her breath, the kid scampers about, looking for furniture to climb.

Dried mud muffles Samael's boots as he moves forward to join the Man-shape. He removes his helm and the two touch heads.

Vesper waits, the hairs on the back of her neck prickling, nervous.

377

A few seconds pass and the two figures withdraw.

Samael steps back further, removing himself from the conversation. The Man-shape catches Vesper's eye, then turns its back. Muscles work in its jaw, bones popping into the position required for speech.

'When I asked Samael to bring the Malice here, I did not expect it to come willingly.'

'Hello,' says the girl, clearing her throat. 'My name is Vesper. Are you the one they call the Man-shape?'

'Yes. And you are making an introduction, identifying yourself in order to facilitate discussion. I plucked the idea a long time ago and had almost lost it. My kind have no need for such things you see. We know who each other are even before we make contact.'

She begins to move forward but it holds up a hand, careful to keep its back to her. 'Do not come closer. I am not yet ready to face the Malice again and I cannot speak as you do and maintain the correct composition with my face.'

'You fought the sword before?'

'Not fought, no. But I watched it fight my master.'

'You were there when Gamma died?'

'Yes. I saw the Usurper end her, and later, much later, I saw her revenge.'

'What happened?'

'Come, I will show you.'

The light in the room is poor and Vesper has to use her Navpack to make sense of its contents. She sees webs strung across the ceiling, their patterns strange and drunken, peppered with ancient flies. She sees vines pushing through cracks in the floor, their purple leaves knife edged, garish.

They grow everywhere except for a space at the back of the room where two figures recline, embracing, an alien parent and full grown child, dead.

Vesper moves quietly towards them, placing each foot with care. The Man-shape and Samael enter the room behind her but do not follow. The kid does not even enter the room.

The smaller of the two figures is covered from head to toe in armour. Originally fashioned in the proud tradition of the Seraph, it, like its wearer, was twisted by the Usurper and remade. Once the metal lived, breathed, but now it is silent, captured in a last spasm of death. To Vesper it looks as if the plates were superheated and then frozen mid melt. In places the armour is stretched thin, like saliva over a screaming mouth. In others it collects in thick lumps. The figure inside the armour is shrivelled away, a collection of too-thin bones.

Both of its arms are missing below the elbow.

The larger of the two figures is a statue, bloated, silver skin tarnished with green which in turn gives way to brownish rust. Tracks of scars run the length of its body, weaving across each other, a litany of repairs. Two wings sprout from its back. Unlike the other features these remain their original size, vestigial reminders of a more graceful past.

The Man-shape speaks, unexpected, making Vesper jump. 'When my master came, it defeated Gamma and took her body as its own. But even the greatest of your world was not enough to contain my master's strength. So the Usurper took the strongest of your Seraph Knights, your Knight Commander, and mixed its own potency with him, making him into this. But then the Malice reclaimed him and sent him here, laced with Gamma's essence, a pick to reopen all of the wounds from their first struggle. When he came, the master welcomed him, drew their essences together once more, allowing the Malice to have its revenge. What was left of Gamma destroyed my master from the inside. It was terrible to behold and yet I find a symmetry in it all that is not without beauty.'

Vesper studies the face, looking for signs of Gamma but all she sees is the Usurper distorting from within, great ridges of bone stamping out her features.

'Now all that remains of my master is an echo in Samael's chest and all that remains of yours is strapped to your back. But still we must bow, even to their ashes.'

A frown begins to form on Vesper's face. 'If you don't mind, I'd like some time alone.'

Samael and the Man-shape withdraw, closing the doors, sealing Vesper inside.

She looks at the sword on her shoulder. Silvered wings wrap tight around an eye squeezed shut. The Navpack is put away, taking the light with it. She takes a deep breath then slowly, carefully slides the sword free of its sheath and holds it in her arms, the flat of the blade pressed to her chest.

They stand like that in the dark, together, a human heart beating on silent steel.

'I think you need to see this for yourself.'

The sword feels cold against her. It does not move.

She lets go with one hand, reaching up to find the edge of one wing. Fingers find feathers, curling underneath, easing back. There is no resistance, just reluctance. Having opened out one wing, she lets go, feels the briefest tug at her fingertips. She pulls at the second, gentle and it allows itself to be moved, revealing an eye, resolutely closed.

Vesper waits, trying to ignore the mix of scents, of alien pollen and decaying matter, of her own sweat.

An eye half opens, peering out under the lid. It does not need the light to see.

After a few moments it closes again, wings pressing in hard against it.

She holds on a little tighter. Sharp edges press through sleeves, bringing discomfort and Vesper feels rage charging the air, terrifying, destructive, directionless. She holds on, enduring and patient, feeling the anger make way for other things. The blade begins to tremble in irregular bursts, shaking them both.

And still, Vesper holds on.

One Thousand and Ninety-Seven Years Ago

Massassi's body slumps in the chair, held fast by crisscrossing straps. Three holes perforate the seat, matching three passageways through her back and chest. Through the three new holes in the roof she can see the sun. To normal eyes the great disc is felt rather than seen, hidden behind a veil of thick smog. To Massassi however it shines like an astral spotlight, highlighting her end.

She is aware of her own essence, how it wants to fade, to give up her shape and break apart. Only her will holds it together. It is tempting to let go. To stop fighting. It feels to her as if she has been fighting all her life and suddenly that inner fire is no longer there. It is a great relief.

The screens that surround her are inoperative, dark, depriving her of one final look at the Breach. Instead, she looks up at the sun.

On its blazing surface she perceives three smudges of dark, little gaps where no light exists. She frowns, or at least she imagines frowning, for in reality, her slack-jawed face does not move, and looks closer.

The holes in the sun are tiny things and she has to strain to make them out. As she watches, cracks creep outward from them, little fingers joining up to make a single line that threatens to grow, to divide the sun in two.

She sees the distortion in the sky shift, as if drawn to that weakness, lines of light that fold the sky, trying to force a breach in the stars to match her breach in the earth.

This will not do. Her life's work must not be undone by her death. Renewed with purpose, Massassi sharpens her focus, draws her essence together once more. It shines like a star, hard and silver through her wounds. She takes back her body, restarting its heart, waking muscles, slapping the release button on her harness.

She drops out of her seat, turning to see a masked figure holding a sniper rifle. The assassin's mask is stretched at the bottom by her jaw, gawping. While the assassin wrestles with the fact that Massassi still lives, reflexes take over, smoothly reloading as they raise the rifle, this time aiming for the face.

Massassi's eyebrows raise, her eyes flash and the essence within the assassin turns to ash. Another life to add to the many she's taken. But Massassi does not falter, who would cry over a drop of spilt water to save the ocean?

Past experience tells her to move quickly. It is not easy holding one's essence together while leaking blood from six holes. If she trusted her subordinates to get it right, she'd call for help. No. Better to do it herself. In the end, she has always been alone and that is how she likes it.

Outside, the world rocks to warheads detonating. People hide, people die and the earth trembles.

Massassi barely notices as she stumbles into walls, pushing off them again, leaving hand-prints of red behind her.

Her body is starting to fail by the time she reaches her workshop. Blood loss and shock combine, trying to force her to lie down. She refuses, grabbing her welding torch and a plate of metal.

The work is ugly by her usual standards, especially compared with her arm, but it is functional. Six caps to plug the wounds front and back, studs of silver, lifesaving. In the coming years her body will demand recompense, a constant diet of drugs and occasional organ repair. She accepts this, ready to pay any price to extend her life.

Hauling herself to a window she looks at the sun once more. The three black marks no longer mar its surface, but a faint impression remains, a hairline scar, prophetic.

The distortions in the sky return to their normal lines as well, drawn back to the south and the breach waiting to open there.

Normality reasserts itself and Massassi slumps against the window, letting her head rest on the plasglass. She lives, and for humanity to survive, she must go on living. It is her strength that holds back the invaders and the tidal wave that carries them. She sees it now. For as long as she draws breath, the sun is safe.

CHAPTER TWENTY-SIX

Vesper returns to the Man-shape's chamber, the sword in her arms, sleeping. Silvered wings drape over the back of her hands. She is greeted by the kid, who sniffs at her hopefully.

Samael takes his habitual place by the left wall and the Man-shape stands by the window, its back to her. 'The Yearning is getting closer. When I look out to the south, I can see the way its essence plays across the sky. I can see it fighting to gain ground. It's still too far away to read in any detail but I have had an interesting thought. Would you like to hear it?'

Needing both hands to hold the sword, she tries to rub tired eyes on her shoulder. 'Okay.'

'Seeing the Yearning through this shell, and through the visions Samael shared, I am struck by how strange it is. Unlike us, it has not tried to adapt to this world. The Yearning shows me how much we have changed since we arrived here. If the I that first emerged from the Breach were to see what

I have become, it would not recognise itself. I see the Yearning and I cannot understand it and I feel fear. Is that not how your kind first reacted when they beheld us?'

'Why do you think that the Malice can stop it?'

'I believe that the Malice will be like a poison to it, as it is to all of my kind. It may take longer to work than it did on my master but in the end, the Yearning will be vanquished.'

'But, the Usurper survived those wounds for years!'

'There is no other way.'

'And, if I did this for you, what would you do in return?'

The Man-shape's frame becomes still for a moment, then reanimates. 'I do not understand. We are not trading, this is what the Malice is here for.'

'The Malice might be, but if you want to send the Malice against the Yearning you need me.'

'Do I?'

'The sword doesn't want to be used by anyone else. I don't think it would end well if they tried.'

'But you, like the Malice, wish to stop the Yearning. Why do you try to trade when you already have what you want?'

'Because there's no point in stopping the Yearning if we don't make things better afterwards.'

'Interesting. What is your price?'

'In return for stopping the Yearning, I want you to take New Horizon from the Demagogue.'

'This is agreeable, the Demagogue has betrayed us and we will have need for a new home if the Yearning comes any closer to the Fallen Palace.'

A grim smile flexes Vesper's face. 'Actually, there's more.'

'Go on.'

'When you take it, you have to free the people there. All the slaves.'

'Without slaves, how will my kind acquire fresh shells?'

'I don't know. Maybe we can work out an alternative but that's my price.'

The Man-shape tilts its head. 'What do you think, Samael?'

'I think the slaves will die if you free them.'

Vesper shakes her head. 'I don't want that to happen!'

'They'll starve,' continues Samael, 'or get picked off by other people.'

'Then you have to look after them. Give them food and proper clothing and shelter, at least until they are able to look after themselves.'

With a pop, the Man-shape's jaw resets itself. 'And how long do you expect us to care for them?'

'As long as it takes.'

'Very well. We have an accord. Samael will take our forces and depose the Demagogue, taking his rightful place as our king. He will release your people and care for them. In return, you will destroy the Yearning and then take the Malice back north, as far from here as you are able.'

'Wait a moment,' Vesper replies. 'Is that what you want, Samael?'

Samael's voice is a soft whisper. 'I want to go back to the sea.'

'It does not matter what he wants. It is what he was made for.'

'But he doesn't want to rule New Horizon, he told me so.'

'There is no one else.'

'What about you?'

'Me?'

'Yes. You've been in charge here since the Usurper fell. Why not carry on?'

'I was made to serve, not rule.'

'By who?'

'By my master.'

Briefly, the sword is jostled by Vesper's excitement. Silvered wings tense, pressing into her hands, warning against further disturbance. She continues in a more measured tone. 'But don't you get it? Your master is dead. It doesn't matter what it wanted. The Usurper isn't here to deal with this and neither are The Seven. It's up to us. Would the other infernals listen to you?'

'They might.'

'Might isn't good enough. You have to make them listen.'

'I am not the Usurper.'

Samael moves to stand next to the infernal. 'You are not the Demagogue, either. Given the choice, they will support you.'

'They will support whoever appears stronger.' It holds up a hand, a human gesture. 'I will need Samael if I am to succeed.'

Vesper shrugs. 'Why are you asking me?'

'Because somehow, he has become yours.'

Eyes widen, remembering his oath, understanding. 'Sir Samael, will you go with the Man-shape and liberate New Horizon?'

He says yes for many reasons. For the glory of the Winged Eye, for Jem and those like him, because it will help the Man-shape, because he wishes to see the Demagogue fall and, above all, because he has an impulse to do so.

* * *

Jem chews his food slowly, in part to savour, in part because his stomach needs all the help it can get. He sits at the base of the Man-shape's tower, letting walls take his weight, looking up at Vesper. 'I swore I'd never go back.'

'I'm sorry but there isn't any choice, unless you want to come with us?'

'To the Breach? Even New Horizon isn't as bad as that.'

'Exactly. And I think you're needed there.'

'Oh yes, New Horizon is in sore need of another hungry mouth.'

Vesper frowns. 'That's not what I mean. Well, actually, maybe it is. I think Samael will try and do right by the people but I doubt he'll understand them. He doesn't need to eat anymore and the Man-shape never did. I don't know if they feel pain like we do or . . . I don't know. The thing is, you've been there and lived it.'

'Yes, it was torture. But so what? I don't see how my suffering helps anyone.'

She takes his hands, squeezes them. 'They'll be scared. You can reassure them.'

'If they manage to take back the city.'

'They'll take it.'

'You don't know that.'

'No, but we've got to try.' She lets go of his hands but he keeps hold of hers.

'You're so young. How are you handling this so well?'

A giggle bursts out. 'Thank you. You really think so? I feel like I've been messing it all up since the day I left home.' Her attention goes briefly elsewhere. 'That feels like so long ago now. Have you ever met Tough Call?'

'No.'

'She's the leader of Verdigris. She really knows what she's doing. I wish I was more like her. Or my father.'

Jem reaches for some more food, hiding his bitter reaction. 'Tell me about your father.'

'He carried the sword too, and me, back when I was a baby. He brought us both from the far south all the way across the sea to the Shining City and fought infernals along the way. My Uncle Harm says that he helped a lot of people. Some of them still send us presents occasionally. But it's easy to forget all that. Most of the time he's just this guy who doesn't say much and doesn't trust me to go anywhere. I mean that literally. Even when I'm not that far away he checks on me all the time. It's really annoying.' Her eyes focus in on Jem again. 'But without him, I wouldn't be here and the Usurper would still be in power. Suns! He must be out of his mind with worry!'

'He sounds impressive.'

'He was, at least, he used to be.'

'He didn't save everyone though, did he? I'm sure he had his failures too.'

'I suppose so. I suppose everyone does.' She squeezes his hands again and pulls hers free. 'I don't know how things are going to turn out but . . . I wanted to ask what you want to do, you know, if we both survive?'

'Isn't it a bit early to think about the future?'

'I don't think so. I mean, what's the point of doing all this if we don't have something to hope for on the other side?'

'Well, in that case, I'd like to see what life is like in the Shining City.'

The toe of her boot worries a loose stone. 'I don't know

much about life in the city itself but I can show you a lot of fields and goats.'

'I'd like that. Do goats taste good?' He sees her appalled expression and smiles, revealing small feral teeth. 'Just kidding.'

'Well,' she says, standing up, 'I have to go.'

'I don't have much faith in The Seven but I hope they'll watch over you.'

'You too.'

Hands are raised in farewell, weak smiles exchanged, and the two part company. One joining Duet to go south, the other going to Samael and the waiting infernal army.

The trudge through the swamp is slow-going and tedious but eventually the Fallen Palace is left behind. Muck clings to their legs, stinking, going hard as it dries. The sword hangs lower on Vesper than usual, slumping, wings curled around her right shoulder, an eye pressed against her back.

The kid trots alongside, nibbling food from Vesper's palm.

Duet's condition worsens steadily. Her left foot drags when she walks and her left arm dangles by her side. Self-abuse is muttered, near constant, as the Harmonised tries to keep pace.

Ahead, strange mists play across the sky. Giant snakes of vapour, twisting and stretching. They press like fingers toward the north while rays of sunlight stab at them. The foremost tendrils thicken when the light strikes them, hardening into branches of crystal, a growing forest of emerald and sapphire. These strange trees draw in the daylight, distorting, weakening, a shelter for fresh mist to build around.

The sight of it makes them both stop.

'All of this is the Yearning?' asks Vesper.

Duet looks at the crystals taking root in the ground and the ones suspended above, dotted as far as the eye can see, left to right, up and down. She grimaces. 'A sting to the heart or the brain should still kill it.'

'What heart? What brain?'

'Everything has a weak spot. We'll find it.'

'Are you sure? The Man-shape thinks the sword will be like a poison but how could such a tiny amount of poison do anything to this?'

'The sword wanted to come here. It has a plan.'

Vesper tries to look at it over her shoulder. Only the tip of the hilt is visible. 'We know it wanted to come south but we've never known why.'

'Yes, we do. To destroy the Yearning and seal the Breach.'

'No. That's what Genner was hoping for. That's what I thought it must be. But what if it isn't? What if there's another reason?'

Duet looks unimpressed. 'What other reason could there be?'

'To die.'

They continue walking, the nearest trees less than a hundred feet away. Mist curls in the air in front of them, ignoring the wind, sunslight sparking off it.

Duet loses focus, reminded of something by the patterns in the air. Realising she has slowed down, the Harmonised moves to catch up, and finds her progress suddenly easier, as if running down a gentle hill. But still Vesper stays ahead, accelerating slightly faster. Duet hears something but can't make it out. 'What did you just say?'

Vesper and the kid glance back. 'I didn't say anything.'

'Hmm. I thought you did.'

'What did you think I said?'

'It doesn't matter.' Another glance from Vesper prompts her to continue, raising her voice. 'I thought you called me.' She mutters something else under her breath, too low for Vesper to catch, then adds, 'I don't believe the sword came here to die.'

'Why not?'

'Because The Seven can't die.'

'Gamma did.'

'No! She lives on, in the sword.'

'Only a bit of her.'

'Isn't that enough?'

'You tell me.' Vesper's wince arrives as soon as the words are out of her mouth. 'I didn't mean that.'

'Yes, you did.' She challenges Vesper with her eyes, daring the girl to disagree. She doesn't. 'I still feel her, did you know that? She's not here, of course. I know she's not here but I feel my other half standing next to me, just like she always did. Her voice is in my head, even more than when we were connected. I wish she'd shut up and give me some peace. She's talking to me right now and do you know what she's saying? She's telling me to stop feeling sorry for myself. She's telling me to stop bothering you with irrelevant things and she's telling me to focus on the mission.

'And I want to do that. Being in this tainted place actually helps. When we're under threat my mind is clearer. My training kicks in. I don't worry if I'm keeping myself together because I am together. I have to be. The sword needs you to bring it here and you need me to protect you. It works, most of the time.

'So, you see, I have to believe that the sword would want

to carry on without Gamma. Because if there's hope for it then there's hope for me.' There is a pause, Vesper just stares. 'Nothing to say? That has to be a first.'

The girl stops, bites her lip. 'Duet, what are you pointing at?'

'Pointing?' She looks at herself to find her left arm is raised, fingers stretched out, fluttering slightly like a flag in a strong breeze. As she tries to understand what is happening, her left foot slides forward of its own accord, pulling her along behind.

Silent winds stir at their backs. Invisible hands that tug and push, drawing them towards the trees.

Vesper grabs Duet's right arm, tries to anchor her. She feels the pressure herself now, dragging at her centre of gravity, tipping it forward.

The kid bleats, turns around and runs. Hooves churn up the dirt, working hard, but frantic efforts only slow the inevitable, all three of them sliding inexorably toward the crystal trees.

Vesper leans back, reaching down for extra purchase. Small stones scratch at her fingers, collect under nails, scattering when she grabs for them.

Without pride, she shouts for help. The kid joins her.

An eye twitches at the sound.

They skid past the outermost trees.

Duet slides faster, her left hand extends slightly too far in front of her, the wrist stretching, elongating.

All three of them scream.

An eye opens and with a snap, wings unfurl. They catch the strange currents and rise with them, the sword sliding free of its scabbard.

The Malice

An angry note slices the air, severing invisible strings.

There is a sound like thunder and the pulling stops, alien winds diverting around them like a river around a stone.

They fall with variety: Vesper on her back, the kid on his front and Duet crashing sideways.

A beat later the sword clatters next to them. It's eye flicks from left to right, tracking currents of alien essence, widening at what it sees.

For a few moments all three lie still while chests rise and fall and air is gulped.

Vesper sits up and reaches out to the sword, her hand resting on one of the wings.

The kid looks around. They are surrounded by the strange trees and the stranger atmosphere. It is hard to tell which way is home. With a bleat, he jumps into Vesper's lap, burying his head, his small body trembling. She strokes him with her spare hand, soothing, the gesture automatic.

Around them, colourful gases swirl, drawing the outline of an invisible dome where the sword's voice holds sway. Nearby trees are shaken by the vibrations, crystal branches shivering, trying to bend away.

'Thank you,' says Vesper. But the sword does not register her voice, its eye stares elsewhere, its wings rigid with effort. The girl turns to Duet. 'I don't know how long the sword can keep this up.'

The Harmonised is studying her left hand, suspicious, rotating it in front of her face.

'Did you see it? Did you see the way it stretched?'

'No.'

She raises her voice. 'I'm not mad! I saw it!'

'I never said you were mad.'

'Yes, you did, you're always saying it. That I'm mad, unworthy, slowing you down. You think I don't hear you but I do.'

'Duet, who do you think I am?'

Behind the visor, her eyes are unreadable. 'You're . . . you're . . . Oh, Vesper, help me. It took my arm and my leg.' She holds out her left hand. 'This isn't mine any more. I can't keep it still.'

Vesper feels the kid burrowing deeper into her lap, the sword humming beneath her fingers, fighting. There is tension in her head, the kind that comes before a storm. Above her the dome shrinks slightly, bowing to the pressure.

Duet starts dragging herself closer. 'Cut it off, like they did for Tough Call. And my leg. I need to be purified. You can use the sword to do it.'

'I can't.'

'You have to.'

'I'm not a knight.'

'It doesn't matter.'

'I'm scared.'

'Do it!'

She takes a breath, takes the hilt.

The sword is light, seeming to rise from the ground by its own accord. An eye comes level with hers. She sees fear in it to match her own and grips the hilt tighter. Wings reach out, gentle, and close her eyes.

But she still sees. With the sword's vision, the world is transformed. The swirling clouds that press around them have rings of teeth, sharp circles that open onto tunnels of emptiness. Not nothing, rather a hungry hole that demands to be filled. The trees are the same. To the sword, they have no colour, their surfaces feeding on the light, sucking it down greedily. In return the trees exhale more clouds of empty, hungry essence. And all of it, all of the endless desperation is linked together, a living growing loss, driven by black need.

Vesper feels horror but not revulsion, fear but not anger. The sword seems caught between a desire to attack and hopelessness, all of its strength needed to hold back the Yearning. All of its strength not nearly enough.

Again, the dome shrinks.

Duet kneels, leaning on her right arm to keep balance. She forces her left arm straight, holding it in front of Vesper. 'Please, I invoke the rite of mercy . . .'

As the Harmonised speaks, an eye looks down, and Vesper sees Duet laid bare. Her essence flutters, half remembered, tattered around the edges where strands of it peel away. Vesper sees a loneliness there, strong enough to kill, that spreads. The essence is weakest on Duet's left where the ill-defined shape of her left arm tries to pull away from her body. It is searching she realises, trying to reconnect with the lost half of itself.

The Yearning sees it too. For the first time since its arrival in the world it recognises something like itself, something that might end its terrible isolation. The Yearning tries to touch it, to take it but the Malice holds it at bay.

Vesper raises the sword. The shapes on the outside of the dome flinch and Duet steels herself, her arm extended, ready.

But instead of striking, Vesper turns on the spot, wanting one last look, one last chance to think, to consider if she is capable of the idea that has just occurred.

'Duet, I need you to do something for me.'

'What? No. Take my arm, quickly.'

She makes her voice harder. 'In the name of The Seven, stand up.'

With a grimace, Duet complies.

'Go to the edge of the dome.'

As she does so, she asks why.

'Because . . . the Empire needs you to.'

The dome shrinks again, its protections brushing over Duet, exposing parts of her to the outside.

There is an immediate reaction. The shapes rush towards her and parts of her essence respond, the fragmented silver ghost that floats around her arm lifts up, drawing the physical limb with it.

Duet tries to step back but Vesper shakes her head.

Behind her visor, features contort, tears spill.

Essence stretches from Duet and from the Yearning, a great emptiness reaching toward a small loneliness, entwining, touching. Tendrils of smoke wrap around her, boneless fingers of a giant hand, swirling and tasting, obscuring her. Like a thin smoke in a storm the edges of Duet's soul are whipped away.

The Harmonised gasps. 'She's gone.'

'Who?'

'Me. Her. She gone.'

Vesper sees ethereal teeth pressing against Duet. The action is not violent however, the many mouths moving carefully, not biting, bonding.

'I can feel it! The Yearning. It's . . . calling me.'

'Yes,' says Vesper, her voice small.

'It's huge and sad, so very sad. So alone. It . . . wants me to join it. You have to help me, I don't think I can hold on for long.'

'It needs you. If it has you I think it will stop growing.'

With effort, Duet turns her head. 'What are you saying?'

'I'm saying I can't fight the Yearning but you . . .'

'No! I'd rather die than be an infernal.'

'I know.' Vesper brings the sword to her chest. 'I'm sorry.'

The dome contracts around Vesper, shrinking past Duet, exposing her.

Unimpeded, the Yearning flows around Duet, whittling away resistance until it finds the core, the need in her to be joined again, the need to belong. This, the Yearning raises skyward like a trophy.

There is a ripple of satisfaction in the mists and then a distortion. For a moment, Duet's body begins to stretch towards the south, the tendrils of smoke elongating with her. Then both she and the smoke are gone.

Sunlight falls suddenly bright, the world reasserting itself, claiming back old ground, burning away stray wisps the Yearning has left behind.

Vesper falls to her knees, clutching the sword to her. Eyes still squeezed shut, she howls in despair, the sword catching the note, echoing it, extending.

Around her, trees shake, chunks of crystal flaking away from brittle branches, smoking in the hostile air. Gradually, the sound dies away, leaving behind the soft sobs of a lonely girl. After a time, they too pass.

The sword has waited long enough. It takes action; wings beat once, languid, pulling Vesper to her feet.

She opens her eyes.

Without the strange mists, the landscape is exposed. The

rocks have been stripped bare of vegetation and blasted clean, their surfaces left smooth, rounded. And everything shines, from the mundane stones to the bizarre crystal trees. Of these, the ones that hang in the sky begin to burn, breaking into fragments that rain musically onto the ground below.

Vesper holds the sword high and opens her mouth. Only a soft song comes from it but it is enough to chime against the blade. The air around her shimmers with sound and, above her head, crystal chunks explode into harmless powder.

Protected now, she walks south. The kid is tucked under her arm, a small ball of fear that refuses to look anywhere but in her armpit. She taps the sword against any trees that she passes, and the crystalline bark shivers, the sound screaming through it, shattering.

She travels for several miles, seeing no one, the sword drawing her on, until at last she finds a great gash that runs across the land, a rough edged chasm yawning wide in the distance. The Breach.

She is the first human to see it in her lifetime. It too has been picked clean of history, giving a false air of timelessness. Since the Yearning's arrival, the Breach itself has been silent. No newcomers have found their way through and there is no hint of any on their way. From this distance, the Breach appears like an ordinary feature of the landscape, fixed, natural. Only by looking inside would an observer be able to tell any different.

In front of it, the Yearning settles, folding itself inward, vapours thickening, darkening, not quite solid but more substantial than air. Essence so potent it becomes a kind of slime, existing partway between the physical and the ethereal.

It still dwarfs the girl but in a conceivable way, as a cloud might dwarf a mouse. Infinitely preferable to what was before.

Even so, she stops. Feet fidget and shoulders twist, suggesting a desire to turn away. An eye swivels to look at her. She meets it and finds its gaze softer than usual, understanding. Guilt stirs inside, stamping down fear, and she nods to the sword, tired, and keeps going.

Within the quivering viscosity that the Yearning has become, something moves. A tiny sphere, a pearl of essence, the purest parts of Duet's need to be joined to something bigger, to not be alone. It travels through the Yearning's insides at incredible speed, orbiting internally within the colossal infernal.

And the Yearning treasures its new companion-component, totally absorbed in self-reflection. The outside world is rendered irrelevant, a bad memory that does not bear revisiting.

It does not notice Vesper as she approaches, nor the Malice singing at her side.

They get closer, the girl not stopping until she is inches from the translucid being. She watches Duet's remains rush past, again and again, noting the way the Yearning shifts each time. She wonders if it is expressing pleasure.

The sword is eager in her hand, keen to finish the job.

But Vesper hesitates. There is a kind of beauty here and an absence of threat. Perhaps the Yearning would remain like this if she left it alone. Perhaps she has done enough. She shakes her head and tears fly from cheeks. Duet's words echo in her mind: 'I would rather die than become an infernal . . . I would rather die . . .'

Her friend's sacrifice has exposed the Yearning's heart and Vesper knows what has to be done.

When the pearl's orbit brings it close she cries out, giving voice to grief, and plunges the sword into what passes for the Yearning's flesh.

Singing steel slides easily inside, the point piercing the pearl, infusing it with deadly malice. She pulls the sword free and watches as the pearl continues on its way, changing. Gradually, the sphere brightens, a tiny star trailing sparks that spread behind it, birthing new spheres that immediately start new orbits, whirling faster and faster until the infernal's innards appear like the night sky. The essence comets follow their orbits doggedly, chasing their own light trails until they catch them, forming bands that burn, widening, blurring together, until the Yearning is eclipsed.

The multitude of lights blend into one, a chorus of wounds that build to a final flare, dazzling, deafening, overwhelming, peaking, then calming, echoing in pulses, each softer than the one before, fading away.

When they are gone, nothing of the Yearning remains.

One Thousand and
Seventy Years Ago

Massassi punches the air as the report comes in. Finally, she is ready. After years of war, the world is hers. From the Dagger states in the west to the Constructed Isles in the east, from her outpost in the far south to the Emerald Peaks in the far north, all comes under her banner. All are loyal to the Empire of the Winged Eye.

And the flag is more than just an image. The Empire's role is to watch and it has many eyes to do so. Human ones scattered far and wide and metal ones on the deep of the sea and the dark of the sky, flying, floating, unblinking. Should the eyes discover a problem, the Empire has other tools at its disposal. Soldiers armed with her weapons, with fire and spinning shot. Swords, imbued with her song and placed in the hands of knights trained in their use. The forces of the Empire wear armour to protect their bodies but protecting their essence is more difficult. Massassi fears that she alone is strong enough to stand in the presence of the infernal and not be broken. To prepare her knights, she trains them in simple techniques to anchor their simple minds. It is much easier for people to cling to a narrow idea than a complex one.

And if the knights lose a little creativity or a little empathy along the way, it is an acceptable loss. But she does not stop there. The best way to protect the essence of her knights is to give them a shield, something to prevent any contact between them and the enemy. For that, Massassi uses other humans. A pair is allocated to each knight as guardians. These pairs work in tandem, drawing strength from each other, giving up independence for a shared sense of self. They fight and live and think together. Massassi calls them the Harmonised. It is their role to hold off attacks both physical and other while the knights bring their swords to bear.

So far, there is only one breach between her world and theirs but Massassi knows that as things degenerate, more could appear. Outposts are constructed in all of the most likely breach points, patrols set over the others. Maps are made, exhaustive charts for every inch of sea and land. New islands are discovered, their populations quickly overrun and assimilated. A whole branch of the Empire is dedicated to the maintenance of these maps and the monitoring of infernal activity. They have many names but are commonly referred to as the Lenses.

Massassi has had to break many hearts to get to this stage. Stealing corporations and levelling cultures, appropriating scientific discoveries and crushing other smaller dreams in pursuit of her own. But, at last, her forces are prepared for what is coming.

She has been conservative in her predictions, terrified that the Breach would open too soon and spill death on the unwary. A year before Breach date, she returns to her outpost, the ex-quarry where first contact was made. Her forces come with her, giant warmechs and multi-segemented snakes of metal, wave after wave of foot soldiers, legions of Seraph Knights and their Harmonised sentinels.

They take up positions around the Breach, covering it from all sides, ready to eviscerate the invaders before they can get a toehold in reality. Armour sparkles in the sunlight, silver buffed with gold. Nervous hearts are mastered with quick prayers to their leader and hands hold steady on a thousand thousand lances.

High, high above, metal eyes orbit, whispering to each other, relaying positions, organising, delivering the picture, complete, into Massassi's HUD. She surveys her preparations and is content. If her empire fails, she will feel no guilt.

At the thought of guilt, faces swim up, a long line of lives snuffed out too early. Some were killed by accident, some by intent, all by her hand. But here, in this place, she is able to return their gaze and say, 'Look! This is what you died for. This is why I had to do it.' She dismisses them easily, empty phantasms compared to what waits before her.

The Breach itself appears quiet, no different on this side from the image she has stared at like an obsessive parent for the last thirty years. The sky distorts around it as it always has, threatening to burst but never actually tearing, a tease of cosmic proportions.

Her troops have unquestioning faith in their leader. They know that something is coming because she has told them so and for them that is enough.

For Massassi, however, there is a flicker of doubt. The phantasms return as quickly as they went, dead eyes questioning.

What if this breach is just a hole in the ground? The horrors on the other side merely imagined by a mad woman? What would justify their deaths then?

She climbs out of her warmech, gliding down into the blast zone that exists between the front line of her forces and the Breach. Her jump boots catch the rocks, absorbing weight, storing energy, then spring off again, sending her forward in decreasing hops.

She skids to a stop in front of it. A tiny line of darkness in the rock. She can see bubbles of silver along its edge, marking the place where she sealed it shut many years before. Her seal has begun to peel away, suggesting the earth has shifted in her absence but it is clear that nothing has emerged.

There is only one thing to do, one way to be sure.

Massassi takes a deep breath and raises her metal arm, allowing the iris in her palm to open. Blowing out air through gritted teeth, she steps forward, pressing her open hand against the crack, and closes her eyes.

As before, she feels them as much as sees them. Formless things that flow through the void, rushing towards her like a great shoal towards a fresh meal or a river of poison towards a sinkhole.

For the second time they see each other across the fathomless distance. Without a doubt they are closer than before and she is able to perceive differences in them, to identify one from another, to see that some are more potent, that the larger ones effect some kind of pull on the smaller.

But they are still far away. Too far. She pulls her hand back, forces herself to remain upright and maintain the appearance of strength for her forces. Her head shakes from side to side, unwilling to accept the implications of this new data.

Her predictions are wrong.

The demons are coming, that remains true. The threat they pose is undiminished, the need for humanity to prepare just as relevant.

But they will not arrive when she thought. Not in the next few months, nor the next few years. Based on her new readings, the invasion will not begin in her lifetime. Not for hundreds, or possibly even thousands of years.

Humanity's only hope against the tide has arrived too soon and all of her power and preparation is suddenly meaningless, a joke.

Her life has been given for this one purpose: to fight the demons. But when they do come, in unimaginable numbers, and with unquenchable fury, she will be dead.

CHAPTER TWENTY-SEVEN

Vesper walks along the edge of the Breach, following curves and jagged corners. Occasionally, she stops to look over the side. The walls of the Breach are smooth and grey, like volcanic rock, long cooled. Small indentations can be seen, darker spots where bubbles have burst. There is nothing to interrupt the vertical view and Vesper finds herself leaning out, squinting, trying to see to the bottom. Mercifully, the sunslight only goes so far, preserving mystery.

She walks on, keen to map its length. But a dry throat and empty belly conspire against her and she is forced give up. One last time, she looks out at the Breach: this is one of the narrowest places she has seen, less than half a mile wide. On the other side, the landscape is barren and she wonders if anything survives further south. Did all the infernals come north with the Usurper or are there more?

Bleak thoughts are shaken away.

The Breach appears dead. A scar left by history. Vesper knows better. She holds out the sword, letting it swing, to look along the Breach's length one way, then the other. An eye narrows, then swivels towards her.

On impulse, she closes her eyes, letting the sword see for her again. Though there are no new infernals rising up, she sees empty threads of essence wafting and feels them play against the sword's wings, gently tugging as they pass.

Eyes open and something passes between girl and sword. It dips a wing towards the Breach, looks at her pointedly, and then down, into the darkness.

'No,' says Vesper. 'I can't . . . I can't go down there. I'm scared . . . and you're scared, too, I know it.'

An eye looks at her, patient, unyielding.

'We have to do this, don't we?' Vesper nods to herself. 'Alright. Tell me what I have to do and I'll try.'

Silvered wings quirk up, reminiscent of a shrug.

Vesper shuffles to the cliff's edge, toes touching nothing. The sword bobs in her hands, made almost weightless by the updrafts of essence.

She senses the sword's intention, starts to protest. 'No, I'm not ready, I—'

And with a sharp tug, it pulls her over.

She falls, quickly at first, then wings spread, and the plummet slows, becomes a glide.

Down.
Down.
Down.

Sheer rock passes her by, the slice of daylight above becoming rapidly distant. She grips the sword tightly but it does not slip in her grasp. It is holding onto her just as tight.

Essence binds hand and hilt securely, she could not let it go any more than she could let go of her limbs.

The kid is another matter. Only a firm arm keeps him close.

Deeper they go, beyond the reach of the sunslight, to the very bowels of the world.

And there, twitching, malignant, is the heart of the Breach itself. After being stretched wide to birth the Yearning, it has shrunk down, a puckered sphincter-shadow of its former glory. In time, it will recover and stretch again, refilling the crack in the earth with alien emptiness.

Vesper does not intend to give it that time.

Essence is visible here, arriving in constant gasps from the Breach, casting a greenish pall.

She glides down to a nearby ledge, stumbling, holding the sword out for balance. Briefly, she teeters, looking out over the crack that goes still deeper, seemingly without end.

With a single stroke of its wings, the sword pulls her back.

'Thank you,' she whispers.

The kid is placed carefully into a nook. He whimpers but does not move, head tucked firmly into his belly.

Together, girl and sword sing. Softly at first, Vesper's voice is uncertain, slipping from high to higher in order to find the right note. The sword waits for her, keeping tune simple, soft, holding back its power.

She finds it, and briefly their voices swell together with strength, then she loses it, finds it again, struggles to hold the sound. She has not been trained for this but the instincts are there. Imprinted early in the days before her conscious memories.

The edges of the Breach retreat from the sound, sucking

inwards, shrinking, wrinkling, like a slug doused in salt. On the other side of it, in the realms beyond, infernal shapes not yet born hear the disturbance, are drawn nearer. They see the Breach, notice the change, see their chance to enter our world vanishing, and, as one, they dive forward.

None have names, none are fully realised yet but they are different in size and potency and potential horror.

As the first three clouds burst into the world, Vesper staggers away, till back hits stone, her mind unable to process what stands before her.

Briefly, she feels repulsed, afraid, then just as she starts to recover, grappling to understand the shapes that exist both inside and out of her perception, the sword's sound changes and she is filled with grief and rage so pure it leaves room for nothing else.

Without thought, Vesper kicks out, into the space above the Breach, the sword's wings beating down, catching currents, powering her leap. Air burns blue around the blade, crackling with energy.

She sings, swings the sword once, splitting a cloud and setting the two halves aflame.

She swings the sword a second time, and a third, shredding two more invaders.

For a moment she hovers there, the sword known as Malice held above her head, three eyes glaring down, daring any more to come forward.

None take up the challenge.

Then, slivered wings fold, and Vesper falls, straight down, straight towards the Breach itself. She grabs the sword in both hands, inverts it, so that the tip points unerringly towards the Breach's centre.

411

Together they sing. Together they fall. A wordless song of woe, of loss, of anger.

The Breach recoils, shrinks still further, but not enough.

The sword plunges into it, searing its edges, blocking the flow of essence.

Vesper feels the pressure. As if they had just plugged a dam and the weight of an ocean was pressing against them. She stands on top of the sealed Breach, feet braced on not quite stone, not quite flesh. Smoke plumes at the point that Breach meets sword, and Vesper feels it shaking in her grasp where it works still to burn, to seal, to shut this door that should not be.

She struggles to hold it in place. The muscles in her arms are too small, the weight of her body laughable against the forces, elemental, pushing against them.

But she has to hold on, to give the sword time to complete its work. And so she commits more than muscle and bone. She gives song and heart and every part of her will.

And still it is not enough. Her throat grows raw from singing, her spirit wanes, and the sword presses up into her hands.

But the sword is more than just a sword. It is part of Gamma, and she is more than just a human, she is part of a family and she carries their strength with them. Vesper sings for them all, for her father, her Uncle Harm, for Genner and the knights, for Samael and Jem. For all those that died for her to get here and those that might live if she succeeds. And when that is not enough, when the urge to stop becomes unbearable: she thinks of Duet.

And her song surges again, filling the air with sound and fury and fire, and then, with a hiss, the sword comes free, leaving a husk where the Breach was. Silvered lines like scars stitch the sides together, binding fast.

The echoes of their song fade, the light going with it. Vesper sways, stumbles. Somehow she staggers back to the ledge, dragging the sword with her before laying down and passing out.

Rough stone pokes at soft skin, forcing the end of sleep. Vesper groans. Around her it is dark, save for a distant slit of gold, far above her. She switches the Navpack to torch mode and hauls herself upright, picking up the sword soon after. It feels heavy. An eye moves sluggishly, glancing at what remains of the Breach. Everything appears as it was and an eye moves to close.

'Wait . . .' begins Vesper, then gasps, her throat raw and burning. 'Wait . . .' she whispers. 'Can you fly us out?'

A wing extends but with the Breach closed, no currents remain to ruffle silver feathers.

She puts the sword away and moves to the wall. It is a daunting climb and the wall looks sheer. For a long time she looks up, then shoulders slump in defeat. She has no idea where to begin.

It is easier to sit down.

Somehow the victory tastes less sweet now it seems she will die here.

'I have to try,' she mumbles, standing once more. A few abortive attempts are made. Fingers slip on smooth stone, knees are scuffed. She swears, falls for a third time and sits down again. Vesper's head sinks down into her hands and stays there.

All becomes quiet.

From a nearby nook, a dark pair of eyes dare to peek out. The kid sees Vesper slumped forward. He sees very little to eat. But more than that, he sees a climb of such immensity, such wonder, that terror is forgotten.

The kid gets up.

The kid looks up.

The kid begins to bounce.

By the time Vesper reacts, the kid has already made a start, hooves naturally moving to the best places, treading a winding path towards the surface.

Vesper follows, trying her best to track the kid's progress, to use the holds he reveals. Sometimes the kid waits for her, balancing easily on ledges too small to see. Often he does not.

Nails crack and fingertips bleed. Muscles ache and limbs tremble. Vesper pauses often, gasping for breath, listening to the sound of little legs clipping merrily above her.

But she does not stop. She does not allow herself to stop. With a grim certainty she realises that she is not done yet. There are still things to do.

And so she climbs.

When she finally reaches the top, she allows herself a brief sleep and a cuddle with the kid, then she strikes out north, putting her back to the Breach.

It is not forgotten though.

There are few distractions as she walks, letting thoughts drift. Vesper murmurs to herself, biting her lip or shaking her head. She sighs often, though not through fatigue.

Sometimes she remembers the kid and strokes his head. Hooves crunch on little carpets of crystal, marking the remains of an alien forest. Rations are eked out, shared.

414

The kid's presence brings only a brief reprieve and soon Vesper's thoughts turn inward again, a frown like her father's returning.

*

Scout pads out of the broken building, weaving through rubble where the door used to be. From his mouth hangs the body of an infernal, one of Gutterface's children. It thrashes around, little arms clawing the air in wild sweeps. Scout shakes it violently, turning the shrieks into stutters.

The Dogspawn finds Samael in the street, presiding over a growing pile of empty shells. Bodies, animal and human, distorted for the pleasure of their hosts, now broken by the Man-shape's army.

He opens his mouth, letting the mangled form drop at Samael's feet.

It lands on the floor with a soft plop, beady eyes peeking through slitted lids, hoping for escape.

Before such ideas can take root, Samael inserts a finger and thumb into a ragged wound in the infernal's stomach, plucking out its essence.

The impish spirit tries to flee, throwing its formlessness about his hand, like a fly against glass. He studies it, a wisp of hate and mischief, curiosity and venom. Just like the others.

Samael begins to work the tiny essence, spreading it out, isolating individual moods and thoughts. He remembers that the Uncivil used to do this. With time he will be able to distill the essence down to its basic form, cutting away the personality until only a pure, neutral substance remains.

While he works, Scout picks up new scents and goes hunting.

The battle for New Horizon has been quick and relatively bloodless. Gutterface met them at the walls with the bulk of the Demagogue's forces but quickly realised it could not win. When the great infernal surrendered the rest fled and now the noises that ring out in nearby streets are of slaughter, not combat, as the last of the Demagogue's allies are dug out of their holes and destroyed.

Undaunted, Samael works on.

It is dark when Vesper arrives at New Horizon, its many lights smudging the sky like a dirty beacon. As ever, the gates are open and, as ever, all the bodies have been swept away. Such precious resources are never ignored for long.

The air is full of unease. New monsters rule the city now, exploring its nooks and crannies, staking territory, jostling for the most gain.

But, however grim it might become, life goes on. Human slaves may be off the menu but bodies can always be sold, one way or another. Drums beat and voices shout, trading insults and prices, the two often interchangeable. Many may have died or lost holdings but every loss is a chance for someone else, and the people of New Horizon waste no chances.

Vesper glances at the horned figures scurrying past, at the groups who clump together, dangerous, and loners hugging to the shadows, willing to do anything but make eye contact. The kid stops and begins to shake, simply unable to cope with further horrors. She scoops him up and tucks him into her coat, away from hungry faces.

Up ahead, a Dogspawn blocks the road, prowling its width, the play of its muscles visible beneath patchy fur.

There is no Handler in sight and the people of New Horizon give the creature a wide berth.

Vesper stops in front of it and raises a hand. 'Hello Scout.'

The Dogspawn barks in acknowledgement and runs off, forcing Vesper to jog to keep his wagging tail in sight.

They travel quickly through grimy streets while people get out of their way, pressing themselves against walls with haste and, often, choice words.

Soon, the Iron Mountain comes into view. A great mound of junk, the outside peppered with lights, the inside riddled with holes and chambers. At first the edges of the junk pile appear hazy, as if viewed through a dark veil. As Vesper gets closer, she sees the veil is moving. The distortion created by thousands of insects swarming together, crawling over neon. Some lights are hot enough to cook, snuffing out little lives with a pop.

Scout stops and sits back on his haunches.

'We're stopping here?' asks Vesper.

He barks in reply.

Soon, Samael can be seen approaching from a side street. He compensates better now but the limp still marks his walk and armour clanks more crisply every other step.

He stops further back from Vesper than usual and Scout suddenly rounds on her. Ears prick up and teeth are displayed.

She takes a step back. 'What is it?'

'He is trying to protect me.'

'From what?'

'From you.'

She follows the Dogspawn's gaze and finds the sword is

in her right hand, humming, ready. She does not remember drawing it. Bringing the hilt to her lips, she whispers, 'What is it? Samael is a friend.'

Wings reach out, brushing eyes shut. Through the sword she sees the world anew. Samael is brighter than before, distinct veins running through his essence, flowing together now, ordered. The tether between him and Scout remains clear. It would be a simple matter for her to sever it.

Behind them, the Iron Mountain looms large and dazzling. She sees the flies lit from within, each a tiny spark of essence, linked by wires, ethereal, that float in the air. Many of the strands tangle together, loose ends drifting, all angled towards something within the base of the Iron Mountain.

'It's not you, Samael. It's something inside there.'

'The Man-shape is in there. It is waiting.'

'For me?'

'Yes. I will take you.'

Vesper follows Samael along a path of trampled machine parts and old packaging. She raises the sword and flies immediately disperse, buzzing angrily to a safer distance.

Samael ducks his head and steps into a passageway, shoulder plates squeaking against narrow walls. They zig zag along it to come out into one of the larger chambers. In an old life, the space was a hangar, part of a sky-ship. In place of tanks and trucks, infernals lurk in the shadows, waiting on the word of their new king.

The Man-shape appears comfortable on a throne of steel and leather. Each leg has been placed carefully, artfully, to create the impression of a human in repose. In truth, the seat is unnecessary as the Man-shape's shell does not tire, an indulgence to alien vanity.

From the chest upwards, the Man-shape is cloaked in darkness. It turns its palms upward in a gesture of welcome. 'What has become of the Yearning?'

'It's gone. Destroyed.'

'And I feel the Malice is all the stronger for it. Can you dim its gaze? My shell only blocks so much of its ire.' She slides the blade back into its sheath, muffling vibrations. 'That is better. I have taken New Horizon and made it my home.'

'What happened? Is Jem okay?'

'He lives. Samael believes he is not beyond restoration. He is with the mortals claimed back from the Demagogue.'

'Did you destroy the Demagogue?'

'Not as you mean it. Our kind is different to yours in this respect.' The Man-shape gestures and two figures shuffle forward. Each appears like a crash victim, badly restored. Vesper covers her mouth, swallowing repeatedly. 'Where once stood our enemy, Gutterface, I have two new members of my court. Their essences have been diluted and blended. Vesper, meet Guttershamble and the Faceless Prince.' The Man-shape gestures again and they retreat meekly to their corners. 'The Demagogue is a different matter. I have sealed it within its palace.'

'Why didn't you kill it?'

'I only kill when I need to.'

'Aren't you worried it will break out?'

'No. After all the exits were sealed, we collapsed the palace around it.'

'But a powerful infernal could survive that, couldn't it?'

'It will have survived, there is no question of that. But I hope it will be too broken to free itself.'

Vesper shakes her head. 'You should have gone in there and killed it.'

'Our agreement was that I take the city and free the enslaved mortals. Nothing more. The Demagogue is too powerful to defeat and remain unchanged. My solution is satisfactory for all parties.'

'Okay then. I suppose we're done. Only . . .'

'Yes?'

'I don't know. It feels like we've started something here. What happens now?'

'Now you go back to your home.'

'Yes, but . . . I know our peoples have fought and . . . well I was hoping there could be a different way. I mean, you're not the Usurper and I'm not The Seven. We might be able to find a way to understand each other.'

'I am listening.'

'I don't have the answers yet, there's a lot to think about but I'd like the chance to speak to you again one day.'

'You are welcome here Vesper, so long as you can muffle the Malice.'

'Then I'll take Samael and Jem and be on my way.'

'Yes. Tell me, how do mortal allies show their appreciation to each other?'

'I don't know but I think you just did.'

'Good. And are you appreciative of me?'

'I am. And we will speak again, I promise.'

CHAPTER TWENTY-EIGHT

They leave New Horizon together, a Dogspawn, a small goat, a half-breed knight carrying a wasted man and a young girl carrying a sleeping sword. They have supplies for those that need them and fresh clothes for Jem and Vesper, though Vesper still wears the old coat. She has grown since she first put it on, the edges brushing ankles rather than heels. Sleeves still hang too long, gobbling everything from sight save fingertips.

There has been a change in the wind and clouds have come, papering the sky grey.

Just outside New Horizon, Vesper comes to a stop. 'Oh . . .' she says.

Jem sits up in Samael's arms. Sunken cheeks have regained some colour and eyes some of their old sharpness. 'What is it?'

'I don't know how we're going to get home. I've been so busy thinking about the Man-shape and New Horizon and Tough Call and Verdigris and the Yearning and, well, everything, that I haven't thought about how we're going to cross the sea.'

'How did you get here?'

'I came in a sky-ship but it was shot down.'

Samael tilts his head, signalling that they should continue. 'I used to cross the oceans. I will take you home.'

'How?' asks Vesper. 'Do you have a ship?'

There is a pause and when Samael's voice does come, it contains warmth, uncharacteristic. 'Yes. It may need work.' He does not add that he hopes it does. Techniques come to mind, bringing with them sensory memories, the feel of tools in his hands and the roughness of raw material, the sense of potential and above all, an impulse to experience it all again.

Jem looks over his shoulder and spits in the dust. 'Goodbye, New Horizon. This is the last time I'm setting eyes on that shit hole of a city, I swear.'

Vesper frowns. 'Not for me. I'm going to come back here one day.'

'Why?'

'Because I made a promise.'

'And do you always keep your promises?'

Her eyes lose focus, attending to a memory but she nods, emphatic. 'Always.'

The journey home feels very different to Vesper. Between the infernal blood in Scout and Samael's veins, and the sword's presence, none of the usual hunters of the Blasted Lands bother them. Things seem almost safe. She finds herself relaxing into the rhythm of travel and because Samael doesn't sleep, he takes all of the night watches.

Sleep and security bring peace of mind and fresh focus. Her thoughts are often elsewhere, practising conversations, worrying about the future and the decisions she leans towards. Sometimes, though, she looks around, at the world of her Uncle's stories. For so long now she has been looking for threats, or expecting trouble that it is refreshing to enjoy her surroundings with new eyes. She sees scars of ancient wars and the daily ravages of nature, animals and plants fighting each other for food, for shelter, for access to the light. She sees other things too. Flowers with petals like insect wings, from one angle transparent, from another a cross-stitch of rainbows. Pink fungus with spiky hair that squeaks when touched. A half-breed rodent, tiger striped, that hangs from nearby trees and dances in exchange for treats.

The kid only eats the first two while Scout, much to Vesper's horror, eats the third.

At Verdigris, the group keeps a low profile and Jem gets some good deals, trading their unwanted things for essential supplies.

It is tempting to speak with Tough Call but Vesper isn't ready, and neither, she suspects, is the city. The flag of the single flexed arm still flies proud but she notices signs of the Empire of the Winged Eye are often displayed alongside. There is a balance here, delicate, that she understands just enough to leave alone.

After they leave Verdigris, Samael leads the way, taking them on a different route to the one she came on. Vesper is sad not to pass Wonderland and speak to Neer again but happy to miss the forest of stalks, and the swarm that lives within it.

They stick to the coastline, trailing it until they reach the northern peninsula. Much of the land has broken away over the years, swallowed by a hungry sea, but five great discs remain, bobbing on gentle waves. Each is a mile across, a miniature settlement in itself. Buildings rise from the discs, their smooth walls blending in, as if the everything was carved from one block of plastic.

The five circles are without power, engines stripped away, their lights dark. A quiet monument to a better age.

Samael stops where the rocks meet the water. 'Wait here,' he says. 'I won't be back for a while.'

Jem and Vesper watch as the half-breed strides into the water. Waves lap ever higher as he progresses, touching first ankles, then knees, waist, chest, until even the plume of dark hair vanishes from sight. Only Scout follows, his head just visible as he paddles after his master.

That night, they shelter in a rocky hollow, enjoying a fire. Jem sits close, fingers spread above the flames, while further away, the kid dozes, one hoof pawing at something imaginary.

They listen to twigs popping and enjoy the woodsmoke that tickles nostrils.

Jem breaks the silence. 'You never really told me how you defeated the Yearning.'

'Yes, I did.'

'Well, yes, you did, but not in any kind of detail.'

'I don't want to talk about it and anyway, there isn't much to tell.'

Jem snorts. 'I find that hard to believe. Will you at least tell me what happened to your friend?'

For a long time, Vesper looks at the flames. Absently, she

bites her lip. 'Duet died fighting the Yearning. She sacrificed herself so that I could finish it off. She's the hero, not me.'

'So she really was as tough as she made out. I can't say I liked her much but –' he raises a battered cup '– here's to Duet.'

Vesper raises her own cup but keeps her eyes on the fire. 'To Duet.'

Days pass, gentle, under a cloudy sky. The kid hops about the rocky beach, finding mossy treasures tucked beneath the stones. Jem grows slowly stronger and begins going for walks. Sometimes, Vesper goes with him and they trade details of each other's lives; favourite colours, stories about family, hopes and dreams.

On quiet nights they can make out the faint sound of hammering, blowing across from the five floating circles.

Throughout, the sword sleeps.

Then one morning, a gleaming arrow detaches itself from one of the giant discs, skimming across the waves towards them. Sunlight glimmers along a smooth white hull and an engine purrs as it catches that light, focusing it into a single stream under the water, propelling the vessel forward.

Scout sits on the prow of the boat, mouth open, wind rippling cheeks and ruffling fur. Behind him, standing at the helm is Samael. Gauntleted hands hold the controls steady, guiding manually, indulgent.

Jem and Vesper walk down to the edge of the beach to meet them.

As the boat nears the shallows, the engine pivots, sending its force straight down and the vessel lifts gently to hover, two feet above the stones.

They climb aboard, and Samael sweeps the boat in a gentle rotation to face the sea once more. 'What do you think?'

Vesper laughs. 'I think its beautiful! Did you build this?'

'Yes. In my old life, a team of us were making this to expand our business. It's a scaled down version of the wave rider models that the Empire tends to use but with thinner plating to make it more fuel efficient. No weapons, of course, we didn't have the clearance, but it meant we could expand the storage bay.' Vesper smiles at him, warm, and he continues. 'Before we could finish it my creator came with the Uncivil's army and we had to evacuate. Every boat in the port was used to push First Circle into the sea and any boats that weren't working were to be stripped for spare parts.'

'But you didn't strip yours?'

'No. When the time came, I couldn't do it. I hid the boat and swore that I'd come back and finish it one day.'

'Well you've certainly done that.'

Samael runs his hand across the top of the main display screen. 'All it needs is a name. If I had one prepared in my old life, it is lost to me now.'

'What do you want to call it?'

'I don't know.'

They all think hard for a moment. Jem is the first to have an idea: 'How about, *The Late Arrival*?'

Vesper is next: '*The Hidden Treasure*?'

Names are bandied about until, finally, Samael says, 'I will call it *Commander's Rest*.'

And with that, the single engine of the *Commander's Rest* flares bright, shooting them out to sea.

*   *   *

The Malice

The weather is clear and the sea merciful, allowing the *Commander's Rest* to make good time. After several loud disagreements, Scout and the kid eventually come to an accord, sharing the space at the front of the boat.

Jem stretches, admiring the rich tan on his arms. 'I can't wait to see the Shining City. I've heard the food there is incredible.'

'Oh, it is,' replies Vesper. 'I don't know why but things taste less watery back home.'

'You must be looking forward to it.'

'I am, I can't wait to see my family again.' She sees him look away, misunderstands. 'And I was going to say, I can't wait for them to meet you. You'll love them, I know it. And they'll love you.'

'Maybe.'

She prods his chest. 'There's no maybe about it. You'll all have to get on because you'll be staying with us.'

'I will?'

'You will.'

He prods her back. 'And what about me, do I get a say in it?'

'No.'

An expression of mock offence is taken but fails to hold. He grins. 'Good. Next stop: the Shining City!'

'Not quite,' Vesper replies, suddenly serious. 'We can't go back yet. We have to go to Sonorous first.'

'Why?'

'I made a promise there that I have to keep.'

Jem shakes his head. 'Maybe you should think about making fewer promises in the future.'

*   *   *

Having declared independence from the Empire of the Winged Eye, having made an alliance with the First, the leaders of Sonorous live in fear of retaliation. The fear has increased since twenty-five sacred swords were broken and their knights locked away. The fear keeps them vigilant. Ships are sent on wide ranging patrols, and the watchtower is constantly manned. Traps are left in the deeps to discourage submersible craft from getting too close.

But all of these measures are set against the arrival of a war fleet and most of those point to the north. As such, the *Commander's Rest* is able to glide into Sonorous' port without even raising an eyebrow.

The island is crescent shaped, the natural formation of the rock extended by metal plates to create a large bay of calm water. Within it, a mix of ships are moored, serene, while crews sweat and cargo rushes back and forth.

Infernals have a strange status here. Sonorous is allied to the First but on a day-to-day basis, the presence of the taint is neither seen nor accepted. It is not clear how the locals would react to the sudden arrival of a Dogspawn and so Scout is tucked away below deck.

Vesper and Samael step off onto dry land, leaving Jem and the kid behind.

They make their way into town, following the Tradeway directly through the port and on past densely packed living blocks towards the prison.

Every inch of space is used, buildings squeezed together on the ground and strewn across the mountainside, staggered, with lifts running between them. Above the main town are the engine levels and machine factories and above that, the featureless block of silver that houses the Harmonium Forge. Between the top of the forge and the bottom of the watchtower are a scattering of private dwellings, a few of which perch on top of the cliffs, their residents paying the price for the finest views.

On the opposite side of the wall, suspended above the sea, is the great prison complex. Each cell dangles from sheer rock, unsettled by the constant winds. Unlike most cells, these ones have no door, tempting their prisoners with an illusion of freedom. There are stories of those that jump.

None of them end well.

The only way to get to the cells is via the watchtower. Vesper takes the long way, unwilling to trust the lifts or to explain herself to those that run them.

They pass through the town without challenge and begin the long hike up the mountain, following the path as it snakes back and forth, climbing, slow.

The number of pedestrians decreases with each new level, until they walk alone, two figures standing out. Vesper pauses to catch her breath and turns to admire the view. From above, Sonorous looks like a claw grasping the buildings, squeezing them together.

Further down the path, a unit of uniformed troops assemble, four rows, red and neat, lined up in front of a crawler tank.

Vesper bites her lip. 'I was hoping they hadn't noticed us.'

Samael says nothing and the two continue, side by side.

The troops follow them at a distance, matching pace, following rather than closing.

More of the Sonorous independent military wait up ahead, lining both sides of the path, weapons ready. They make no move as the two draw closer. There is room to pass between the lines but only if Vesper and Samael walk single file.

She stops. It is too late to go back but she finds it hard to commit to going forward.

Samael stops a few paces after. 'What is it?'

'This was a mistake. I'm sorry, Samael, I wish we hadn't come.'

'You had to come. I understand.'

'But look at them.' She hangs her head. 'This is a death trap.'

'They're more scared of us than we are of them.'

She looks at the rows of masked faces. 'Seriously?'

'They are just people. You are the voice of The Seven.'

Suddenly, the rows of masked faces gain character, distinct. She detects the tension in their limbs and the nozzles of rifles quivering in the air. On sudden impulse, she draws the sword and watches as they flinch one after the other, a set of dominoes teetering on the brink as the note hums through them. One shrieks, involuntary, the other soldiers pretending hard that it didn't happen, that this is just a normal day.

Vesper straightens and walks between the red uniformed walls. On either side, people hold themselves rigid, trying to strike the middle ground between looking away and making eye contact.

Ahead lies the watchtower squatting heavy on the cliff, its flat head butting the sky. Standing before its door is a figure all in black, loose clothes flowing in the wind around armour.

The sword hums, growing steadily in volume as she advances towards it. By the time she and Samael are within speaking distance, the sound has deepened into something approaching a growl.

Unlike the others, the figure shows no concern at their approach.

From behind the cliffs, two sky-ships rise on streams of light, hovering either side of the watchtower. Broken swords hang from their wings, chiming together, off key and despairing.

The figure takes a step forward, spreading its hands. 'Do you remember me? I remember you. You have shot me, incited others to attack me and now you come again in anger. Guns and lances and swords, that is your way. It is not mine. I am the First and it is my custom when dealing with your . . . kind, to attempt to reach an accord before resorting to violence. However, it seems that despite the . . . futility of your situation, you have no wish to talk.'

Vesper continues walking until she stands barely three metres away. She plants her feet and stares straight into the mirrored black of the First's helmet. 'I do want to talk. My name is Vesper. I bear the sword and speak for it. I've not come to fight.'

'Strange then, that you come with the Malice bared.'

'Well, you do have two sky-ships and half an army here.' The First does not react and she continues, hasty. 'I'm here to make you an offer.'

'This is unexpected but welcome.'

'I haven't come here to attack Sonorous or to attack you. I just want the knights that you took prisoner. Let me take them with me and we'll all leave you in peace.'

'That is not an offer. It is a demand. And if I do not return your . . . people to you, what then?'

431

Vesper swallows, tries to keep her voice calm. 'It is an offer. I'm offering to hold back the Malice. I'm offering to stand between you and it.'

'You think that you are in a position to threaten me?'

Vesper glances at the sky-ships and the weapons trained on her. She looks back at the rows of armed soldiers and lastly she looks at the First, remembering what it is a capable of. 'I think . . .' she begins, 'that you're scared. If you weren't, you wouldn't have bothered with all this. I think that the men in those cells have suffered long enough. You've broken their swords, they can't hurt you anymore. I think their freedom is a small price to pay for peace. The Malice has sealed the Breach. It has destroyed the Usurper and the Yearning.' She closes her eyes, letting the sword see for her. 'You are nothing in comparison.'

'The Malice is broken.'

'No, you are broken and Gamma is dead. The Malice is sharper than ever.' Eyes still closed she takes another step forward. 'Do we have an accord?'

The First steps back, bumping into the watchtower's door.

Vesper steps forward again, closing the space between them. The sword shakes angrily in her hand and the air around it shimmers with heat, sparking blue. 'Do we have an accord?'

'You will take them and leave? You swear it?'

'Yes.'

'Then stop, stop! We have an accord. Your . . . people will be set free.'

Vesper's eyes open, triumphant. She pulls back the sword a fraction, nodding to it. 'Good.'

*   *   *

432

A line of knights kneel by the docks while Samael prepares the boat. Jem and Scout stay below deck, tucked away in storage, hidden.

By contrast, the kid stands on the prow of the ship glaring at the newcomers.

Vesper walks along the line, talking to the knights as she passes. Solemn faces drain her enthusiasm, her smile sagging by the time she gets to the end.

Samael gives the signal and one by one, the knights climb on board. Not all of their armour could be found and many suits are incomplete, some dressed completely in scavenged clothes, another slight to be borne.

Last to arrive is a tired looking man, every part of him seeming to slump, aside from the dirty red hair that sprouts defiant, irrepressible.

Vesper hugs him, eliciting a surprised gasp. 'Genner! You're alive! But I saw you fall. I'm so glad you're alive, I thought you were dead for sure.'

'So did I.' He chokes something back, looking up to stop tears from spilling. 'But the First wanted me alive. It wanted to talk.'

She hugs him again. 'It's over now. You're safe. You're all safe.'

'Yes, thanks to you.'

'Why do you all look so sad?'

'We might not look it but we're grateful you came for us. Sonorous prison is no place for a knight to die.' He nods to her deeply, the gesture halfway to starting a bow, and moves on.

She watches him, a frown developing. 'Wait!' she calls as he steps onto the boarding plank. 'What do you mean die?'

Reluctant, he turns to face her. 'We failed in our duty to protect you. We disgraced ourselves. The knights broke their swords, swords passed down from the Maker to The Seven and through generations of Seraph. They cannot be replaced. If we are lucky the Knight Commander will grant us honour in death.'

As he speaks, Vesper's head shakes, disapproving. 'What? But I saved you! You can't just go and die!'

'What use is a knight without a sword? What use is a leader that let that happen?'

She stands there, rendered speechless by the naked shame on his face. He inclines his head and joins the others on the ship.

The *Commander's Rest* departs in silence, slipping out from the calm bay into open sea. Vesper sits up top next to the kid. He butts her shoulder gently and she strokes his head.

Behind her the knights sit pressed together, bodies packing the deck. They watch Samael with open suspicion, exchanging looks with their neighbour, muttering.

About an hour after leaving, Vesper stands, too abrupt. The rocking of the boat sends her sidestepping to the right, rapid, before feet find purchase. Next to her, the kid is mockingly stable.

Taking more care, Vesper makes her way towards the middle of the deck. Emotion burns twin smudges on her cheeks. 'Listen to me!'

Surprised, the knights and Samael look up.

'When we first came to Sonorous, you did everything you could to save me. A lot of people died so I could live. I know that everyone here would have given their lives to protect the sword. But, when the First came, I didn't ask you to die. I asked you to live, even though you had to break your swords to do it.' She pauses, the flow of words suddenly dry. 'I – I hear you whispering about Samael. I bet you're wondering where his armour came from. I'll tell you. It came from the bodies of knights that died in the Battle of the Red Wave.'

Horror radiates from the knights. Angry lips press together, fingers curl into trembling fists.

'Don't look at him like that! Don't you dare judge him! He went where nobody else dared to go and he found it and he's putting it to good use. Samael hasn't given up.' She looks at them, hoping for something, finds only confusion. 'Don't you see? We have to keep going.'

In a low voice, one of the knights replies. 'But he hasn't lost anything.'

Vesper's hands prod the air as she speaks. 'Of course he has. We all have. Gamma's body was taken by the Usurper and destroyed, but part of her lives on. Who better to serve her than those who understand? Who better than you? She doesn't give up. Samael doesn't give up and so I swear to you that I won't give up.' She sweeps them all with a look. 'When we get back to the Shining City, I'm going to tell the Knight Commander that thanks to you and our unit, to Genner . . .' she pauses for the briefest moment, 'to Duet, and thanks to Samael, I was able to take the sword to the Breach, to seal it and stop the greatest infernal ever from coming into our world. But it isn't over. Gamma still needs you. And so do I. So the Knight Commander isn't going to give you honour in death because there's too much to do.'

The old knight shuffles from his seat, onto his knees. He

begins to intone the litany of the Winged Eye. Another follows, then two, then more, like a wave, prostrating themselves before her.

'Wait!' she says, silencing them. 'There's more.' She goes below deck, anger and pride strangling caution and opens the storage container.

Jem blinks up at her, Scout wags his tail. She grabs a wrist in one hand, the scruff of a neck in the other and drags them both up into the light.

'This is Jem,' she announces. 'He survived in New Horizon and helped us. He is a friend and deserves your respect.'

But none of the knights are looking at Jem, their attention held entirely by another.

'That's a Dogspawn!' cries one.

'Yes,' replies Vesper, eyes flashing. 'His name is Scout and he protects me, too.'

At an unseen command, Scout lays down, head resting on crossed paws.

'But . . .' stammers another knight. 'It's tainted. We should kill it.'

Vesper shakes her head. 'No. The taint may be bad but it can be beaten by the power of The Seven. When I was in Verdigris, the sword turned back the power of the taint, healing people that would have been killed by it.'

Genner finally speaks up: 'You're saying the power of The Seven has touched this animal?'

She pauses, lips moving as she thinks about what to say, what it might mean. How the truth is one thing in her mind, another in theirs. 'Yes. The sword has saved him. He serves The Seven now and has protected me more than once. And he's friendly, too, see?'

She pets him and Scout's tail bangs on the deck, innocent.

The knights relax into a state of shock. Fists open and jaws slacken. Vesper returns to her place up top, Scout goes with her.

Later, Samael finds her there. 'What you said on deck. About me. Thank you.'

She smiles at him. 'It was true, every word. And I couldn't stand the way they were talking about you.'

'Yes. All the same, when we arrive at the Shining City, I would ask that you let me stay with my boat.'

'Why?'

'Because I don't belong.'

She takes breath to argue but looks into his mismatched eyes and changes her mind. 'Where will you be?'

'Here, on the sea.'

Her smile loses some of its sparkle. 'Of course. Will you ever come back?'

'Yes. And when I do, I'll come to the place where I've dropped you off. If you ever need me, leave a message there.'

CHAPTER TWENTY-NINE

Vesper and Jem walk hand in hand between neatly arranged trees, an army of spears, perfectly straight, smooth, that explode with life at the top, branches and leaves lacing together like tangled hair. Sunlight dapples through the gaps as they walk, winking and warm.

The kid trots in front, content, and a unit of knights led by Genner march behind, incomplete armour polished, chests out, chins high.

They break from the trees to see hills stretching ahead, uniform humps carpeted in lush green grass. Each one is a dwelling, an upper chamber in a dense network of interconnected rooms tucked under the earth. Between the hills, pillars of silver rise, epic, dwarfing trees and people alike.

From their underground dwellings, the citizens of the Shining City emerge, forming lines. They are here to celebrate the return of their heroes. Dignified smiles are prepared and children automatically assemble in clusters, tidy, ready to sing.

As they get closer, Jem seems to shrink in on himself. He sees the myriad faces turned towards him, beatific, cheeks radiant with health, eyes shining and hopeful. The spotless clothes with their simple, crisp lines. The overwhelming sense of order, of every person knowing their place and slotting into it like a well made piece of machinery. His eyes meet theirs and, in synchrony, they smile.

Mindful of his teeth, he does not smile back. Suddenly, his tan seems patchy, more burned than beautiful, the bones painfully prominent under the skin.

He slows down and lets go of Vesper's hand.

Fingers slip, half free until hers tense, catching them. Vesper's head whips round, concerned. 'Are we going too fast?'

'I'm fine. You go ahead.'

'We'll go together.'

He gives her a half-smile, lips together. 'This is your moment, enjoy it.' With another tug, his hand comes free. 'It's okay. I'm right behind you.'

A little shadow clouds her face. 'Okay.'

As they get closer the people begin to sing quietly. Their harmony sends a pleasant tingle through the air. Vesper raises the sword and it spreads silvered wings, basking in the sound.

The citizens part, forming a living, singing corridor. At the end of it stands another group of Seraph Knights, and at their head stands the Knight Commander. At his signal, they all salute.

Vesper returns it, and behind her knights do the same with empty hands.

Just as the two groups meet, a woman joins them. She is called Obeisance, Caretaker of The Seven. Her body is hairless, nailess, wrapped tight in a cloak of feathers. Only face and toes peek out, bare and unblemished.

With a creaking of armour, the knights and their commander kneel.

Obeisance only bows. 'Bearer, on behalf of the Shining City and the Empire,' she says quietly, voice carried via chips direct into the minds of the listening people, 'I welcome you home.'

'Thank you.'

'It will bring great relief to your family to know you are safe.'

'Oh my suns! Father! Uncle! It must have been so hard for them.'

'It was, and by extension,' she adds wryly, 'for the rest of us.'

'I don't understand.'

'From the moment they realised you were gone, we have received constant . . . visits, from the previous bearer and your uncle.'

'What happened?'

'Best you not know the details. Suffice to say, your father was all for taking a sky-ship himself and going after you. If he had been able to fly one without our help, I daresay he would have tried. He's been coming daily with requests.' She pauses. 'And demands.'

'Oh.'

'No matter. This is the second time you have come to us in glory, though I doubt you remember the first.'

It takes Vesper a moment to understand, then she smiles. 'I was very small.'

'You were,' agrees Obeisance, something approaching

warmth in her eyes. 'But no longer. Now you are our champion, chosen of The Seven.' Unsure what to say, Vesper inclines her head.

The older woman looks at her for a moment. 'And, I imagine, you are hungry.' She gestures, the cloak making it look like a bird extending a wing. 'Come.'

They walk together into the heart of the Shining City, Knight Commander on one side, Obeisance on the other. Jem follows alone, stranded between them and the knights behind.

At first, Vesper feels awkward but after a few questions she is soon lost in the retelling of her journey. They listen gravely to her description of encounters with the First and the situation in Sonorous and are incredulous when she tells them about New Horizon. Some details she keeps to herself, or alters slightly. Neer, Wonderland and its secret inhabitants are not mentioned, neither is Scout. She speaks highly of the knights that travelled with her but her highest praise is saved for Genner, Samael and Duet.

As Vesper talks about the state of the south and the need for cooperation with Tough Call and the Man-shape, troubled lines form on the Knight Commander's face and Obeisance becomes increasingly distant.

The sword tugs at Vesper's arm, indicating a desire to change direction. She lets it point as it wishes. 'Is the Sanctum of The Seven that way?'

'Yes.'

'I thought that was where we were going.'

'Surely, but first, let us take you to a place where you can rest.'

'But I need to see Them.'

Peter Newman

'And you will, but first, you must rest and be cleansed, ready for Their pleasure.'

'No,' replies Vesper, wincing as Obeisance locks eyes with her. 'I'd rather it be now. They need to see me as I am.'

Two men stand on a hill next to a farm. One watches, the other listens, a hand on his companion's back. About them, goats graze, leisurely. Though the second man is blind, he knows the first has seen something, feels it through the play of muscles under his palm.

'Is it her?'

There is a long pause. Amber eyes scan the horizon, aided by a powerful scope. The man lowers the scope and nods slowly.

'Good, let's go to meet her.'

The first man doesn't reply. He is already marching down the hill.

Ahead of schedule, Vesper approaches the sanctum of The Seven, a giant cube of silver suspended in the sky, rotating, slow; windowless sides reflecting suns above and the city below.

Giant metal stairs lead from the ground towards the sanctum but only travel part of the distance, the last step leading to empty air.

At the bottom of the stairs, Vesper stops, forcing the Knight Commander and Obeisance to do the same. She turns to Jem. 'You should wait here.'

He looks up and then back to Vesper, painfully aware of the others' eyes on him, judging. 'No problem.'

'Can you look after him?' She nudges the kid forward with her boot.

442

'Sure.' He reaches down for the kid but the kid has other ideas, skipping clear. Blushing, Jem tries again and manages to scoop up the struggling animal.

'Thanks. I shouldn't be long.'

'Are you,' he begins, pausing to get a better hold on the kid's waving legs. 'Going to be alright?'

She looks at the sword.

The sword looks back.

'I think so.' Her smile is weak. 'Take care.'

'You too.'

Obeisance starts up the stairs first, taking them at a stately pace. For all her grace she moves deceptively quickly and both the Knight Commander and Vesper struggle to keep up.

'She's been climbing these stairs every day since she was able to walk,' he explains, panting. 'I try not to make a habit of it.'

For a time they both concentrate on the task ahead, the Knight Commander's robotic knees squeaking into the silence. Legs labour and muscles begin to burn while Obeisance moves further and further ahead. When she reaches the top, she does not hesitate, stepping out into open air.

Vesper grimaces, then gasps as the other woman's feet find purchase in the ether. Obeisance continues to rise, her cloak making it appear as if she flies rather than walks the remaining distance to the sanctum.

'How did she . . .?'

The Knight Commander pauses, and Vesper joins him, both catching their breath. 'They say The Seven carry you the rest of the way. You have to put your trust in Them.' She raises the sword, closing her eyes as he continues. 'It isn't easy. I've gone up there several times but it doesn't make any difference.

Obeisance says that every day our faith is tested anew. I think for her that's literally true. I find that the best thing to do is get myself to the top step and take a deep breath, then I think about all—'

Eyes still shut, she touches him on the arm. 'It's alright. I can see them.'

'Excuse me?'

'The steps. I can see them.'

'Ah, well, in that case . . .' Paling, the Knight Commander trails off.

Vesper steps out, and up, and up, coat flapping crazily in the wind. As she ascends she sees a detail in the flawless walls. A small square of darkness, opening, and within it, Obeisance.

They make their way through the sanctum together. Corridors of silver reflect infinitely, dizzying, the images split by designs etched onto every surface. From the right angle, these designs become faces, or wings, or swords, multiplied and fractured and multiplied again, picking at sanity.

Obeisance is careful to stare straight ahead.

Vesper keeps her eyes closed, letting an eye see for her. It twitches left to right, suspicious.

At last, they reach the inner doors. Obeisance presses her lips to them, whispers, then steps back, pulling the doors open.

Vesper steps past the other woman. 'The sword wants you to wait for me here.'

Obeisance complies wordlessly, closing the doors as soon as Vesper is inside.

The inner chamber is tall, the roof lost in darkness. Flames flicker on the walls, illuminating seven alcoves. Six contain images of perfection, male and female, wings enfolding them, protective. One is left dark. The Six appear frozen, no breath stirs their chests and beneath their lids, eyes remain motionless.

Vesper takes a deep breath. 'Hello?'

Her voice bounces about the chamber, echoing and rising until it fades into the upper reaches of the roof.

She bites her lip. 'I was hoping to talk to you. I mean, I am talking to you, but I was hoping you'd be more awake than this.'

'This . . . this . . . this . . .' says the room.

The Six say nothing.

Vesper lowers her voice and steps closer. 'The Yearning is gone and the Breach is sealed. Things are quiet, at least for now. But it won't always be that way. I don't understand why you don't come out. The Empire needs you. There are so many people suffering and they're all waiting for you to act.'

The Six say nothing and Vesper's cheeks begin to warm. An eye narrows angrily.

'Gamma died and you abandoned her. And, and you left what's left of her to deal with what's out there, alone. It's too much. People have died, are dying right now. Your people! You're supposed to be protecting us. You're supposed to be leading us.'

The Six say nothing.

'Out there,' she points towards the door, 'the Empire is collapsing. We've lost the south and most of the colonies. The sea belongs to an infernal! The world is changing. I've been out there and seen it. And it scares me. It scares all of us. We're waiting for you to give us a sign.' She holds the sword high, letting its eye sweep the silent figures. 'The sword is waiting, too. Please. We need you, now more than ever. Wake up. Wake up and help us make sense of all this. Please.'

The Six say nothing.

She grits her teeth. 'Well?'

Nothing.

She lowers the sword, opens her eyes. 'Fine. Stay here in your hole.'

Her head droops, and she looks down at the eye looking up. 'Fine,' she says again, turning her back and walking away.

Outside, Obeisance waits, the very picture of patience. She bows deep as Vesper pushes open the doors, eyes never leaving Vesper's. 'May I ask what transpired?'

Vesper takes a deep breath, prepares her lies. 'The Seven are pleased. They want me to carry on serving them.'

'In what capacity?'

'For too long we have pulled back from the troubles in the south but now, with the news I have brought, They feel it is time to reach out to our troubled neighbours again.'

'They are rising?'

'No. At least, not yet. But I know that they want me to make things better. And they want you to help me.'

Obeisance looks at Vesper for a long time, until sweat begins to bead on the girl's neck, running down her back. 'Of course,' she says. 'I was bred to serve The Seven. My wishes are but an extension of theirs. In my time serving them, I have found that interpreting those wishes can be difficult but I'm sure that together, we will do what is right.'

Vesper swallows. 'Good. There's just one more thing I need to do, then we can get started.'

* * *

The Malice

Alpha of The Seven sleeps. He dreams of times long past, happier times that seemed to last forever and yet make up a tiny fraction of his lifespan. Each memory is held, perfect, as he walks through them, polishing and treasuring.

And yet someone speaks out of turn. Not the honeyed words of his creator or the cherished singing of his siblings.

He strips the words away, restoring memory to its previous state, but the other words come back. Halting and simple, the words of a mortal.

Behind them he hears his sister Gamma and at once remembers her death.

The protective walls of reminiscence crumble and pain grasps him, dragging him towards the present where bitterness is a taste, ever-present, in the mouth. He has hidden a long way down, wrapped in layers of memory and denial and the return to consciousness is slow. But still he comes, inching out of his self-imposed oblivion, stung into action by the words of a mortal.

Anger sparks, building within, towards the words, their meaning, the mortal who uttered them and the world that spawned it all.

Away from the Shining City, the hills are just hills, unmanu-factured, random. Vesper and Jem walk towards one of the larger ones, on the other side of a huge field. Further up, two figures approach, both using sticks, each casting twin shadows that stretch out towards them.

The kid runs ahead, ignoring the other goats that litter the hillsides. A few glance at him as he passes, most keep to themselves. Eventually, he recognises a familiar hill and climbs it. At the top, he reaches two buildings, stopping at the second, the smaller one.

From within, a pair of dark eyes watch, warning against further approach.

The kid straightens. He is not the same creature that left the farm. He is older, bigger and seasoned by travel. Head high, he struts into the barn.

There is a brief silence followed by the sounds of kicking, bleating and things being broken.

A few moments later the kid scampers out of the barn at speed. He stops a few metres away, turns and spits.

Inside the barn, something moves and the kid panics, charging down the hill and over a few more, until he has put several hills between himself and danger. He is, on reflection, still quite young.

The goat walks heavily to the entrance making sure that the kid isn't hiding nearby. Any curious looks from the older males are met with a fierce stare. Knowing their place, the males are quick to look away. Satisfied, she snorts, turns, and goes back to her bed.

Meanwhile, as she gets closer, Vesper's feet get quicker, anxious to be home. Jem does his best to keep up, until he sees the two men more clearly. When he lets go of her hand, she flies from him, throwing herself into her father's open arms.

He squeezes her tight and she laughs, breathlessly, happily.

Her father sees the hilt of the sword resting on her back, sleeping, one wing curled over her shoulder. A frown begins to form but before it can take root he notices the young man standing behind Vesper and his eyes widen.

Jem stares right back, dark emotions pulling at his face.

A soft clearing of a throat breaks the moment.

'I've missed you, too.'

Vesper laughs again, pulling out of the embrace. 'Uncle Harm!' She goes to him, more gently than she did her father and the two hug. His hands find the tangles in her hair and his nose wrinkles.

'You need a bath!'

She prods at him, mock offended. 'That's all you have to say!'

'You need a haircut?'

A gasp becomes a smile, becomes a laugh, shared.

'Oh, both of you: this is Jem. He's my friend. He can stay with us, can't he? He doesn't have anywhere else to live.'

Her father's mouth drops open.

'Of course,' says Harm, beckoning Jem over.

He comes, bubbling feelings tucked swiftly away and shakes hands with the two older men. 'Nice to meet you,' he says to Harm, voice warm, narrow eyes locked on Vesper's father.

Detecting something but not seeing it, Harm adds, 'Help me back to the house, will you, Jem. Let's give these two a moment to catch up.'

Jem nods and they go ahead together.

'When we get to the house, I'll give you the grand tour. Don't worry, it won't take long, and then we can settle down and have something to eat. Do you like goat's milk?'

'I've never had it.'

'Then you're in for an experience. We drink a lot of goat's milk here. And tell a lot of stories. Well, mostly that was me but I suspect that's about to change. I haven't been across the sea in over twelve years. What's it like? I'm dying to

449

know. I don't suppose you went through Verdigris on your travels because . . .'

Vesper and her father wait while her uncle's chatter moves further away. Both smile.

'He hasn't changed.'

Her father shakes his head.

She sighs. 'I have.'

He nods, his eyes searching her face, noting tiny scars and worry lines in the grime. On impulse, he embraces her again.

'I'm okay. I'm just tired. There's so much to tell you I don't know where to start. Can you let go a moment? It's hard talking into your chest.' He blushes, half stepping back, one hand lingering on her sleeve. 'You never told me what it was like when you went to The Seven's sanctum. Did they make you angry too?'

An eyebrow raises, then he nods, emphatic.

'I'm not coming home.' She holds up a hand. 'I'm sorry if that sounds harsh but let me explain. I love it here and I'll visit of course but I need to go back to the Shining City. I have things there I need to do.'

He frowns, eyes full of questions.

'While I was away I spent most of the time wishing I was here, where it's safe. It would be so good to just hide here with you and Uncle. But now I've seen what's happening, I can't pretend otherwise.' She pauses, awkward. 'Maybe talking to your chest would be easier.'

He hugs her again and she continues: 'It's all a mess and I don't know how to fix it exactly, but I know that someone has to. In the Shining City, they're all waiting for The Seven, or The Six, to save them, but The Six aren't going to do anything, they're useless. But I know the Knight Commander and Obeisance will listen to me because of the sword. I'm not sure if I can do this but there isn't anyone else, so I have to try.'

He nods, his chin rubbing the top of her head.

'The thing is, well, I know you hate the city and, most people, but . . . will you help me?'

Strong hands go to her shoulders, one resting on top of a silvered wing. Gently, they squeeze. He looks at her for a while, proud tears misting amber eyes, then takes a breath. 'Yes.'

ACKNOWLEDGEMENTS

This is the second book I've had published and a lot of the wonderful people I need to thank remain the same (and remain wonderful).

First off, I want to thank my Wife of Awesome +5, Emma. She's there from the start of the first draft to the end, and beyond. Thanks for all the support, chats over coffee and your wisdom.

I also want to thank my editor, Natasha Bardon. Once again her suggestions have made the book so much better than it was. So thanks! The Malice would have been both shorter and less satisfying without you.

And thanks to the Harper Voyager book ninja for their continuing work from the shadows.

Covers are everything, and I'm so lucky to have Jaime Jones back on board. I have to look at the covers of these books a lot and Jaime makes that a thing of pleasure and pride.

A huge thanks also has to go to Juliet Mushens, my agent.

Who is, and always will be, the best. I can't imagine my career without her, nor would I want to.

Lastly, I want to thank all the people who supported The Vagrant and (hopefully) this book too. For all the reviews, encouragement, fan art and general loveliness. This is exactly where I want to be and you've all helped to make it possible. Thank you.